DEAR MUSTAFA

A NOVEL

STEVEN DAMRON

Random Events Publishing

Copyright © 2023 Steven Damron

www.stevendamron.com

ISBN 979-8-9891991-0-5 (paperback)

ISBN 979-8-9891991-1-2 (ebook)

Cover designed by Miblart.

Cover photo by Josef Palermo.

When you're drowning you don't think, "I would be incredibly pleased if someone would notice I'm drowning and come and rescue me." You just scream.

– John Lennon

If you could say it in words, there would be no reason to paint.

– Edward Hopper

But I have to tell you this: this whole thing is not about heroism. It's about decency. It may seem a ridiculous idea, but the only way to fight the plague is with decency.

– Albert Camus

The chances of factual truth surviving the onslaught of power are very slim indeed; it is always in danger of being maneuvered out of the world not only for a time but, potentially, forever.

– Hannah Arendt

To my friends who died.
For my friends who didn't.

I

SAN FRANCISCO, JUNE 15, 2001

Peter was quiet, lost in the process of inventing a color. Light flooded his airy South of Market studio on this fogless spring day. He was reliving a color nightmare. Daubs of an evolving red contrasted with the bucolic background color left dried on his palette, like blood splats on a quilt of lichen. He mixed in yellow with his trowel, transforming the oil paint into an explosive orange red. Applying this to the canvas would blow up the image, blast the outline of the shed to smithereens. Add a different color? Start over? When would this nightmare end?

The phone rang, breaking Peter's concentration. He looked from the canvas to the table, where he examined his sketch of the shed. The phone rang again. Peter couldn't adjust the paint to the color he remembered, and now, as he reviewed the sketch, he wasn't sure this shed fit with the abstract landscape on the canvas. Another annoying ring. The shed read almost New England, even though he'd drawn the thing in all its bright red glory while squatting not a dozen steps off a quiet Mendocino country road. The persistent phone rang a fourth time. No progress today. Peter pushed aside the drawing on the table, smooshed together the colors on his palette, and walked to the phone.

"Hi, Peter, it's Erica." It was the New York gallery on the line, a call he'd anticipated a week ago and then forgot about after a few days. It wasn't a good sign when these sorts of long-distance negotiations petered out. "Hello? You there?"

Phone pressed tight against his ear, Peter took a breath. "Of course."

"I meant to get back to you sooner," Erica said, "but a major client asked to meet with several of my artists and I have a show opening tonight. I wanted to let you know my decision before the weekend."

Another breath. "I assumed no reply was your reply."

"No," Erica said.

"So it's a no?" Peter asked.

"No," Erica laughed, "it's a yes, yes, yes. As long as we can open your show September eighth."

Three months. Not even. Didn't leave much time. He'd nearly given up on an invitation. Now Peter was shocked. Ecstatic and shocked.

"I can't get everything to New York that soon," Peter said.

"Don't worry," Erica said. "Relax. Celebrate your good news with friends. Right now I have to celebrate another opening."

"Thanks so much," Peter blurted before they said goodbye. He paced back and forth. There was no way to finish everything by September, much less ship it. He began questioning whether his work was good enough for New York. The invitation had to be proof it was. But maybe not. Adrenaline excitement shook Peter's hands. Like any self-respecting artist unable to concentrate, he put away his brushes.

Celebrate? Maybe clean the studio instead. It was pointless to paint. The New York gallery show marked a new direction for Peter. He needed a distraction, a chance to absorb the significance. Celebrate or clean? No friends around this weekend and, after last night, no romantic interests left to impress. Dinner had been as bland as Peter's date. Dessert was even worse. Spooning a flan, Mr. Bland enquired sardonically how Peter was enjoying what was, to Peter's surprise, their second date. "Am I supposed to remember everyone I've slept with?" was Peter's unfortunate apology.

Cleaning it would be then; a soothing, mindless afternoon of spring cleaning. After Erica's news, the studio required a preparatory cleanse. It commenced in a dark corner at the far end of the studio. Even the cobwebs were dusty. The last major clean was a dozen years back, after the Loma Prieta earthquake cracked the walls and pushed supplies off the shelves. A half hour into the effort, cobwebs safely suffocated in plastic bags, Peter, climbing to the top of a metal shelf, stretched to reach a long-forgotten box. It was Rano's box, a box someone must have placed here not long after the earthquake, a box Peter couldn't wait to open. Not quite a decade since someone placed it here, Peter calculated as he stretched, not quite a decade since Rano died from AIDS. He wasn't sure what intimacies were inside. Surely photos of friends and Rano's favorite dildo, but possibly some less amusing artifacts from their relationship.

Peter's unbalanced nudge accelerated to a shove and the decrepit cardboard box flew from the shelf and crashed to the floor. Scrabble tiles exploded from the wreckage, bouncing to form gibberish. Peter climbed down. Photos were scattered like bodies over a debris field, photos of Peter and Rano, of Brice, of other friends, of Linh, of Angel, of Angel's boyfriend and other faces like Angel's boyfriend, faces that Peter recognized but could no longer name. Prehistoric floppy disks crammed with Rano's unfinished writing strangely circled the black dildo—larger than Rano, but not much. Among the other memorabilia strewn across the floor was a black book, clasp broken; a journal wide open, open to a page about Peter, a page that, as he read it over and over, brought back dark memories of a long-ago night, the night of Carl's attack. "I'll explain what Peter did after Carl attacked us another time." What did Rano mean by that?

Cleaning came to a halt as the excitement of Erica's call dissipated. Peter sat cross-legged on the floor, flipping through a few pages. Each journal entry was addressed to someone he didn't know, someone named Mustafa. He read a few more entries before returning the journal and the rest of the mess to the box. Ten years after the fact, Rano found an odd way to remind Peter that he also had wanted to work in New York, that he had wanted to move to New York with Peter. If Rano were here, he'd let Peter know whether his art was good enough for New York. Peter's heart beat too quickly as he climbed to replace the box on the high shelf. All these years later, he wasn't sure he had the strength to finish his art, to leave San Francisco, to make the trip to New York without Rano.

April 30, 1989 – Anniversary

Dear Mustafa,

Tomorrow is May Day. I was reading about May Day protests and remembered that Carl and I met on May Day thirty years ago, a few months, my dear son, before your first birthday. I was the street urchin who knew how to wear a bathing suit. Carl was the vacationing sadist who made sure I accompanied him back to San Francisco.

What I couldn't have known when I agreed to Carl's offer to live in America was that I would not return to our sunny Algerian coast after Carl captured me, that I wouldn't see you these thirty years. In the excitement of a new country and a new city, it didn't occur to me. I was too young then to know the limits of my street smarts.

It wasn't entirely Carl's fault that I haven't seen you, Mustafa. Peter played a role, too, although I haven't let on. It's better that way. Peter can be stubborn. I'll explain what Peter did after Carl attacked us another time. It's why I haven't seen you.

Today, though, Carl is on my mind, not Peter. Well, the memory of Carl. He returned to Algeria more than once, never with me. He never explained why I couldn't accompany him. Probably more trips with the same scary French assholes who introduced us. Probably exploring his fetish for dark guys. Naturally there were other street urchins with talent similar to mine. Similar, mind you, but not as prodigious. Also, Carl must have worried I would stay in Algeria if he brought me back. He always worried I'd leave him. He never bothered to understand me.

If Carl had bothered to understand me, he would have known my only interest in returning to Algeria was to see you. Well, perhaps I would have visited the family who forsook me and tracked down a few of the other street urchins who became my chosen family. Perhaps I would have checked out the bookstores and cinemas to see if anything changed. I wouldn't risk returning to Algeria, though, if I knew how to phone you, hear your voice, see your smile.

Even without bothering to know me, sadistic Carl should have known my departure from him was as inevitable as my departure from Algeria. I moved to San Francisco for my freedom, not his bonds.

Please excuse me if I repeated myself here. I don't remember everything I've told you about Carl. I do remember I haven't told you about the way Carl blackmailed me before he died. I'll tell you that when I have more time, dear Mustafa, because it concerns you as well as Peter. What's important to know, though, is that Carl never revealed to me where you moved, so I haven't found you. Yet.

Right now, I have to go to another funeral. Two funerals, actually, one for Eric, the other for David, best friends in the time of AIDS.

2

NEW YORK, SEPT 8, 2001

Peter had no idea what New York City magic Erica conjured, but somehow she installed his art just in time for opening night. She'd given him one final task—arrive on time. Brice was not helping. He was glued to the storefront of a vintage poster shop.

"I realize the mechanical dancers in that window are adorable," Peter said. Since he was sleeping on Brice's couch, he didn't want to sound too upset. "However, in case you forgot, tonight is my opening."

"Relax," Brice said, adjusting his hands to shade the black and yellow reflection of Chelsea traffic on the window. "I want to see how the mechanism makes them dance so realistically."

Peter leaned back on one foot and tapped the other. The frenzy of packing and shipping happened. Hanging the art went smoothly enough. Erica was expectedly supportive. She'd primed the art-world pump, scheduling private viewings with clients, building press support for her new talent, sounding out critical interest for Peter's rich abstract landscapes. However, this was New York. Even with a gallery's imprimatur, one bad review could put Peter's takeoff into a tailspin. He'd learn New York's judgment soon enough. Right now he wished Brice would give these mechanical dancers a rest.

"Erica wants me to make a final inspection," Peter said at last. "Wants to brief me on the guest list."

"Would you mind if I go inside and ask the clerk who made the mechanism?" Brice asked, leaning forward. "The way the dancers move reminds me of Charlie."

"Charlie?" Peter asked. "The go-go dancer who died after you dumped him?"

"Charlie was more than a go-go dancer and he didn't die because I dumped him," Brice said sharply. "You know that."

"Sorry." Peter was tense. That was no reason to needle Brice. Charlie was another sweet dancer who shouldn't have died of AIDS. "I really need to get to the gallery."

"Just give me a second inside," Brice said, pressing his forehead against the glass. "We have like a half hour."

"Oh, and I forgot," Peter said. "Linh called while you were showering. She's stopping by early. She has a few minutes before she flies out of JFK."

"In that case," Brice said, swinging around, "I'll come back later." He took Peter's arm and headed toward the gallery. "I haven't seen Linh in like forever."

Brice looked dashing this evening. Demonstrating some of the mechanical dancers' moves, he went on about the store's window design, about how he'd never seen a retail display with dancers that good. Peter half paid attention, half thought about Rano. There hadn't been a good time to tell Brice about Rano's diary. This certainly wasn't it. Peter wasn't sure he wanted anyone else, let alone Brice, to read it. Things with Brice were already complicated.

Brice babbled on. Radiating enough opening-night excitement for both of them, he seemed intent on distracting Peter, calming his nerves. He was nearly pirouetting as they turned the corner off Tenth Avenue. Right this minute, though, Peter wasn't interested in Charlie or store windows or mechanical dancers. In spite of the difficult things Rano wrote, in spite of the upsetting posthumous revelation of a son named Mustafa, Peter wished Rano were here, on his arm, reassuring him. He missed the comforting warmth of Rano's good energy.

"Who's this fireball with you?" Erica asked from the gallery door. "Billy Elliot?"

"You remember Brice," Peter answered. "I'm staying at his place."

"Got us here on time," Brice said, shaking Erica's hand. Brice's dance moves hadn't slowed his brisk New York pace.

"Luckily a little early." Erica let go of Brice's hand and locked arms with Peter. "Brice, dear, could you give me a minute with Peter. There's a nice cafe down the block if you wouldn't mind?"

"Okay, but what about Linh?" Brice asked. As the words left his mouth, a black car elegantly rolled to a stop.

"Looks like Linh has arrived in style," Peter said. He'd had a short catch-up with Linh on the phone while Brice showered. Now he wanted to know what inspired the limo.

"Give us ten or fifteen," Erica said to Brice. She tugged Peter toward the gallery before he could greet Linh. "Have fun with your friend."

"No problem," Brice replied, stepping off the curb and effortlessly extending his hand to assist Linh out of the car.

Erica pulled Peter inside the gallery and locked the door behind them. Through the shades, all Peter caught was a glimpse of Linh stepping out of the car and strolling down the block with Brice.

"Something wrong?" Peter asked Erica. Even during installation, he'd never seen Erica so disheveled.

"I had to fire Jodie just now," Erica said, surveying the mess on the floor. "What fucking timing."

"Your assistant?" Peter asked. It wasn't a good time to delve into details. There were grocery bags on the floor next to a broom, like someone walked in and dropped everything. The air conditioning shifted small piles of debris across the floor. "How soon do people arrive?"

"I found some suggestive emails she sent my boyfriend," Erica said. "Ex-boyfriend. Fuck. I'm sorry. This never happens before an opening."

"Okay," Peter said. He didn't need a clock to know there wasn't enough time to clean up the gallery and make Erica presentable. It felt like a bad omen, like there was no point waiting for what now were bound to be disastrous reviews. He might as well hitch a ride to JFK with Linh and fly home tonight.

"I'm going to buy ice for the drinks," Erica said. "A walk will clear my head. Would you mind moving the food to the kitchenette and sweeping the floor?"

Peter didn't have a chance to reply before Erica dashed out the door. Poof. What was going on? His mind raced. What would he do if a client knocked? Or if a reviewer showed up? As panic set in, he focused on Erica's requests. Carry bags to kitchenette. Pick up broom. Sweep debris drifting across floor.

Focus helped. When Peter looked up for a dustbin, he found himself alone with his art. For a moment, New York's cacophony faded. Peter turned up the gallery lights to inspect his paintings. Erica had arranged them just right. She'd found relationships he hadn't noticed before, as if they fit just this way, as if she'd solved a puzzle. Sitting down where he could appreciate the entire exhibit, he searched for a word to describe how well everything worked in this space but couldn't find one. Maybe it was New York. Maybe it took New York to make sense of his work. As his anxiety waned, he forgot about the time. Peter felt surrounded by family. It seemed as though Rano could arrive any moment, fresh from a stroll along the Hudson River.

"It looks fantastic!" Linh shrieked, shoving through the door with Brice in tow. "And so do you!"

"Look at you!" Peter jumped up and wrapped his arms around her petite frame. He was excited to see her, although concerned a squeeze might sully her ensemble. Where was Linh buying threads these days?

"Sorry Brice and I took so long," Linh said, letting go. Her straight black hair bobbed from side to side as she swayed through Peter's exhibit. The debris scattered across the floor in her wake. "This work is super, Peter. I'm so proud of you."

"I wish you didn't have to fly off," Peter said, enjoying Linh's lively motion.

Brice was standing to the side. He'd studied the paintings earlier, during the installation. Now he seemed subdued, his earlier enthusiasm clouded.

"If you want to check out the mechanical dancers that reminded you of Charlie," Peter said to Brice, "you could meet me back here later."

"I can stop by that poster store any time," Brice said, pushing the dirt on the floor with his foot. "How come Erica isn't here? Do you need some help cleaning up?"

"Yeah," Linh said, returning to Peter's side. "What kind of opening is this? Where's the champagne and caviar?"

"Erica had a little family emergency," Peter answered, wondering how much time they had. "I'm a bit nervous about what to do. At least you guys are here."

"Let's set up the food and drinks," Linh said, producing a joint from her tiny purse. "But first, I have a long flight to Monaco ahead of me."

"Monaco?" Peter asked.

"A little detour on the way to the Berlin art show." Linh snapped a flame from her lighter and took a hit.

Linh's European tour surprised Peter. No wonder she was excited. The partly smoked joint in her hand explained Brice's muted mood. It had been weeks since Peter got high. It would be insane to get high before talking with collectors and reviewers. Linh was right. The show looked great. At this point Peter couldn't change what was on the walls even if he wanted to. There was no way to help Erica's romantic disaster. What Peter didn't want was to worry about details, about the debris on the floor or the refreshments. The weed smelled good. Peter wanted to bask in his New York debut. He decided he would appear less anxious if he took a hit, so he did.

As the three friends passed around the rest of the joint, they tidied up the gallery, arranged the food and drinks on a table, and giggled. The pot was perfect. Peter stopped worrying about anyone else coming. He hadn't felt this relaxed in weeks. Linh gobbled half a platter of celery and carrots while she arranged the wine glasses. There was a knock at the door.

"I'll answer it," Linh said, hugging Peter. "I have to take off anyway. Enjoy your opening. I know you will on this stuff."

As Linh let the first guests through the door and waved goodbye, the full force of the marijuana knocked Peter off his feet. This New York stuff was a whole different level, a strain that would keep Linh high her entire flight. Luckily Brice greeted the guests who were arriving. Luckily Brice turned up the air conditioning to clear the smoke. Luckily Erica returned before her gallery filled up. Luckily because Peter wasn't sure he was conscious. He thought he heard Erica outside her office, where he was resting with his eyes closed, letting the high wash over him.

"Are you afraid?" Erica said after she found Peter. She coaxed him to stand. "Nice job setting up the drinks. Let's meet your new fans."

"I'm not sure I'm ready," Peter said, opening his eyes. "How did you do it? You look fabulous."

"Thanks," Erica said, tugging at Peter's jacket. "If I can do it, so can you. We couldn't ask for a better crowd. My favorite critic from the *Times* showed up."

"The *Times*?" Peter asked. "That's overwhelming."

"It's do or die," Erica said. "Don't be too solicitous with the critic and, oh, yeah, make sure to chat up a guy named Thomas."

MAY 1, 1989 – BOUKALATES

Dear Mustafa,

Yesterday, I went to the funerals of my friends Eric Tonningsen and David Lesser. It's devastating that both of them departed from this planet during the same month. They were opposites and best friends, Eric the quiet one, David the screaming queen, Eric the dark-haired Scandinavian beauty, David the ruddy Jewish provocateur.

I met Eric at San Francisco State. How could I not notice his fastidiously groomed curls? I pinched myself as he approached the lectern under the pretense of asking questions, but really to invite me to a gay political meeting.

Eric accompanied me to my first ACT UP meeting. Afterwards, he introduced me to the foghorn in back who annoyingly interrupted all the speakers, but was always right. That, as you may have guessed, was David.

Eric and David shared an enormous Victorian with a crew of gay boys and fag hags. The parties at their Cole Street house were legendary. I don't know how I got invited so often. I was much older than the rest.

Peter was sure Eric invited me because he wanted oral sex. Why am I mincing my words? You're an adult, Mustafa, and I need to treat you like one. Peter said Eric wanted to suck my cock. Of course, Peter trotted out that old put-down whenever he was jealous. I replied to Peter that I'd let him watch if he joined me at one of the Cole Street communal parties, parties that usually featured some or other drug, sometimes an unrehearsed entertainment of sorts, and always laughter. Peter never joined. Not, mind you, that I ever got a blow job from Eric.

David grew bitter towards the end. I avoided him. His humor became toxic. He seemed angry at anyone who wasn't dying with him. Of course he was angry. Life was cruel to his alluringly smooth body. It stole the allure before he turned thirty, leaving behind a plastic bag of dust and bone chips.

I avoided David these past months because I couldn't let myself get dragged down. I plan to live, to finish my book, to write several more books on technology and ethics after that. My T cells are stable. My energy is good. I keep up with the kids at the parties.

The party I remember best with Eric and David was last summer. They hosted a tasseography, a reading of tea leaves. Like so many of their events, this also was a make-it-up-as-you-go affair. Eric and David would take turns predicting a guest's future. Eric quietly made serious predictions about a next job or about a family predicament. David laughingly conjured up something completely ridiculous like marriage to sexy young Prince Edward. Eddie's in the theater, David said with a wink, and you know what that means.

Where there was tea, of course, there had to be pot, so things got loopy. After a time, someone asked me if Algerians practiced tasseography. The question caught me off guard. I don't think about Algeria much anymore except sometimes when I'm writing you. I suggested that if the others wanted to learn about Algeria, we might switch from tasseography to the ritual of boukalates. I told the crowd I hadn't been to an actual ritual in my homeland because it's for women. They laughed.

I explained how the ritual works. I presume you know how this works, of course. I barely remembered after so many years. I hope you're proud of me for at least trying to remember enough to introduce my friends to a bit of Algerian culture. I'm sure you'll let me know someday of any errors I made.

Algerian women sit at a round table, I said, drawing circles in the air with professorial authority. They place a ceramic vase on the table, a vase called a "boukala," filled with water. Each participant throws an object into the water and they cover the vase with a scarf. After incense and incantations to conjure the jinn, poems are read. A poem is also called a "boukala." Many poems, "boukalates." Boukalates can be about good things, or about bad things, but they're always about romantic things. After each poem is read—my hands fishing for an imaginary object in an imaginary vase—a virgin removes one of the objects from the vase. Then the group discusses how the poem relates to the owner of the selected object. For that woman, the poem becomes a prediction, an Algerian tasseography of sorts.

Good luck finding a virgin around here, I remember David saying. You'll be pleased to know that in the interest of multicultural harmony and world peace, David and Eric agreed to boukalates. Instead of love poems, Eric wrote a dozen of what we called "intimations," short predictions about what might happen to any of us who survived AIDS. David wrote a dozen more about what might happen to those who didn't. Meanwhile, someone poured water into a wooden salad bowl and each of us tossed an object into the water. Instead of incense and incantations, everyone smoked more weed to summon the spirits. This was a ritual for the ages.

Why I remember any of this after so much pot is because of what happened during the third boukala, when Eric read one of David's intimations. It predicted what would happen to the work of any of us who died. I thought David's intimation quite remarkable because it suggested that somehow, even after we died, our work, whatever it might be, would come to fruition—like a reincarnation. We discussed what this third reading meant, what the word "work" could mean, that this would be wonderful for anyone in our party, even for any of us who survived AIDS and died of some normal disease like cancer. David said this intimation would be a mitzvah, especially were this game played in Israel rather than Algeria. Then everyone laughed hysterically when we realized we were so high we'd analyzed the boukala before we fished out an object from the salad bowl. Who deserved this marvelous boukala? We passed the bong around once again before David pulled a key out of the salad bowl. It was my house key. I hope this brings you joy as it did me. This lovely mitzvah, dear Mustafa, was for me.

That party has haunted me ever since. I don't plan to die. I plan to live, to write several books. I worry, though, what would happen to my work if AIDS snatched me. What did my boukala mean? Is there some way, any way, I could complete my work after I die?

Every time I think about the destiny of my work and the boukala I received, I remember Eric and David and the hazy evening reading boukalates. These friends dying so young from AIDS, they barely started their lives. Bless them.

3

New York, Sept 9, 2001

Peter watched Brice pour celebratory martinis. Good thing they were strong. He needed the courage to tell Brice that he'd discovered Rano's journal and seen Brice's name on several of its pages.

"I'm surprised Rano didn't destroy it," Brice said, sitting down after the news. "Why did you want to climb down that rabbit hole?"

"Don't even try to guilt me," Peter replied. Two majestic stuffed olives stared at him through the condensate on the glass. "I skimmed a few pages and closed the thing."

As Peter sipped the chilled spirit, he peered over New York's skyline, surveying the vista south across Chelsea, down the Hudson River, all the way to the Twin Towers, and beyond. Earlier the sun glinted off glass in a thousand random directions. Now Brice's perch absorbed light like a lighthouse in reverse. Millions of lights sparkled, highlighting clubs, spelling words, trying to add meaning to the night. It was ten years to the day that Rano died. Of course Brice would remember. On this particular trip, it was comforting to stay with Brice, even if it was in the teeny, tiniest Manhattan shoebox.

"Cheers!" Brice extended his glass. "Finally, we get some time to ourselves. What a glorious evening."

"New York's best remedy for summer weather," Peter said, bending over to clink Brice's glass. The bitter, cold martini was a perfect remedy for the oppressive humidity. New York had a remedy for every known human condition. As Peter sat down in the combination living room, dining room, kitchen, and foyer, he noticed, or thought he noticed, a tear rolling down Brice's cheek. Brice was as lithe now as the dancer he'd been years before. His pose on the other chair was a reincarnation of Rudolf Nureyev.

"Something must have possessed you to open Rano's journal after all this time," Brice said, dabbing his eye with his napkin before placing it on the table. "What was it?"

"Fuck if I know." Peter looked again over the skyline. The blinking lights of an aircraft went dark as it passed behind the Twin Towers. Brice's curiosity about the journal irritated

Peter. He knew exactly what possessed him, exactly what happened. The journal had crashed to Peter's studio floor three months earlier and, as if it had a mind of its own, opened itself to a page about Peter.

"Well, anyway, here's to Rano," Brice said, lifting his glass again. "That was, what, 1991? I can't believe it's been a decade."

"To the day," Peter answered, turning back to Brice from the captivating skyline view. "I've thanked you before, but I can never thank you enough for being there at the end."

"How could I not? Rano was extraordinary, a force. Besides, it was you who always did the hard work, even when Rano threw his tantrums."

"I was lucky his final descent was quick," Peter said, sipping the cool concoction. "No time for tantrums."

"He went downhill faster than a drag queen stumbling on stilettos."

"Remember the dance you performed afterwards, at his service?" Peter asked. "Everyone said it was like you were making love to Rano."

"How could I forget?" Brice answered. "It was the last time I danced in front of an audience."

This surprised Peter. Brice moved like he'd never stopped dancing. Peter knew Rano had a thing for Brice. Rano said so. Whatever Rano's interest in Brice had been, it rarely bothered Peter back then and it hardly mattered now. Brice was one of Peter's dwindling living connections to Rano, one of the few friends left who had experienced and appreciated Rano.

"It was important to Rano that you made the effort at the end," Peter said.

"Me? All I did was hop on a plane to San Francisco. I was like one of those priests in the movies, the guy who shows up to perform last rites just before the final gasp."

The two sat quietly for a moment. There were things to say. Enjoying martinis was easier. Brice's kitchen clock ticked loudly, tocking over New York's din. The candles on the table flickered in a nearly hypnotic rhythm with the clock. They were placed in a bed of decorative twigs that perfumed the apartment with a woody scent. Eucalyptus? Peter's mind turned pages of the journal, the diagrams Rano made to work out ideas, the clumsy line drawings of objects around his hospital beds, the choice descriptions of meals they'd shared, the news that Rano had a son somewhere in Algeria. Why had Rano hidden that from him? He wondered what else Rano had kept secret. Peter felt ashamed that Rano wouldn't disclose something as important as a child, too ashamed to reveal this secret child to any of his friends. As desperately as Peter wanted to quiz Rano about Mustafa, about why he kept Mustafa's existence from Peter, the only answers were in the fragile pages of Rano's journal.

"I loved your opening night," Brice said, interrupting the martini contemplation.

"I hope the *Times* did, too," Peter said. He swirled the olives, unsure whether to reveal that Linh's pot had fried his memory. "I'm feeling a bit over my head."

"I don't know what it is, but there's something about your recent work I really like." Brice shifted in his seat. His workouts showed through his unbuttoned shirt. The New York queens had a thing about muscles and hairless skin. It felt overwrought to Peter, but it was pleasant enough to look at. Maybe it was this smooth allure that had attracted Rano a dozen years earlier.

"I started traveling up to Mendocino to study the ocean and the trees," Peter said. It was more than that, but Peter didn't know how to explain it. He'd broken through something he didn't understand yet, something probably staring him in the face if he ever figured it out. "Maybe that's what you're seeing. I needed a new inspiration, a new muse."

"More like a new pot supply," Brice quipped.

"That's abundantly available along the coast, as well as magic mushrooms if you know how to spot them." Peter put down his glass. Barely under the surface, the two olives looked at him again.

"You're a bad boy."

"No, not anymore," Peter said. "Pot doesn't mix with painting, so I paint."

"It didn't seem that way last night," Brice said, reaching across the table and putting his hand on Peter's. Brice's hand calmed Peter, but the intention of its comfort was unclear. "You're just like Rano. He never wanted to get high. At least until he was sick."

"Oh, no," Peter said. "I think Rano and I tried everything once,"

When Peter and Rano met, they got high on something or other nearly every weekend. They stopped after Rano got the teaching position at San Francisco State. Reading the journal, it became clear that Rano started to take his career and reputation seriously, that he had desires and ambitions Peter hadn't grasped. Rano seemed to have developed a plan for himself, a plan that would leverage his wit and intellect to transform the study of ethics. Rano was that smart. When friends giddily enquired whether Rano's cock was really as large as everyone said, Peter's pat response was that Rano's cock could never measure up to his brain.

Brice took his hand off Peter's and hopped over to the cabinet. He fumbled around for a moment and switched on music. It was something classical, something Peter recognized. Brice twirled back into his seat with a joint in one hand and a lighter in the other.

"Since you're on vacation from painting, you want more pot?" Brice asked.

"Hmm. Isn't this Copland?"

"Yes, a dance from *Appalachian Spring*." After a couple long drags off the joint, Brice offered it to Peter.

Peter took the joint, but didn't light it. They listened for a while. The music was orchestral, folksy. It was obvious now that Brice wanted to get high and have sex. Peter was too nervous about reviews, too anxious from unresolved feelings about Rano on the tenth anniversary. The music was familiar, but he couldn't quite place it. He sipped his martini, then stroked his short beard absentmindedly. "Didn't Rano listen to this?"

"It was the first thing I played for him," Brice answered. "Rano lit up."

Peter realized it was the same recording he'd found in the player at home the day after Rano died.

"Rano asked me to explain classical music, American music," Brice said. His eyelids closed slowly, then opened. The weed was kicking in. "I brought him all these recordings and we'd talk about them. Copland and Bernstein, Duke Ellington, Fats Waller, Carole King. I was a disorganized musicologist, but he loved it all. He wanted to know more than I could tell him. Who influenced whom, the idioms, the sources."

"That's Rano," Peter said. "Wanting to know everything."

Brice nudged the lighter closer to Peter.

"Hearing the Copland again makes me feel like he's nearby," Peter said.

Brice stared. The cannabis gave his eyes a reddish intensity.

Peter put the joint on the table and raised his glass to toast Rano. They clinked glasses again. The two olives bothered Peter. He swirled them in his glass before chewing them. The combination of drink and music had turned the evening maudlin. The Copland dance ended. After last night, one martini was plenty for Peter. It was a remedy for the humidity, but not for Rano.

"Are you sure you don't want a hit before bed?" Brice pressed.

"I don't want to have weird dreams."

"Rabbit holes." Brice giggled. He looked pretty high.

"It's the journal," Peter said, looking over the vista again. The Twin Towers made Peter feel as though Rano had joined him in New York, as though somehow they were standing together again. Maybe it was the martini. "You want to read Rano's journal, don't you?"

May 9, 1989 – Escape

Dear Mustafa,

This is my second diary or journal or whatever you prefer. I wrote my first diary many years ago as I was escaping Carl. In case you ever read either of my diaries, I want to explain them to you, tell you how I came to understand the importance of writing and of words. What you can't put into words may sabotage you.

Rummaging through a box of my early academic notes and manuscripts this morning, I found my first diary. The text of that diary is strange. I wrote in Arabic, French, and mostly English. My written Arabic is practically nonexistent. I was convinced Carl couldn't decipher Arabic, though, so I expressed my most confidential thoughts in illegible scribbles. Now I can't decipher the scribbles, either.

I attempted to write in French, too, but Carl understood enough French to decipher my Algerian slang, so it didn't matter whether I wrote French or English. My written English was best. Carl made sure of that. If there's one unconditional gift Carl gave me, it is English literacy. I couldn't have become an academic otherwise, couldn't write the necessary papers. The sections of that diary written in English were clear. I saw my thought process, the way I worked out ideas.

Reading my decades-old first diary, I realized how much it helped me consider my options with Carl, helped me work out my feelings. I could see an earlier edition of myself coming to my senses. When I escaped from Algeria, I didn't understand the value of a diary, how writing a diary focuses thought. Without the aid of a diary, I escaped from a bad situation in Algeria to something even worse with Carl. Later, as I planned my escape from Carl, writing my first diary helped me think clearly, helped me escape to something better, eventually to Peter. As I wrote, I realized how Carl manipulated me with his secrets, especially secrets about you, dear Mustafa.

It may seem odd to you, Mustafa, but when I grew up in Algeria, I wasn't literate enough to keep a diary. I didn't write well enough. I barely wrote Arabic. I did read beaucoup French books to pass the time. There was nothing else to do on the beach. The tourists who paid for my services, the men I found amusing enough to spend more time with, the ones who might teach me something over a fresh sea bass or a tasty merguez, they seemed relieved when I insisted they buy me a book afterwards, as if giving me a good dose of French literature would absolve them of the sin of having given me a good dose of sex.

I rarely wrote more than a few words in French to friends. *Donne-moi l'argent*, or *rencontrer au café*. I knew a few English tourist words, enough to attract and transact. Please understand, Mustafa, that I didn't choose that line of work. I had no options. It was the only way someone in my circumstances could eat. I'm not proud of it nor do I expect you to be, but you must respect those circumstances. It was Algeria long ago, mostly before you were born. I ate well.

As impossible as it would have been to write a diary when I lived in Algeria, it would have helped. I might have understood better, even writing in nonsensical French, the kind of devil Carl was before I took his deal. That's as deep as I would have been able to write when I was a teenager. Deeper, actually, than I could have written then. My need to buy what Carl was selling thirty years ago on that picture-perfect postcard of an Algerian beach is so obvious now.

I ran across another thing in my box of treasures this morning, a document that reminded me of why I started this second diary. It was a transcript of a speech Vito Russo gave in New York's capital one year ago today, on May 9, 1988. I started this diary the day after I got my first HIV test. I started it for all the reasons Vito spoke about a year ago. I needed to deal with everything going on, with friends dying, with the unpredictability of my infection, whether my HIV will remain dormant or advance to AIDS.

A year ago, Vito reminded me to fight. He reminded me again today.

At a time when I feel guilty about skipping ACT UP activities in order to work on my research, Vito's speech inspires me to reflect on my own HIV status, on the ways I choose to slay this hideous viral dragon. It makes me understand how this struggle is different from my struggle with Carl, how the struggle with HIV is so much larger than I am. The struggle with AIDS is a Victor Hugo novel compared to the sad tale of a waif waylaid by Carl, the sadistic slime bag.

I must never stop fighting for a cure. I must spend more time with ACT UP.

As with the first diary about escaping Carl, I don't know what the outcome of this diary will be. I don't even know if I consider it a diary at this point. This writing is more focused than my first diary, more journalistic, more topical. I wrote my first diary because I wanted to know myself better. I'm writing this diary to save myself.

I'm writing this diary to you, Mustafa, because I want you to know me. Perhaps I have graduated from diary to journal. "Epistolary journal," to use a fancy term. This journal, then, is a testament that my thinking and writing have improved. I write it for you to understand everything about my life, regardless of your sexuality, but especially if you share my sexual predilections.

I don't mean to offend you by writing that. There is growing evidence, after all, that homosexuality is genetic. If you're gay, too, I wonder if you will try to escape Algeria as I did. Perhaps you have escaped already. Or perhaps it is possible these days for a gay boy to survive in Algeria as something other than a street urchin. I hope I can guide you one day and, in case we never meet, that this journal will suffice.

As I write this, I don't know how many books I'll complete. Nor do I know how many new places I'll live. With HIV, I don't know if I can visit Algeria again. I don't know if you will come to America. I don't know if I'll ever see you. I don't know whether Peter will provide for me fully, satisfy my needs beyond shared domestic activities of cooking and cleaning, of sleeping together, of less and less frequent sex.

I do know that I need to escape HIV, even more than I needed to escape Algeria. I know that the first diary helped me escape to something better. I know this diary or journal or whatever it is—these letters to you are my way to escape HIV. I write for me to escape, for you if I don't.

4

NEW YORK, SEPT 11, 2001

They sat at the table, reading the newspaper silently like an old couple.

"I'm glad you stayed an extra day," Brice said at last. "Even if it's only to meet a collector."

"Still no review of my show in the *Times*," Peter said, dropping the paper and standing.

"Yeah, I know." Brice rescued Peter's airline tickets from under the newspaper. "That's been bothering you."

"I wanted to have it for the collector tonight," Peter said, emptying the coffee pot and adding milk. "Erica insisted that I postpone my flight back to San Francisco, no matter what it cost."

"I bet you'll be reading a glowing review on the flight to San Francisco tomorrow," Brice said, examining the airline tickets. "Oh, for a second, I thought you bought two tickets for the same flight. But now I see one's for today, the other for tomorrow."

"A review tomorrow doesn't do any good for my meeting tonight," Peter said. "But Erica said this guy really likes my work. If Thomas buys anything, Erica said, it practically guarantees selling out."

"You're dining with Thomas?" Brice asked. "I met Thomas at your opening. We're supposed to talk business, too."

"Business?" Peter asked, glancing at Brice. "Or monkey business?"

"Business," Brice answered. "What did he say about your art?"

"Erica introduced me to Thomas," Peter replied. "I remember that much. I have to admit things got a little blurry after Linh's pot."

"It's a good sign Thomas wants to meet, right?" Brice asked.

"I don't know." Peter gazed out the window, sipping coffee. "I should've flown back to San Francisco today. It's not just the cost of the ticket. I need to be in my studio. My job is painting. Erica's is selling."

"I wish there was something I could do to take your mind off money," Brice said, slipping the tickets back in their jackets. "It's perfect outside. Would you like me to take off work today?"

"That plane seems really low."

"They always look too low," Brice said. "Look at that clear blue sky. Let's do something outside to relax you before you meet Thomas."

"No, it's really low. Come over here. A jet. You know, a passenger jet."

"Well, you're not a passenger on a jet right now because you're meeting Thomas tonight. A walk somewhere would clear your mind."

"It's wobbling. The wings are teetering. It looks like it's headed right for the . . ."

"It's the coffee talking. You drank enough to power a flight to San Francisco."

"Oh, my God, it's gone. It vanished inside the World Trade Center."

Brice's shoebox apartment shuddered.

"Oh, wow," Brice yelped as he leapt to Peter's side.

"Oh, my God, a fireball."

"Holy shit." Brice stared out the window for a few moments, slowly lifting Peter's airline tickets. "Holy shit."

Peter looked over at his tickets, then back at the smoke rising from the tower. "Oh, my God."

JUNE 24, 1989 – COMPROMISE

D ear Mustafa,

The answer to this question is a bit of a riddle.

Q: What is a drag queen's least favorite animal?
A: The chameleon.

Allow me to explain.

Tomorrow is San Francisco's gay pride parade. According to the promotional posters plastered on every Castro nook and cranny, this year's theme is "Stonewall 20: A Generation of Pride." Perhaps fierce drag queens will save us from AIDS the way they saved gay establishments like the Stonewall Inn. Their uncompromising force of will derives, in part, from a sense of having nothing to lose. A drag queen can't hide in the closet, can't blend into a crowd like a chameleon.

As with drag, there can be no compromise with AIDS. A person with AIDS can't die unnoticed in the closet. Come out, come out, wherever you are!

I write this knowing full well that I myself have compromised. Obviously, I'm out of the closet, so that's not my compromise. I have been out since I left home to prance along the beaches in Algeria. That jinn could never go back in the bottle.

My compromise is more complicated, more insidious. My grand bargain was to stay in San Francisco with Peter. I realize that has nothing to do with fighting AIDS and finding a cure, except it does for me.

I wanted to teach in New York City and, out of the blue to a surprising degree, Columbia University wanted to hire me. I know my work is important. Not to brag, but Columbia's unsolicited offer wasn't the first validation. In New York, I would have had many more resources than I have here to break ground in my field. I begged Peter to move east. He's really all I have in America. I trust him without question. For better or worse, Mustafa, you should know Peter is my family here.

Peter refused to move to New York. He was open to changing our living arrangements. He suggested we fly back and forth, me spending a week in San Francisco one month, him spending a week in New York the next. He even suggested I stay with Brice. These suggestions seemed too risky, too likely to wreck our family.

Peter said that he was working out ideas, seminal ideas, that his painting relied on the geography of the Bay Area, the relationships between the ocean, the coast, the vegetation, the wildlife, the history, the spirits, and the nearby mountains. He'd never revealed so much to me about his work. He didn't see a way forward in New York City and worried he'd have to start all over, worried New York landscapes might not work. Even though I gave up everything in Algeria to move to San Francisco, even though I knew a transcontinental move could shake up Peter's perspectives in good ways, Peter's truth wasn't something I could argue with. Back then, he was a headstrong twenty-something man grappling with his own demons.

My choice came down to compromising my work or compromising my family. I regretted turning down Columbia, but I reasoned that I could accomplish nearly as much in San Francisco. It just would take longer. I settled in. I found Leslie the Librarian. She's been excellent help navigating resources at SF State and elsewhere, probably worth two Columbia research assistants. Any good lipstick lesbian is worth at least two RAs, and Leslie is beyond lipstick. Occasionally, I've considered positions at other local institutions, but it's hard to beat my commute and impossible to replace Leslie.

And then AIDS attacked our community. And then my HIV test. And then a new reality that my life was at risk and so, also, my work. It was far too late to put on a condom to protect against the spread of compromise, too late to undo the compromise I agreed to. I was infected with compromise and the terms of my compromise mutated uncontrollably. "Publish or perish" took on added significance.

I don't want to regret the compromise I made. I pray that Peter's work makes my compromise worthwhile. I compromised for our relationship trusting that, as a result, Peter would excel at his art while I excelled at my research. I fear that I will regret my compromise if he does not excel or if I do not finish my books. This possibility angers me.

Who anticipates a plague during his lifetime?

My original choice between compromises, the choice to compromise my work rather than compromise my family, has led me to another choice between compromises. Do I compromise my work yet again, this time to fight AIDS? Do I attend every ACT UP meeting, join every committee, recruit new members? Or do I compromise my fight against AIDS to give myself the benefit of time, as much precious time as I can squeeze out of life, to make advances in my corner of the ethics world?

You, dear Mustafa, make my decisions harder because I also want to meet you. I will travel to Algeria to find you as soon as I complete my first book. Soon, dear son, soon. For all I know, Mustafa, you have grown into the same headstrong young man who Peter was when I made my great compromise.

Compromise is inevitable. The chameleon fits in to survive, but if all we do is survive, if we never express ourselves, never stand out, what is the point of survival? Compromise wisely, young man.

I want to believe Vito Russo, believe that a cure is coming, that I am going to live with HIV, not die from it. If I choose not to fight against AIDS, if I choose not to fight for a cure, what regret will follow if I were to die from AIDS?

Is there regret after life?

5

NEW YORK, SEPT 16, 2001

Brice returned to his apartment with the *New York Times* and two iced coffees.

"Any update on your flight?" Brice asked, placing the styrofoam cup with coffee and milk next to Peter.

"No," Peter said without looking up from his drawing.

After the planes struck the Twin Towers, no one could find words. Then, when they finally spoke, they couldn't stop. Except, of course, Peter. Looking over Peter's shoulder at the visual improvisations of the view south, Brice saw scribbles that looked as if a ruthless dentist had extracted two prominent canines without benefit of anesthesia. Brice sat down and opened the newspaper without reading it.

The longer Peter was stuck in New York, the smaller the apartment felt. Brice had given up on physical intimacy with Peter. He wanted an update about when Peter might catch a flight home. It wasn't worth turning on the television again, though. The images would upset Peter. Besides, all the stations were repeating the same stories over and over. In contrast, the pages of the newspaper burst with details, speculation, the stench of death. Stuck inside the apartment with Peter, Brice had nothing but time to read, to contemplate, to try to understand. Outside, everything was still a noxious jumble, a jumble that crashed into his apartment every morning on smudged newsprint.

Brice had to remind himself that none of this was Peter's fault. The attack was devastating. It sobered the city and country. At first, as the jumble unfolded, the main thing was to get in touch with Peter's friends and family; let them know, without mentioning that, by that point, Peter was freaking out in a fetal position in the middle of the floor, that he was okay; let them know, to everyone's relief, that he hadn't boarded the flight to San Francisco, the flight that didn't make it; let them know that Erica, the gallery owner, asked Peter to stay an extra day to meet with a significant collector. An extra day that was turning into an extra week, into an extra life. A life without flight. Unimaginable. No fucking flights anywhere.

While Brice struggled to maintain a semblance of sanity over his cramped dominion, the entire nation projected its sadness, anger, sympathy, and hate on the defanged metropolis. The city struggled to find remedies for its unspeakable condition. Drinking and crying helped some, reading and talking helped others, but the soreness persisted. No one was sleeping soundly. Brice stayed up listening to music and watching Peter. On nights that Brice managed a wink, the pile of new drawings each morning was more evidence that Peter never slept, that he continued all night to draw the panorama of buildings and lights. As far as Brice could tell, Peter's brush with death put dreams beyond his reach.

While the nation mourned outside, Peter's incessant sketching created a veneer of privacy in the claustrophobic nest. Brice interrupted only to ask what Peter wanted to eat or to coordinate schedules. He contemplated a return to work to give himself breathing room from Peter, but work was pointless.

Brice looked at the *Times*. One detail stuck out—how few of those who perished in the massacre managed a final phone call. Most, vaporized as the jets struck or pulverized in the collapsing towers, didn't. It was different from AIDS. AIDS was a slow-motion massacre, a massacre with time for hundreds of thousands of farewells.

Reports of the fortunate few New Yorkers who spoke with a loved one reminded Brice of his final conversation alone with Rano. In wheezy whispers, Rano had asked Brice to take care of Peter, support Peter as a son might support his father. After catching his breath, Rano then revealed he had a biological son in Algeria, a son he'd never known, a son he wanted Brice to keep secret. Brice took Rano's last requests to heart. He'd written and called Peter frequently in the weeks and months following Rano's death. Over the years, Brice visited Peter in San Francisco or hosted Peter in New York. All that time, he kept the secret of Rano's son from Peter and from everyone else.

Now Brice had to question these promises to Rano. At first, Brice had enjoyed Peter's overdue visit. Peter's gallery show dazzled Brice. Peter always painted well, but his work had evolved remarkably since the last time Brice traveled to San Francisco. Brice felt a renewed attraction as he watched the installation of Peter's show, and then perhaps a tinge of envy as he observed the reaction from the opening-night crowd. Soon after it became apparent Peter wouldn't be flying anywhere soon, Brice wondered if this delay were a belated offering from beyond the grave, if, a decade later, Rano somehow paddled back up the River Styx to arrange Peter's extended visit, to remind Brice of his promises.

As time passed after the gallery opening and the missed flight, though, Brice didn't know what to make of Peter's unpredictable mood swings. While waiting for reviews, Peter's reticence intensified. Then, as coverage of the massacre droned on and on, smothering coverage of everything else—especially of cultural events—Peter seemed to lose the gift of speech altogether. It was like those last visits with Rano. Peter had been quiet then, too. He must have been just as panicked when Rano died, but he'd hidden his panic behind meticulous organization and minute-by-minute care schedules. Now his quiet volatility was shrinking the already miniscule confines of Brice's apartment into an emotional pressure cooker.

It was time. Brice needed to release some steam, needed to discuss his confused feelings. He rustled the newspaper on his lap to get Peter's attention. Peter remained lost in his drawing. Brice tapped the paper like an impromptu bongo, then cleared his throat several times, all to no avail.

Brice stopped rustling the newspaper, stopped tapping it. He stopped clearing his throat. Peter was replying to Brice in the way he knew how, by drawing. In spite of the cramped quarters, in spite of Peter's overflowing anxieties, a desire for Peter grew inside Brice as he watched Peter's creative juices quench the madness. Of course, Brice realized, he couldn't interrupt Peter, couldn't draw his attention. By all rights, Peter should be dead. If life went as planned, Peter would be buried in Pennsylvania. Brice knew Peter wouldn't talk about any of this, at least not soon. Peter wasn't processing his fortunate survival with words. He had to draw.

Brice picked up the *Times* again, perusing it carefully. It was clear from the reporting that, even now, nearly a week later, no one knew how many had perished after the Twin Towers collapsed, after the Pentagon exploded, after the flight to San Francisco, the flight Peter missed, burrowed snuggly into Pennsylvania countryside, snatched from the sky before it could slam into Pennsylvania Avenue.

Bits and pieces of the puzzle were falling into place. Thousands had perished, certainly, but the authorities were still digging, still sifting, still counting. The President spoke on TV, the politicians held hands and sang nonpartisan songs. Financial markets sputtered. The only thing rising was smoke at Ground Zero. Reports said there had been as many as ten or twenty hijackers, that others might have escaped. Middle Easterners. Not from Algeria, it seemed. Maybe Rano hadn't paddled back from the dead. It was, after all, the Hudson flowing by the rubble, not the Styx.

One by one, stories of heroism and stories of misery escaped the rubble. One by one, the tragic missing person posters all over New York took flight from their precarious attachments and, like many of the souls they represented, floated through the air and landed on pavement. One by one, clear memories formed from an abstract landscape of terror.

"Hey!" Brice exploded, shaking the newspaper at Peter. "Your review. It's here."

Handing the newspaper to Peter, Brice pointed to the article. As extraordinary as it was for anyone Brice knew to get a notice in the *Times*, the review's arrival detonated a sense of normalcy in the apartment, as though the outside world hadn't forgotten entirely the survivors pushing on with things. A small miracle of linearity and causality displaced a bit of chaos. Watching Peter read and reread the review, Brice could feel the steam venting off.

"So much for my career as an artist," Peter said, slapping down the newspaper on top of the drawings littering the table.

"The review was better than that," Brice said. Peter's childish self-pity annoyed Brice. "It's much better, and you know it."

"I'm stuck," Peter said, tears welling in his eyes. "I can't paint again." He leaned on the table, resting his head on his hands. A siren passed by on the street below. Peter's torso began to shake with uncontrolled gasps.

"Listen," Brice said, retrieving the newspaper from the clutter of drawings. "The reviewer says, 'The lyrical quality of these California landscapes is achieved with a masterful technique reminiscent of a Hopper or perhaps an O'Keeffe.' That's brilliant."

Peter's crying grew into a quiet sob. Realizing Peter hadn't heard a word he said, Brice put his hand on Peter's. Peter continued sobbing. His breathing slowed. The kitchen clock ticktock seemed to stop in a sympathetic response.

It had been a decade since Brice had seen Peter fall apart like this. He moved to Peter's side of the table and put his arm around Peter's shoulder. He almost could hear Peter's heart pounding. Peter cried longer and, after it seemed he could cry no more, he sat up to hug Brice and rest his head on Brice's shoulder.

"You can't stop painting," Brice said. "You did that already, after Rano died."

"I'm sorry, it's not the review," Peter whispered in Brice's ear. Then, after a few more breaths, "You're right about that."

Brice hugged Peter tighter. Peter started crying again and kissed Brice's cheek softly.

"It's been ten years," Brice whispered back. It was time to release the rest of the pressure. He rose, pulling Peter up from the chair, then leading him to the bedroom.

"The night Rano died."

July 13, 1989 – Birthday

Dear Mustafa,

Another birthday without AIDS. A blessing in light of my HIV status. Good health breathes life into my wish to meet you soon.

It's not the big five-oh. Your father isn't an old man quite yet, Mustafa. I'm determined to make it past fifty. Far beyond. In these times, though, gay men celebrate any chance we get. Peter and I invited friends over for a party, friends I thought I could enlist for ACT UP. I can't keep up with my ACT UP commitments, so my birthday celebration was a two-for-one, socializing and activism.

Peter wanted to serve something Algerian. I suggested a mezze platter. Mezze may not be the best example of our Algerian cuisine, but it is easy for Peter to order. He bought dishes from the nearby Middle Eastern restaurant along with an almond tart for dessert. I helped him brew mint tea. I told him it's called "Berber whiskey" in Algeria. I'm not sure why Peter wanted to delve into my ancestral culture. Maybe because I told him about boukalates recently.

I hardly feel Algerian anymore. I realize that may shock you, but my identity is American. Actually, even my dark skin feels American. After nearly thirty years, I believe I've even got the hang of American discrimination, of being called derogatory names, of being ignored by retail clerks, of being scrutinized by security guards, of being spat upon.

I still find America's post-slave culture something of a mystery. It's hard enough for me to understand America's flavor of injustice towards people who aren't lily white, but I certainly don't understand how to frame it in the context of post–Civil War emancipation, of chattel slavery without direct ownership. It's like the bank took away houses from the white folks, but they continue to act as if the houses were theirs.

I didn't spend my birthday ruminating on racism, though. I used the party to recruit ACT UP members, sharing with guests the speech I found recently by Vito Russo.

Reviewing some of my recent journal entries, it seems I have a bit of a crush on Vito. What's not to like? He's sexy, articulate, and an activist.

Manfredo was first to arrive at the party. He's had full-blown AIDS for a few months. I assume the others who joined us at our house have HIV, but I didn't pry. We're all scared of AIDS. Many gay men, even Peter, are too scared to test. Knowing HIV status helps control the spread of the virus, but a positive result can feel like a death sentence. There's also fear of quarantining HIV-positive men and of loss of work. That's how scary test results are to many of us. Each of us knows the disease could strike any time. It's a comforting distraction to talk about something else, anything else, but it's the thing on everyone's mind. Like a drunk uncle occupying the remotest bedroom in the house, there's no vacation from it.

Vito's speech provided a ray of hope for us. I read sections of the speech aloud. We discussed what actions we could take, what we could do to prevent more AIDS suffering. Everyone wanted to know ways to get active politically. Vito's speech provided inspiration, provoked commitments to fight.

Manfredo plays on the gay soccer team, although you might not guess it from his pudgy frame. Normally, he's quiet. At the party he began to cry as he told everyone what he's been going through. He showed us a couple KS lesions. There weren't many dry eyes around the table. Luckily, Manfredo isn't getting worse, hasn't developed other symptoms. The doctors started him on AZT right away.

Manfredo's show-and-tell got everyone talking about their maladies. What a birthday party conversation! Our dining room sounded like an old folks' home, except everyone was gay and young.

I told my friends about these gruesome headaches I've had the last few days. All of us jump to the conclusion that we have full-blown AIDS every time we have a sour stomach or a runny nose. Manfredo and Peter think something must be triggering my migraines. I told them I've never had migraines. The others laugh and tell me, honey, no queen with AIDS has ever died of a headache. Thankfully, no headache on my birthday.

Evenings like this remind me why I fell in love with Peter. He's not all terrible. It was thoughtful of him to throw a birthday party and to allow me to commandeer the conversation, to read at such length from Vito's speech. He doesn't always like when the activist side of me emerges, although he admitted afterwards I may have done my fair share for ACT UP, recruiting several new members.

After the party, I should have thanked Peter. Instead I got angry at him. I didn't realize how angry until I wrote this entry. He told me I should work harder on my research. He said other people can recruit for ACT UP. He's in bed waiting for me, or asleep already. I'm not sure if I'm angry about what he told me. It could be unresolved feelings I have about our relationship, feelings I don't understand yet, concerns that started when I tested positive. Perhaps I have been unfair to Peter. I have tried not to be cruel about it. I should be transparent with my feelings.

Instead anger brews inside.

Instead I brought Brice into our relationship to compensate for what's missing.

Maybe that wasn't such a good idea, but at least I can blame it on Linh. She's more Peter's friend than mine, and she's the one who introduced Brice to us. I know I have this rage. If I understood its source, I might be able to tell Peter about it.

I hope you are not angry at me, Mustafa. I'm coming to find you the second I finish my book.

6

NEW YORK, SEPT 28, 2001

Erica observed Thomas from across her gallery, waiting for the right time, figuring out the right angle. He'd been examining one of Peter's landscapes for a time. She knew this landscape well. It was the first of Peter's paintings she'd seen. In her never-ending talent hunt, she'd traveled to San Francisco for the annual show of up-and-coming Bay Area talent at the Yerba Buena Center for the Arts. Peter's landscape dripped with uncertainty, a demure house on the coast caught in the afterglow of a glorious sunset as though it hadn't been able to say what it needed to say, hadn't been able to provide something the sun desired before the day ended. The technique was impeccable.

Erica pulled her blouse tight and brushed her short blonde hair behind her ears before she walked surreptitiously across the gallery. She didn't want to startle Thomas. This was not a time to pounce. But she could use a sale right now. After 9/11—the designation the press landed on for the morning of hijackings and subsequent massacre—she nervously watched as financial markets finally opened and then plummeted for a week. Even reliable art buyers like Thomas seemed skittish.

"You might have saved Peter's life, you know," Erica said.

"But I barely met him," Thomas said. His eyes didn't move from the art.

"Oh, that's right. So sorry."

Crap. Erica had forgotten to reschedule the dinner with Thomas and Peter. Now it was too late. A stupid drama in her Park Slope apartment building sidetracked her. Like everyone else in New York absorbed in the disaster playing over and again on television, Erica had lost track of appointments and commitments in the days following the collapse of the Twin Towers.

"My neighbors went missing after 9/11," Erica said.

"Oh, dear," Thomas said, turning slowly to face Erica. The gallery lights reflected off his smooth dark pate. The intensity of the light brought to life a luxurious palette of silky browns and reds in his jacket, a lovely detail viscerally discernable from across the room and quite glamourous up close. "Are they okay?"

"No one knew how to contact them," Erica answered. "The police took a report, but didn't follow up."

"I know how that goes."

"My next-door neighbor worried the missing neighbors had a cat," Erica said. She almost mentioned her landlord was predictably useless when she'd called to check about a cat, but remembered Thomas also was a landlord. "This neighbor wanted to call the fire department, but the other neighbors convinced her the fire department had higher priorities than breaking down doors to rescue cats."

"That's the truth," Thomas said. "I still can't believe I don't know one person who died."

"Same here," Erica said, wondering how she was going to steer the conversation back to Peter's painting. Two weeks had passed, and it still seemed impossible to avoid the topic of 9/11. "Kind of a miracle."

"Oh, so your missing neighbors showed up?" Thomas asked.

"Once air travel resumed," Erica said. "You know what? I forgot to ask them about a cat."

Thomas turned back to Peter's painting. Erica was relieved that he seemed more interested in the paintings than in reviving 9/11 memories. Maybe people were moving on from the horror. Maybe the art market was ready to come back. If not, the next rent check wouldn't clear.

"Something about Peter's work changed in the last year or so," Thomas said, breaking the silence. "Something more than adding houses and structures to his landscapes."

"He did start painting up the coast in Mendocino about a year ago," Erica said, relieved that Thomas wasn't insisting on a meal with Peter.

"Better pot, I hear," Thomas said, grinning mischievously.

Erica picked up clues during her trips to San Francisco that Peter might have used drugs. And from some of his early works. It was a valid business concern, of course, although prices for artists whose drug habits progressed all the way to lethal overdose often compensated for their lack of output. Erica guessed that a gallerist who happened to represent the next Basquiat probably would do just fine. To her face, Peter had denied partaking in anything stronger than pot and wine these days. She believed him, although he'd seemed a little hazy on opening night.

"In Peter's recent work, each house, each structure appears to tell a story," Erica said to Thomas. "I don't know how he'd be able to get high all the time and paint like that."

"It's insane that this is his first New York show," Thomas said.

"Peter took a long break that put his career on hold. He stopped painting for five years after his lover died of AIDS."

"But Peter looks like the very picture of health." Thomas' eyes revealed grave concern, as though he'd just received a mortal diagnosis.

"Yes, very healthy, and my doctor clients tell me AIDS isn't the death sentence it was."

"Finally, thank God."

Thomas turned back to look at the landscape again. Erica relaxed. Thomas wouldn't spend this much time if he didn't like Peter's work. She could use the sale. Not a single piece of art sold since the 9/11 attack. It seemed she'd addressed the concerns that might block a sale. She'd come to recognize a rhythm in the way Thomas made acquisitions. He moved slowly and decisively. She had to take time to strike a deal. The time looked right.

"I can see you like this painting," Erica said. "There are several more in back if you'd like to see others."

"I'm not sure. It's brilliant work. I'd hoped to spend time with Peter, though. Get a sense of him. It gives me a connection to the art when I know the artist. Otherwise, I'd collect the dead ones."

Thomas moved closer to the art. He was consistent about meeting artists. After Peter's opening night, he'd invited Peter and Erica for dinner at his place in Harlem. Like many people who grew up in Connecticut, Erica wasn't comfortable in Manhattan above 96th Street. She said she'd prefer dinner at a trendy new place in Chelsea. Thomas' "um-hmm" had let her know that he recognized her fear of Harlem and would let her get away with it only because she represented such gifted talent.

"Well, unfortunately for a meeting and fortunately for Peter, he finally got a flight back to San Francisco," Erica said. Arranging meetings with other artists was easy. They lived closer, most within an hour or two of Manhattan. Now Erica had no idea how to make a deal go through. "You know he was supposed to return to San Francisco on that plane that went down in Pennsylvania."

Thomas turned to Erica again. This time his brown eyes were open wide. "He rebooked his flight so we could have dinner?"

"Yes," Erica answered.

There was a long silence. Even the traffic noise from outside paused. Erica could hear herself breathing. She looked at the landscape on the wall. Something about Peter had changed since she first saw this work and tracked him down. He seemed more confident then. His work improved in the past year, but he seemed less sure of himself in the past few months.

"An artist with nine lives," Thomas said. "I'm sure you'll understand why now I really must meet Peter."

September 2, 1989 – AIDS

Dear Mustafa,

Severe headaches after my birthday, not migraines. Turned out to be encephalitis. Peter got me to hospital, Peter's hospital. Don't remember much, just how hard it was to get admitted with headache. "Go home, take aspirin."

Was there for three weeks. three. Doctors didn't know what I had at first. Something rare. Not good sign when it's something rare rare these days. Something rare = AIDS. Got out with intact mind intact. Feeling bad I've missed everything ACT UP friends are doing. Need my health need to get back to research. No research, no Algeria, no Mustafa.

Mostly intact. Had trouble with balance first week home. Better every day since I returned returned. Tired. Still have random memory problems. Not as scary now as in random hospital. The times I was present enough to know what was going on, I freaking out. Mostly intact. Health. Tired. Tired. Couldn't remember where I was born for couple days, even after doctor told me. San Francisco.

Doctor says I dodged bullet.

Now officially have AIDS. Of course, rare disease, not something common, not pneumocystis, not KS, not pneumocystis. Not me. Something hard to diagnose with with.

Tired.

no clear therapy.

Now officially on AZT. Learning about the side effects. Not pretty. Dodged bullet, but more on way. Mostly intact. Random.

First time contemplated possibility never seeing you. Cried.

7

SAN FRANCISCO, OCT 13, 2001

Angel was excited to visit Peter in his art studio, excited and apprehensive. His was the excitement of lovers meeting after a long hiatus—the fantasy of renewed passions, the fear of sags and furrows. The building door was unlocked. Angel entered the rickety two-story building and tread over the threadbare carpet, past door signs for oddball political causes, for porn studios, for artists, for other questionable tenants. It wasn't the South of Market shithole he remembered. The building where Angel once had spent so much time with Peter was coming up these days, along with the rest of the neighborhood. Through the hallway, the buzz of small enterprise now overpowered the silent work of cockroaches. The interior style was evolving into something Angel associated with Section 8 chic.

Angel's excitement grew as he ascended the creaky stairs. He hadn't expected Peter's invitation, the groggy phone call earlier in the day. Luckily, Angel had stopped doing lines a week ago, hadn't dropped any ecstasy. It seemed like a week, anyway. The headaches were gone. Angel wanted his taut body to look good in front of the mirror, not so haggard, not so mangy. Today was another clean day.

Angel's backpack applied zero pressure to his shoulders while he climbed. Sales were good the past few days, which meant Angel had plenty of cash. His distributor split town for a week, though, which meant La Farmacia—as his backpack was known to clients—would continue to be light on his shoulders for a few more days. Angel reached the second floor. Apprehension supplanted excitement. He had no idea what Peter had in mind. At least there was plenty of coke, if that's why Peter called.

Angel pushed open the unlocked door and stood at the entrance of the sunny studio. Peter looked hot. Same sturdy legs, same scruffy beard. A little more gray. They embraced. Peter held on. His sober hug felt genuine, different from pharmaceutically uninhibited physical contact. A warmth filled Angel as he stepped inside the studio. It felt better than the last time they were together, much better.

"Wow, you've really cleaned up here," Angel said, looking around the studio. The sun reflected off the polished floor, casting a blueish tint on the walls. Angel hardly recognized the place now. It was quite a few notches above Section 8. It was the kind of place he was looking to rent.

"I should be painting more and cleaning less," Peter said. "Really nice to see you here after so many years."

Unlike other chapters of Angel's memory, the chapter about staying in the studio was as pristine as the blue polished floor. That chapter took place after his boyfriend died, which was right after Rano died. Peter and Angel had helped each other while their boyfriends died, first Angel helping Peter and then, a month later, Peter helping Angel. Wham, bam, and unexpectedly Peter and Angel found themselves bonding, sharing the usually unusual experience of youthful widowers grieving their losses. Ashes scattered, they turned to each other for support, seeking some way, any way, to comprehend what transpired during those calamitous months. Sex and drugs had been easier, mucho sex and mucho drugs even better.

"I don't see many paintings here," Angel said. He saw drawings, lots of drawings, on the large table in the middle of the studio, but only four paintings on the walls. "I could use a space like this if you're not working."

"I shipped all my new work to New York for a gallery show last month," Peter said, walking over to the table covered with drawings. "How can I rent this place to you? I'm stuck. I can't paint to save my life. I don't even know if I'm renewing the lease."

"How could you not renew the lease?" Angel asked. He knew Peter loved this space, the abundant light, the skanky neighborhood. So many improvements since Angel's last visit. Angel had muchos recuerdos here, too. But the studio was always an integral part of Peter's San Francisco existence. "Where will you paint if you don't renew?"

"That's what I'm saying," Peter answered. "I started working on New York skylines based on the sketches I made there. I just can't paint. If I can't paint and my work isn't selling, how can I afford to renew the lease?"

So much for living here again. Angel sighed. Back to the drawing board for digs. He didn't know much about art, but a show at a New York gallery had to be a big deal. He walked over to the table, close to Peter. All the drawings were skylines, some recognizable with jagged rows of rooftops, others less clear with scribbles and colliding lines, all dark, most furious. It seemed like grist for at least one painting.

A stream of traffic rumbled by outside. Examining the smoke and destruction in the drawings, Angel put dos y dos together. Peter must have been in New York and sketched the destruction of 9/11. Hard to imagine actually being in New York when the jets struck the towers. The sketches had to be Peter's way of talking about it. Most of Angel's clients were still talking about where they were when the planes struck. Angel even remembered where he was that day. After snorting all night with three guys in Pacific Heights, the host got an urgent phone call at dawn. He turned on the television. A jet exploded in the unblemished World Trade Center tower while they watched. Angel couldn't deal with that image. It made no sense. He snorted another line.

"I was supposed to return on that flight to San Francisco," Peter explained over the traffic noise. "You know, the flight that didn't make it, the flight that went down in Pennsylvania. I changed my ticket the day before."

"I was flying high enough for both of us that morning," Angel said, browsing through Peter's drawings. "That Twin Tower shit totally freaked me out, watching the plane hit the tower. Cabrón, no wonder you can't paint."

"Yeah, maybe missing my appointment with death is part of it," Peter said.

Sometimes it took Peter a while to say what was on his mind, especially the personal shit, but today was nonstop gushing, by Peter's standards, like a busted fountain or something. This reunion was heavier than Angel expected. If only his damn distributor was still in town, he could procure some quality weed. That would calm down Peter. Angel turned to comfort Peter with another hug, but he was halfway across the room.

For Angel, this studio always was an oasis in the morass of the building, of the neighborhood, of his life. He'd moved in two days after his boyfriend died, a day after the asshole landlord evicted him. Peter had been a saint to offer Angel a safe haven. Today the space had something else going on, though, some loco vibe Angel didn't recognize. He looked at the drawings again. There was some serious bad shit in those lines.

Peter picked up a book from a shelf next to a window and carried it back to Angel. It was both peculiar and familiar, a black leather cover with a broken miniature silver fastener dangling on a strap. Angel knew he'd seen this, but he couldn't remember where.

"Do you know anything about this?" Peter asked, holding it so Angel could see its cover.

"Oh, it's Rano's diary," Angel answered. Surprise. Here was Rano, appearing again so many years later. Maybe the crazy energy Angel felt in the room was emanating from this notebook. Or maybe it was just part of Angel's adjustment to reality without pharmaceutical enhancements. "I think Rano wanted me to destroy it. Wouldn't he have wanted something like this destroyed? It's been too long to remember."

"I wish you had destroyed it," Peter said, placing the black book on the table. "It's so sad, so confusing for me to read. I'm ashamed of some really important things I didn't know about Rano."

Peter was talking up an emotional shitstorm today. Angel only knew of the diary by accident. Anxious to see what Rano wrote, Angel reached over for the notebook. Peter swatted away his hand.

"No one sees Rano's journal," Peter said, pulling the notebook close to his chest and hugging it. "At least until it stops keeping me awake at night."

"Okay, puta, you don't have to kill me for being curious," Angel said. The diary shit seemed as bad for Peter as the 9/11 shit. Worse, Angel sensed, watching the way Peter clutched it. Angel didn't want to talk about the diary, or "the journal," as Peter called it. He also sensed that Peter was holding back something major, that as much as the diary bothered him and as much as 9/11 bothered him, there was, as per usual, some other shit Peter hadn't revealed yet. Right about now would be a really good time to smoke a joint. Changing subjects had to suffice. "If you'll keep your hands to yourself, I'll show you which drawing I like best."

Peter nodded and Angel reached over again, pulling out one of the skyline drawings and placing it atop the others. The iconic Twin Towers were missing from New York's skyline. In their place, smoke distending from Ground Zero to the sky reflected eerily off the thousands of windows witnessing the towers' absence.

"Funny, this is one of my favorites, too," Peter said, grinning as he placed Rano's diary back on the table next to the drawing Angel liked. "I drew this at Brice's place, right before we fucked."

Chinga tu madre. That was not information Angel wanted to hear. Peter had slept with Brice the night Rano died, too. That was other information Angel hadn't wanted to know. Peter never spoke about it, but somehow the comfort Brice offered Peter that sad night got back to Angel. Today Peter was talking way more shit than Angel wanted to hear.

"Did you invite me over to tease me about what's in the diary, or to give me the details about fucking Brice, or just to offend me?" Angel asked.

"Sorry," Peter replied, putting the diary back on the shelf by the window. "It's just that I'm flipping out a little right now, remembering the Twin Towers collapsing and thinking about the flight that crashed and trying to paint and everything. I'm too stressed-out to be properly stressed-out. I thought it would be nice to smoke a joint, chill out, catch up with you."

"Should I be flattered that, after all these years, when you want someone to smoke with, you call me?" Angel asked, lifting La Farmacia from the floor and shaking it. "It doesn't matter. No pot aquí."

"Really?" Peter asked incredulously as he returned from the shelf. "You always have the best."

"Really," Angel answered. He put the backpack back on. "It's weird with you today."

"Really?" Peter repeated. He paced over to the kitchenette, rummaged in the fridge for a beer, and twisted off the cap. "What's weird is the last time you were here. Remember that? The time you heard the cops sneaking up the stairs and practically leapt out that window over there. The time you ditched me and hightailed it all the way to Phoenix. The time you left me here high and dry without a phone call or even a postcard. I worried about what happened to you for weeks."

"Oh, fuck, that's right," Angel said. Peter was right. It was a low-class, if necessary, exit, a long-forgotten chapter in Angel's memory. No arrest that night, though. No arrest for many years. Angel was nimble, knew the moves. He sensed the heat a mile away, knew when to beat it. Business had been good in Phoenix. Then in Los Angeles. Until that time, until that little incident with the law earlier in the year. "Felony," they called the charge. A return to San Francisco had been in order after that. Angel slipped his thumbs through the backpack straps. "You're right, cabrón. I'm sorry about that. And sorry I don't have any weed. No weed makes it hard for you to relax and hard for me to make payroll."

"I'm driving to Mendocino this afternoon," Peter said, tasting the beer. "Wanna join?"

"I can't drive up there today," Angel said. Sitting in Peter's car for an hour or two was an invitation for more strange energy, if not actual torture. It reminded Angel of those grinning invitations from the old priest to go for a ride when God knows what would happen. "Besides, what would I do? Watch you not paint? I need to find a place to rent today."

"Too bad," Peter said, taking a longer swig. "I met a guy up there who sells great pot, the best I've smoked since forever."

Okay, this was different from entertaining Peter in a car. This was business. This was a potential new supplier. As strange as Peter was acting today, Angel appreciated how Peter watched out for him. The bond they'd formed taking care of their dying boyfriends still meant something. They'd always be there for each other.

"Maybe I could join you, after all," Angel said.

"What happened to finding an apartment today?" Peter asked.

"I heard there might be nice opportunities up the coast." Angel winked and rubbed his shirt up and down in a way that revealed his ripped abs. It was a signature move that never failed, especially with Peter.

Peter smiled and put down the beer. "Okay, let's go."

September 30, 1989 – Art

Dear Mustafa,

When I lived in Algeria, I had no inkling how significant visual art would be in my life. I sometimes wonder how much you've learned about art (or literature or music). I don't remember Algeria having an art scene, at least anything like America's art scene. No Algerian I knew had money to spare for anything but the simplest home decorations.

Then Peter entered my life and I had an around-the-clock artist. He doesn't talk much about art with me, though. I experience his creativity viscerally. I know by his mood, for instance, when he's had a good day painting.

All that changed during Brice's last visit to help out with my brain infection recovery.

First, some background. I'm still adjusting to AZT. Feel shitty, but better every day. Brain function, normal as far as I can tell, except I get tired fast. Doctors say I was lucky. Just a touch of encephalitis. They don't know what caused it and they have no idea what treated it. Sometimes I think I'd do better without doctors.

I've been able to maintain a reduced teaching schedule. Not researching as much as I want because I have to rest, but I find energy here and there. Leslie the Librarian stopped by to offer support and drop off a package of research books. Mostly, she stopped by to make sure I was okay. She's sweet. Her chicken "penicillin" soup is the best. Of everyone in my life, she's the one who seems to understand best the significance of my academic work. The bond of our homosexuality may have kindled her initial interest in my work, but now she's as excited for research results as I am.

I feel bad missing ACT UP meetings. I hope my comrades understand. It's not like I'm the first member to miss meetings due to illness. After my hospital stay, it looks like I have a big choice coming up, the choice between participating as an AIDS activist and completing my research. This keeps me up at night. It's a compromise I dread. My decision may determine whether I ever see you. I can see it approaching as clearly as the distant headlights of a truck winding along the Algerian coast.

But back to art, which is where I started. Brice flew out for a week to help with my move home. Convenient time for him to take a break from his business, the stretch between back-to-school windows and Halloween windows. Brice made me happy. I wasn't in great form. Peter appreciated the help, though he gets jealous sometimes. Brice understands that. He ingratiates himself with Peter.

The most fascinating thing happened while I was recuperating in bed. I was so bored, I listened in on Brice's conversation with Peter about New York artists who decorate retail windows. "Snooped" is a better word. I was bored and tired, but then I noticed how enthralled Peter seemed, animated in a way I hadn't seen for years.

Also, this was the first time I noticed Peter and Brice bonding. Maybe I'm the one who should be jealous. Here's my transcription of notes I jotted down during their conversation.

Brice - There's this rumor Bonwit Teller is going bust.

Peter - What's Bonwit Teller?

B - Girlfriend, please. Super high-end fashion. It's as iconic as the Twin Towers. I mean, if you're actually gay.

P - Hmm, didn't Rano buy something there? Yeah, that plaid suit. He loves to wear that suit for photos.

B - I introduced him to Bonwit Teller. Security watched Rano the whole time, like he was going to steal the fucking shoelaces. Imagine their surprise when he walked out wearing that plaid suit.

P - How much did that suit cost?

B - You don't want to know. "Centuries working on the beach" is all Rano said. He loves posing for photos in that getup. He insisted I take photos of him in front of the World Trade Center. So zany.

P - So who cares if this store goes out of business?

B - What?!?! Problems started when Bonwit Teller moved its flagship store into Trump Tower. As far as I can tell, Trump Tower is a self-aggrandizing erection with as much taste as Velveeta on a dog turd. Not an address for fashion.

P - And now they're folding. So what?

B - A quick history lesson about Bonwit Teller and gay artists. They practically invented the art of window dressing. In a stroke of public relations genius, the store invited Salvador Dalí to decorate its windows.

P - Dalí did store windows?

B - That was 1929, the year Dalí and the poet Lorca were carrying on their surreal relationship. Many significant gay artists followed in Dalí's footsteps.

P - Such as?

B - Jasper and his boyfriend dressed Bonwit Teller windows in the 1950s.

P - Jasper Johns and Robert Rauschenberg?

B - They worked under the closeted pseudonym Matson Jones. In the '60s, Andy Warhol took over the Bonwit Teller windows from Matson Jones.

P - Gay artists practically held court there.

B - Now you understand. For gay artists, Bonwit Teller going out of business would be as unfathomable as the Twin Towers collapsing. Bonwit Teller owes its fuck-you fashion attitude to the queens who decorated it. Gay sensibility hidden in plain view on Fifth Avenue.

Peter asked about other artists who'd dressed retail windows. Brice mentioned artists he knew, including an artist who died last year, an artist named Basquiat. Of course, I hadn't heard of Basquiat, but that name got Peter's attention. Brice said artists like Basquiat used retail windows to display their work when they couldn't sign with galleries. Peter asked a lot of questions. He sounded ready to jump into business with Brice.

Needless to say, I was pleased to see Peter and Brice getting along. When I was confirming this later with Brice, he told me Basquiat overdosed on heroin. Basquiat was brilliant, Brice said, and only in his twenties when he died.

That seems like such a fucking waste of talent. I'm dealing with news of two more friends who died while I was in the hospital. My dentist, Paul Miller, died. No more drilling with Doc Miller. My violinist acquaintance Dusann Bobb died, too. I already miss him practicing Bach's lovely Air on the G String.

Now I'm dealing with my own case of AIDS. I'm scared to research my book because I can't help my ACT UP friends, and I'm scared to help my ACT UP friends because I can't research my book. Most of all, I'm scared that, either way, I won't see you. Along with the possible demise of Bonwit Teller, it feels like the entire gay world is collapsing, like an era of homosexual men boosting the arts and sciences is ending.

What pissed me off, and the reason I'm telling you about this, is that Basquiat overdosed in an era when so many of us are struggling to save ourselves from AIDS. I realize addiction and depression are problems, but in the face of a pandemic, in the face of what is the genocide of our entire community, Basquiat seems so selfish.

Maybe, I'm realizing just now as I write this, maybe selfishness is in the nature of artists. Writing this is only pissing me off more. I really need to do something to stop this. I need to get out of bed and get back to work.

8

New York, Oct 14, 2001

Brice pushed the penthouse buzzer. After a moment, Thomas opened the oversized door. "Thanks for coming."

"Is it me, or has everyone gone off the rails since 9/11?" Brice asked as Thomas took his jacket. "The subway got to your stop just before the porn started."

"I'm not sure what you mean," Thomas said, pressing a switch that lit up the entire apartment.

"I boarded an empty Harlem express and felt lucky to have the car to myself," Brice said. "Then, at 42nd Street, this couple got on and started making out. Like I wasn't even there. It got quite risqué."

"It couldn't have been any more risqué than what goes on in Central Park." Thomas started down the hall.

"It was practically like sitting in a porn theater," Brice said. Maybe this wasn't the best topic to kick off a business meeting, especially since Thomas also was the art collector interested in Peter's work. But the city seemed crazy since 9/11. "I got off the train just as they started getting off."

As Brice followed Thomas to the living room, he counted three or maybe four bedrooms along the hallway. Thomas pointed out a plaque above the door to a study crammed with books. *Colors fade, temples crumble, empires fall, but wise words endure.* Thomas boasted it was a trophy his late lover won debating the Columbia professor who wrote the elevated words.

Artwork was everywhere. Serious artwork. High pre-War ceilings gracefully accommodated the largest of the canvases. Brice didn't recognize the artists, but he knew the art was smashing. So was the view of the park. Uptown lights glowed around the silhouette of sylvan Central Park hills. In the distance, Times Square radiated midtown excitement miles into the sky. Flights descending to La Guardia passed regularly, engines quietly whooshing, lights flashing. On a round table in the vast living room, white wine and bowls of mixed nuts were waiting.

"When we met at Peter's gallery opening, you reeled off an impressive list of clients," Thomas said, pouring Brice a glass. "How's business after the terrorist attack?"

"I'm anticipating the frenzy to replace Halloween displays with holiday displays," Brice answered, inspecting the wine. After the attack, retailers asked for many more last-minute changes than usual. Not minor adjustments, but major redesigns that kept Brice awake at night. Brice worked the magic he could, but there was only so much improvisation possible with a warehouse chock-full of custom decorations ordered months in advance. None of this mattered for tonight's discussion. "Everyone wants simpler displays," Brice continued after a sip, "more spiritual, less literal. No matter how cute, a chorus of electrically powered dancing elves looks a bit extravagant after 9/11. A lone flickering candle more than suffices. I'm lucky that every year it's a question of how much I want to expand."

"As I mentioned at the opening, it's a great time to get established in Harlem," Thomas said, leaning over to click the music system remote. "President Clinton's moving his office to 125th Street. Upscale is moving uptown."

"Isn't that *Billy the Kid*?" Brice asked.

"Good ear," Thomas replied. "You move like a dancer."

"I danced until I tore a ligament ten years ago."

Without prompting, Thomas launched into a story about meeting Aaron Copland years ago at a party. As it happened, Thomas said, there was a benefit after a ballet performance of *Billy the Kid*. Patrons at the party kept asking Thomas to get them a drink. He wasn't sure that's why Copland came over, but once Copland started small talk and put his hand around Thomas' shoulder, the guests stopped presuming Thomas was a waiter. With everyone pressing for a piece of the maestro, Thomas managed only a short conversation. He asked Copland the inspiration for his ballet, if it was Billy's heroism in the face of frontier justice or Billy's stand against the establishment that attracted Copland to the material. As Copland turned to the next guest, the only inspiration he mentioned to Thomas was the astounding musculature of the dancer who originated the title role.

While Thomas told his story, Brice looked over Central Park again. The wine was as spectacular as the view, just the right temperature. He put the nuts he was holding into his mouth one by one and chewed slowly, wondering what Thomas actually had in mind. Thomas was excited to tell this story about the dance world, but why? For Brice, this was a straightforward business meeting. Thomas would introduce his retail tenants so Brice could dress their windows and improve their holiday sales. That, in turn, would improve Thomas' bottom line.

Sitting on a luxurious couch, looking at spectacular art and views, enjoying a perfect Chardonnay, listening to Thomas' story about Copland, Brice realized how much he missed dancing. Sure, the retail window business was a more satisfying way to pay the rent than sitting at some desk all day. It more than paid the bills. Perhaps it was the timing of Thomas' story. Perhaps it was the beauty of Peter's gallery show. Perhaps it was the wild abandon of the subway lovers. Brice wasn't sure, but whatever it was, something told him he was wasting his time with retail windows, that he should dance again.

After Thomas ended his story, after he repeated the line about the muscled dancer who inspired Copland, he picked up the wine bottle and refilled Brice's glass. It certainly seemed Thomas regaled him with this story because there was something at stake besides retail windows. Thomas hadn't invited him here just to do a deal. The silence made Brice uncomfortable, but not uncomfortable enough to get to the point, to ask Thomas to introduce his tenants. Brice examined an abstract oil painting, waiting for Thomas to bring up the real point of their meeting.

"Look how I'm monopolizing our conversation," Thomas said after a long sip of wine. "Tell me how you know Peter."

Brice looked down at his full glass of wine, realizing that's what Thomas' story was really about, realizing Thomas was interested in Peter for more than his art. Thomas was setting the stage for Brice, finding common ground before inquiring about Peter.

"Peter and I were introduced through a mutual friend," Brice responded after a sip. "We were introduced by a lovely Vietnamese woman who probably understands Peter's art better than I do. His art has matured masterfully."

"Yes, his art is quite something," Thomas said. "He has explored masterfully, to borrow your word, the interplay of abstraction and realism. I sometimes wonder how the death of Peter's lover influences his work, whether he's working out something through this interplay."

There wasn't time for Brice to get into Peter's history with Rano, much less Peter's current dilemma with the journal. In fact, there wasn't time for much more chitchat at all. Brice needed to get back to the mess at work before he drank too much. However, Thomas' interest in Peter's art, his articulate interpretation of the paintings, made Brice realize something about himself.

"You're helping me understand the significance of Peter's art," Brice said, setting down his glass. "I envy his latest work because he's pushed on and achieved so much."

"I'm not sure I know what you mean," Thomas said.

"It's not important," Brice said. Of course it was important, but there wasn't time. This was a business meeting, not therapy. Brice's envy of Peter was for Peter's persistence and the breakthroughs that resulted, persistence that Brice abandoned a decade earlier. Now Brice was confused about his own attraction to Peter. He'd have to sort it out later. "Unfortunately, my time is short, so, if you wouldn't mind, I'd like to learn how I can help your retail tenants."

OCTOBER 8, 1989 – DENMARK

Dear Mustafa,

It's been one week and the world is still here. Civilization has not collapsed. Peter's family would claim the Second Coming is nigh. If Peter were in touch with them, that is.

What earth-shattering event took place a week ago, dear Mustafa? News that I'm sure didn't reach Algeria.

Denmark legalized gay unions a week ago. That must have shaken America's Evangelical community off its foundation, knocked a few crucifixes off walls. For everyone else, our china is unbroken, our furniture in place, our meat and vegetables still fresh in softly whirring refrigerators. Life goes on as if nothing had happened, even though everything homosexual changed.

This legal cataclysm has got me asking two questions.

First, if Denmark can do it, why can't America? It's this nation's conundrum. She's part practical businessman, part praise-be-to-Jesus quack. Part hardworking immigrant, part belligerent foreign tourist. Part Nobel Prize winner, part illiterate laborer. Part white, part black. Part straight, part gay.

America has trouble talking about the black part. She can't even acknowledge the gay bit.

It comes down to identity—nationality, race, religion, sexual orientation, whatever you please. Identity locks you into a worldview, traps you in the constructs of your ghetto. Danish Lutherans and American Evangelicals read the same bible, but you wouldn't know it based on homosexuality.

American churches raise too much money from their anti-gay propaganda. Whisper innuendo about gay pedophilia and megachurch donation lines ring off the hook. Can't kill the gay golden goose. My opinion doesn't matter, though. If you identify with American evangelicalism, you will carry its homophobic baggage in spite of the cognitive dissonances you encounter on your journey.

That, my dear Mustafa, is the power of identity.

Which brings me to my second question: What do train robberies have to do with identity? Hang on. Allow me to make the connection.

While I was recovering last month, Leslie the Librarian left me a paper about the history of train robberies. Her note suggested links between the ways technology and crime change. It seemed random, but Leslie has a way of connecting dots.

As trains replaced stagecoaches throughout America's Wild West, robbers upped their ante. There were fewer trains, but they carried more passengers. They had more gold and money than stagecoaches. Trains made magnificent targets, carrying the equivalent of twenty or thirty years of normal salary while steaming through uninhabited territories. Stagecoach robbers upgraded their techniques to exploit the larger opportunity, even derailing entire trains to steal the loot. Likewise, train operators upgraded their security, paying Pinkerton to track down every last robber.

In short, after train technology aggregated the booty carried by stagecoaches, robbers earned higher returns with fewer heists.

That got me thinking about today's technological Wild West. In today's Wild West, I asked myself, are there stagecoaches carrying small booties? What is the booty they carry? Is there a train about to replace these stagecoaches?

Today's precious cargo is no longer gold. It's not patents. It's not trade secrets. It's information.

Digital information.

With digital information, the bank gives me cash at ATMs. The phone company logs my every call. More and more of my information is digital. My book is saved on computer disks. Even my DNA, my very essence, is digital.

As I thought about Denmark and same-sex unions and the power of identity, I connected several dots. Today's robbers could steal my information and, even more valuable, my identity. I'm not sure a stagecoach carrying my identity is worth a robber's time, but what about stagecoaches that carry the identities of a J. P. Morgan or a J. P. Getty? Those are valuable identities.

But suppose there was an information train carrying thousands or millions of identities. Whatever that train might be, it's worth derailing.

Sorry if this is messy. I have good questions, but no great answers yet. My new technology friends can help.

The important thing to remember for now, dear Mustafa, is that each of us is a little Danish.

9

DANBURY, OCT 15, 2001

The off-hours train ride to the Danbury station was uneventful, if slow. It felt much slower than usual to Erica. The conductor's indecipherable public announcements didn't help gauge progress. Erica worried her father would have to wait at the station.

The train was nearly empty. Erica spread the contents of her bag on adjacent seats as she skimmed through art magazines and reviewed her client list. The gallery and apartment rents nearly emptied her bank account. Business was off at Erica's gallery, like all the galleries. She searched for signs the market would change, ways to approach clients who were on the fence. Nothing obvious, nothing she hadn't thought of.

Erica recognized the announcement for the final stop in spite of the distortion. She put away her things and looked out the windows. The woods were ablaze with orange and red foliage. She instinctively looked for animal tracks. The long shadows made it hard to discern details. Something about the scene resembled one of Peter's works. Erica wondered whether one day he might paint East Coast landscapes.

"What's wrong?" Erica's father asked as he walked around his car and opened the trunk. He was maturing into a sweet old man, belly bulging over his belt, white hair thinning.

"Nothing," Erica replied, afraid to mention her dismal business, much less ask for money. She dropped her bags in the trunk and hugged her father. "Why?"

"I love seeing you, but you should come up sometime when there's not a problem."

"It's just that I can't track down an artist to return his unsold art," Erica said. As the words left her mouth, she regretted them. Her answer wasn't forthright. She was avoiding her big problem. "He isn't answering his phone."

"That doesn't sound so bad," Frank said.

Erica got in the car. Her father was right. She did travel to see him when she had problems. The last time she'd come up was when the landlord took nearly a week to fix the toilet. The time before, she'd just broken off with Mark. He never seemed to finish school and she couldn't abide his student lifestyle. That was a tough call. Their sex was delicious. Erica's father was right. Whenever she felt like crawling into a box to avoid the world, she would jump on a train to Danbury. Her father rarely challenged her rationalizations.

While Frank's dilapidated Toyota sedan rattled along the road to the house, the sun set behind them, intensifying the brilliant hues of the trees. Frank rattled on about the President's decision to invade Afghanistan, how important it was to show terrorists America's resolve. Erica's father obsessed more and more about politics and sports ever since her mother died four years ago in a car accident. He lived for his high school coaching job with its attendant after-school practices and games, a satisfying job that left him too much time alone at home. Erica wanted her father to socialize more outside work. She encouraged him to try activities where he might meet women, but he dismissed the gardening and hiking clubs. He said he relaxed more doing those activities by himself. When she suggested a pet, Frank told Erica as long as she was nearby, that was all the company he needed.

The house hadn't changed since Erica's mother died, except the television was on most of the time. It was like an unkempt museum of her parents' relationship. Erica put her bags upstairs and roamed from room to room for a time, switching lights on and off, straightening a couple pictures, admiring the fashionable shoes still in her mother's closet. The shoes made Erica miss her mother. She had fond memories of growing up here, of playing in this house, of time with her parents. Except for the dust that made Erica sneeze, the relationship museum tour was a pleasant enough distraction from thinking about her problems. Cool evening air seeped in the house. Erica went downstairs to adjust the thermostat.

Frank was planted in front of the television, listening to the news anchor assess the hunt for Osama bin Laden, the 9/11 mastermind. He addressed the television, urging the troops to "get that guy." As Erica watched the intensity in her father's eyes, she knew nothing would change with her father. He had no desire to join a gardening club or any other after-work activities that might improve his social life. That was okay. It wasn't what Erica wanted, but it was how her father was. Erica could live with that. What choice did she have? She stepped between her father and the television to announce it was time to start cooking.

At dinner, Frank served lasagna, the same lasagna he served every visit. Erica had resurrected her mother's recipe and taught Frank how to cook it. Most weekends, he'd make a big batch of lasagna for the week. He always kept some frozen in case Erica showed up. While Frank went back to the kitchen to get sodas and 100% Real Parmesan, she sniffed the lasagna to make sure it was okay.

"So, what's really wrong?" Frank asked, sitting down.

It always comforted Erica to share a meal with her father, to enjoy his familiar sky-blue eyes. She could hear the television jabbering away in the living room. Sitting with her father, the gallery seemed quite distant. She wouldn't be forthright if she mentioned her gallery. What was wrong was that her father was more concerned about Afghanistan than what happened to his wife, more concerned about killing terrorists than what he should do with his life. He was stuck. She couldn't change him, but she could change herself.

"I want to get back together with Mark," she replied.

OCTOBER 20, 1989 – EARTHQUAKE

Dear Mustafa,

The earth shook on Tuesday. One second, everything was normal; the next second, the world split in two. Reports say it was 6.9 on the Richter scale. I still duck under tables during the aftershocks. Everyone has jitters. Someday, Mother Earth will heal and the ground will feel safe again.

Our apartment shook, but it wasn't as bad in the Castro as elsewhere. The only damage Peter and I found in our clunky Victorian dwelling was the box of cotton swabs that crashed to the floor. We couldn't remember all the things we were supposed to do after an earthquake, except to check for gas leaks. No gas leaks. Checked with neighbors in the building to make sure they were okay, too. They were okay, too.

If you saw the images of this earthquake broadcast over and again on television, Mustafa, you might believe San Francisco was wiped out. It was nothing like earthquakes in Algeria.

You were old enough to remember the El Asnam earthquake in 1980, the earthquake that killed five thousand and triggered a tsunami. I saw photos in American magazines. I was in Algeria for the 1954 coastal earthquake in the same region, around Chlef, or Clef as the Berbers call it, that killed over one thousand. That shaker also triggered a tsunami. The earthquake here was bad, but nothing close to either of those Algerian earthquakes.

In the midst of the chaos here, I remembered a story about the 1954 earthquake, a story that might amuse you, Mustafa. A distant cousin, another black sheep in the family like me, moved to Chlef. I have no idea why a small city like Chlef, but maybe because of a scandalous French art collective that resided there.

Anyway, the family story I heard was that this cousin was presumed dead. The early-morning earthquake demolished his apartment building. But no one could be sure who died and who was alive since there was no systematic way to sort through the rubble.

Then, a day or two later, someone heard this cousin of ours whistling a few blocks away from the rubble of his building. They knew it was him because he walked around town whistling this tune all the time—I like to think it was "La Vie en rose," but in fact, I have no idea. People on the street stopped what they were doing to excavate the whistler's room. There he was, in his birthday suit, still holding on to his man, the lover who'd died during the quake. The astonishing thing is that, even after a day or two in this horrid condition, he instantly went to work digging out others in the rubble so that everyone overlooked his transgression. It was the luck of a melody that saved him.

In San Francisco, there was no power in our apartment Tuesday night after the earthquake. No whistling, either. It was quiet, the din of televisions and radios silenced, telephones dead. The next-door neighbor shattered the silence of our collective shock, inviting anyone in earshot to take advantage of his barbeque. Our neighbors cooked meat and vegetables before they spoiled—a feast.

Peter and I invited people to share our canned food if needed in the following days, but we weren't sure about water at that point. Lots of jokes from the assembled crowd about drinking from the toilet.

There were plenty of distant sirens, only a few nearby. That convinced the gathered grillers that, for once, we had a disaster that hadn't wiped out the Castro. We hung flashlights in the yard and opened bottles of wine. If there's anything the gays are good at, it's throwing a party in the midst of a disaster. How else could we get through this fucking AIDS crisis?

Power came back on Wednesday. Water was running. Television and radios droned constant updates. Peter got to his studio finally. Said it was a wreck, things scattered everywhere, supplies scattered across the floor, paintings off the walls. Said not to worry. He didn't think anything important was lost. He sees it as an opportunity for a thorough cleaning. He'll need help. He doesn't like when I visit the studio, so I don't expect I'm the help.

The basics were restored by yesterday. The damage is limited, especially compared to Algeria, but still incredible. People were crushed in their cars when the double-decker freeways pancaked. That seems the worst of it. Too early for a final death toll, but maybe a hundred. Like the famous 1906 quake, the worst property damage in San Francisco is from fires. The ancient fire boats pumped bay water on the Marina while it burned into the night. They helped, but they didn't quench the fires in time.

I know I'm being self-centered, but the entire week my main frustration has been my inability to research. First the distraction of power and water. Now I can't track down

Leslie the Librarian. I should be checking that my friends with AIDS have what they need after the quake. Everyone I've heard from is okay. I assume the others are okay because it's less stressful than worrying they've been displaced.

You might not care about any of these details. But this was my first major earthquake, the first time I felt a major earthquake. I survived. I take that as a good omen, dear Mustafa, that I will survive other disasters.

And then there are those who didn't make it.

On Tuesday morning, hours before the earthquake, John van Deventer died in hospice. John was a budding photographer. Beautiful black and white photos of Bay Area nature, the amber waves of wild grasses crowned with the grace of majestic oak trees. His death will go unnoticed. The single fatality on the Bay Bridge, a nurse's aide named Anamafi Moala whose car fell through the broken upper deck, she will be spoken of long after John. John and Anamafi were both twenty-three years old.

IO

GUERNEVILLE, OCT 16, 2001

In a mildewy room at a sleazy Russian River resort, Peter took the rolled-up dollar bill from Angel and snorted another line of cocaine.

"I have to stop," Peter said, taking his hand off Angel's soft cock and lying back in bed. Fuck. He wasn't painting, his work wasn't selling in New York, his lease renewal was coming up, and he was wasting a fucking week smoking and snorting. Fuck, fuck, fuckety, fuck.

Lying back on the bed, Peter's mind was racing at a hundred miles per hour, trying to get back on track. Angel snorted another line and continued his coke babble. Guys he'd fucked, places they'd fucked, how hot it was fucking them, the times they'd fucked outside, how big their cocks were, the curved-shape cock he liked best in his ass. Peter tried to block out Angel's babble. He closed his eyes. He wanted more than anything to sleep before the sun came up, but his mind kept racing. He wanted to tell Angel to shut up, but knew it would create a bad vibe, bring down both of them, way down. Halloween was around the corner, and this was already too scary. While Angel described an orgy where two black dudes took turns fucking a hustler at a Las Vegas casino, Peter wondered about his siblings. His parents would never come around, but his siblings might have escaped the gravitational pull of the Bible Belt black hole, might have realized homosexuality was harmless, nothing more than a gift God gave Evangelicals to raise money. Peter felt the bed rocking and opened his eyes. Angel was rubbing his dick and talking about ways he'd figured out to get hard after doing a few lines, even though a lot of guys couldn't. Only Angel wasn't getting hard. Peter closed his eyes again. Angel was asking Peter if he wanted to get hard, too. Angel put a hand on Peter. It felt good. Angel rubbed Peter's smooth chest, then moved his hand to the hirsute south. Peter imagined that people in the Bible Belt must have fucked on cocaine. The Evangelicals had to know the sins whereof they spoke. They knew of the rising spirit. There could not be an experience closer to God than sex on coke, even if it were nearly impossible after a few lines to achieve an erection for the resurrection. Angel kept telling Peter about the ways he got hard. Peter liked Angel's hand exploring his crotch and concentrated on getting hard. He opened his eyes again. Angel's chest was so perfect. It made Peter want to get on top of Angel and fuck him. The way Angel was looking at him, Peter knew Angel wanted to get fucked. Peter concentrated, but his dick wasn't responding. Not even Angel's incantations of sexual exploits could raise the limp spirit. Angel remembered aloud the night he stumbled into a gang bang in Buena Vista Park, a group of guys fucking a Japanese guy relentlessly until they heard the rustle of cops sneaking up the hill. Angel pulled out of the Japanese guy, pulled up his pants, pulled the Japanese guy by the hand, and ran like crazy. They escaped. Back home, Angel got the Japanese guy high, then called some friends to come over and fuck him some more. Peter closed his eyes and took Angel's hand in his own. Angel babbled on. Peter heard the hot tub outside switch on, heard its gushing bubbles, heard someone splash the water before entering. It sounded delicious, refreshing, better than lying in bed perspiring to death. Peter opened his eyes and looked at the clock by the bed. They'd been snorting in this room for hours. It felt like days. Peter's sinuses were parched. He slowly sat up and told Angel he needed a break, told Angel he was getting in the hot tub outside. Angel said the hot-tub water was disgusting. Peter got out of bed and put on his underwear. He told Angel he'd be back in ten or fifteen. How could Angel think the hot-tub water was disgusting? It wasn't like the sex he'd been describing was exactly germfree.

It was dark outside. No moon. Peter stumbled twice on the path across the lawn to the tub. From his wordy salutation, the other guy in the hot tub sounded like he was toasted, too. Why else would anyone be in a hot tub at five in the morning? It was hard to see the other guy, hard to tell if he was sexy through the bubbles. The water did look a little disgusting. Peter's mind kept racing. He almost did another line on the way out of the room, but it was time to come down. At one point, he'd been so high he almost started telling Angel details of Rano's journal. That's when he got a clue he was getting messy, that he should slow down. If he relaxed in the hot tub, he wouldn't feel so crappy as the coke wore off. Peter slipped off his underwear and slid in. Oasis. Wet, warm oasis. He noticed the other guy's leg moving up his own leg. Didn't take long. Resting his head on the edge of the tub, Peter watched the dark sky slowly fill with light. Images rushed through his mind. Christmas with his family. The first Christmas tree with Rano. Angel's taut body the first time they fucked. Brice. The New York skyline. The sketch in his studio. Peter wondered if this sequence of images was what people described seeing when they'd almost died. He still felt the other guy exploring. He didn't reciprocate. In the glimmer of dawn, Peter could discern the emaciated face of his hot-tub partner. It had been months since Peter had seen this once familiar wasting. It was easy to forget about AIDS. Friends had stopped dropping like flies. Peter lifted the exploring leg and slid away. He closed his eyes. The shame of not knowing about the existence of Mustafa until he opened Rano's journal washed over Peter. More images flew through his mind. Rano in the hospital. Bathing Angel's boyfriend. Sewing Rano's panel for the AIDS quilt. The first Christmas tree without Rano. Fucking Angel in front of this Christmas tree. Peter heard the other guy getting out of the tub. He didn't open his eyes. More images. Then nothing.

The blasting stutter of logging-truck air brakes shook Peter awake.

As the first rays of sun shot over the Guerneville hills, Peter understood he wouldn't make it to Halloween if he didn't stop. He squinted. The door to the room was wide open. What the fuck? Was Angel letting anyone in the room now for sex? Peter pushed himself up and out of the tub. No towel. Fuck. He made an unnecessary fig leaf with his underpants while performing a brief walk of shame.

Everything was in the room. Everything except Angel. And La Farmacia. Was Angel doing deals? All Angel had was some pot he'd scored from Peter's guy in Mendocino and whatever cocaine was left. Peter felt his exhaustion pushing against his drug jitters. He gulped some water, nudged the door almost shut so Angel could slip back in, dried off, pulled on enough clothes that Angel wouldn't attempt sex, flopped onto the bed, and shut his eyes.

Peter's mind kept churning. He couldn't fall asleep. A distant siren wafted through his ears into his mind. Jesus. Air brakes and sirens. It was supposed to be quiet out here. Peter relaxed his muscles, cleared his head, but the persistent siren grew louder. Much louder. Peter pushed a pillow over his ears. He couldn't hear the siren now, but he heard the muffled screech of tires skidding to a stop. Car doors thumped shut and men were yelling.

As if a coke crystal dislodged from a deep nasal crevice to energize him, Peter opened his eyes, shot out of the room, and dashed through the building to the parking lot. There was Angel wearing nothing but sandals and handcuffs. One of the police wrapped a blanket around his naked body and opened the cruiser door. Angel looked away from Peter and got in.

October 23, 1989 –
Dependencies

Dear Mustafa,

Aftershocks startle me even now. I duck under the closest table at the slightest movement. I freak out when the upstairs neighbor climbs the stairs, dropping to the floor, sliding under the bed.

No time to research or write because we've been helping friends and discussing the best way to get Peter's studio back in working order. As much as Peter discusses these things.

My main concern today, however, is Leslie the Librarian. I finally reached her yesterday to check in, to see if everything is okay after the earthquake. Of course, I also called to find out when she would resume her current literature search. We didn't get that far.

Leslie said her apartment suffered no damage from the earthquake. It was worse than that, she told me. She got uncertain mammogram results the afternoon of the earthquake. She's been in limbo ever since. Talk about aftershocks. Her doctor's office told Leslie that he couldn't return to the office until sometime this week. Unlike Leslie's place, the doctor's Marina home sustained extensive damage from the fire after the earthquake. This fucking earthquake.

I feel terrible about Leslie's predicament. It's not a complete surprise. After several glasses of a strong Zinfandel one evening not so many months ago, Leslie came out about her breast cancer, told me her doctor performed a mastectomy a few years back. After the treatment, she said, her doctor gave her the all clear—clear margins, clean lymph nodes, all that.

On the phone yesterday, I told Leslie I understood how she feels. When she fretted about the uncertain results, I reminded her of her doctor's all clear, told her not to worry, told her it's probably just some screwup with the X-ray machine or the film processing.

Every time I wait to see a doctor, I explained to Leslie sympathetically, I could worry what the latest blood work will reveal or what new malady will afflict me. It doesn't help that I feel fine. I've got fucking AIDS, so I worry. However, I continued, I remind myself there are more productive things than worrying. Besides, given my recent medical history, I want to enjoy life as much as I can because, who knows, I might lose my mind any second.

Of course, Leslie noted, it's possible I lost my mind before the encephalitis. She laughed and then said something surprising. Leslie said I should concentrate one hundred percent on my research and stop helping ACT UP. Life is short, she said. If you want my help on research, she said, I need you to put aside everything else. I'll find someone to go to ACT UP for you, she said.

After the call with Leslie, I reflected on the boukalates ritual with Eric and David, on the intimation I received that my work would come to fruition no matter what. Maybe Leslie is right. If I don't finish the book, there's nothing to come to fruition. If I don't finish the book, there's no trip to Algeria.

That made me think about you, dear Mustafa, worry again that if we don't find a cure, I may not see you—even if I do complete my book. Will my ACT UP work, my small contribution, make a difference to finding a cure? Maybe not, but I feel like I'm giving up hope of ever seeing you if I give up fighting for a cure. It would be so much easier if Carl had told me where you are. Fucker. Sorry, I promised to tell you about that. Then this fucking earthquake interrupted everything. I'm on my last gay nerve. Any more disasters and I'm setting my hair on fire.

Yes, there's been a horrific earthquake. Yes, Leslie is worried her cancer is out of remission. Now she's got me worried about my writing, about finishing my book. She's forcing me to make a choice between ACT UP and my research. This dependency on Leslie hobbles me. I need her help and encouragement to finish my book. This week without Leslie's assistance has felt like an eternity.

Disaster reveals who we are, reveals our dependencies. What happens if I give up ACT UP?

I want to help with earthquake relief, but I can't. I have to write. I can't afford to have people depend on me for earthquake help.

I want to help with AIDS, but I can't. I have to write. I can't afford to have people depend on me for AIDS help.

However, even though people can't depend on me for help, I have to depend on people to write. I'm being selfish. Leslie is asking me to be selfish.

These days and weeks without progress torture me. It feels like Carl has somehow returned from the dead to haunt me, like he is rolling around in his grave to create the aftershocks that still startle me.

II

New York, Oct 21, 2001

Most times Thomas took the B or C train to seek advice from the rabbi at Congregation Shearith Israel. Despite the rainy weather, on this day, Thomas trudged through Central Park so he could view the reservoir from its west side, remembering his late lover Maurice and their adventures in the park. Maurice was born in 1917, the same year New York installed a fountain celebrating the completion of the reservoir, a key component of its new Catskill water supply system. Maurice died in 1994, the same year as former first lady Jacqueline Kennedy Onassis, the same year the city named the reservoir after her. These reservoir celebrations made monumental bookends for Maurice's solidly twentieth-century life.

It was deserted here, resting against the iron rail separating the path from the water. And wet. Very wet. Rain pelted the surface of the reservoir. Thomas and Maurice had met by chance at this spot on a warm, smoggy evening in 1969, Thomas having returned intact from Vietnam, Maurice having scraped together funds to buy his first Manhattan building. Then, as they explored the Ramble to celebrate the Summer of Love, an unforgettable summer shower drenched them with love. Theirs was love at first sight, a veritable Upper West Side Story, each family assiduously avoiding the other for years until it became obvious there was no tenable alternative to acceptance.

The African American from Harlem and the Sephardic Jew from the Lower East Side made a remarkable Manhattan couple. Maurice taught Thomas his business. Thomas taught Maurice his love of music and dance. Their mutual fondness for visual arts evolved on frequent forays to art galleries. As the real estate business expanded, they were the belles of the charity balls, the go-to invitees for arts institutions promoting their inclusiveness. Thomas and Maurice understood this, but turned it into a fashionable game of getting under the skin of less inclusive high rollers, making them as uncomfortable as possible without going all the way, as it were. Thomas and Maurice were, after all, a devoted and monogamous couple—as monogamous, at any rate, as any gay couple living near Central Park could hope to be.

Thomas and Maurice's devotion to one another excluded only religion. Neither converted to the other's faith, but Thomas got friendly with the rabbi when Maurice hosted his quarterly "Jews Do's" fundraiser dinners at home. After Maurice died, Thomas found the rabbi had an understanding ear. On those occasions that Thomas wished he still could consult with Maurice, he often headed down to the synagogue.

Thomas had walked to this place in the downpour because he needed to understand better his feelings for Peter, the artist. This place seemed to hold important clues from Thomas' past even though the place itself constantly changed. When Thomas first spied Peter on the other side of Erica's gallery, it upset him, upset the companionless equilibrium he'd reached after Maurice's death. Chatting with Peter wasn't exactly the same as when he smiled at Maurice in this spot by the reservoir the first time, but it was the first time since Maurice's death, the first time in seven years that Thomas met someone he instantly sensed he wanted to know more about. Much, much more.

Standing here drenched, Thomas was reminded of details of his history with Maurice. At the gallery opening, Peter physically reminded Thomas of Maurice that day in the park. Both Peter and Maurice had short salt-and-pepper beards and receding hairlines. Both were slightly pigeon-toed when they walked. Both absentmindedly rolled an empty wine glass between their hands when they happened to have a wine glass while talking about something important.

That last trait was something Thomas actually noticed a few days after he met Maurice, during an intense discussion about the merits of Harlem real estate investments in the midst of the city's volatile real estate market. Maurice had argued that the completion of the World Trade Center would reignite the flagging real estate market. Thomas had fretted over the country's political and economic climates. So, of course, how could Thomas not be surprised at the opening-night gallery party to glimpse Peter rolling a wine glass between his hands as he described his art? From across the gallery, Peter appeared to be Maurice reincarnated as a painter.

Beyond the physical traits, Thomas was drawn to Peter's work. The reviews of Peter's show were kind enough, but Thomas saw a special talent, a talent that eluded the reviewers. It was more than the brilliant technique. The structures Peter had incorporated in his recent landscapes—the houses, the stables, the outbuildings—brought a depth of meaning to his work. They told a story that Thomas felt was just starting. It seemed Peter had much more to say.

Thomas also understood that the artist and his art were two different animals, that falling in love with an artist was pointless if it was only for his art, and this was his conundrum. Meeting Peter awoke something stirring inside Thomas. Everything about Peter screamed to Thomas that now was the time, that here was a man who could, if not replace Maurice, then engage Thomas in ways that mattered. Thomas' physical attraction to Peter was strong and his curiosity about Peter grew as he contemplated buying a few of Peter's works.

Thomas was anxious, though, that he was getting ahead of himself. His meeting with Brice yielded little insight into Peter or into any possible interest in Thomas on Peter's part. Thomas wanted to pester Erica to fly Peter back to New York or to invent some pretext for Thomas to visit Peter in San Francisco. He wanted to pick up the phone and call Peter. He also wanted, desperately wanted, further engagement with Peter to proceed organically, as though it were spontaneous, as if they'd just met by chance at the reservoir and then found themselves drenched in love. Thomas felt vulnerable, perhaps because of his standing, perhaps because he'd never known any relationship except Maurice, perhaps because of something he didn't understand. He wanted to know if any feelings with Peter were mutual, yet it felt like Peter barely noticed him. Maybe Peter wasn't into black guys. Maybe it was that simple.

Thomas turned towards the synagogue, pulled tight the hood of his slicker, and marched through the rain. The rabbi would be waiting.

OCTOBER 28, 1989 – DANNY

Dear Mustafa,

I want to tell you about the scooper at the Double Rainbow ice cream shop across from the Castro Theatre. In case you're concerned that I take life too seriously, the young scooper provided me a pleasing diversion from the terror of the plague and from the drudgery of work. He started there around my birthday. When I wasn't sick, I'd buy ice cream at least once a week just for the pleasure of chatting with him, to adore his beautiful brown wavy hair and beguiling smile. He gave me plenty of free samples each visit. His youth was a pleasant antidote to death and dying. As he scooped my chosen frozen cream, I would lean against the big sign warning me not to lean on the display, imagining how the same downy hair on his forearms must be sprouting over the rest of his youthful body. Maybe that's too much information, Mustafa, but I'm not ashamed of my lust. Lust is universal, a lovely distraction for even the most religious among us. If you don't believe me, I can catalog the unusual sexual activities I've seen at the climax of Eid celebrations.

All I know about the scooper's past is that he moved from Pocatello, a railroad stop in the middle of nowhere, to the Emerald City, as he referred to San Francisco. He escaped the train yards, the drunken beatings he got at home. Our usual banter was lighthearted. Our ice cream parlor trysts stretched as long as we could make them last, until paying customers interrupted the scooper's attentive flirtation.

We enjoyed each other in the store, and I fantasized what was to come. When he said he wanted to attend college, I volunteered to help him enroll at SF State. Each visit, I wondered if anything would come of my offer. Yesterday, when I stopped for my lick, the young scooper wasn't there. I assumed it was the earthquake. I assumed he'd lost his apartment or was helping friends. But it turned out he won't be there. I didn't know his name until his replacement told me Danny Chrisman had died.

Fuck.

In the frenzy of earthquake recovery, it's like AIDS took a vacation. This earthquake is so different from the AIDS disaster.

The press can't say, "Sorry, we haven't confirmed what happened yet and, since whatever it was only affected a few people in, you know, those kinds of communities, we'll report on it later."

Government can't say, "Why are you upset? You have water and power, don't you? Sure, a few freeways collapsed, but the freeways didn't collapse on you, did they?"

Why hasn't AIDS shaken us like an earthquake? Does AIDS have to demolish buildings and swallow automobiles for the press and the government to take action? Does property loss take precedence over loss of life?

I'm writing this, dear Mustafa, because Leslie so much as demanded I leave ACT UP in return for her assistance. She's insisting that I prioritize my research above everything. I don't know how to go forward if I drop my AIDS work completely. My poor Leslie had to have another mammogram because the first one was botched, so I won't be hard on her, but she's asking the world of me. I don't take her request lightly. I need her support. My research is unlikely to succeed without her.

But I think about Danny, and it makes me want to do a hundred times more for AIDS. I want all my friends to do a hundred times more. More protests, more ACT UP disobedience, more unrest, more newspaper and TV stories. Unseen AIDS must be seen. I want everyone to see the gory details of the AIDS story.

Classes starting again at SF State. Stores open. No power interruptions. Things getting back to normal, whatever normal was or is. Peter says his studio is back to normal. We discussed what "normal" would mean after AIDS. We also discussed the new name for the earthquake. Funny how we need names for disasters. "AIDS," "Loma Prieta," "Hurricane Hugo." Disasters need names like books and artwork need titles. Hard to talk about something before it has a name, hard to ascribe to it any attributes.

Sorry I've gone on a bit, but I realized this week that the response to Loma Prieta was universal because all of us who experienced it shared common ground, as it were. We all understood the terror of the earth under our feet giving way.

Those of us with AIDS don't share common ground with most of America. We live in, you know, one of those communities. Those of us with AIDS depend on people in power who have no experience with AIDS and whose only notion of homosexuality is that it's a repugnant lifestyle. My reality is that I am at the mercy of these people. That is sobering.

12

SAN FRANCISCO, OCT 21, 2001

Brice dropped everything after the early-morning phone call from Peter and caught a taxi to JFK. It felt eerily similar to the ride he took a decade ago when he dashed for a flight to see Rano the final time. At the ticket counter, Brice didn't wince at the astronomical price for the last available seat, a seat which, naturally, was a middle seat adjacent to the rear lavatories. After a few martinis, he stopped worrying about upcoming holiday retail windows. Two words Peter had said during their brief call—"heart" and "hospital"—were all Brice remembered, all he needed to know.

Maybe it was the in-flight drinks, but SFO seemed all turned around since Brice's last visit. Interminable airport construction had hatched a shiny new international terminal that the talkative cabbie pointed out as he extricated them from the tangle of new roads. Brice didn't hear much through the martini fog. Luckily, it was clear sailing up the Bayshore Freeway to San Francisco General Hospital. Inside the hospital, though, it took a tedious hour to locate Peter. As the martini fog burned off, Brice felt more himself. He waltzed into Peter's room.

"You must be Brice," the nurse said with a wink. His biceps were as thick as Brice's thighs. He snapped closed the chart and stepped out. "Don't be long. Your friend needs rest."

"Are you okay?" Brice asked Peter, relieved by the heart monitor's regular beep. "You look fine. A little TLC from Nurse Buff would do the trick for me, too."

Peter didn't look up, didn't answer. Maybe things weren't as rosy as they appeared. It couldn't be that bad, though, the way the nurse winked. Maybe there was something in the drip. Maybe Peter was being his quiet self. Maybe Nurse Buff was just flirting.

"Is your heart okay?" Brice asked.

"Yes and no," Peter said. He still didn't look up from his bed. "No heart attack."

"I was so worried," Brice said, happy at this news. When Peter had asked Brice to fly, Brice had remembered his promise to Rano—his promise to support Peter as a son would a father—and flew without reservation. Now he realized it was more than that. Brice had grown more fond of Peter than he realized during Peter's New York stay.

"It's worse than a heart attack," Peter said, looking up. "Angel is in jail and it's my fault."

"Wait, Angel?" Brice asked. "Didn't you blow off Angel years ago?"

"Angel got in trouble and moved back to San Francisco," Peter said. "We did some weed and coke. Angel got arrested. It was my fault for letting him wander outside so high."

"Just like old times," Brice said, shaking his head. He knew Peter was stressed by everything going on, but why was he riding the Coke Express with Angel again? "Did the coke cause your heart problems?"

"Went to bed with chest pains," Peter answered. "Couldn't fall asleep. Called 911, and then you. Thought it was the coke. Now the docs think it's my fucking gallbladder."

Peter looked down. He was quiet. Brice considered how soothing another martini would be right now. He hated hospitals. He'd had enough of them with Rano and other friends who died. Last time Brice remembered Peter panicking like this was shortly after Rano died, when Peter invited Angel to share his studio.

"They don't seem to be in a hurry about your gallbladder," Brice said after a while. "Are you okay?"

"I'm sorry I asked you to fly out," Peter answered. "I got scared. I'm losing it. I can't paint again, and I don't understand why."

"Don't worry," Brice said. "Now you've got Nurse Buff and me to take care of you."

Peter was quiet again, picking absentmindedly at the tape that secured his IV line. He seemed scattered, unable to concentrate. This was going to be complicated. Brice knew Peter and Angel bonded when their lovers died weeks apart. Everyone knew. When Peter stopped painting then, everyone blamed it on Rano's death. Everyone except Brice. Brice blamed Angel and the drugs, although he had no way to know. As he listened to the monotonous heart monitor, reality seeped in for the first time since the phone call. It was dawning on Brice he would have to return to New York soon to install holiday windows. There was going to be too much for Brice to deal with during this visit.

"Hey," Peter asked, perking up a bit, "did you ever go back to check out those mechanical dancers."

"What mechanical dancers?" Brice replied. Peter was all over the map today. It was as disconcerting as friends losing their marbles in the AIDS wards.

"You know," Peter said. "The ones that reminded you of that kid who died, the kid you dumped."

"Charlie?" Brice asked. "Oh, no. Oh, geez, I mean yes. Please, can you please stop saying I dumped Charlie. It sounds like I killed him."

"Did you go back to that poster store or not?" Peter asked again.

"It closed after 9/11," Brice said. "Yes, I went back. The sign said the owner died. He was installing posters in the Twin Towers."

"Oh, my God," Peter said. "He died and I didn't?" Peter stopped picking the tape and rested his hands on the bed rails. "So, you never got to see the mechanical Charlie dancer."

"No, no, I didn't," Brice said. "I never found out who made that spectacular mechanism."

"I remembered that when I was high with Angel," Peter said. "I remembered so much. I remembered the mechanical dancers. I remembered photos of Charlie. He looked so sweet. Why did you dump him?"

"That was so long ago," Brice said, hoping Nurse Buff's return would interrupt the conversation.

"Really, I want to know why," Peter said. "He seemed perfect."

"He was," Brice said, walking to the door. He looked up and down the hall. No sign of anyone, let alone Nurse Buff, to distract Peter. Brice sat down and rested his hand on Peter's. Stories were as good a way as any to kill time at hospitals, and this was as good a time as any to get this particular story off his chest.

"I met Charlie at a rehearsal," Brice said. "He was from Utah, too. We were both ex-Mormons. That blissful smile of his was all I ever needed. I think about it almost every day."

"He was beautiful," Peter said. "And that red hair."

"Well, Charlie told me on our first date that he was positive."

"That took some courage back then."

"Charlie had such grace," Brice said. "He said he'd understand if I didn't want a second date. I didn't think twice. I told him as long as we played safe, it'd be okay."

"That also took some courage back then."

"Honestly," Brice continued, "I didn't want Charlie's HIV to be an issue. This guy had made it on his own after his family disowned him, like I did."

"I remember watching him twirl and twist in the cage at The Saint," Peter said. "He was dazzling."

"That earned him way more than rent," Brice said, looking at Peter for a moment before he could say more. "I used to say I dumped Charlie. The truth was different. I didn't understand I was lying when I told Charlie his HIV status wouldn't be a problem.

My fear of seroconversion didn't have words. It found ways to express itself, though. After a few months, I started sabotaging our relationship. When I slept with Charlie's best friend, it all unraveled."

Brice stood up, took a plastic cup from the tray, and poured himself water from the pitcher. He thought about Charlie's smile and his red mop often, but he rarely thought about the cruelty of this sabotage.

"I called Charlie about a year later. I'd come to understand how my fear of seroconversion fueled my sabotage. I wanted to apologize, maybe have a drink. Maybe even a date. I was confused, though, when Charlie's best friend answered Charlie's phone. I wasn't sure what to say. Was he mad at me for using him? Was he dating Charlie? Anyway, I finally asked for Charlie. That's when I found out the celebration of Charlie's life would be the following week at The Saint."

"Oh, geez," Peter said, wiping his eyes with the back of his free hand. Brice handed him a tissue. "Thank you. When I remembered Charlie again last week, an instinct said I needed to know more."

The nurse knocked and entered. "They're keeping you overnight," he said to Peter.

"I can't go home?" Peter asked. "But my friend Brice is here to take me."

"Sorry, can't let you go with what's in that drip," the nurse said, checking where Peter picked at the tape. "But my shift is over, and Brice has to leave now, so maybe he can take me instead."

NOVEMBER 11, 1989 – FORWARD?

Dear Mustafa,

While recovery from the Loma Prieta earthquake continues, we homosexuals continue to battle AIDS. Just in case anyone forgot. I can't sleep some nights after hearing about the generous response to the earthquake, not because of the generosity, which reflects the best of humanity, but because of the insulting response to AIDS.

The Marina took the biggest hit. One couple we know had an apartment there. Rent controlled, which compounds their loss. Red Cross only helps for a few nights. After that, they wish you luck. This couple is staying with one friend after the next until they find a place. I'm hoping they find a place before they end up here. They drink like fish.

The images of destruction are breathtaking. Haven't had time to see much of the damage in person. A lot of the damage is hard to see in person, hard to access. The Bay Bridge will be closed for months or years. Same with the freeways that collapsed. After a disaster of this magnitude, it takes time to survey and comprehend the devastation.

I look for hope everywhere and anywhere. The earthquake has provided unexpected pleasures. Entire neighborhoods, for instance, suddenly have no traffic congestion. Around the Opera House, that frilly Beaux-Arts drama queen of an edifice, no cars race to beat traffic lights at barricaded freeway on ramps. The city is eerily quiet without freeways. I would write that it's quiet as a funeral, but it's different. The city hasn't died from Loma Prieta. It's more like San Francisco is trying on an old dress that tumbled out of the closet and, quite to everyone's delight, the dress fits. There is already talk of tearing down the double-decker freeways running through town instead of repairing them. People like the way this old dress feels, they appreciate how things used to work, they recognize that new fashions aren't always what they're chalked up to be.

One healthy attribute of an earthquake is that it shakes loose old memories. Friends phone to see if you're okay. Some calls are expected. Brice called. He was so worried. Said he'd try to fly out soon, wanted to know if I needed any help. I told him about Peter's studio, which is fine now. Besides that, there isn't much else.

Other friends call unexpectedly. Linh called from New York, too. We haven't heard from Linh for nearly a year. She was worried about her family here. She couldn't get through and wanted Peter to check on them. She called back twenty minutes later. They were fine.

Coming directly after Brice's call, Linh's call reminded me that she met Brice after she moved to New York and that she was the one who introduced Brice to Peter and me. Loma Prieta jogged my memory about that and much more.

In the midst of San Francisco's devastation, there are some auspicious signs. I see a new normal emerging after the worst of the disaster. There is hope and rebuilding. It helps me paint a picture of a world at the end of the AIDS crisis, a world in which I meet you, dear Mustafa.

From the outside world there's good news, too. I'm not talking about the collapse of the USSR. Who knows whether that's good or bad? I'm talking about US politics, about elections that presage better government response to AIDS.

I don't expect you to care about any of this, but it's like a beacon to our political future. New York elected its first black mayor last week. Virginia elected the first black governor in America. Blacks elected to leadership roles shouldn't be a big deal. It's been well over a century since Lincoln signed the Emancipation Proclamation. Unlike Russia, which has been changing governments like it's changing underwear for the past 125 years, America has stuck with the same government, a white government that can't work out its slavery fetish.

This election is auspicious, but it's not a cure. Nowhere near a cure.

As it does with all calamities, the Religious Right claims that the earthquake is a sign from above, a sign that Goddess disapproves of the gays. I take these elections as a harbinger of resistance to the Republicans, a sign that minorities matter. A message that President Bush should fucking fund AIDS research and education.

The most significant action from the new administration? The First Lady held a baby with HIV. Nice symbolism. We don't need symbolism. We need money, support, protection. Bush isn't turning out any better than his predecessor. Reagan was elected ten years ago, just as AIDS came on the scene. You know what his response was, Mustafa? To tell a gay joke at the Republican National Convention. "What does 'gay' stand for?" Reagan asked. "It stands for 'Got AIDS Yet.'" Fucking infuriating.

I'm upset as I write this because dead friends are piling up. Last month it was Ray Hailey, Josh Persky, Robert Flaherty, and Neil Unger. A bumper crop. Ray's annual summer margarita parties jammed the hottest Castro boys into his backyard. Josh died much too young, as young as the kids I teach. Twenty-one? Twenty-two? Robert was a lawyer turned restaurateur, and quite tasty himself. Neil, dear Neil. Peter and I didn't realize he had a thing for black guys until we arrived at Neil's service. Peter was the only white guy there.

I had to start a list of my dead friends. After my brain infection, I forget things. It all seems to be coming back, but I worry I might not remember a friend no longer with us. I might pick up the phone to call him, and then hang up when a stranger answers. With a list of my friends who died, I can check it, avoid embarrassments. I hate myself for forgetting the names.

Why am I writing all this? Am I trying to fool myself? The reason I'm upset isn't just more dead and dying friends, isn't just the horribly insufficient government response to AIDS. The reason I'm upset is because I told Leslie the Librarian I would cease my ACT UP work.

Leslie's second mammogram showed a new growth. She starts chemo next week. She said she'll research as much as she can during the treatment. Leslie has every right and reason to give up on me unless I devote myself to research. Her life now is as precarious as mine.

AIDS is forcing me to choose, to focus. The whole point of this journal is to examine my treacherous path with AIDS. As I read over the last few entries, I know Leslie is right.

I tell you my decision, dear Mustafa, not as a surrender. I can never give up on you. I want to meet you now more than ever. I can't tell you how this decision ate at me. Any father who doesn't want to know his son is an unworthy father. I promise you that your father is worthy.

You should be proud that I'm teaching this term. It's a good omen. Either my brain is working well enough to teach or the school is desperately short of staff this term. I like to think it's the former, but it doesn't matter much. It feels good to teach, even on the days when I don't have energy. There's no embarrassment forgetting a student's name. The students come and go each term. They're young, healthy. They remember what I teach them. I want you to meet some of them soon.

13
NEW YORK, NOV 22, 2001

On a supercheap Thanksgiving Day flight from London, Mark returned to New York rejuvenated. The longer he could stay awake, the easier it would be to cope with jet lag. It took a while to unpack after he lugged his bags up the five stories to his East Village studio. He couldn't squeeze his heavy outerwear in the closet. The new boots from Paris landed on the mound of shoes. Everything else went in the hamper.

After unpacking, Mark cleared one spot on his desk for the research collected during his journey and another for the stack of mail the super left for him downstairs. Riffling through, he uncovered a handwritten envelope from Erica, which he set aside. As much as he expected it, as curious as he was to open it, the letter seemed passive-aggressive, something best ignored. He arranged the bills in a pile and dumped the rest of the mail in a paper grocery bag for recycling. The room was still warming up. It hadn't cleaned itself while Mark was gone. He picked up a dirty cup in the sink and rinsed it, then put on a kettle for tea.

The new stack of research notes on Mark's desk made him proud. He'd traveled around Europe for over two months to meet with computer programmers and researchers. He was studying computer languages for his postdoc, how the semantics of each coding language shaped the way computer programmers expressed themselves. He'd planned to travel during the chilly, untouristed winter until the travel agent showed him a fall itinerary that accommodated all the meetings he needed without blowing through his meager travel budget. The trip was a goldmine. It also was timed perfectly to create distance from Erica's maddening capriciousness.

The kettle whistled while Mark was showering. He toweled off quickly, ran his fingers through his curly red hair, donned his brown plush bathrobe and bunny slippers, took the five steps to the stove, and poured hot water into the clean cup. To this he added a bag of ginger lemon tea. After a bit, a tablespoon of honey. After a bit longer, a shot of Irish whiskey. He looked around the kitchen. No other ingredients.

Mark sat down at the desk, put on his glasses, and took a few sips from the warm cup. The envelope from Erica was decorated with hand-drawn flowers. He picked it up and contemplated whether to open it. He didn't have to open it to know that it was another entreaty to get together again, another invitation to continue their on-again, off-again relationship. He turned towards the bed as fantasies of their time there pleasured his mind.

She drove him crazy. It was always too easy to return to their lovemaking. Her silky hair and pert breasts were sirens, pulling Mark to bed whenever they beckoned. Her precoital purring squeezed Mark's erection before they touched. Her luscious pussy was his dick's addiction. Afterwards, limbs entwined, they could whisper and caress and giggle for hours, the bed encompassing their entire universe. If only the rest of the universe disappeared, Mark and Erica could be on-always rather than off-again.

Mark swiveled back to his desk, put down the envelope from Erica, took a last sip from the cup, and rummaged for a piece of paper to write on. He'd meant to apologize for the email exchange with Erica's assistant, Jodie, before his trip. It was a sophomoric prank gone wrong.

After Erica dumped Mark, he'd been drinking away his sorrows with a school buddy. A few whiskeys into a game of guessing each other's password, while Mark was downstairs buying a fresh bottle, his friend guessed "abc123" and emailed suggestive notes from Mark's account to Jodie. Jodie replied. Mark would have stopped it right away—he wasn't even interested in Jodie—but the damage was done by the time Mark returned to pour the next round. A few days later, the drunken flirtation from Mark's account ended up hurting Erica for no good reason.

The warm tea and whiskey weighed on Mark's eyelids. An apology to Erica could wait. There was one last task before Mark fell asleep. He picked up a pen and wrote.

Dear Anna,

I so enjoyed meeting you on Guy Fawkes Day at that cozy party in Knightsbridge. You're spectacular in every way, more spectacular than I know how to write.

What I liked most was the time we had to converse, the wit and perspicacity you bring to each discussion, to any topic. If I had only one wish, it would be another chance for us to speak.

No one seems to understand me like you do, to show any interest in the admittedly droll subjects I study day in and day out. Comparative computer languages. A surefire conversation stopper at any cocktail party.

And, of course, I'll never forget our private undercover Guy Fawkes "fireworks" display.

Sorry if I'm too forward. It was a lovely fortnight. I would like many, many more with you.

Should you deign to reply, I would be overwhelmed yet again.

Fondly yours,
Mark

Mark transcribed a London address on a blank envelope, folded the letter, and sealed it in the envelope. He couldn't keep his eyes open any longer. Before he got into bed, he changed the sheets.

December 3, 1989 – Photo

Dear Mustafa,

I'm feeling down. First Loma Prieta. Then Leslie's cancer. Then quitting ACT UP. I miss my comrades. Giving up on AIDS advocacy makes me worry that I'm not doing enough to see you.

However, finally there's time to tell the story I've promised you, Mustafa, the story about Carl and Peter.

Carl went haywire after I left him. He thrived on control, and he was furious to lose control of me. Once I got my citizenship, he lost power over me. Once I could support myself, he lost more power over me. When I moved out, moved to Ed's place where Carl couldn't find me, he lost all control over me.

Things were volatile whenever we ran into each other. Things turned ugly a few years later, after Carl found out Peter moved in with me. Carl stalked me, trying to force my return. Looking back at it now, I wonder if he had an early HIV infection. Something made him really crazy. Often when Peter and I dined at a restaurant, Carl appeared and made a huge scene. How he knew where we'd be eating, I never figured out. He wrote me letters threatening to have me deported, claiming my paperwork had irregularities.

One evening Carl cornered me at the Midnight Sun. He told me that he knew where you lived, Mustafa, and then threatened to harm you unless I returned to him. I threw my cocktail on his face and dashed out.

I never told Peter about that incident. For one thing, Peter didn't know about you, didn't know you existed. It was early in our relationship. Telling Peter seemed like a bombshell that would blow our budding relationship to bits. The only American who knew of my fatherhood was Carl.

For another, I didn't know whether Carl was lying to get me back. He'd gone back to Algeria enough that his claim could be true. He described a few physical details about you that I had no way to confirm, details that seemed horribly creepy. I worried that Carl might have done to you some of the nasty things he did to me. He did things I was scared shitless to tell anyone, even Peter.

Carl became a monster. One night he went berserk. It wasn't the first night he showed up at our apartment. He yelled and pounded on the door, waking Peter and me and the neighbors. After a while, he stopped. The usual pattern. Relieved, I fell back asleep.

Sometime later I woke, startled by a cold hand covering my mouth and the stench of alcohol. I shook Peter's arm. Peter screamed at the sight of Carl, who must have climbed the back stairs and entered through an unlocked window.

While Peter leapt across the bedroom to phone the police, Carl stumbled to the kitchen and grabbed a chef's knife. He returned slowly, silent except for the knife slashing the wall. Peter and I held each other in the bedroom, terrified at the dim specter approaching in the hallway. Who knows how the police responded so fast. At the sight of their blinking lights, Carl, not a foot from the bedroom door, dropped the knife and fled out the back.

I don't want to get bogged down in legal details. The long and short of it is that Carl got out on bail and sent me a letter with a grainy photo he claimed was you, Mustafa. For all I knew it was a photo he'd taken when he met me. I had no way to know for sure. After so many trips to Algeria, though, he might have found you. His letter said if Peter and I pressed charges, he would make sure I never found you. I worried he might do more, like molesting you. Or worse.

Peter, of course, wanted to press charges. He wanted to protect me, wanted to make sure Carl knew there were consequences. That put me in a bind. I tried to dissuade Peter from prosecution, suggesting that Carl needed mental health help, that his arrest would shake some sense into him. What I should have said is that Carl could reunite us, Mustafa. I was too worried the revelations of a son in Algeria—let alone the revelations of what Carl did to me and perhaps to you—would separate Peter from me. How could I risk my relationship when I wasn't sure Carl was telling the truth?

If I'd told Peter about you, his choice would have been between our safety and the possibility that I find a son neither Peter nor I really knew. I couldn't put Peter in that position, so I let him press charges. He was right based on what he knew.

What Peter couldn't know—what I never wanted him to know—was that after Carl went to jail and lost his job, my chances of finding you vanished. It was the same hopeless feeling I had after my AIDS diagnosis. I haven't given up on living, and I won't give up on you. If there's any silver lining to this story, it's that Carl died of AIDS soon after he got out of jail, so he couldn't have returned to Algeria to harm you.

Now, Mustafa, you are a mystery. I don't know who raised you, whether you're devout, what interests you. I would like to know. I would like us to share something, even if it's that I don't matter to you.

Whenever I consider telling Peter all this, I conclude it still would put him in an untenable position. That's because I realized later, when I looked at that photo of you and reread Carl's threat, that Carl did have information about you. On the back of the grainy photo, Carl wrote your name, Mustafa. I have never told anyone your name.

14

SAN FRANCISCO, NOV 25, 2001

Peter sipped coffee on the patio at Cafe Flore while waiting for Linh. It was a temperate Thanksgiving weekend, warm by San Francisco standards, but still a tad nippy in the shade. There wasn't a day since Rano's journal tumbled off the shelf in the studio that Peter didn't think of Rano, didn't want to talk with Rano about the journal, about what Rano might have left out of the journal. Today was no different.

To take his mind off Rano, Peter flipped through the pages of the *Bay Area Reporter*, his weekly search for the obituary section. Back when the obits filled more column inches than the rent boy ads, they were easy to spot. Peter remembered six or seven years earlier when the obits began to thin out, not so many years after Rano died. Today they were hiding somewhere in the back of the first section.

"Who died last week?" Linh asked, peering over Peter's shoulder at the three obituaries he'd finally found.

"No one I know," Peter said, standing and wrapping his arms around her. "You look like a million dollars."

Peter rarely felt self-conscious about his clothes, but Linh's couture startled his sensibilities. Smiling and standing next to her, his jeans and pullover were conspicuous for their absence of color. The baseball cap Linh wore backwards seemed out of place, but somehow she pulled it off. Peter's underdeveloped fashion sense didn't keep him from appreciating the fine cut and soft touch of Linh's blue-and-yellow-striped wool dress.

"I hope you haven't been waiting long," Linh said, negotiating her tight dress into a chair.

"What's with the threads?" Peter asked, setting his empty coffee cup on top of the obits.

"My ship came to port," Linh replied. "I decided to afford what I'd only been able to relish."

That reminded Peter that, after Linh's visit to his gallery opening, Brice had mentioned something about Linh's good fortunes. Brice said Linh's Internet company went public or something. The Linh who'd arrived to the opening dressed to the nines was a stylish revision of the Linh he'd always known. Today she was a total knockout.

"I'm relishing that choker," Peter said, impressed by how subtly its blue sapphires emphasized Linh's eyes. "I'm lucky you could squeeze a fashion lemon like me into your schedule."

"I'm sorry I didn't have more time this trip," Linh said. "Things are complicated with my family."

"How's your aunt's bánh mì shop?" Peter asked. Things always seemed complicated keeping the family sandwich shop afloat. It must have been closed for Thanksgiving, which explained the timing of Linh's trip. Peter remembered the shop also being closed that year he tried ordering Vietnamese sandwiches to avoid cooking turkey.

"After 9/11, demand for good, cheap food shot up," Linh answered, adjusting her shawl. "The shop is great. The problem is my aunt's newfound enthusiasm for Christianity."

"Sounds like my family," Peter said.

"Yes, I suppose so," Linh said, handing Peter his coffee cup and picking up the newspaper. "Anyway, I've had enough Jesus talk after a weekend with my aunt. I need a gay diversion. Would you get me a cappuccino?"

"Sure," Peter said, realizing Linh needed something to warm her up. As he waited inside for the barista, he also realized how much he missed visiting with Linh. When she'd lived in San Francisco all those years ago, she'd stop by his studio at least once a week. After Rano died, rambling mind melds with Linh had been the most satisfying substitute for talking with Rano. Linh knew Rano, understood his quirks. She knew Peter even better. Peter couldn't wait to discuss Rano's journal with her. She was as close to a confidante as he ever had, especially after a joint or two.

"Here you go," Peter said, placing the coffees on the table.

"Thanks," Linh said, putting down the paper. "None of the obits are for anyone who died of AIDS."

"I remembered celebrating the first six-month stretch when no one I knew died," Peter said. As the obits dwindled, so had caregiving and grieving. "Suddenly I could focus, start painting again. Over five years ago now."

"These obits reminded me that Brice flew out to see you at the hospital last month," Linh said, stirring sugar in her cappuccino. "Brice said you got lucky."

This could be awkward. It wasn't the conversation Peter wanted to have. What did Brice tell Linh? Did he tell her about Angel's return to San Francisco? About their

Russian River coke binge? About Angel's arrest after he left the motel room wearing nothing more than his drug-laden backpack?

"Don't go all quiet on me," Linh said after a bit. "I'm just glad you didn't have a heart attack."

"I was lucky it wasn't a heart attack," Peter said. "As lucky as I was to miss that hijacked flight on 9/11. I had a pain in my chest. My pulse seemed too quick."

"According to Brice, it was nothing worse than heartburn. Or gallstones or something."

"It all cleared up at the hospital by the next day," Peter said. "I was grateful, but so embarrassed when Brice showed up."

"You don't have someone in San Francisco you can call for emergencies?" Linh asked.

During those moments Peter had gripped his chest and contemplated death, during the endless wait for the ambulance, Brice was the first person who popped into his mind. Angel was, in fact, closer. Under different circumstances, Peter might have called Angel. It wasn't a good time to reveal to Linh, however, the messy situation with Angel. Peter didn't want to explain to Linh why it was impossible for him to call Angel. On account of Angel's prior in Los Angeles—the felony conviction that prompted his return to San Francisco—he was now in jail, facing a second strike. After abandoning Angel in the Russian River motel room, Peter felt obligated to help Angel.

"Well, anyway," Linh said after a long silence, "I don't care about what's going on between you and Angel. I care about you."

"After the 911 call, Brice was the first person who came to mind," Peter said, wondering again what Linh knew about Angel. "Maybe because of how Brice and I reconnected when I stayed at his place."

"Ah, yes," Linh said, placing the paper back on the table. "I always thought the two of you would get together after Rano died. But Angel seems to distract you."

Peter knew that phoning Brice had been the right thing to do. Brice's trip to San Francisco confirmed it. After Peter's brief hospital stay, they spent a couple of days together before Brice returned to dress the rest of Manhattan's holiday windows. Peter didn't tell Brice everything about Angel, though. How did Linh know so much?

"Did you see this article about the gay guy who died on that flight you missed?" Linh asked, rotating the paper so Peter could read it. "Mark Bingham. They want to name a community center after him."

"Oh, the rugby player," Peter said. "The guy who led the charge to break down the cabin door and take back the plane from the hijackers. They want to name a community center after Mark Bingham?"

"He's an easily digestible gay hero for Americans," Linh said, picking up the paper and browsing its pages. "A photogenic guy who saved the White House. Sorry he had to die to get recognition, but he was an outstanding example of the community."

"There were thousands of gay heroes who died at the height of the AIDS crisis," Peter said. "No one is naming community centers for them."

"Seems like everyone thinks AIDS is over with these sex ads," Linh said, putting the paper back on the table for Peter to see. "Look. These come-ons have something for everyone. Don't care for *Soccer Jock*? Maybe *Leather Top* will do. Don't like *Puerto Rican 24*? Why here's *Hot Hawaiian Filipino. Xtra Hung Dad* not your cup of tea? There's always *Cum Starved Muscle Punk*!"

"Funny you mention rent boys," Peter said, taking the final sip of his coffee. Sexual fetish was always a fun topic with Linh, but not what he wanted to discuss today. "If I don't sell some paintings soon, I'll need another way to pay my rent."

"You have to keep your studio," Linh said, folding the *Bay Area Reporter* and putting her cup on top of it. "We've had such great conversations there."

"I remember all of them," Peter said, finally finding a segue to Rano. "If I hadn't met Rano, I might have been one of those rent boys."

"After your bus ride from Kansas, your come-on could have read *Corn-Fed Beef*," Linh said, pointing at the sex ads. "Or *Naked Boy Draws You* with those tourist sketches you used to draw on Pier 39."

"Rano saved me from all that, gave me a proper home, a place to start painting. He'd say sex work during the AIDS crisis was more dangerous than breeding rats during the Plague."

As Peter remembered those words, he strained to hear Rano's voice, to hear how the French part of Rano's accent softened the Arabic. He wanted Linh to help him figure out Rano's journal. Peter had made a big mistake putting Carl in jail. It was a mistake he couldn't have known until he read the journal, but still it was big. Peter had kept Rano from finding his son. Linh would understand.

Linh's cell phone rang. She spoke a few Vietnamese words before she flipped her phone shut and put it back in her purse.

"My car to the airport is arriving," Linh said, tilting her cappuccino to spoon out the last of the foam. "This is my problem with money. It's controlling my life, controlling when I come and where I go. I'm sorry I didn't stay long at your opening night in New York, and I'm sorry I can't stay longer now. Tell me what you're working on."

"I'm stuck again," Peter said. He needed to talk to Linh about painting, too. She wasn't exactly a muse, but he trusted her intuition about art. "After Rano died, I contemplated how I formed memories of lost friends, friends disappearing in life's rearview mirror."

"I sensed that," Linh said, looking at her watch and checking the airline ticket in her purse, "when I saw your gallery show."

"Many friends who died of AIDS," Peter continued, "left me a junkyard of memories—obits, photographs, letters, T-shirts, cassette tapes, books. Others left a junkyard in my memory. As my brush found its way over the canvas, I contemplated not so much my memories of these vanishing friends, but how I formed these memories. Now I want to paint something about New York, about 9/11, but I don't know what it is yet. I can't find my way into the material."

"All the artists I've met in New York get stuck, too," Linh said. "When they do, they start making self-portraits. It's predictable. Artists can be so self-absorbed."

"I'm not much at portraits," Peter said. "I haven't made a portrait since Pier 39, since my first weeks in San Francisco."

"There's my car," Linh said as a black sedan pulled up in front. She leaned over to hug Peter and whispered in his ear, "Shred Rano's journal and get back to work."

As Linh shuffled out to Market Street in her tight dress and waved goodbye, Peter sat frozen. Why had Linh whispered that? After the black sedan pulled away, he browsed the rent boy section again. If Rano had kept his son a secret, Peter wondered, what else did Rano keep secret from Peter? What else did Peter's friends know about Rano that he didn't?

December 31, 1989 – Beginnings

Dear Mustafa,

Thank Goddess this decade is nearly over. I spent the final day of the decade researching. Lots of progress, even with Leslie the Librarian out for chemo. I figured out a better way to incorporate my new ideas about digital identity and theft into my earlier work, the stagecoach and train robbery metaphor I wrote about.

As the year ends, I want to reminisce, for your benefit and for mine. I want to look back at how you, dear Mustafa, came to be. Before I tell you that story, though, first I want to look back at the beginning of the journey to my field of research.

It started in the Summer of Love.

The Summer of Love. That's a fine memory. The floral version of the American dream blossomed right here in San Francisco. Flower Power headquarters was located at the corner of Haight and Ashbury. Hippies moved into communes with their children, flower children flaunted the system with pot and protests, peaceful protesters inserted flowers in the barrels of police rifles, Black Panthers raised their rifles on the steps of the state capitol. The summer of 1969 was the culmination of America's protests against the Vietnam War, of its countercultural struggle against a system gone haywire.

Make love, not war.

I'd escaped Carl. Even though I was working and going to school, I can't tell you how nice that was. With my newfound freedom, I made time for free-love antics. The late-night parties after The Cockettes performed. The drug parties in the Haight. The South of Market bath houses.

Ah, the bath houses. Shut down now on account of the plague, but once the bastion of blatant bad behavior and the center of seedy gay social life. At night, South of Market was dangerous, so dangerous that only longshoremen and police showed their faces. No one else dared walk those empty sidewalks after sunset. Except the gays. Who would bother us in that Goddessforsaken neighborhood? After a few drinks at one of the sleazy South of

Market bars, we'd slink over to Ritch Street Baths, or 8th & Howard, or the very nastiest of the nasty, the Hot House. The closeted boys would join us after dinner with their girlfriends, driving them home, giving them a peck. Once they crossed to the south side of Market Street, those peckers cruised the dark hallways where their lurid sexual preferences remained secret.

Secret and not. It was the unwritten rule that everyone kept everything at the bath houses a secret, except that it was impossible to keep secret what we found out about each other's sex. Who topped, who bottomed, who flipped. Who liked oral, who liked anal. Who fucked one-on-one, who fucked in groups. Who showed off, who lurked. Who snorted coke, who got hard. Who was endowed, who was a bottom, or might as well have been. Who played roles, who didn't. Well, everyone played some kind of role.

Sometimes we even snagged a name and phone number.

The morning after our sexcapades, we'd brunch at Hamburger Mary's or Cafe Flore or The Cove. We'd gossip. You wouldn't believe who I saw last night taking it at the Eagle. Or, did you know so-and-so likes double penetration? Or, I didn't know someone could spend so many hours working a glory hole.

But I digress.

The Summer of Love. Our shenanigans in the years following were liberating. But it was about more than sexual liberation for me. My gay doctor—how comforting to have a doctor who anticipated my problems before I spoke—my gay doctor explained to me that sexual liberation was the result of The Pill. He said birth control freed women from unplanned abortions and shotgun marriages.

This gay boy from Algeria didn't know as much as he should about The Pill or its history. Luckily for you, as it turns out, this gay boy also didn't pay attention when his older brothers taught him about birth control. In my world, condoms were for venereal diseases and only when the client provided one. As far as I know, The Pill hadn't arrived in Africa by the time I left.

The Summer of Love conversation with the gay doctor gave me the seed of an idea. As I write this, I realize that conversation was, in fact, the very first time I contemplated the relationship of culture and technology.

Leaving his office, my head filled with observations about the cultural implications of The Pill. Americans invent a pill that modifies human reproduction. Why Americans? What if Algerians invented it? Would an Algerian Pill have worked the same way? How did The Pill affect Algeria differently from America? It's clear what American women did with The Pill. Did Algerian women have to choose between The Pill or their religion? Did white American men ship The Pill to black Algerian women to promote the white race?

Later, these questions turned into my master's thesis. I wrote about The Pill as well as other examples of the relationship between culture and technology. It was brilliant. That's not my narcissistic judgment. The originality and importance of my thesis gave me a choice of PhD programs with a full ride.

A decade before the Summer of Love, I created you, dear Mustafa. I created you with your mother, Aaliya, who worked in one of the better bookstores in the coastal city where I worked. To protect you, Mustafa, and your mother, I have kept the name of this city and other details to myself. I considered, for instance, that you might want this journal translated. One way or another, it could fall into the wrong hands. I won't give any zany religious zealots a reason to harm you or Aaliya.

Whenever my "associates" agreed to buy me a book after consummating our transaction, I often invited them to the shop that Aaliya's family owned. While Aaliya was a year or so my junior, she knew much more about books. It was unusual for a young woman to work at a bookstore, but she was good for sales and her family knew it. Customers asked for her help not only because she was charming and beautiful, but also because she had a gift for matching reader with book. We were both precocious in our own way. That was my attraction.

It was Aaliya who first suggested we meet for coffee. With all the men I paraded through her shop, she must have known my business by then. We never discussed it. She knew I liked books and that was all that mattered. She remembered what I'd read and asked me about the characters, plots, and writing styles of each and every title. I was enthralled with someone who cared about my opinions. Captivated, really. She laughed through my criticisms of *Les Misérables*. We argued over the best French writers and singers. I loved Édith Piaf. I don't remember Aaliya's favorite singer. I grew quite fond of Aaliya.

I won't provide all the details of our trysts. Certain specifics are best kept from the children. Suffice it to say things clicked. We had our own Algerian Summer of Love ten years before it was chic. Our affair was scary and fun and confusing for me, an adventure I hadn't imagined. I even stopped my business activities, thinking perhaps I'd finally outgrown my homosexual phase.

One day, after months of amorous activities, I visited the bookstore looking for something to read on the beach. I'd found Camus intriguing and stopped by the shop to ask Aaliya for help finding his book called *The Plague*—a prescient title given how things have turned out. My visit was, of course, mostly an excuse to see Aaliya, but she wasn't there.

I was informed she'd fallen ill. In fact, I was asked to leave the shop and never return. I missed her instantly. I missed our conversations. I felt helpless. I worried about Aaliya.

Eventually I went back to work. I had to. My homosexuality was quite intact. For months, I'd walk near Aaliya's shop, keeping an eye out for any sign of her. I suppose this was my way of mourning. I remained suspicious about Aaliya's illness. She'd been sick the last time we met, but sick in a way I suspected only women got sick. I was new to all this.

A year later, long after I'd stopped obsessing over Aaliya, long after I'd stopped walking through her neighborhood, stopped looking for her, she appeared in a street market, testing the firmness of tomatoes. Aaliya wore a new head covering, so I wasn't certain at first. As she picked up one tomato and the next, though, I recognized her gestures. She looked more beautiful than I remembered. It took me a minute to realize the bundle she cradled in her arm was a baby, to deduce that I must be its father. I walked to the cucumber section, facing her across the vegetables. When she looked up and saw me, the color ran out of her face. She put down the tomatoes, pulled our baby close, and regained her composure. The only thing she said before she turned and walked off was, "His name is Mustafa."

I never saw Aaliya or you again. I couldn't make out your face through the swaddling. I don't pray, but if you do, please pray that I will see your face someday. I hope you grew up healthy. I'm sure you're well-read, which gives me some solace.

Now, two decades after the Summer of Love and three decades after my Algerian Summer of Love, here in the midst of my research paperwork, I'm celebrating my first New Year's Eve with AIDS. If the '70s were the sexually liberated fallout from the Summer of Love, AIDS was the killer venereal disease going around the decade after. The '90s better deliver the cure. AZT is keeping me alive, but not everyone.

It's hard to plan for the years ahead, dear Mustafa, let alone the decades. Last week, I bought a self-help book to draft a will. It was too depressing. I couldn't finish it, couldn't decide what to leave to Peter, what to give friends, how I might leave something for you.

After several months, the AZT seems to be working. That was all the excuse I needed to procrastinate on organizing my meager estate. So, happy fucking New Year, my dearest Mustafa. No will and no last testament necessary because AZT is The Pill for me. I've been liberated. I'm going to live forever.

15

NEW YORK, NOV 28, 2001

Erica watched coffee drip into the pot. Her celebratory drink for surviving another month. Since 9/11, she'd become less flamboyant and more practical. She'd cut back on new shows, negotiated a rent reduction, halved her personal expenses. No new assistant to replace Jodie until business improved.

All this time, Thomas made noises about buying Peter's landscapes. On this rainy November afternoon, it was the deal most likely to keep Erica's business solvent. All she needed was for Thomas and Peter to meet in person. The phone rang. Erica dashed from the coffeemaker to her office, hoping for news from Thomas.

"Hey, it's Mark."

Erica gulped. Of course Mark waited to call until she was desperate for business. After she'd found out Mark was in Europe, she stopped leaving messages and sent a few letters in hopes that he would reply whenever it was that he returned. Here he was. Why now? After so long a time, the call felt like a first date, except without the bad coffee and sanitized family histories.

Mark glossed over his tardy response to Erica's messages. At first, while he babbled on about research breakthroughs, all Erica heard was sex. Their sex, which was great. That was obvious from the very first day they met at a wine and cheese event, from their tipsy flirtations over a selection of soft Vermont cheeses, flirtations that tumbled into a bed of delightfully creamy sexual innuendos. She missed watching him grow erect those times she moaned from across the room and slowly unbuttoned her blouse. She missed him inside her. She missed his arms around her afterwards, their fingers intertwined. She could learn to live with someone who squeezed the toothpaste tube from the middle.

After futile attempts to chitchat, Mark lurched into a description of Guy Fawkes Day celebrations, describing a swank Knightsbridge party he'd attended, comparing the fireworks to Independence Day fireworks. Erica's happiness to hear Mark's voice transformed to shock as adrenaline sped up her heart. When Mark's travelog continued in France, Erica knew by the tone of his voice there was something he wasn't telling her. She was pretty sure she knew what he wasn't mentioning. He avoided it, but at least he wasn't lying about it.

Although Erica understood she had no rational claim to outrage about another woman—Erica herself was the one who'd cut it short with Mark—her anger brewed of its own accord. On those rare occasions she'd thought about Mark finding a new girlfriend, she was sure it would take him eons. One visit to his messy playpen would cast doubt in the mind of any sane woman seeking a relationship with another adult.

On the phone, Mark still was going on about the cities he'd visited. From the way he wrapped up, Erica knew her rationalization of his long-term availability was just that, a rationalization. There was another woman. Whoever it might be, all Erica wanted right now was to scratch out her eyes.

It was Erica's turn to talk. She needed a moment to gather her wits. On the train back from Danbury, she'd decided to give Mark one last shot. She convinced herself that she'd missed the mark, as it were, with Mark. As a practical matter, given her biological clock, it was less risky to learn to live with his obsessive research and his unkempt quarters than to campaign for another candidate to father her child. Dedication and messiness were not deal breakers, not when the two of them enjoyed theater and film together, not when they explored cheap ethnic restaurants and discovered a prized dish, not when they giggled over their own snooty wine and cheese review parodies after taste testing five-dollar bottles and toothpicking Whole Foods samples. The call with Mark was making Erica feel desperate. Desperation did not suit her cause. The phone conveniently signaled another call coming in. Erica asked Mark to hold while she checked the incoming call.

"Hello," Peter said on the other line.

"Where have you been?" Erica asked plaintively.

"Are you okay?" Peter replied. "Something sounds desperately wrong. I can call back later."

"No, no, no. It's just a call on the other line."

"Well, then, I'll be brief," Peter said. "I can't paint anymore."

"What happened?" Erica asked. What could have fucking happened? Where had Peter disappeared these past weeks? In a haze of drugs? Or had he been whisked away by a sugar daddy? Why the fuck would Peter stop painting? It would be impossible to sell his work if anyone found out. "I was worried about you, but I couldn't reach you."

"Things are okay now, but I'm stuck," Peter said with exasperation in his voice. "Since I can't paint, I've decided not to renew my studio lease."

"I thought you loved that studio," Erica said.

"Every place has its time," Peter said. "I'm closing shop."

"Can we talk about this? I have a buyer who wants to meet you."

"Thomas?"

"Yes," Erica said. "How did you know?"

"A friend told me."

Yes. Right. A friend. Of course. Erica tilted back on her chair and wondered if this was a dodge, if Peter was trying to cut her out of a deal. She must have misread Peter completely. How could he possibly know of Thomas' continuing interest? He'd barely met Thomas. It made no sense that Peter would abandon painting, especially after the recent evolution in his work, after the gallery show and the glowing reviews. She tilted a little too far and the chair nearly fell backwards.

"You sure you're okay?" Peter asked again.

"No." Erica paused, swiveling around to a more stable position in the chair. "Tell me how to call you back."

Peter gave Erica a number and hung up. Erica hesitated before switching back to the call with Mark. Across the empty gallery, she watched the cold rain pouring down outside. Without a meeting between Peter and Thomas, it was curtains, and it was curtains anyway if Peter gave up painting. For the first time, Erica couldn't think of a way to keep the gallery afloat. She felt like she'd been shoved, like Peter had pushed her down a dark shaft so vertical that even if she survived the fall, she would never be able to claw her way back to the surface.

"I have to help a customer," Erica said, returning to Mark on the phone. "Could we have coffee sometime?"

January 1, 1990 – Resolutions

Dear Mustafa,

Peter and I prepared a yummy dinner last night. Too bad you couldn't join us. Roast chicken, beets, string beans. My appetite is good. I ate two slices of almond tart.

We had a conversation about Peter's art. He doesn't talk about it much. He never invites me to his studio. He says it's time for a show now that he's finally completed a set of landscapes he considers worthy. Since he doesn't have a gallery to represent him, a proper show won't take place soon. He sells works here and there to friends and at open studios, but he can't be serious without a gallery. This really hasn't worked out the way I'd thought. Other people who have seen his work claim it's top-notch. It's confusing to me. If the work is top-notch, why doesn't Peter have a gallery? Better I don't ask.

I wished Peter good luck, but there's really not much I can do. I need to put my energy into my research and writing. I don't know anything about business, much less the art business. I haven't even seen his painting since he started the California landscapes.

I was going to tell Peter about my work, my writing, but he'd nod off or start cleaning dishes like he usually does.

We watched the Times Square ball drop at midnight. Peter served champagne and caviar. He toasted my health, which was kind. I'm not as ornery when I'm healthy. I thanked him. It felt comfortable with Peter, like an old couple whose love celebrates the warts and all.

That's our problem. We are a perfunctory couple. It's not that I want drama. It's that I want something deeper, something beyond cooking and cleaning.

Ten minutes after midnight, I was in bed and Peter was out the door, celebrating in the Castro. All I remember when he returned was the alcohol on his breath. I was up with the sun. He's still snoring.

That gives me time for resolutions. Won't take long.

I have three resolutions this year. First: take my AZT. It's not perfect. I feel shitty more often than not. But I have my T cells. All I need this year is T cells. Lots and lots of them to keep me alive so I can see you, Mustafa.

Second: help Leslie fight her cancer back into remission. We spoke yesterday. She's starting another course of chemo in a week. More research delays.

Third: complete a draft of my book by year's end.

Brice called yesterday while Peter was shopping. He's exhausted from work. So many windows, so little time. But he snagged a cheap flight at the end of the month. A propitious start to the year.

16

SAN FRANCISCO, DEC 9, 2001

Thomas found himself sitting alone in the Big 4 lounge at the Huntington Hotel. The wood-paneled walls and leather chairs had the air of an English manor. The chicken pot pie at the next table filled Thomas' nose with memories. It had been ages since his last sojourn to this San Francisco gem. The 49ers game glowed on the television above the bar, something that would have helped Thomas pass the time if he followed football. He checked his watch. It was ticking. Peter was twenty minutes late for their meeting. Thomas swirled his glass of pinot noir and debated between chicken pot pie or salad.

When Erica first suggested this trip right after Thanksgiving, Thomas resisted. He was adamant that Peter travel to New York. Privately, he still wanted Peter to demonstrate initiative, if not in getting to know Thomas himself, at least in learning about Thomas as a collector. Erica was relentless. Her tone had more than a hint of desperation. After a week, it became clear Erica was frustrated, so frustrated, in fact, that finally she said if the artist wouldn't come to the collector, the collector must go to the artist. She insisted Thomas fly to San Francisco. Knowing how treacherous the art business was after 9/11, Thomas agreed.

For Thomas, the Huntington was a pleasant trip down memory lane. The venerable hotel was where Maurice preferred to stay when they'd traveled to the Bay Area, and San Francisco was a comfortable destination. It was rare here that anyone got completely bent out of shape by any combination of being gay and being black and being Jewish. The last meal Thomas ate with Maurice in San Francisco was right here at the Big 4, memorable because of the dinner company.

Maurice had recognized the people at the table next to them that evening. They were, as it turned out, Amy and Armistead, local authors celebrating recent screen releases of their books *The Joy Luck Club* and *Tales of the City*, respectively. Not by accident, a spoon fell between the tables. Apologizing to the adjacent table with a smile, Maurice picked it up. After introductions, the quartet found itself in an animated political conversation about the military's hypocritical "Don't Ask, Don't Tell" accommodation for homosexuals. That led to Maurice telling the sympathetic authors about the relevant work of certain New York based advocacy groups, and ended up just short of Maurice asking for their support. Although Maurice got their phone numbers, he died not long after returning to New York.

Thomas never followed up with Amy or Armistead. It wasn't that Thomas didn't participate in politics and arts organizations the way Maurice did, because he was engaged and continued participating in causes after Maurice's death. It wasn't that Thomas didn't enjoy the company of the two authors that evening, because he loved listening to them describe what happened during the process of transforming their books for the screen, loved the jokes they told about unworkable costumes and awkward scenes, loved the details of rewriting lines and pacing scenes for the camera. It was that Thomas' social life had existed largely in Maurice's shadow. He wasn't the natural schmoozer Maurice was. Thomas couldn't bring himself to interrupt strangers at an adjoining table with a premeditated spoon drop, especially if he recognized their celebrity. Phoning the authors after Maurice's death would just remind Thomas of this shortcoming. After nearly a decade without Maurice, Thomas worried that his social universe was collapsing rather than expanding, that he was missing out on what was going on, missing the mischief Maurice always got them into.

Thomas' stomach gurgled. Just as he motioned to the waitress to order a chicken pot pie, Peter breezed by. He was more attractive than Thomas remembered. Thomas was discouraged that Peter didn't seem to recognize him. It couldn't be that hard to remember what he looked like. The only other black guy in the neighborhood was the bartender, the black guy whom Peter did greet. Peter watched the ball game while the bartender mixed his drink. Then Peter looked around the room and waved to Thomas.

"Sorry I'm late, man," Peter said, extending his hand as he seated himself.

"I was just ordering." Thomas shook Peter's hand. "Would you like something?"

"I'm good with this," Peter answered, stirring the dark concoction in his glass. "Thanks."

Thomas changed his order to a salad. After the waitress left, he reassessed Peter. It had been a few months since opening night at Erica's gallery. Peter was quiet. He looked nervous. Or stressed. Maybe lost in thought. Thomas couldn't tell. Thomas himself was nervous. He decided to regale Peter with the story of his last meal here with Maurice. It would calm both of them. It also would reveal to Peter that Thomas was single.

Thomas embellished the story of meeting the two authors the way Maurice would have. It wasn't Maurice who dropped the spoon and made the introductions, it was Thomas himself. The two San Francisco authors sitting at the next table that night weren't just having a tête-à-tête, they were celebrating after the actual opening-night party for *Tales of the City*. Thomas hadn't just snagged their phone numbers, he'd invited them to a dinner with their significant others and cast members the following night. The new friendships hadn't died after Maurice's death. Thomas convinced the two authors to pledge substantial sums to the charities. "After Maurice's death," Thomas repeated.

Peter listened without interruption. As Thomas finished his story, Peter mentioned he also knew Armistead. In fact, he'd accompanied Armistead to the San Francisco opening-night party for *Tales of the City*. Peter described Armistead chasing the actor who played Mouse. He was surprised Armistead hadn't gone straight home because he hadn't been in any condition to go out afterwards, and even more surprised that Armistead would have ended up both at the Big 4 and without his coterie.

San Francisco was a smaller city than Thomas realized. A fishing village, actually, by New York social standards. He was mortified by the creative license he'd taken. He'd created a predicament for himself. He'd made an unforced error, as the 49ers commentator might note if the television weren't silent.

"Did the guy who played Mouse come to the dinner you and Maurice hosted the following night?" Peter asked.

The waitress placed Thomas' salad on the table. Thomas poked at it with his fork. He'd lost his appetite. He wasn't sure how far to take his story revisions, how to extricate himself from the Mouse trap he'd built for himself.

"You couldn't have missed the actor who played Mouse," Peter said. "The cast was handsome, but Mouse stole the show."

"Oh, yes, Mouse," Thomas said, rubbing his forehead to remember a story that never happened. Thomas couldn't remember if he'd even watched *Tales of the City*. "Mouse was a looker, wasn't he?"

"If Mouse was there, he must have come with Alan's boyfriend," Peter said. "Well, Alan's ex-boyfriend at that point because guess who did end up with Mouse after opening night."

"I don't remember Mouse coming with anyone." Thomas poked his salad again. "Probably because I don't remember the dinner very well."

"Seems like you'd remember everything," Peter said. "Wasn't it your last San Francisco dinner with Maurice?"

At least, Thomas thought to himself, Peter knew Maurice was no longer in the picture. This conversation was turning into a lot of effort.

"Anyway, I haven't seen Armistead in a while," Peter continued. "I'll see if he can join us when we meet at my studio tomorrow."

The bartender interrupted all the conversations in the room when he turned up the volume on the television. The bar patrons demanded to hear the announcer explain the pause in the game. The referees were huddling after reviewing an instant replay. As they broke up, the announcer said the play stood as called. The opposing team got a first down on a 49er unforced error. Anticipating a loss after this fourth quarter setback, the patrons ordered another round. As the fans booed the call, the bartender turned down the volume.

"That might be amusing," Thomas said, anxious about losing this match. "I can't imagine he'd remember me after so many years."

January 28, 1990 – Breaks

Dear Mustafa,

While Leslie the Librarian has been on chemo, I asked a couple students to help with research. That almost compensates for Leslie's absence. I wish I were as good at tracking down information as she is.

I got a lucky break. Before Leslie started chemo, she sent letters to a dozen CTOs of Bay Area technology companies. These, my son, are the leaders who know the most about technology in the most advanced technology companies on the planet. Leslie said it was a shot in the dark. She dug up the names and addresses from financial filings, industry magazines, phone calls—pretty much any way she could.

We received a couple of declines and then didn't hear anything for weeks. After the holidays, though, the replies poured in. They seem very interested in my ideas about digital identities. When I checked in on Leslie, I was happy to report that most people she contacted agreed to an interview. She was happy to report, in turn, that she expects to return full-time late March.

After a month of diligent work and a lucky break, another kind of break seemed in order. Brice flew out for Super Bowl Sunday. Super Bowl, Mustafa, is tantamount to a high holy holiday in the United States. Brice is from Utah, where they play lots of football, so he tried to teach me about the points. Even he couldn't remember for sure all the different ways to score.

Soccer—the unseemly name America gave football after misappropriating "football" for a game that has little to do with feet touching balls—seems so much more intuitive than football. The rest of the world is content with soccer's simplicity. One goal is one point. Just shoot the ball through the posts. The rest is foreplay. Why does America show so little interest in foreplay?

The main thing about football is the touchdown, and a touchdown is six points, or seven points, or eight points. Who cares? San Francisco scored a lot of them today. The main thing about today's game is that Brice and I scored a lot during the fourth quarter. As the score reached 55 to 10 in favor of San Francisco, even I knew it was a blowout. When the TV announcers grew bored, we had to do something to keep the game entertaining. We scored our own "touchdowns."

At first it didn't bother me that Peter skipped the Super Bowl to watch the new Tom Cruise film with Angel. Why should it? Gave me time alone with Brice. Tom Cruise plays a paralyzed Vietnam vet. *Born on the Fourth of July*, I think it's called. It's got Oscar buzz, as they say. I wouldn't mind watching Tom Cruise, even paralyzed, but not as a Vietnam vet. I'm sure it's terrible whatever this vet goes through, but I've already got enough grievances with AIDS.

As Peter stayed out later and later, I felt a touch of jealousy. Angel is quite stunning, his youth, his chiseled physique, his altar boy manners, that thick mane of jet-black hair. Everyone craves sex with him. But that's not what was making me jealous. That's like people wanting sex with me because of my cock. Who cares? Besides, who knows if Peter and Angel even have sex.

It's Angel's personality. He's shy at first, always quiet in a crowd. But when he's comfortable, he's open and honest. He listens. That's my jealousy. He pays attention to what I say. It's unexpected. I didn't think a perfect physical specimen like Angel would even notice me. Instead, he's like the one student in a hundred who really hears what I say and takes it to heart. Peter used to listen to me that way.

I haven't been a good partner. Since my HIV test, I've had too much to write. I want to put down all my thoughts. After HIV progressed to AIDS, it's urgent. Sometimes I feel desperate, like the oxygen is running out of the room. I can't breathe.

As much as I enjoy time with Brice, he's a huge distraction from my work. Brice teaches me things. The music, the art, the dance. But I do get antsy before his visits end. It feels good to be appreciated, to have sex with someone who's over his fear of seroconversion. Feeling good, though, doesn't type words into the computer.

Even though this visit with Brice has been more satisfying than previous meetups, the last thing I should have done is spend a long weekend away from work. I feel guilty with Leslie in chemo. I should be working harder to compensate for her time off. It was the only time Brice was able to travel, though, the break between Christmas and Easter. He'll be gone tomorrow.

I worried whether Peter would return after the Tom Cruise film. What poetic justice if Peter hadn't returned, if he'd left me for Angel. Then Brice would be decorating windows in New York, and I'd sit here all alone, trying to stay healthy.

I need Peter. I don't want to need him, but I do. Things would be so much different without AIDS. Maybe I should forgive Peter for keeping me from knowing where you are, Mustafa. Then I could address other issues.

17
NEW YORK, DEC 10, 2001

Erica sipped her second cappuccino at the East Village diner she chose not for its food but for its proximity to Mark's studio. Still Mark was late. After a sleepless night, the warm sunlight filling the diner was comforting. As she ordered a third cappuccino, Erica spotted Mark's red hair bobbing up and down from a block away. At least he didn't cancel, didn't use one of his unoriginal excuses about subway service to Brooklyn, or a proposal deadline, or laundromat timing.

The closer Mark got, the less Erica remembered the routine she'd worked out during her subway ride, how to comport herself, what topics to start with. She could make out his face now. She hoped their mutual animal magnetism would kick in. She certainly felt it. His puffy down coat couldn't hide his slender features. She pushed away her cappuccino because she was too excited to drink more. Mark pushed open the door. Erica felt her nipples harden.

"I've missed you," Erica gushed as she squeezed him.

"It's nice to see you," Mark said, pulling himself away and sitting down.

The fast-returning waiter pivoted away from the table.

"I'm sorry," Erica said.

"Sorry for what?" Mark asked, pulling off his coat and picking up the menu. He was wearing his shirt open to midchest, making it easy to count the freckles.

Erica didn't want to lie, but she couldn't think of anything truthful to say that wouldn't make her look any more desperate than she appeared already. That, and images of Mark dawdling in bed with a new girlfriend, kept running through her head. Why else would he be late and not make an excuse? Erica sat down, bit her lip, and picked up her menu, as if she hadn't read it five times, hadn't decided twenty minutes ago what she wanted. What she wanted *them* to have. Now, though, her idea to share the lumberjack breakfast seemed ridiculous. After a few minutes hiding behind her menu, she peered over the top.

"I made a mistake breaking off with you," Erica said.

"Let bygones be bygones," Mark said.

The waiter darted back to the table with Erica's third cappuccino. She ordered a Cobb salad. When Mark ordered the lumberjack breakfast Erica had wanted to share, she was sure Mark's new girlfriend had given him lessons in how to get under her skin. Silence lasted for what felt like hours.

Apparently angling for a truce, Mark asked about the gallery. Erica admitted things were touch and go but said she felt more confident than ever about her roster of artists. She expected a deal shortly, a deal that would stabilize her bank account. She told Mark that, in fact, her favorite collector had traveled all the way to San Francisco the day before to meet the artist whose show opened just before 9/11. The collector would visit the artist's studio later the same day.

"The artist whose lover died of AIDS?" Mark asked.

"Yes," Erica answered. "The death of Peter's lover put his artistic career on hold for several years."

"So sad, all those lives cut short. What did Peter's lover do, before he died?"

"A professor, I think," Erica said, absentmindedly pushing her cappuccino cups to-gether. "Something about ethics and computer codes, or computer identity, or computer something. Something you'd understand."

Erica relaxed a bit. This was the Mark she knew. She couldn't ask directly, though, the questions she wanted to ask, about whom Mark was fucking, what she was like in bed, if she could make him drip without touching him. Why did she care so much?

Erica asked instead about Mark's European trip. Mark told Erica about his comparative computer language research, what he'd found out in Europe. He gave more details than during their phone call, but not romantic details. Boring technical details. So many details that it became clear Mark was avoiding what really mattered, the one thing Erica wanted to know, that there was some chance, any chance of getting back together.

The only good thing about Mark going on and on was that he didn't give the let's-be-friends speech. But he kept avoiding the other woman Erica knew he must be seeing. His romantic reticence bothered Erica so much that she felt that feeling again, the feeling of falling down a dark shaft with no way to claw her way back up. Only this time it was worse. When she'd felt this after her call with Peter, after Peter said he'd stopped painting, she'd figured out how to scratch her way up the dark shaft. She'd phoned Peter over and again to see how he was doing, reached out to him, FedEx'd little care packages.

Over the next week, Peter opened up, realized he had to paint again, discussed with her once more how to market his paintings.

Listening to Mark, Erica felt worse, as though she hit the bottom of the dark shaft and someone was shoveling dirt on her, as though someone wanted to suffocate her. This time she was the one who'd made the mistake. She didn't know how to communicate with Mark, if there were any way to salvage their relationship. Mark continued describing meetings in Germany, in France, in England, the differences between coding in one computer language and another, the implications of his research for the Internet. Erica could hardly breathe. She motioned for the waiter.

"Please take these," Erica said, handing the cappuccino cups to the waiter, "and bring the check."

"But I haven't brought your food."

"That's okay."

FEBRUARY 11, 1990 – NEWS

Dear Mustafa,

Today's news brings hope that global civil rights progress is possible and quells my angst about leaving ACT UP. I'm sure you, too, saw this news in Algeria. Big, big news. South Africa released Nelson Mandela from prison.

Russia's nascent democracy is winning the headline competition here, but that's because white people are more interested in Russia than South Africa. No one could be surprised the Berlin Wall wasn't enough to keep Europe's democratic ideals from migrating east.

How consequential is this Russian news, though? It's just Russia giving democracy a whirl after centuries of failed czars and dictators. Russians are too smart for their own good. They invent brilliant ideological constructs to rationalize horrible governments. How long until they revert to another czar?

Of these two international stories, Mandela's release is the story with true longevity.

Mandela is a catalyst as significant as Gandhi. As Gandhi turned the tides on centuries of colonialism, so Mandela is turning the tides on centuries of racism. Mark my words, Mandela is the seed of a pan-governmental revolution.

Progress in the long arc of the isms—of colonialism, racism, sexism—comforts me after setbacks from AIDS and from the Loma Prieta earthquake. The sands of time continually deliver these disasters, mirrors that reflect both the beauty of decency and the ugliness of sanctimony. The isms persist in these reflections until a Gandhi or a Mandela transforms culture.

Although every country has its own brand of racism, I'm sure the effects of Mandela's release will reach far beyond South Africa, as far as Algeria and even America. It took me months and years to appreciate how different America's racism is from Algeria's.

Algeria suffered the brutal colonial flavor of racism. After the French put down the Berber pirates and stole the dey's wheat, they spent decades stripping the country of its leaders and tribal identities. Whole tribes were massacred. The lucky ones were deported to Syria, Tunisia, and Morocco. I'm barely old enough to remember reports of tens of thousands of Muslims massacred around Sétif after the Nazis surrendered. The French took domination seriously.

Moving from Algeria to San Francisco required an adjustment. Not that San Francisco is a bastion of colonial genocide, or even of the overt racism of America's south, but racism isn't hard to find here. I've experienced it in the kinds of questions police ask me. I've experienced it when shoppers assume I'm the help at a store. I've experienced it in our gay community. Even card-carrying, flag-waving queens have prejudices. The big black cock fetish that I know too well. The personal ads with their "more into rice than beans" preferences. The bars where white men and black men expect to hook up, the bars where they don't.

I've had to assimilate, to learn America's version of black.

Mandela's freedom, dear Mustafa, symbolizes freedom for black people everywhere, freedom for you in Algeria, freedom for me in America. It bolsters the possibilities of equality. In the middle of this AIDS crisis, it's a ray of hope that the human race is capable of civil rights progress.

Perhaps I'm using this news to rationalize my departure from ACT UP, to rationalize that a cure will be found for AIDS even if I don't fight for it directly. Mandela's release, unfortunately, has not freed me from researching and writing my book. Trust me when I tell you that I'm toiling away so I can visit you soon. We'll toast Mandela!

18

SAN FRANCISCO, DEC 10, 2001

After Peter buzzed in Thomas downstairs, he flew around his studio, throwing away food scraps and recycling beer bottles. In front of the full-length mirror, he zhooshed up his hair to camouflage the thinning. The studio lease was up at the end of the month. Erica said Thomas was interested in buying not one, but several paintings. It was more than saving the studio, though. After chatting at the Big 4, Peter also found himself interested in Thomas.

There was a knock at the studio door. Peter checked himself again in the mirror. The color of his belt and shoes matched. Glancing at his face, checking how evenly he'd trimmed his beard, he caught himself caring more than usual about how he looked.

Peter opened the door. Thomas wore a fetching sweater with what looked like silver and gold threads running through it, threads that glittered in the studio lights as Thomas entered.

"So this is where the magic happens," Thomas said, perusing the space.

Not much longer, Peter thought to himself, not without a deal. No sales, no lease renewal. Peter also looked at the studio walls. There wasn't much art. He'd hung a few of his old paintings and taken his New York skyline drawings down from a shelf. Everything was arranged nicely, but the large space felt barren.

"Coffee?" Peter asked.

"Done," Thomas said, placing a sizeable bag on one of the studio tables. "I found a pastry shop on the way here."

Peter poked around in the kitchenette for two clean plates. He smelled the milk in the mini-fridge before he set it next to the array of apple tartlets and croissants Thomas laid out on an extemporaneous paper bag platter. The pastries smelled like Thomas pulled them right out of the oven.

"Why three cups of coffee?" Peter asked.

"In case our friend Armistead joins us," Thomas answered.

Peter's puerile ruse the day before at the Big 4, the ruse about knowing Armistead, seemed to have caught Thomas off guard, as though Thomas himself had made up a story of knowing Armistead. The San Francisco gay scene was small, but not so small that Peter knew everyone. Peter also lied about attending the opening-night party for *Tales of the City*. He'd been invited, but why bother attending a stuffy corporate party when he knew he'd hear the best dirt from friends? The more Peter had improvised about Armistead the day before, the more Thomas squirmed. Peter wanted to let Thomas in on his prank, but he couldn't tell if the third cup of coffee for Armistead was tongue-in-cheek or serious. Not much to do now but play along.

"Armistead said he'd try to swing by," Peter said. "Depends on how long his meeting in Oakland goes."

Thomas' "um-hmm" made Peter second-guess his Armistead strategy. Thomas seemed to know Peter was prevaricating. Maybe Thomas did know Armistead. Maybe Thomas had spoken with Armistead. Maybe the third cup of coffee was actually for Armistead.

Thomas poured milk into his coffee and headed to the table with the New York skyline drawings. "I like this one," Thomas said, pulling out the same drawing that had caught Angel's eye a couple months earlier, the drawing Peter had finished after 9/11, finished right before he fucked Brice.

"Yes, it captures something about the way New York felt after 9/11."

"Will you paint it?" Thomas asked.

At this particular moment, that was a difficult question for Peter. In spite of Erica's encouragement, in spite of his desire to keep the studio, he wasn't convinced he could paint again. He glanced at himself in the mirror, now unsure who was looking back.

"Perhaps it's not for me to say," Thomas said, "but it has the ingredients for a great painting."

"I've never painted an urban landscape," Peter said after a bit.

"It doesn't look like you've been painting much at all lately," Thomas said, looking at the studio walls. "I've seen lots of your current work tucked away in Erica's storage room. It's prime time, by the way."

"Oh, thanks."

"I like the interplay of abstraction and realism in your paintings," Thomas said. "I see something real forming out of the beauty of the abstract."

"Something like that," Peter said, trying not to sound too impressed with Thomas' interpretation of his work. Even the *New York Times* had missed this concept entirely in its glowing review. The second Peter had spotted Thomas at the Big 4 the previous day,

Peter did remember their chat on opening night. Thomas was the one who'd asked good questions about Peter's use of structures, about the relationship between the realistic structures and the abstract landscapes. How could Peter have failed to form a memory of the man who inadvertently saved his life, who delayed his return to San Francisco?

"Why have you stopped painting?" Thomas asked.

"9/11 scared me, started me on a path of reevaluating everything, of deciding what's really important," Peter answered. "I never thanked you, by the way, for saving my life, for delaying my departure. I would be buried somewhere in the remote Pennsylvania countryside if you hadn't insisted on dinner."

"Thank Lady Luck." Thomas walked around the gallery, viewing Peter's older work.

Peter felt uncomfortable with his dissembling answer. Sure, 9/11 bothered him. It bothered everyone. But it wasn't the reason he'd stopped painting. At least the Armistead lie started as a ruse, a game. This felt worse. Peter couldn't bring himself to tell Thomas, or anyone, what was keeping him from painting. The humiliation of Rano's secrets was more than Peter wanted to discuss with Thomas at this point. They barely knew each other.

"I hope you don't have any artwork stored over here," Thomas said, pointing at the storage alcove at the far end of the studio.

Peter walked over to Thomas. There was a slow drip from the alcove ceiling and a puddle on the floor. Everything on the shelf under the drip was soggy, including the box full of Rano's things on the highest shelf and especially the journal resting next to it.

"It smells mildewy," Thomas said. "Probably been leaking for some time."

"Luckily nothing valuable over here." Peter stepped up on a chair to inspect the ceiling leak and the soaked top shelf. The mineral fiber ceiling tile was so saturated that Peter's light prodding punctured it. Water pooled above the perforated ceiling tile poured down, drenching Peter and splattering on Thomas. What was left of Rano's box melted, half its contents spilling into the lake forming on the floor.

While Thomas fetched a mop and paper toweling from the kitchenette, Peter grabbed at Rano's journal. Its binding broke and the saturated paper plopped downwards from the top shelf to the shelves and floor below. Some pages were torn, others mulched beyond legibility.

"That's quite a dildo," Thomas said as he returned.

"The 1988 entries are destroyed," Peter said, holding together the pages he could. Peter started to cry as he assessed the damage. Thomas' reassuring hand on his shoulder couldn't help. Rano's words were melting before his eyes. "Oh, my God. Even some of 1989."

FEBRUARY 12, 1990 – LOSS

While writing my exuberant entry about Mandela, I somehow lost a fucking floppy disk. No idea how it escaped my briefcase. Poof! Three long days of work disappeared.

I was so angry, I nearly reverted to pen and paper. The magic of cut-and-paste, though, whets my appetite for a clickety-clack computer keyboard. Not to worry, Mustafa. I will finish. Should the computer and disks fail me completely, writing these very pages by hand has kept my poor penmanship from degenerating to utter illegibility.

I can fall back to pen and paper any time. Writing by hand, however, would slow down my work and that, in turn, would separate us longer. I'm sticking with the computer so I can see you soon. Assuming I don't lose more disks. Which invariably I will.

One of the more technically inclined students explained a simple backup strategy. I've started copying disks after each writing session so I won't lose any work. When I explained I planned to make backups of the backups, the student called me neurotic. I replied to her, yes, of course, I'm writing a book.

For further protection, I'm limiting each disk to one chapter. That way, when I invariably lose another disk, and its backup, and the other backup, and the paper printout, I will lose no more than a chapter. It feels like wearing a condom over a condom, like something bad could never happen.

Who am I kidding? Computers burst into flames if I just look at them. If anyone could erase an entire book's worth of floppy disks unknowingly, it would be me.

I'll need a librarian to keep track of my disk proliferation. Leslie is still on chemo. Maybe Brice can help me. He's great at organization, the way he installs a new retail display, puts each piece in the right box, ships the boxes to the right location, brings the right tools to each window. No time for screw ups. If he could just write my book for me, I'd have to consider leaving Peter.

Brice said he's coming out for my birthday. I'm trying to persuade him to come sooner. I know what you're thinking, Mustafa. I shouldn't invite him. I should write. What can I say? Brice says the Easter and Passover retail windows will keep him busy through mid-April. I told him not to wait, I'm feeling great.

19

NEW YORK, DEC 12, 2001

Brice was right on time to meet Linh at Big Cup for an overdue reunion. On this chilly December afternoon, Linh was easy to spot. The colors of her reversed baseball cap coordinated stunningly with her festive Givenchy sweater. She was sipping coffee in a cushy chair, lost in the *New York Times*.

"Hey, Linh," Brice said, smiling and stooping to hug his friend.

"Can I get you something?" Linh asked.

"How about an original Mapplethorpe?" Brice replied.

"Hang on."

Brice watched as Linh walked over to whisper an order to the cutie behind the counter. He teased Linh about Robert Mapplethorpe regularly. Mapplethorpe had become a running gag in their friendship. While Linh was flirting, Brice remembered he'd met her just before she met Mapplethorpe.

In those days, Linh often donned skintight boy clothes to gain entrance to the gayest of the gay bars. Eyeing the puerile knockout, club bouncers stood like liquor license sentinels, blocking her entry until she produced identification. They had to. Linh looked fourteen, fifteen tops. Surprised by her actual age, bouncers never broached the subject of her gender as she sailed by. When Brice met Linh at the Mineshaft on that warm mid-1980s night, they lurked in the back, taking in the titillating action together. As little interest as the beyond-butch men showed in a fem boy-girl like Linh, she wanted them all. She told Brice she aspired to be the main attraction at a Tom of Finland amusement park. S&M bars thrilled her.

After a few weeks of comparing notes with Linh on the nastiest of nasty leathermen cruising in the darkest of dark bars, she met Robert Mapplethorpe at a raunchy West Village bar. It was Linh's first celebrity encounter, before Mapplethorpe was exactly a celebrity. Mapplethorpe seemed interested in something physical with a cross-dresser as flamboyant as Linh, but the right time came and went without either making a move. At some point, he'd shown her his taboo S&M prints. Linh had seen plenty in her short life, but she needed to talk to someone about Mapplethorpe's photos. Linh's confidant was Brice and, from that day on, the two trusted one another like siblings.

Linh returned with a chocolate cake in one hand and a latte in the other. The latte was topped with milk foam in the form of a penis.

"Sugar with your Mapplethorpe?" Linh asked.

"Too bad you didn't buy one of his photos when you met him," Brice said, coating the foam phallus with a sugary condom. "They were cheap then."

"Yeah, but now I can afford his work again," Linh replied. "You know how it is. Lucky in cards, unlucky in love."

Linh sank into the cushy chair and the two friends caught up on their lives. While Linh complained about last weekend's hookup, Brice took a bite of the rich cake. Linh always seemed to know what Brice wanted. The cake was like sex in his mouth, firm and moist.

"You sound more tortured by that hookup," Brice said through gooey dark frosting, "than when you started your customer service job."

"At first, the technology intimidated me," Linh said. "After a week, though, connecting customers to the Internet was like sleepwalking."

"Practically a piece of cake," Brice laughed, waving another forkful. That job worked out just fine for Linh. After three years of helping customers at the Internet startup, she mentioned to Brice one morning over bagels and coffee that she'd become a millionaire many times over. "What could have been so bad about last weekend's hookup?"

"He got harder when we talked about my money than when we fucked," Linh answered.

"Did he at least appreciate your fab outfits?" Brice asked.

"I wouldn't know how to dress without your advice," Linh answered. "By the way, thanks for the tip on the Barney's sale."

"By the way, what does 'lucky in cards, unlucky in love' actually mean?" Brice asked. After all these years, Linh still confused Vietnamese and American sayings.

"You can figure it out," Linh answered, loading a fork with chocolate cake.

"By the way," Brice changed subjects, "did you see Peter in San Francisco? He was out of sorts during my last visit. I can't tell whether it's that journal of Rano's or the lack of art sales or something else. He's so quiet about personal things, even when he's lucky in love."

"I saw Peter for like a second," Linh replied. She paused to enjoy the cake before she continued. "We met after I had a rather complicated weekend with my aunt."

"Has he started painting?" What Brice wanted to ask Linh was whether Peter said anything about him, about their unexpected time together after Brice's emergency flight to San Francisco. Brice felt like things were warming up with Peter, moving forward after his gallery opening. It was as difficult as usual for Brice to read Peter's feelings, though, during their phone calls afterwards.

"No," Linh replied after another bite of cake. "No, and it must be something in that journal of Rano's that's blocking him."

"How can you be so sure?" Brice asked, wanting to know what Linh knew about Rano's journal, whether Rano wrote about his secret son, about Carl's possible abuse. "It could be the journal, but Peter also missed that flight on 9/11 that crashed in Pennsylvania. That could knock anyone out of commission."

"You know Peter as well as I do," Linh replied. "He always avoids talking about uncomfortable shit. Peter is, after all, a painter, not an orator. He never talks about that journal. I'm sure the reason he never discusses it is because Rano wrote things that upset Peter. Nothing Peter can do about it now. Water under the bridge. That's the saying, isn't it? I told him to forget it and move on."

"Yeah, but maybe it's the lease on his studio that's bothering him," Brice said, trying another angle." Maybe he can't paint until he renews the lease. Maybe I should offer to help cover the cost so he can paint."

"I'm sure it's the other way around," Linh said. "He's not renewing the lease because he can't paint."

"Anyway, I hope Peter doesn't destroy Rano's journal," Brice said, watching Linh take another bite. "Rano was so brilliant, I'm curious what he wrote."

"You just want to know what Rano wrote about you," Linh said.

"Okay, maybe," Brice conceded. Linh wasn't taking Brice's bait. She didn't seem to know what was in the journal. She wasn't giving Brice any clue about Peter's feelings towards him. It would be embarrassing to push harder. This wasn't the day Linh would bring him romantic encouragement from Peter, not the day to be lucky in love. "Regardless of the journal, one of us needs to spend time in San Francisco to help our friend get back on track."

"Funny you should say that," Linh said. "After a long and difficult conversation with my family, I've decided to move back to San Francisco."

Brice put down his fork. Even though they'd seen less of each other since Linh's startup windfall, Linh was someone Brice would miss around New York. Linh was a confidant, a trusted adviser, a bosom buddy. Brice didn't have anyone as close in New York.

"I made all this money," Linh continued. "I still need to do something with my life, something more significant than landing a lucky job. The Bay Area has more tech startups than here. My relationship with my aunt and her family is complicated with her religion and my wealth, but I can never forget how much my aunt did for me. Plus, there's a vibrant Vietnamese community. I never really gave San Francisco a fair shake."

Brice didn't know what to say. He wanted to encourage his friend's new adventure, but he wanted Linh close by. Maybe staying close would be possible with the Internet, but Brice would never be able to take his friend's hand or enjoy her daily wardrobe accent through a computer screen.

"Don't look so sad," Linh said. "I'm not leaving right away. Besides, there is something good in it for you. My move gives you another reason to spend time in San Francisco with Peter."

April 12, 1990 – "Love"

Dear Mustafa,

Tonight is the first regular episode of *Twin Peaks* on TV. Peter insisted I take a break from work. Now that Leslie the Librarian is back from chemo and helping me again, I didn't feel so bad taking off Sunday evening for the two-hour opening-night show which, by the way, totally rocked. And who doesn't mind an hour or two of Kyle MacLachlan on the screen? Even if you aren't gay, Mustafa, you can appreciate my sentiment.

Peter thought *Twin Peaks* would be a good excuse to start a Thursday night TV party series, so we invited the old *Dynasty* party crowd to join us. These television programs, dear Mustafa, are a vital, if silly, part of American culture. Gay men in particular love to critique the costumes and gossip about the actors.

Anyway, Peter and I dug through the drawers for our old *Dynasty* call list and phoned everyone. Half of them are dead. That was depressing. Most of the survivors begged off because taxes are due in three days. When did our friends become so responsible?

Three friends are coming over for the next *Twin Peaks* episode. That's how bad it is. We used to get ten or twenty for *Dynasty*. I count my lucky stars I have AZT. I'm going to make it through. But the friends who died and the friends who are too sick to join tonight's *Twin Peaks* party, they made me sad today. It made me want to return to ACT UP, to fight AIDS again.

The three friends coming over? Ugh. One's not so bad, the lawyer. A little pretentious, but he helped us deal with Carl. Bill and Eduardo, on the other hand, always find some oblique reference to my penis. I guess I'm over it now, but really, as many times as I tell people penis size is not worthy of conversation, up it comes again.

This gets under my skin. That's what I want to write about to you, as odd as it may seem for a father to write to his son about his penis.

I wrote at length about my penis in my first diary, the diary I started while escaping Carl. I ran across that diary last year and parts were instructive. For one thing, it was nice to find my English much improved. Some of the entries in the first diary are cringeworthy.

For another, I was reminded of Carl's obsession with my big black cock. I'd suppressed my memory of his fetish, of the things he did. It was crazy. I forgot how, in my presence, he would describe to strangers the shape of my cock, boasting to a gay waiter or retail queen about its size. I forgot that he would command me to drop my pants and show off, humiliate me in front of friends. His obsession saved my life since it got my cock from coastal Algeria to coastal California.

In the aftermath of Carl, I felt ashamed of the way everyone cared to know my penis before they cared to know me. If they bothered to acquaint themselves. After Carl, I wanted to date anyone who didn't care about my cock, or at least was more interested in my other endowments. That's what attracted me to Peter, what made Peter refreshing when we met.

I stopped writing my first diary years ago, when Peter came along. Reviewing it, I felt like I'd worked through my issues with Carl. He was both terrible and wonderful. I have to acknowledge both sides of him.

No I don't. What the hell am I writing? Carl was an asshole, a terrible, terrible man who happened to rescue me from a terribly bad situation in Algeria. If I had an average penis, I'd still be in Algeria. More likely, as you must know, dear Mustafa, I'd have been buried there long ago by religious zealots or political revolutionaries who'd surely have taken my ass against my will to confirm my abominable lifestyle.

It might not be obvious yet, but today's topic isn't my penis, actually. It's about how I've found my relationships. At least, that's the topic I had in mind. I'm drifting now as I often do when the topic is relationships. I have nothing to add to what I wrote before about your mother. I don't feel like I need to write more about Peter, either. He isn't terrible the way Carl was. He's not perfect, though. I should talk with him. I'm lazy after all these years. I've given up. It's easier to endure domestic complacency than deal with what's bothering me.

Have I given up on what I wanted to achieve? I'm working hard on my book, researching and writing nearly every day. To be honest with myself, though, I should be on my second or third book by now. I should have moved to a university with a more prestigious ethics or philosophy department. To be honest, I still want that. I'm good enough to achieve it. I want to prove that to the world. Instead of hosting *Twin Peaks* nights with guests who envy my penis, I should host evenings with technologists who can aid my research. Note to world: Rano has much more to offer than his big penis.

So where does Brice fit in all this? I'm not sure, perhaps due to my own history. After those years doing business on the beach, I had trouble connecting physical and emotional love. Brice is completely different from Carl and from Peter. He calls me on my shit, he demands I respect him, he engages me in honest discussions about feelings. Even without penetration, our sex connects. I'm learning to like this. Like it a lot. But it's also a waste of time. We won't live together, it's too risky to change my situation with Peter. It's an unwinnable tug-of-war between developing a healthy relationship that can't happen and finishing a book that must.

Carl was terrible, pure and simple. Peter isn't terrible that way. Like Carl, Peter has given me things I wanted. Carl got me out of Algeria. Peter provided a notion of family. But each of them has extracted a toll on me. At least with Carl, as horrible as our implicit bargain was, I knew from the day we met the price I would pay.

20

SAN FRANCISCO, DEC 14, 2001

Angel tiptoed over the druggies blocking the street entrance to his new place in the Tenderloin. There was a cosmic irony living in the neighborhood that was at both the geographic heart of San Francisco and the epicenter of its drug activity. It cautioned Angel not to shove the riffraff out of his way. He was tired after his early-morning shift at the Mexican bakery, too tired to take the stairs, too tired to wait for the elevator. Angel looked forward to seeing Peter soon, although his anxiety was growing. There were only a few minutes to clean up, to change into clothes that didn't smell of sugar and flour. He clambered to the fourth floor.

"Chinga tu madre," Angel muttered, looking at the disaster in his single-occupancy room. Someone had broken in. If they'd known how little there was to steal, they would have passed by. Angel couldn't help thinking that someone in the building must have found out his history as a dealer, that someone thought they'd find La Farmacia in his room. No escaping the past.

This was the only accommodation he'd been able to land after almost two months in the slammer. Angel's second stint behind bars had been something between a come-to-Jesus wake-up call and a midlife crisis. While awaiting sentencing, the criminal defense attorney Peter hired—a lawyer who recognized Angel from Peter and Rano's quaalude-enhanced *Dynasty* television parties—told Angel more than once that a third strike, another felony conviction after this one, would require any judge to sentence him to a nonnegotiable life in jail. Maybe it was because Angel couldn't make bail and stayed sober during the weeks before his sentencing, or maybe it was because he had celebrated his thirty-ninth birthday in an unforgivingly cold jail cell, but, for some reason, during the hearing, as the judge repeated the defense lawyer's admonition about three strikes, Angel took to heart his legal predicament. Even though Peter's pretentious three-piece lawyer negotiated time served and community service—a sentence Peter called a once-in-a-lifetime *milagro*—the term "life sentence" took on a new significance when it was one strike away.

That complicated this morning's appointment to visit Peter's studio. In the past, when Peter invited Angel to the studio, he usually wanted to get high. Angel valued the bond he felt with Peter. Their early shared history, helping each other as their respective lovers were dying, was the pure raw steel of that bond. How both of them ended up HIV negative, who was to know? Angel believed it was a protection somehow conferred by their bond. After the funerals, he and Peter helped each other process their respective losses in a series of drug-fueled sexual adventures. Later, before Angel left abruptly for Arizona, they acknowledged to each other that the drugs were better for avoiding their sorrow, for avoiding the specter of AIDS, for avoiding their unimaginable losses, than for coming to terms with their devastation. Nevertheless, the heat of their ongoing passion tempered that original bond.

With all the uncertainty from his past profession, Angel had relied on Peter more than anyone after he decided to live sober. That's what made Angel worry about meeting Peter, worry about drugs. It wasn't a good time to lose any part of his meager support system, especially Peter. This Chicano could not afford a fancy rehab program. He could barely afford his room. The only twelve-step program Angel had the energy to attend was the twelve steps from his building to the bus that took him to work. Angel's trepidation grew as he questioned whether the bond with Peter was unalloyed under any circumstances or might crack from the pressure of rekindling their relationship without drugs.

Angel looked around his small room again. He started putting things back in their places. It didn't take long to see that the thief had no interest in his secondhand wardrobe. It didn't take much longer to fold his clothes and put them away. The boombox was still in the corner. To the right side of the sink, Angel picked up scattered snacks, cans of soup, and sandwich makings. To the left side, he straightened out his toiletries. This was a pattern he knew too well, watching his life spin out of control in thousands of directions and then putting it back together. As Angel pulled out his flip phone to charge it, he realized the one thing stolen was its charger. He slipped the dead phone back in his pocket.

Angel considered canceling his visit to Peter. Besides the temptation of drugs with Peter, Angel needed to secure his room. He could leave it unlocked long enough to call Peter from the pay phone downstairs and postpone their visit. That also would give Angel a chance to arrange for the door repair with the building super and nap until a locksmith showed up. It would save him bus fare and the anxiety of an unsecured room. Angel would rest without fear of temptation.

Then Angel remembered Peter's call asking for help. Peter's voice was trembling. He described the mishap with Rano's journal, the way water drenched it, destroyed half of it. Peter begged Angel to help him mend it, saying that he didn't trust anyone except Angel, that Angel wouldn't judge Peter by the journal's contents. The trembling request reminded Angel of those times long ago when Rano was dying, when Peter asked for help getting Rano to the hospital or cleaning up after Rano. It was an honest request for help, not a concealed invitation to get high.

Peter's call jiggled Angel's memory of Rano asking him to destroy the journal. Obviously, Angel hadn't destroyed the journal, but how it got to Peter's studio was a mystery. He wanted to see this journal. If he broke into Rano's private life, though, he might be no better than the thief who'd broken into his room.

Angel looked at the broken lock. He already was late for Peter. He didn't want to lose anything else, didn't want to spin out of control again. He couldn't afford to. If someone else robbed him while he visited Peter, he might have to wear the same smelly clothes until his paycheck next week.

"Chinga tu madre," Angel muttered. This might be his only chance to find out what Rano really thought about him. He went downstairs and walked the twelve steps to the bus.

June 2, 1990 – Students

Dear Mustafa,

Spring term is over. Students gone, but not my memories of them. Leslie the Librarian and I are on a tear. She's only at half power so far, but that's enough to help me finish several chapters of the first draft, enough that my resolution to finish the draft this year looks like a brass ring I can snatch on a not-so-distant rotation of my research merry-go-round.

The recent work I've been doing on digital identity looks like a gold mine. I hope you, Mustafa, are as pleased as your father to learn the CTOs from local tech companies are fascinated that I'm examining brand-spanking-new computer technology through the centuries-old lens of ethics. Some have gone so far as to discuss grant money for my work.

I found more new research territory during a cameo appearance at The Stud. I was cruising a UC Berkeley grad student. After a little academic chitchat, it turned out he was studying different ways to connect computers with networks. If he weren't so damn sexy in that hairy Middle East kind of way, I don't think our conversation would have gone past a few snide insinuations about the inferiority of each other's academic institutions. I feigned interest in the way computers connect and signal each other to make more time for us to connect and signal each other.

Our signaling intensified, our eyes checking bulges and our hands engaging in light touches and friendly slaps. I looked into his rich Arab eyes and laughed about what this conversation might sound like in a Libyan bar or an Egyptian bar or a bar in whatever country he was from.

That random hypothetical changed our signaling completely. What, he asked, if computer protocols were based on Arab culture. What, I countered, if they were based on Chinese culture. The sexual tension may have dropped a notch or two, but overall attraction increased ten notches as we talked about how culture influences technology.

There it was, the germ for a line of study. It fits perfectly with my digital identity work. As far as Leslie can determine, no one is investigating computer networks, culture, and ethics this way.

I haven't run into the Berkeley student since. His friend grabbed him and they ran off to meet a gaggle of Stanford students. He told me his phone number which, sadly, I forgot. I hope we talk about this again.

On another, much more mundane student topic, I turned in grades. This, Mustafa, is the tedious part of my existence. Perhaps you have something tedious like this in your life, too. I always wonder what you do, whether you've found a challenging or enjoyable occupation. I also wonder whether you're straight, educated, and religious.

Testing and grading take too much time from my research. If even one or two of my students gave me the kinds of ideas I got that night at The Stud, I wouldn't mind the effort of grading. Or at least if they looked as hot as that Middle Eastern grad student.

It's so bad that now I can predict on the first day of class which students will negotiate grades at the end of the term. It's something about the way future grade negotiators arrive late, as though class is the most insignificant event on the planet, or the way they indicate with incessant doodling that they are ignoring the lecture, or the way their eyes glaze over when I utter a polysyllabic word.

This is the first year I feel comfortable with teaching as my way of life. It's in my skin now. Maybe it's because, now that I have AIDS, I have nothing to lose. I want to shake the failing students who ask for better grades and yell at them, "You have nothing to lose if you at least tried before you failed."

Anyway, this new research area feels ripe for new insights. The grunt work of teaching drives me up the wall. I want my eyes and hands on the new research all the time. I've become obsessed with it, even more than I was obsessed with my earlier research. The idea about the influence of culture on technology is yielding more paths of study than I have time to follow. The school administration thinks it might yield grants from government agencies as well as the technology companies.

Funny that my research originated with a chance meeting with a gay doctor and that a whole new line of research that riffs on all my previous research came from a chance meeting at a gay bar. Membership in the gay club has its advantages. Are you a member, Mustafa?

21

NEW YORK, DEC 26, 2001

It was the awkward social week between Christmas and New Year's. Thomas had celebrated Christmas with his family, serving Christmas dinner at his penthouse. The stocking his grandmother made for Maurice all those years ago was above the fireplace, next to Thomas'. Every year since Maurice died, one family member or another would recall a story about Maurice while hanging his stocking. This was the first year that anyone had asked if there would be another Maurice in Thomas' life. Maurice's youngest sister asked as Thomas was explaining the new artwork in the house. Thomas smiled and continued describing what he saw in Peter's art. After the family left, Thomas mused on the two stockings until the fire died out and he went to bed.

Today, the day after Christmas, Thomas lounged on the couch by the fireplace. The help had the day off. He would clean up the disaster later. After yesterday's madness, all Thomas wanted this morning was to sip his tea, enjoy butter-slathered stollen, and meditate on the art. He certainly did not want to worry about next week's New Year's Eve party. The year 2002 seemed too distant. Nor did he want to plan his annual Easter egg hunt in Central Park. That was an eternity from now. He had the rest of the week to dream up themes for his two favorite events.

Thomas had installed two of Peter's landscapes in the living room. Everyone remarked about them during the Christmas party. Peter's paintings didn't jump out. They weren't the kind of art that threw bolts of lightning, that advertised themselves from across the room, that screamed, hey, come look at me. They lured a viewer and, once close, seduced the viewer with details and relationships. These seductions often lasted several minutes, occasionally as long as an hour, as details and relationships revealed themselves, as patterns and thoughts emerged.

This morning, Thomas sat mesmerized on the couch. There was something about the way Peter contrasted realism with abstraction, something that intrigued Thomas, as if the realistic structures in the foreground were an inexplicable transformation of the abstract landscapes in the background. He lost track of time until he noticed his tea was cold.

It was chilly in the cavernous room. Thomas stacked three logs onto the grate, added kindling, and lit a match. Soon a new fire crackled. Back on the couch with a steaming cup of tea, Thomas looked at the landscapes again, pondering Peter rather than his art.

An observation Erica had tossed out at her gallery, that Peter might be using drugs, concerned Thomas. It caught him by surprise. He didn't press Erica for details. He didn't remember anything about Peter or his studio that seemed remotely related to drugs. Of course, that also had been true of his cousin Tammy who, as it turned out, wasn't disappearing frequently, as she claimed, to visit a boyfriend in Delaware. No one even thought to put "Tammy" and "drugs" in the same sentence until one night Tammy's brother found her, by chance, passed out in a Jersey City bar. In the back. Without much in the way of clothes.

Erica's statement that Peter was using drugs was either true or not, either a problem or not. If Thomas were to have any kind of relationship with Peter, there wasn't much he could do but keep his eyes open. As he thought through it, though, the thing that bothered Thomas more was his intuition that Peter hadn't been honest with him. When he'd visited San Francisco, Peter didn't tell pernicious lies, but he seemed to stretch things in an apparent effort to impress or please Thomas. Thomas himself was just as guilty of this as Peter.

Then something happened in Peter's studio. Thomas watched Peter as a goopy journal dripped through his fingers. He saw Peter crying as the pages dissolved. He glimpsed a part of Peter that needed help, but didn't know what to ask. At that moment, Thomas felt he'd peeked behind a mask. It was a mask that only Peter could remove. Thomas might be able to help, but not directly.

After the collapse of Peter's studio ceiling, Thomas and Peter had a heartfelt conversation. There wasn't really a choice. With the journal of Peter's late lover dripping through Peter's fingers, with Peter in tears, Thomas had to help somehow. He mopped up as Peter salvaged parts of the journal. It was clear that Peter knew the entire journal. Peter checked specific entries before he examined the remaining pages. He'd been relieved to find one particular entry intact, an entry he referred to as the "original sin." Thomas was familiar with original sin in several contexts, but not in the context of Peter and this journal. He coaxed Peter to sit, relax, eat a pastry, drink some coffee. Peter never let on that anything in the journal bothered him but, from Peter's attention to the journal, Thomas deduced that something in this journal, perhaps this so-called original sin, kept Peter from painting. He realized the most important thing he could do for Peter was help him move on, get past whatever it was in the journal that was holding him back.

From the comfort of the couch, Thomas examined Peter's landscapes again, finding new relationships between their abstract and realistic surfaces. Of course Peter was having trouble painting. He was unlikely to paint details like this so long as he was hiding behind a mask. Peter couldn't be in an honest relationship until he found a way to remove it.

Thomas knew it wasn't his place to discuss this with Peter or Erica. Each time he met Peter, his interest grew. But they hardly knew each other. As he looked at the paintings again, he came up with a plan that might move Peter along, a plan that would benefit Erica as much as Peter—a good thing because it required Erica's help. Thomas refilled his cup with hot tea. The more he thought about his idea, the more he liked it. The holidays were not the time to divulge this. He'd wait until the New Year to stop by Erica's gallery and see if she agreed.

Thomas sipped his tea. It was luxurious to warm himself by a fire, to feel the slow transformation of solid wood to evanescent heat, to treasure the two festive stockings swaying in flame's glow. It would be lovely, Thomas thought, to share this warmth. He wondered when he would see Peter without a mask.

June 17, 1990 – Algeria

Dear Mustafa,

Normally, I don't care about Algerian politics. I've been in San Francisco thirty years. Algeria is a previous life for me, its culture at complete odds with my queer identity. It's possible to be gay everywhere, of course, but my gay existence in Algeria is not a pleasant memory. If you are gay, Mustafa, I hope you have found a suitable compromise. Perhaps it's easier than it was thirty years ago. It couldn't be much more difficult.

Word from Algeria this week, though, caught my attention. The Islamic party won the local elections, beating FLN by wide margins. As corrupt as the FLN became, its loss creates significant political uncertainty. The Islamicists who won are the same strong-headed jihadis who traveled to Afghanistan to give the finger to FLN's patron, the Soviet Union. If they flex their religious muscle in Algeria like they did in Afghanistan, FLN's corruption will look benign by comparison.

If I care about it, I care because I know too well how strict Muslims treat gays. It's as bad as Evangelicals here. Algerian clerics are as evil as the Anita Bryants and the Jerry Falwells. Sure, educated Algerians tolerate homosexuality, but what about gay working-class boys and girls? Where will the rent boys get help with AIDS? Good luck coming out to your family and your clerics. Good luck when your father walks in while your legs are spread for a man.

American gay refugees fleeing their intolerant families have the advantage of reset-tling safely on the coasts of their own country, in San Francisco, Los Angeles, Laguna Beach, Palm Springs, Boston, Provincetown, New York, Key West. That's what Peter did, moving here from Kansas. There wasn't a single gay mecca in Algeria that came close to the tolerance of these American cities. Gay life in Algeria is bound to deteriorate further after this populist election. Thank Goddess Carl hijacked me from those beautiful Mediterranean shores to San Francisco.

Which reminds me. I found that grainy photo of you—the one Carl sent me—after talking to one of the CTOs that Leslie the Librarian enlisted to help my research. He demonstrated how his company's facial recognition technology measures attributes like the distance between eyes to generate a unique mathematical description of a face, something he called an "eigenface." Based on an eigenface, computers estimate the likelihood that someone is in a photo. It's mind-boggling.

While watching the computer correctly identify faces in a dozen photos, I remembered the grainy photo of you and asked the CTO if he might be able to help me find someone. To my delight, he agreed.

I looked for a month and finally found the photo last week! Leslie is scanning it into a computer so I can give a digitized version to this CTO. I don't know if he can make an eigenface for you. It seems impossible he could match your face to a known image. It's a long shot, but I want you to know I'm trying everything to find you.

22

DANBURY, DEC 27, 2001

Frank confirmed Erica's arrival at the Danbury station the next morning, hung up the phone, and returned to his recliner. Her Christmas stocking lay empty on the coffee table. Filling it could wait for the morning before the drive to the train station.

It was freezing outside, but otherwise a good time of year for Erica's visit. High school football season was over, basketball was easy to manage by comparison, and no one worried about baseball season until after the holiday break. The visit would bring a change of pace that Frank needed. As he sat down in front of the television these holiday evenings, its glow outlined a growing butt divot in the seat cushion. The deeper and deeper divot was a sad record of his dismal social life.

Frank bundled up in a beige fleece blanket, pushed back the recliner, and flipped to a cable news channel. It didn't matter which one. All of them were covering the Afghanistan war and speculating about a new war with Iraq.

Recent news from the Afghanistan war bothered Frank. He failed to comprehend how a military coalition of sixty nations was unable to find the 9/11 mastermind. Sure bin Laden was smart, sure he knew his way around the secret tunnels snaking through Afghan mountains, but sixty countries unable to find their man? What kind of coalition was this? As much as Afghanistan bothered Frank, though, at least this war had a just cause. The bad news about Afghanistan wasn't bad enough to change channels.

What pissed off Frank on the TV wasn't the war. It was a report that the President was considering another war before wrapping up the Afghanistan conflict, a second war against Iraq. Frank wanted to believe the President had just cause, but his premise for this war wasn't adding up. In Frank's youth, he'd witnessed firsthand in Vietnam a war without a just cause, without a real premise, a war that couldn't be won. Starting another of these pointless wars was unconscionable.

Fighting dust, on the other hand, was not. As a news commentator questioned the veracity of intelligence reports linking bin Laden's Al-Qaeda with Iraq's government,

Frank left the comfort of his recliner to mosey around the house, duster in hand. Time to clean up for Erica's visit.

Dust was Frank's fond old enemy, an admirable enemy that never surrendered. He discovered his enemy gathering in crevices, resting in remote corners, hiding in plain view. Dust was a lazy enemy. Persistent, perhaps, but lazy. Very lazy. Unlike his combat experience, tonight's lazy enemy gave Frank freedom to attack at the time and place of his choosing.

The dust skirmishes took place mainly in closets, mainly in the rugged highlands of the upstairs bedrooms. There were some doozies. In one closet, the dust nearly outflanked Frank, escaping to the shag rug below before his duster could make the kill. Luckily, the nearby vacuum unit joined the ground fighting. The noisy carpet beater put an end to those clever bastards. As with most combat, however, Operation Duster Storm wasn't as quick and efficient as planned. In the bathroom, the dust waded through puddles to escape, creating a goo that gummed up Frank's duster. The dust might be lazy, but it didn't surrender easily. Frank called for air support, commanding a sponge helicopter to hover low over the dirt paddies. Before the dust knew what hit, the bathroom mop-up operation was over.

It was well into the night's dust campaign that Frank inspected the chest of drawers in Erica's bedroom, inspecting drawers one by one for the enemy. As Frank slid open the third drawer down, he noticed his Purple Heart medal. He'd forgotten about this, forgotten where he'd left it. Frank remembered that he couldn't find the medal last time he looked, but he couldn't remember the last time he'd looked. It had gone MIA.

Frank put down the gummed-up duster, took the medal downstairs to the kitchen, and opened the bottle of Scotch he kept for such occasions. The medal transported Frank around the world to Vietnam. Most people didn't notice his slight limp or wonder why he always wore long pants, even on the hottest summer days. The searing injury had come at the end of a long night of battle. Shirtless in the jungle heat, he bit down on a shell casing while applying a splint to his leg. Then Frank cradled his commander in his arms while they waited for evacuation. The painful wait seemed like an eternity to Frank. It was eternity for his commander.

The Scotch smothered his brutal memories. Vietnam was something Frank couldn't talk about. Tonight was no different. Except for the refrigerator and the cuckoo clock, the kitchen was silent. The only good things about Vietnam were that it paid for his teaching degree and that it gave him life-and-death lessons, lessons he tried to pass on to each athlete he coached. There was nothing else good about that pointless war.

At dawn, Frank poured the rest of the Scotch over a bowl of cornflakes. It remained on the table uneaten as the sun rose. He couldn't tell if he'd drifted off, if he'd dreamed the battle. The night had been like revisiting the hell of Vietnam in slow motion. Frank brewed coffee to sober up before driving to the train station.

After a shave and shower, after tidying up from the night's battles, Frank drove to town slowly. He waited in the car with the heater full blast and the window cracked open, trying to clear his mind. The smattering of snowflakes distracted him until the horn from Erica's train bleated. Frank walked through the station to meet his daughter, putting on the smiling mask he always wore to cover the scar on his leg.

"What's wrong?" Frank asked.

Erica put down her suitcase and hugged Frank. The other passengers were gone by the time Frank took Erica's bag and walked her to the car. On the drive to the house, he expected to hear about romantic woes, but was pleasantly surprised when Erica told Frank good news. She went on for a bit about a young talent she planned to debut in January, before the next Armory Show, about the immigrant story behind this artist's abstract works, about the beautiful visual references to her war-torn country. Even better, she said Thomas, her favorite collector, had bought quite a few of Peter's landscapes, enough that she didn't have to worry about money for a while. Still better, Thomas said that Peter, her stubborn painter, promised to start painting again.

Frank was happy to hear Erica bubbling about her work. It was a pleasant relief from the loneliness of the house. The television had been poor company. He felt relieved returning home with family. The valiant dust wars general didn't want a parade. He wanted someone who would listen, perhaps understand. It wasn't the right time to hear about Erica's love life problems. He placed Erica's luggage inside the front door and turned to her.

"I found my Purple Heart last night."

"I didn't know it was missing," Erica said. "I don't remember ever seeing it."

"I'll get it from the kitchen."

Frank was excited and nervous to show Erica the medal. He'd never shared much about Vietnam with her. He was ashamed of his tour of duty, of the atrocities he witnessed. He was more ashamed of his one indiscretion. Returning from the kitchen, his mouth went dry. The pain of the wound returned. The limp worsened, almost as bad as when he returned from Vietnam.

"Are you okay?" Erica asked, placing a Christmas gift on a side table so she could hug him.

The hug reassured Frank. After a quiet moment, he glanced over Erica's shoulder and saw her Christmas stocking, still empty on the coffee table. Last night's battles had taken a heavy toll.

"I'll be fine." Frank said. He let go of Erica and held out the Purple Heart. "Why don't you take this as a Christmas gift?"

"I can't do that," Erica said. "I have no idea what it must mean to you."

"Then I'll have to tell you about it," Frank said.

"I'd like that very much," Erica said. She picked up the Christmas present on the table and handed it to him. "I will accept it, though, only after you tell me what you think about the new show at my gallery."

June 27, 1990 – Hospital

Dear Mustafa,

I overdid it. Everyone is furious with me, especially Leslie the Librarian. She wants to know why I did it. She's so upset, she stopped helping with my research.

I don't blame her.

You know what I did without me saying, don't you, Mustafa? Yes, that's right, I participated in ACT UP protests. How could I not?

Ed Railey died last week. I thought I'd finally make it through an entire month without anyone dying. Then I saw Ed's obituary. We met when I first moved here. Ed was my age. When he moved down to LA to open his interior design studio, we lost track of each other. All I can remember is that girl was the gold standard of partying.

Our nights at the Trocadero! My dear Mustafa, the Troc was all the rage. Music pounding, lights flashing, boys dancing. Ed would slip upstairs to lay down lines of coke in the bathroom after inviting the sexiest guys to snort. Then they'd go at it in one of the stalls. Sometimes two of the stalls. RIP Ed. I couldn't have escaped Carl without you and your lube-stained, coke-dusted sofa.

I was too furious not to protest. The world must change.

The International AIDS Conference was at Moscone Center the day after Ed died. ACT UP was protesting for better access to AIDS care for women and people of color. I had no choice. I broke my promise to Leslie. It felt liberating to protest with my comrades again.

President Bush was invited to this conference, but declined in order to attend a fundraiser for Jesse Helms. More than any single person, dear Mustafa, Senator Helms has thwarted efforts to fund AIDS research and care. He has introduced homophobic bills that prohibit people with HIV from entering the US and prohibit needle exchanges that slow the spread of HIV.

I was enraged that Bush sent a surrogate. This pushed me over the edge. I had to change the world.

Out I went with ACT UP. It was beyond glorious. We mobilized the entire event. As the Secretary of Health and Human Services addressed conference attendees, everyone stood with their backs turned. Then we marched out of Moscone Center to the Pride Week festivities.

I joined the festivities, of course. That's where I got into trouble. After a couple beers and a little dancing in one of the disco tents, I felt weak. I told a friend my head was beginning to ache. Then I passed out. Next thing I know I'm here in the hospital.

It's not Leslie's rant that is bothering me this foggy afternoon—I'll find a way to make it up to her. AIDS is bothering me. My case in particular. I wanted to get out of the hospital this morning, and they won't discharge me. Something about my blood work. The doctors are monitoring my brain, which seems just fine judging by this rant, and my T cells, which are down a little, but not much.

I've been trying to get out of here for three days. The first time I came to the hospital with a headache, they wouldn't admit me. This time they won't discharge me. Are they expecting some kind of superhero doctor to appear at Davies Hospital? One with HIV-destroying superpowers? Where's busty Raquel Welch from *Fantastic Voyage*, coursing through my arteries in her miniaturized submarine to end the evil viral attack? She's the heroine I need, totally camp and fabulously effective.

Instead of a superhero doctor, I got Angel, which may be a better deal. Angel came to see me this morning, and Peter hasn't shown up yet. Peter didn't show up yesterday, either. Not sure what's up with that. I asked Angel to bring this journal since he's the only one who knows it exists.

Don't get me wrong. Angel is a lovely Catholic boy. Serious Padre, Hijo y Espíritu Santo shit. He came from nothing, nada. He's dedicated to his lover, embraces their relationship. He works hard. The whispers say he deals pot here and there to make ends meet, but who cares? He's salt of the earth. And there's always great weed at his house. Angel is the one I can count on, the one who goes to church and then appears with my journal.

Besides bringing my journal, Angel brought news of Manfredo's death. I don't know how well they knew each other. Manfredo had been over to the house many times. Played on the gay soccer team. The AZT must have stopped working for him. Makes me sad, makes me worry that we'll never get a cure when someone lives as long as Manfredo on AZT and then dies.

I'm also worried that I'm finding out more about Peter from our friends who visit the hospital than from Peter himself. I tell myself Peter just needs a break. But we've been living together nearly a decade, we're adults now, we take care of each other.

That's what's really bothering me, dear Mustafa. Peter and I have had our problems, made our mistakes. Will Peter come through for me? Would I come through for him?

23

SAN FRANCISCO, DEC 31, 2001

Angel hung his apron on the wall hook, wished the remaining bakery staff buen año nuevo, and left for AA. He looked forward to meeting Peter afterwards for a poor man's New Year's Eve celebration. It wasn't clear whether it was a date, but it didn't matter. Before they made their resolutions, they would celebrate Peter's good fortune missing the 9/11 flight and Angel's sobriety.

Usually Angel took a Mission Street bus, but today he wanted fresh air before the AA meeting. His probation required attendance and he dreaded it. The meetings were a recurring nightmare featuring the dysfunctional customers of his previous business. The chica who dropped Molly because she was just doing what mamacita did. The dude whose grandfather raped him for years while his mother turned a blind eye. Coke numbed the feelings. Getting reacquainted with a similar cast of characters at AA felt like going backward toward 1992 instead of forward toward 2002.

As Angel passed by antique stores and produce stands, telltale scents of taquerias permeated the heavy winter air. He put his hand on his panza and kept walking. The last thing he needed was more food. What he needed was a way to apologize to Peter about Rano's journal.

Before Christmas, Angel had mended the remnants of the journal as best he could. Peter couldn't pay, but Angel saw the work as perhaps a way to pay off the karmic debt from not carrying out Rano's request to destroy the thing. Sections Angel found about himself in the journal were kind for the most part. The revelation about the son named Mustafa, though, that was big news. Angel didn't know what to say to Peter other than he'd done the best he could reassembling the surviving pages. Then there was the unmentionable treachery of Carl. Mending the journal hadn't canceled any karmic debt.

The journal ate at Angel every day. If he'd destroyed it, Peter would be none the worse for his ignorance. Angel understood Rano's rationale not to tell Peter about Mustafa. He also realized Peter must have been devastated to discover he'd unwittingly kept Rano from finding his son. What Angel couldn't work out was how to help Peter. In the countdown to New Year's, the situation gnawed at him more and more.

Maybe it was guilt for not destroying the journal, maybe it was dread of AA, maybe it was the changing nature of Peter's friendship, but the scent of salsa lured Angel to the warmth of Pancho Villa where he could munch away his anxiety. He rationalized his purchase because two fish tacos were less filling than a burrito and he'd have something healthy in his stomach in case Peter showed up late for their celebratory dinner. He took his tacos to the only seat he saw, a seat at the end of a table of revelers starting their celebration early. It was a noisy table of natty young men. One of them put a bottle of Corona in front of Angel, saying he'd bought three extra beers by accident. Below the table, he squeezed Angel's leg.

Angel couldn't remember the last time a stranger did something for him, and the gesture cheered him, made him feel part of this handsome group. It wasn't like he was going to drink with Peter for New Year's. Una cerveza couldn't hurt.

July 13, 1990 – Peter

Dear Mustafa,

Friday the thirteenth. Returned from the hospital a couple of weeks ago. My first full-blown AIDS birthday. Having AIDS keeps mortality front and center more than testing positive ever did.

Leslie visited today. After a couple of weeks without progress, I finally freaked out. I need her help. Yesterday, I implored her to forgive me. I told her it was my birthday and asked her to come by so we could talk. She and I kissed and made up about my ACT UP transgression. I acknowledged that the interviews she lined up with the local technology companies have provided oodles of new ideas. I acknowledged that I can't write up all those ideas without her help. I acknowledged that I broke my promise and promised never again to break that promise. I may have been a bit manipulative. I'm not proud of that, but my Algerian beach business honed those skills.

Mustafa, you have to understand that, in spite of any manipulation on my part, I meant it when I promised Leslie I would focus on my research. Please don't take that the wrong way. As exhilarating as the ACT UP protest was at the AIDS conference, I hit a physical wall. My immune system capitulated. I have to apply my energy judiciously. Healthier ACT UP members will carry on. I've concluded that the chances I find you are about the same whether I protest or research.

I promise to see you, dear Mustafa.

On a lighter note, Brice is here celebrating my birthday. It's something when he's around. Sometimes I even forget about the AZT side effects. Our sex is great. I wonder what it would be like without condoms. I crave that particular physical intimacy. Even though he says he worked through his seroconversion issues with a boyfriend who died, I haven't convinced Brice that raw oral is safe.

Peter and I don't talk about it, but he knows what's going on with Brice. He gives us space. He's nicer than he has to be with Brice, but Peter and I have been family for too long to make a stink about this arrangement. Peter and I understand each other. Goddess knows we've compromised for each other, made sacrifices. I know I have. Besides, I never flaunt my thing with Brice, don't create awkward situations for Peter, don't play one off the other.

I sometimes wonder if Peter is interested in Brice, too. He gets quite chatty with Brice now and again. Borderline flirtatious. Maybe there's a threesome in our future??? If I have a fucking future.

Peter and I have a friend, Jeffrey, who was in a long-term three-way relationship. Jeffrey's three-way relationship was out there, even by San Francisco standards. Because one of the threesome died, no one will know whether a threesome can be stable over the long term. I suppose some Arab men have many wives. Maybe San Francisco isn't as advanced as I thought. Anyway, Jeffrey survived. He has the advantage of mourning with another surviving lover instead of mourning alone.

My frustration with Peter is growing and it's harder to hide. For one thing, I'm not sure Peter will be a good, let alone great, artist. I hope so, but I'm not convinced yet. He told me at the beginning of the year that he was ready to show his landscapes, yet he has done nothing. No viewings, no sales, not even an open studio to foster interest. I've compromised plenty to give him this opportunity. I fear disappointment.

I have to be careful about getting mad at Peter. I may have reasons for being mad, but it's not smart. I know part of my anger is an anger I've heard from other men with AIDS. It's anger targeted at the surviving partner, anger at the unfairness that the other partner will go on. I know I am angry at Peter about that. I'm predictable.

There is another anger I have, though, an anger I don't understand. Perhaps it's different from anger. Perhaps I'm feeling disappointment or an unnerving frustration. When Brice is around, I sense it more, likely because of the contrast Brice brings. Of course I can't leave Peter for Brice. It's too risky for me. "Grass is always greener." That's one of my favorite American aphorisms, along with "there's no accounting for taste." I know what it's like to live with Peter, I know what it's like to have an affair with Brice. Two different animals.

24

SAN FRANCISCO, DEC 31, 2001

Peter sat in his studio, leafing through Rano's journal. Something in it kept him from painting, but what? At first, Peter felt humiliated that Rano had kept Mustafa a secret. As he read and reread the journal, he found passages that troubled him more—the decision against moving to New York, the decision to press charges against Carl, the accusation that he'd betrayed Rano.

It had helped to talk to Thomas about the journal on the disastrous day the flooding dissolved half of it. It unexpectedly helped when Angel patched it up, knowing someone trustworthy had read Rano's words. What unnerved Peter today was Rano's anger about dying first, before Peter' success. Hadn't they talked through that?

Peter placed the precious remnants of the journal on his desk, trying to focus on the parts of Rano he loved, the concern Rano had for his students, his brainiac knowledge, the way Rano let Peter take care of him the final year. Maybe these happier passages would give Peter a way back into his painting.

The year's final chore was hanging the pristine 2002 calendar. Paging through the old calendar, Peter reflected on how oddly this odd year ended. After he'd promised Thomas to continue painting, Thomas bought his art, bought a lot of his art—a half-dozen works with a few more on hold. It was the bonanza Peter needed to renew the studio lease. As Peter flipped the calendar to December, he noticed the final entry. Shit! He'd promised to celebrate New Year's with Angel.

By the time he showered and changed at home, Peter was already late. He paused anyway at the entrance to the Eureka Valley–Harvey Milk Memorial branch of the San Francisco Public Library. The municipal building's clean lines and cinder block construction contrasted with the neighborhood's colorful Edwardian homes and businesses. This branch hadn't always been known as the Eureka Valley–Harvey Milk Memorial branch. On the brisk night Peter and Rano met, over a quarter century earlier, it was called simply the Eureka Valley branch.

That night so long ago, Peter spotted Rano a few blocks away from the library, at the meat market that congregated on Castro Street after the bars closed. Rano sashayed down Market Street, leading Peter astray. They cruised one another the entire way, Rano maintaining fifteen paces as he teased Peter with his hips and lips. At the street corner, Rano turned and skipped ahead, then lured Peter into the dark side of the library parking lot.

Standing in the parking lot now, Peter wanted to remember as much as he could how they'd started, to understand the secrets Rano kept from him. They'd met at the end of his second week in San Francisco. Rano was like nothing he'd seen in Kansas, so carefree, so tantalizing. When he entered the parking lot that long-ago night, Peter's eyes narrowed to make out Rano's obscure form. The corner where Rano crouched felt dangerous, hidden from plain view, but not hidden enough for private exposure. Stepping close to Rano in the darkest extreme of the corner, Peter felt Rano's hands explore his crotch, caress his excitement, loosen his belt, unbutton his jeans.

Peter's heart raced. He was more aroused and more terrified than he could remember in his almost twenty-five years. Just as Rano exposed Peter, Peter shot his wad. That might have been the end of it. Rano sighed disappointedly and slipped away, leaving behind Peter unbuttoned. The whole tryst had taken place in the blink of an eye. Rano disappeared in the night. Peter felt his face flush as he wiped his gooey hands on his clean 501s. Buttoning up, he returned to the street and found no trace of this captivating nocturnal ignition. Rano was the first great thing that happened to him in San Francisco, and he was gone. Peter felt lost.

This parking lot seduction replayed in Peter's mind most times he walked by the library. On this damp, breezy New Year's Eve, as much as he hated being late to meet Angel, Peter relished every detail, searching for anything that might shed light on the journal. He took the unusual step of inspecting the scene of the crime, the corner of the parking lot that was no longer so dark nor so hidden. He didn't find magic here anymore. Aside from the spectacular spider web glistening in the stark rays of the streetlight, it was nothing more than an overgrown corner of an ordinary parking lot. That made Peter sad. It made him covet his time with Angel, Brice, Linh, and the few other remaining friends who could tell stories about Rano. Peter had to keep Rano's memory alive.

Peter never knew any different from Rano. Rano was Peter's only long-term relationship. His only serious relationship, really. The craziness with Angel after Rano died didn't qualify as a committed relationship. Nor did the occasional fling with Brice. Dating had been a recurring nightmare. As difficult as Rano had been before he died, as hard as it had been this past year to discover Rano's journal and then feel half of it ooze through his fingers, Peter still loved Rano like crazy, still missed Rano's smooth skin, his embrace, his goofy giggling in bed.

On the long-ago afternoon Peter rolled across the Bay Bridge on a Greyhound from Kansas and took in the rolling San Francisco vista for the first time, he'd fantasized about finding someone like Rano, a father figure, a sexy man-child, a kindred spirit. Against all odds, a month after their library tryst, Peter ran into Rano again at the meat market. Peter was sure their second meeting wasn't chance. The ineluctable reunion was a sign they were meant to be together. After sex, they slept like spoons in a drawer.

Slowly waking up in Rano's cramped apartment, they stayed together a full day, learning about each other, eating, strolling around the Castro, sharing their family histories. According to Rano, his family had caught him with his legs in the air under a strange man and disowned him on the spot. He was left to fend for himself as best he could along the coast of Algeria.

Peter recounted to Rano a similar story. Peter's midwestern family had been slow to figure out his sexuality, but piously evicted him upon discovery of the gay porn stash under his mattress. With nothing more than meager savings in his pocket and worldly possessions in a duffel bag, Peter bought the fateful Greyhound ticket.

As Peter finished his story, Rano embraced him for what felt like days. The bonds of a new family formed. It was the first time Peter felt safe since his familial exile. During that first night sharing a bed, during that first day sharing family stories, he knew Rano was his man. He learned soon enough how cagey Rano could be, that Rano took weeks or months to trust anyone. Peter's patience and persistence paid off, or so he thought.

After the discovery of the journal, Peter wasn't sure anymore, wasn't sure of Rano's feelings, wasn't sure if he'd been anything close to what Rano deserved in a relationship. He couldn't put his finger on why he felt so ashamed. Some days, Peter convinced himself all Rano wanted from him was a surrogate for Mustafa. Others, the intimacy of Rano's notes to Mustafa ripped apart Peter's insides as if he were being exiled from his Kansas family all over again. Maybe he had wanted someone like Rano too much. Maybe he ignored warning signs he didn't even know to look for. Standing in the corner of the dark library parking lot, Peter found no answers.

The streetlight blinked off and the glistening spider web, curved like a sail in the breeze, disappeared in the dark just as Rano had done. Peter was the only one who could remember how it all started, how he'd found Rano a second time on Castro Street, how happy he'd been when Rano showed up for their first formal date at the Museum of

Modern Art, how ecstatic he'd been when Rano finally agreed to move in together a year later. Peter turned away from the hidden spider web and hurried towards the church. Angel would be out of his meeting by now, waiting.

Angel required Peter's encouragement to start AA. Peter convinced Angel that AA was cheap insurance against a third strike, that as uncomfortable as the meetings were, they were a vastly more enjoyable social activity than life in prison. Angel's group met at a Castro neighborhood church. Peter often took Angel to dinner afterwards, partly to ensure Angel's continued participation, partly to confirm Angel was eating something besides Mexican pastries.

Walking the ten blocks to the church, Peter contemplated the evening ahead with Angel. Christmas trees glowed in apartments and cheery holiday lights blinked outside, outlining windows and doors. The streets looked like colorful line drawings. Peter wasn't at all sure he wanted to go out when he could stay warm inside at home. This celebration with Angel would take effort.

For one thing, it would be an awkward New Year's celebration without drugs or alcohol. Previous celebrations with Angel featured some combination of those substances in the nude. This would be a new kind of night out for them. Maybe not entirely new, of course, since they'd spent time as friends before their respective lovers died, but different from their unhealthy mourning afterwards. Peter was enjoying sober Angel. Sober Angel demonstrated both reason and care.

What Peter dreaded more than an evening of damp, breezy sobriety were resolutions for the New Year, resolutions he was sure Angel had made and would want to discuss as they toasted midnight, hoisting champagne flutes filled with cloying apple juice. Sober Angel also had become somewhat sentimental. Peter remembered the resolutions Rano wrote in his journal. Crisp, no-nonsense resolutions, resolutions with the best intentions that, more often than not, ended up disappointing Rano, turning him inside out.

For Peter, a New Year's resolution seemed all but impossible. He knew he should resolve to paint. All his friends were encouraging him to start again. That was the obvious resolution, if only to pay the rent.

More importantly, though, Peter made a promise to Thomas he intended to keep, especially after Thomas bought so many of Peter's works. Thomas was different from other collectors, so perceptive, so supportive. Keeping this promise to Thomas would assuage Peter's shame about lying to Thomas, lying about Armistead Maupin, lying about why he stopped painting. If only someone had destroyed Rano's journal. Then there would be no need for a New Year's resolution to paint because Peter wouldn't have stopped in the first place.

The implications of Thomas' generous acquisition of Peter's works went beyond renewing the studio lease, beyond Peter's promise to paint. Erica had been right. After Thomas' purchase, sales of Peter's work spiked, as if Thomas' purchase validated Peter's work more than the glowing critical acclaim. By now, Erica had nothing left of Peter's works to sell. She told him it was time for him to restart the art factory. She planned to fly out in February, expecting to see Peter's new work. He had to paint.

And now Peter found himself in a quandary. Every bone in his body knew he had to paint, but Rano's journal as good as sucked all the paint out of the tubes. Maybe, as Linh suggested, he should give self-portraits a whirl. Maybe trying something different from landscapes would start the creative oil flowing again. He could paint self-portraits in the comfort of his studio. He wouldn't have to travel to New York to study its skyline. But there'd be months of trial and error to develop a concept that worked.

And now Peter found himself outside a church in San Francisco, found himself even more confused than he was at Brice's place after 9/11, more confused than he was after missing the doomed flight, found himself outside a church scouring the AA stragglers for Angel, found himself an artist with unusual critical acclaim and marketing success, found himself too consumed by his late lover's journal to mix paint or stretch a canvas.

And then Angel wasn't outside the church. Peter poked his head inside the meeting room. No Angel there, either. He asked the remaining attendees if they'd seen Angel. They weren't supposed to say, they said. That's why it's called "anonymous," they said.

"Fuck," Peter said, pissed at his own tardiness. The attendees gave Peter a look and inched away. Peter knew Angel likely would relapse at some point. It just seemed a little soon. Worrying about Angel's sobriety was not the way Peter wanted to celebrate—or avoid celebrating—New Year's Eve.

Peter walked around the church and gazed at a cherub above its entrance, a cherub he'd never noticed above an entrance he'd never paid attention to, a cherub that seemed to Peter a little, well, buff. It was the Castro, after all, not Kansas. The cherub blushed ever so slightly in the glow of a liquor store neon sign, as though Peter had caught it doing something naughty.

AUGUST 13, 1990 – AZT

Dear Mustafa,

I'd like to tell you my HIV story. It's graphic. Nothing about this disease is pretty. I hope you aren't infected. Regardless, please use condoms.

My first HIV test was in 1987. When it came back positive, the doctor tested again. Could be a false positive, he said. I kept thinking I had to be one of the lucky ones who never gets infected, whose T cells lack HIV receptors. I escaped Algeria and I escaped Carl. Now, I would escape the virus. I never pray, but I prayed every night that week the result was a false positive. I promised myself never ever to have sex again without a condom if my first test was a false positive.

The first HIV tests were rushed to market to protect the blood supply. False positives didn't matter. A few liters of healthy blood lost here and there due to low-quality HIV testing didn't matter as long as donated blood was HIV-free. Gays with false positive results? They should be happy if a follow-up showed they weren't infected. Hell, they should be happy just to be alive.

My second test confirmed what I feared, what I knew was likely. The positive result was correct.

Once the straights had their safe blood supply, all bets were off for helping the gays. Imagine the confusion during those months when the straights had to reckon with the possibility of infection, the prospect of AIDS and death. Gay diseases weren't supposed to kill straight people—just the way black diseases weren't supposed to kill white people. Blood supply secure once again, HIV could be swept safely into the gay disease dustbin. Once again, AIDS was Goddess' punishment for the sin of being gay. Since all Christians are straight, no reason now to fear infection. Once again, HIV became a lucrative marketing gimmick, a glorious reason to hate gays and donate to Jesus.

After my positive tests, I was asymptomatic for months and months, long enough to allow myself to relax, to believe my immune system was fending off a T cell calamity. Then the headaches, the shortness of breath.

The good news is that AZT came along when I needed it. The bad news is that it's been making me more and more nauseous. My last birthday cake smelled disgusting, made my stomach turn. But I have T cells galore. The underground reports say more antiretrovirals are on the way. Soon, I expect to have T cells and eat my cake, too.

What bothers me most about feeling crappy all the time is that it's impossible to sustain work on my book. And I want to travel, take a week with Peter or with Brice, take a break from San Francisco. I'd love a trip to somewhere, anywhere, even as close as Yosemite. How is it I've never been? It's only a couple hours' drive from San Francisco, but I can't maintain my dignity when I travel more than a couple minutes from a toilet.

I can't travel and writing is haphazard. The AZT makes me nauseous, gives me cramps, but I force myself to concentrate for fifteen or thirty minutes, enough sane minutes in a row to type a few paragraphs. I started getting fevers and congestion like I got before the AZT. Peter convinced me to see my doctor. I assure Peter everything is okay because I'm on AZT, but he says I should have it checked out. I know he's right. I want to be mad at him, but I know he's right. My dear Mustafa, after my last hospital stay, I'm as nervous now for my T cell results as I used to be for my HIV results.

In spite of my sporadic writing, the book is starting to feel important, maybe even groundbreaking. Leslie keeps pushing it along. Many of the chapters are based on past lectures, which I record and she transcribes as a first draft. Now I'm on to this new line of computer network and identity research and it's paying off. Really innovative. I'm seeing the information train that's replacing the information stagecoach.

Last month, I managed to make it to the new Ansel Adams gallery on Fourth Street with Brice's help. That was a long trek without a toilet. Strange that Brice is teaching me about art when I live with an artist. Stranger to wander around a building that was formerly a public health clinic. Not just any public health clinic, Mustafa, but the clinic where all the gay boys checked in after a weekend at the bathhouses or the parks or the back rooms. While Brice gushed about the composition and lighting of Adams' iconic Yosemite waterfall photograph, all I could see were the ghosts of queens waiting their turn for tests. Weren't those the days, when all we had to worry about was syphilis and gonorrhea? After a few minutes, the treatment rooms faded from my mind and the photographs came into focus. Yosemite, New Mexico, the Southwest. Brice gave me a case of wanderlust as he explained the photography.

Brice and I explored other parts of San Francisco, too, parts of San Francisco not distant from a bathroom. Cafes and movie theaters are safe bets. I long for a dalliance at Lands End or a walk in Muir Woods, but those are dangerous places on account of my digestive system. Brice wanted to walk around the freeways that collapsed after the Loma Prieta earthquake. As much as I'd love to have seen the twisted steel and concrete up close, I declined.

On his visits, Brice often mentions a move to New York. I tell him I'm satisfied with San Francisco, even though that's not entirely true. I have to hide my frustration about staying in San Francisco from Brice. In addition to its cultural and intellectual assets, New York would accelerate my research. I drool at the resources Columbia has to offer. At this point, though, how would I ever move? The way my body is, I drool too much already. I have to live with the regret of never living in New York, make the most of what I have here.

On Brice's last day, we made it as far as the San Francisco Museum of Modern Art. Brice and I viewed photos from the museum collection. I don't go to museums much, but Brice wanted to introduce me to gay photography. Mapplethorpe, of course, who died last year. You may know of him from his controversial S&M photographs. Many more photographers. Brice exposed my lack of art knowledge.

Photography is easier for me than other media. Maybe it's the reality of the art. Maybe it's because the gay photographers capture images every gay man relates to. Part of coping with HIV is watching the talent in our community die helplessly. Brice pointed out a photographer named Peter Hujar. Hujar died two years before Mapplethorpe. They must have known each other in Manhattan. Hujar's portrait of his young lover was breathtaking. The light, the shadows, the pose. Everything. Love in a frame.

Your father learned something about beauty.

25

NEW YORK, JAN 9, 2002

Lunch was a long affair whose main course was an audacious business proposal. Thomas checked his watch. Yes, lunch had gone into overtime. He was supposed to be on his way to Erica's gallery. Thomas snatched a copy of the proposal and raced downtown in a taxi, partly thinking through the complexities of his lunchmate's business deal, partly thinking about how Erica might help Peter. The details of the business lunch were exasperating. A la-di-da hedge fund wanted the top floors of an uncelebrated midtown building with panoramic views. The deal was quite lucrative, but required delicate negotiations to move many longtime tenants downstairs. Thomas' attention kept returning to Peter. He could wait to call his lawyer to counter the offer.

The favor he wanted to ask Erica was a personal matter. As the cab approached the gallery, Thomas worried about the risks of his idea. He wanted Erica to offer Peter a 9/11 anniversary show in her gallery. But what if Peter didn't agree? What if Peter found the suggestion objectionable or even offensive? Nothing with Peter seemed clear. Thomas paid the cabby and sloshed through the wintery slush.

Inside the gallery, Thomas hung his coat. Most of a new show was on the wall. A few paintings waited on the floor. Erica's voice wafted around the corner. Her cadence indicated the end of a phone call. While Thomas waited, he checked out the new show, pacing from one canvas to the next. As good as Erica was at arranging art on her walls, as good as she was at drawing connections between different artworks by their juxta-positions, this was not one of Thomas' favorite artists. He felt like he was drowning in overwhelming blue and green abstractions. The words the artist drew on each of her works diminished their appeal to Thomas as their initial impact wore off. She wrote funny phrases, nonsensical word combinations. The jumble of letters jolted Thomas' attention at first, then cluttered the artworks, reducing them to babel.

Thomas looked over at Erica's office. He didn't have much time, and Erica's unending phone call was getting on his nerves. Maybe Thomas wasn't in the right frame of mind to look at art today. He sat down on a sofa and watched pedestrians slogging through the miserable snow obstacle course. This particular art was not giving Thomas what he was missing right now—clarity.

As often happened when Thomas had an unexpected pause, he thought about Maurice, about how he missed Maurice in these moments. Maurice always clarified things for Thomas, or helped Thomas find clarity. Marice could talk about almost anything with Thomas in ways that would make the thing apparent, provide an insight. If he couldn't make something apparent, he would ask questions until Thomas himself made sense of it. Maurice was a patient listener, a gratifying lover.

Thomas never expected to find another Maurice. It would be unfair to have that expectation of Peter or anyone else. What Thomas sought, though, was the comfort Maurice provided. Comfort didn't mean stability, although Maurice and Thomas had acquired all the trappings of stability. Comfort meant the support to taunt instability, to try the untried. The way Maurice made Thomas comfortable was to make unexpected sense of things, to shovel a path through the slush on the sidewalks, as it were. No one would be able to make sense of things the way Maurice did, but Thomas wanted to know other ways someone might comfort him. He didn't know what to look for. He didn't know whether Peter could provide him comfort. He wasn't sure how to tell, but he was sure the situation wouldn't become clearer unless Peter made progress with his painting.

"Would you like coffee?" Erica asked, emerging at last from her office.

"Yes, I would," Thomas answered. As much as he liked coffee, however, Thomas' doctor at the Veterans Administration ordered him to cut back—heart murmurs didn't mix with coffee. "But unfortunately, I don't really have time today."

Thomas watched Erica as she walked to the kitchenette and poured herself a cup. She had a way of prowling through the gallery. She sized up a situation before she made a move. He could tell she was sizing him up by the way she looked around the space while she stirred in sugar. Even at a busy gallery opening, she would stand to the side, then pounce when she saw the right opportunity. Sometimes, Thomas felt like she already knew what he was going to say. He wondered if this trait was what made her so good at finding talent, the waiting, the timing of her evaluations, of her moves. Something, however, seemed off in Erica's evaluation of this new artist, the artist who drew words on her paintings. Erica had moved a bit too soon with this one.

"Peter is painting again," Erica said, walking back to Thomas. She paused to sip her coffee in a way that didn't invite celebration. "Peter told me he's painting a series of self-portraits."

"That's odd," Thomas said. After the mishap with the flood, Thomas and Peter spoke for nearly an hour while Peter saved what he could of the journal. Thomas took it as a good omen when Peter stood up to examine his skyline sketches. All this was quite memorable because as Thomas was leaving the studio, Peter reached out to hug him, an embrace that lasted longer than Thomas expected. Thomas remembered his heart skipping beats. It wasn't the coffee. "Different from the sketches he showed me of what he wanted to paint."

"I'm not sure I can market portraits by a painter I've promoted as the next great landscape artist," Erica said, joining Thomas on the sofa.

That, Thomas thought, was a tactful way for Erica to enquire whether a switch from landscape painter to portraitist would fly in the art market and, in particular, whether Thomas might purchase self-portraits by Peter. It wasn't a question he was sure he could answer. His first instinct was, yes, of course he'd buy Peter's self-portraits, especially if it would encourage Peter to paint.

"How would you describe Peter's self-portraits?" Thomas asked, realizing he was in an uncomfortable spot. He wanted Peter to paint, but Peter's new adventure in portraiture also could be a new adventure in avoidance.

"I can't tell you yet," Erica responded. "I'm flying out to San Francisco for business in February. I'll see his new work then."

"I may be projecting my own artistic notions," Thomas said, "but I was under the impression that Peter was painting new works based on his post-9/11 sketches of the New York skyline. I was looking forward to those."

"Peter made sketches of the skyline here?" Erica asked. "I'd be interested in those paintings, too. A skyline series certainly connects better with his previous work."

"I imagine it would be easier to market those," Thomas said. "I mean, you're right, skylines have more continuity with his landscapes than portraits, but 9/11 is relevant, too."

"Funny you should mention 9/11," Erica said, placing her coffee cup on the side table. "For the first anniversary, a few galleries are coordinating their 9/11-related shows. It's a great concept. Unfortunately, I can't participate. None of the artists I represent is working on anything vaguely relevant."

"Perhaps you could offer Peter a 9/11 show when you visit him," Thomas said. "A show based on his sketches."

"That's asking a lot," Erica said. "Peter doesn't have much time to develop a new series with that deadline."

Thomas and Erica sat quietly for a moment. Thomas pondered whether he had asked too much. Erica was right. It was a lot to ask Peter to deliver an entirely new project in a few months. On the other hand, she did see the relevance of a skyline series to Peter's past work, even if she might not appreciate the deeper significance of a skyline series to Peter.

"I worried you might not like Peter's idea of painting self-portraits," Erica said. "Frankly, I'm undecided whether I can show them."

"Then you'll propose to Peter a 9/11 show if he paints a New York skyline series?" Thomas asked.

"Perhaps," Erica replied. "I noticed one of the buildings you own has empty office space with skyline views."

"Yes," Thomas said. He couldn't figure out how Erica knew about this. The building was one of those buildings that no one noticed, but all Manhattanites had visited once in their lives. "I was discussing a deal for that space at lunch."

"I have a stronger case for Peter to paint a New York series if I offer him a New York studio," Erica said.

"Oh, I see," Thomas said, wondering just how much more complicated the la-di-da hedge fund deal could become. "You want me to provide Peter with a studio. I have plenty of other properties that would be easier."

"It has to be in that building," Erica said. "I know the location. The views must be spectacular."

"They are," Thomas said, considering whether to offer space in his penthouse instead. "Of course."

"By the way," Erica asked, "what do you think of the new show I'm installing?"

"We'll have to discuss it next time we meet," Thomas said, glancing at his watch. He tried not to sound too relieved. It was an honest, if convenient, excuse. "I'm late for my next meeting."

AUGUST 26, 1990 – ADRIFT

Dear Mustafa,

I'm scared. The doctor took me off AZT last week. AZT made me feel like shit most days, but my T cell count improved for months.

Today, after a physician's assistant checked my chart, he called the doc. That's never a good sign. The doc said that I'd built a resistance to AZT, that my T cells had plummeted two months in a row. He said we'd have to wait for new treatments.

Losing AZT feels like losing a lifeline, like floating past the Golden Gate out to sea. Nothing else to hang on to. Rumored treatments are not alternatives to AZT. Nine fucking years after the first report of AIDS and the best trick the pharmaceuticals have up their sleeves is a recycled cancer drug.

What's left for me to hang on to, my dear Mustafa? The prospect of seeing you grew quite distant as I walked home.

Some days I spend hours at a library or a bookstore reading anything I can get my hands on about the immune system, about drug testing protocols, about experiments in other countries. I should be writing a book on AIDS.

The knowledge gives me an illusion of control, a way to manage my emotions. On rare occasions I've known something a doctor didn't, it's never changed my treatment. I've learned how components of the immune system battle antigens. I've learned the statistical value of double-blind tests. My ACT UP contacts update me about all the experimental treatments in Mexico and Europe, treatments claiming full recovery.

Some days I fantasize I'll find one of these foreign treatments before anyone else, that a new treatment will give me something to hang on to. These fantasies don't last long. College professors don't earn the kind of money to travel overseas for months of treatments that may not work. I can't even afford to search for you in Algeria, Mustafa, because I have no idea how long it would take or whether I'd survive AIDS there.

The sad reality is that even if I had the resources for foreign treatments, it wouldn't matter. Take Rock Hudson, a stunning American movie star. Hudson had plenty of money and connections. He was white. He acted straight. He flew to Paris for a cure. He must have asked First Lady Nancy Reagan to recommend his admission to a military hospital there, the one claiming to treat AIDS. Assuming he asked, because why would he not ask his friend Nancy, the bitch must have refused because he didn't get the treatment. It would be hard to imagine Hudson's disappointment, his utter humiliation.

I've written a short play about Hudson's humiliation just for you, Mustafa. It goes like this:

Rock - Please, Nancy, please, I'm sorry if you're upset after you heard that story that I like spreading my legs in a sling and letting guys fuck me and fist me, but this is serious, this is my life on the line now.

Nancy - Oh, Rock, honey, Ronnie and I love hearing about your sex antics. Seriously, though, you are fucking kidding me if you think we're risking a single vote in the heartland.

The thing both Hudson and I wanted was to hang on to something in the face of death. For Hudson, it was that new treatment in Paris. Even with all his prestige, he couldn't hang on. For me, it was AZT.

In the end, the Paris treatment didn't matter. It never worked. Hudson died a couple months later. The Republicans retained the White House in 1988. All the money and connections in the world wouldn't have kept him alive.

For the gay community, Hudson's death couldn't come soon enough. Perhaps we owe a weird debt of gratitude if Nancy did ignore Hudson's pleas. Hudson's was the first death that put AIDS on the front page of every newspaper in the heartland.

News flash!

Dear Mustafa, there's this update. The Ryan White Act passed last week, five fucking years after Hudson died. It's the first major piece of American AIDS legislation, the "landmark" AIDS bill every gay man has been dying for. I wish the Ryan White Act were a lifeline. I wish it were something I could hang on to.

How can I?

Here's what I know, Mustafa, from my days in the libraries and bookstores. Nine years after the first reported case of AIDS, there are 100,000 dead Americans. There are another

100,000 like me, infected with HIV. Other than AZT, there is no viable treatment in sight, let alone a cure.

Allow me to explain the absurd political situation. To pass a bill for people with AIDS, legislators needed a compromise, a compromise that would humiliate gay men the way Nancy Reagan must have humiliated Rock Hudson. Nothing against the bill's namesake, because Ryan White fought as hard as anyone for this bill, but he was a hemophiliac, not a homosexual. Supporting a Rock Hudson Act would have forced legislators to acknowledge that men fuck each other, would have risked votes in America's heartland.

For young American men, the AIDS scourge is already twice as deadly as the Vietnam war. The US government spent hundreds of billions of dollars on Vietnam, on a war Defense Secretary McNamara determined it couldn't win. How many more need to die for the federal government to spend serious money on AIDS? If 100,000 straight white men were dying of a disease, the government would have spent billions of dollars already. The Ryan White Act marks the first time the federal government will spend over $100 million on AIDS.

Here, gay men, here's a drop of money in your bucket of infected blood. Now go away.

Its political cost is so high, its name so humiliating, its benefits so embarrassing, how do I maintain a shred of self-respect if I hang on to the Ryan White Act? My friends say to lighten up. They are encouraged by any ray of hope. They tell me, of course it's not everything we want, it's political compromise.

AIDS, I tell them, is not a disease of political convenience. AIDS, I tell them, is not a straight white man's disease. AIDS, I tell them, is death, not fucking compromise.

I've lost my AZT lifeline, dear son. I try to maintain hope, but I don't know how I can hang on. I'm gay and I'm black. That's two strikes against me. Dearest Mustafa, I want you here next to me more than anything. I want to see your face and hear your voice. Pray for me, pray for your father. I have nothing, nothing, nothing to hang on to.

26

SAN FRANCISCO, JAN 13, 2002

Peter nudged the closet door back and forth until the attached full-length mirror aimed directly toward the easel in the middle of his studio. Then, walking to the easel and facing the mirror, his eyes shifted for a time between a blank canvas and his reflection. The time had come. Peter seated himself. He didn't care what he painted or how good it was. He'd made a New Year's resolution to paint. As long as he had the studio, he'd told himself in front of the television as the ball in Times Square dropped, he had to use it for something besides reading newspapers.

To Peter's right, a palette rested on the table alongside a stack of his favorite New York skyline sketches. The splotchy paint on the palette was dry. Nine months dry. The dry paint formed a miniature model of Mendocino's coastal range, camouflaged in colors of lichen and wild grasses. Next to the desiccated palette, well-rested brushes were anxious to spread colors after a long vacation.

The mirror reflected the landscape of a naked man in a relaxed pose on a stool. He was in his early fifties with mixed hair and a close-cropped beard. The trim body was neither firm nor flabby, with patches of brown hair under its arms, between its small nipples, and above its genitals. The legs were long and skinny, the arms and fingers delicate. Halfway along the right side of the torso, a birthmark the size of a small russet potato interrupted the unblemished white skin.

Peter had never examined himself this way. Despite the cold, his penis had grown more than a little. He broke his pose to rub his hands together and take his mind off his cock. Even with all the space heaters full blast and vigorous hand rubbing, goosebumps covered his arms. As much as Peter tried, it was hard not to shiver. Shivering didn't matter. What mattered was Erica would arrive in a few weeks and Peter had nothing to show. He squeezed out paint from four tubes on the palette. While he examined the condition of the brushes, the front door buzzed.

Shit. When was the last time someone dropped by the studio unannounced? He'd have to go downstairs to make sure it wasn't a druggie or the homeless guy who kept breaking in. Peter threw on clothes and flew down the stairs.

"Sorry I didn't call first," Angel said, standing on the sidewalk. "My phone battery died."

"That's okay," Peter said. He guessed Angel, too embarrassed to phone after missing their New Year's celebration, preferred to apologize in person.

"I was on my way to church," Angel said, looking down at Peter's bare feet. "If I interrupted something upstairs, I can come back later."

Peter planned to paint all day. He'd finally built up the courage to paint again, even if it would be the self-portraits Linh suggested rather than the New York skylines he'd promised Thomas. But here was Angel at his door, sober, with a bouquet in his hand. The last time Peter could remember a sober Angel arriving anywhere with flowers was a dinner party before Rano died. So much for painting today.

"Please come up," Peter said.

The two were quiet as they climbed the stairs and entered the studio. It was the awkward silence of dancing around an enormous relapse elephant and waiting to see who would address the disconcerting pachyderm first. Inside, Peter put on his socks and shoes, smoothed his disheveled clothes, and then rummaged in the entry closet for a sweatshirt. When he turned around, he saw Angel plopping the flowers into four beer bottles clustered in the middle of the table.

"You painting again?" Angel asked, taking off his worn pea coat and sitting down. "You painting those skyline sketches of yours?"

Peter didn't want to discuss his painting, especially after being interrupted. What he wanted was to address the elephant in the room. From a profile view, it appeared that Angel was nibbling a few too many pastries at the Mexican bakery. He was less the young boy etched in Peter's memory, more a middle-aged man. Even if drugs and booze had started to wrinkle Angel's face, at least the recent abstention from those excesses renewed his skin's healthy glow. The cherubic face of this man arranging flowers was the lone survivor of the former altar boy's years of dealing.

"Oh, no," Peter said, remembering Angel's questions. "I haven't started painting quite yet."

"I thought I smelled paint," Angel said. There was another silence as Angel rearranged the beer bottle vases. "Whatever. I completely understand now why you're not painting."

"Well, that makes one of us," Peter said. He couldn't make sense of Angel today, showing up unexpectedly with flowers, avoiding the topic of his New Year's relapse, claiming knowledge of Peter's painting block, something private to Peter, something that Peter himself didn't comprehend. "Perhaps you could explain why I haven't been painting."

"Because of Rano's journal," Angel said. "When you asked me to reassemble the remnants, I took a look. I mean, I know half of it was destroyed, but I'm no fool. I wanted to know what he said about me. Then I read what he said about you."

"Have you told anyone about the journal?" Peter asked. "I worry what people will think about it, what they'll think about me if they read it. I'm ashamed that Rano never told me he had a son in Algeria."

"Who would I tell?" Angel responded. "My nearest and dearest friends at the bakery? The addicts who break into my room every month?"

"You must have made some friends by now," Peter said. Then he considered Angel's limited probationary life, working at the bakery and spending solitary evenings as far as possible from the temptations of bars and other questionable establishments. Not great for socializing. "No one from AA?"

"What I share at AA is none of your business," Angel said, glaring at Peter. "What I say to people at AA, cabrón, is that I'm concerned about my friend who paints. I say that my painter friend is my only true friend, the one person in the world I trust. I say that my friend's paintings are good enough for museums, except something keeps him from painting. Nada about repairing Rano's journal, nada about what's in it."

Peter wasn't sure what to think. Here was Angel making Rano's journal the topic rather than the relapse, asserting that the journal was what kept Peter from painting. It probably was the journal, but how would Angel know? As Angel continued fiddling with the flowers, Peter noticed an odd combination, the smell of gardenias and oil paint. Angel was sweet to bring flowers, but it was keeping Peter from his work. The entire situation seemed as preposterous as the combination of these scents.

"I hate it when you get so quiet," Angel said. "Why do you care so much who knows about the journal? Why do you keep hiding it from people?"

Peter walked to the easel and looked at himself in the mirror again. What he wanted right now was to paint. The relapse elephant would have to remain in the room silently for the time being. Peter leaned over the palette with a small trowel, mixing a bluish background color from the four lumps of fresh oil paint.

"I was just about to start painting when you arrived," Peter said, testing different color combinations. "Make yourself at home."

For a moment, Peter debated stripping again. His naked reflection had provided an entirely different set of details to render. With clothes on, he had new lines to consider, the way the folds of cloth created shadows, the texture and color of the fabrics. It was the same person underneath, but the clothes revised the landscape.

While Peter looked at himself in the mirror, contemplating the clothed reflection of himself, Angel filled a glass with water in the kitchenette and then walked back to the storage area. The titillation of painting in front of Angel was different from the titillation of painting naked. Even though Peter wanted to start with a nude painting of himself, it wasn't the time to tempt sex with Angel. Clothes stayed on. The colors he'd squeezed onto the palette were all wrong for these clothes. As Peter selected tubes of paint for his clothed self-portrait, Angel returned.

"When was the last time you painted a portrait?" Angel asked, setting down the glass of water and a stack of floppy disks on the table.

"When I moved here," Peter replied, putting down his paint brush. "I sketched tourists at Fisherman's Wharf to earn money for food."

"These may help you start painting again," Angel said, handing one of the floppies to Peter. "Really painting. Painting without guilt."

"Isn't it time for you to go to church?" Peter asked. What in the world did these floppy disks have to do with anything? They were impeding him right now, not encouraging him.

"Were you posing naked when I rang the buzzer," Angel asked. "When you met me downstairs, you looked like you were escaping a four-alarm bathhouse fire."

"Yes," Peter answered. "I wanted to start my self-portrait series without clothes."

"I'll head to church so you can go back to painting in the nude," Angel said, "but I had to show you these. I noticed them when I was repairing Rano's journal."

"I don't understand what floppies have to do with painting," Peter said. "Are those Rano's floppies?"

"They must have Rano's book on them," Angel answered, sliding the other floppies towards Peter.

"There can't be much left on decade-old floppies with water damage," Peter said, running his forefinger around the edge of the disk. "Besides, even if I knew someone who still owned a floppy drive, and even if these floppies were readable, what would I do with them?"

"Before I tell you what to do with them, I have to apologize about New Year's Eve," Angel said. He looked away from Peter, stared out the window. "I care so much about you. It made me nervous about our celebration. I got anxious about where things are between us. A handsome boy offered me a beer. I drank it to relax. And then another. And another. And then I don't remember."

"I wasn't completely surprised," Peter said. "After helping you with the lawyer and the apartment and the job, though, I was disappointed. I don't know how to help you now. I was mad at you for suggesting New Year's and then flaking out."

"I know," Angel said, turning back to face Peter. "Afterwards, I thought about how to apologize. I couldn't just ask for forgiveness. I had to do better. I had to do something that showed you how much I care."

"So you're showing me Rano's floppy disks?" Peter asked. He put the disk in his hand on top of the stack of disks on the table.

"Yes, it came to me last night as I thought about Rano's journal," Angel answered. He stood up and walked to the door. "I understand why you don't want anyone to read Rano's journal. It's not just that no one knew about Mustafa. It's that you're embarrassed by things you did. Those are your issues. But Rano wanted the world to read his research. If you love Rano, it's your responsibility to free the words trapped in those floppies."

OCTOBER 15, 1990 – DEPRESSED

Dear Mustafa,

I've been feeling too sorry for myself to write you. I felt physically better after I stopped AZT, but not mentally. I lost my commitment to teaching and researching until today. Very little research progress, even with Leslie the Librarian unearthing treasure troves about computer security and personal data. Also, the story of how this technology called the Internet was invented. It's all fascinating, even when I'm too depressed to work.

I had to stop feeling sorry for myself. My mental state and lack of output jeopardized my resolution to finish a draft of the book this year. It's still possible, but it will overwhelm anything else in my life. I can't afford to get sick.

Two unexpected things happened that improved my outlook, helped me find my way again. I tell them to you, Mustafa, in hopes they might help you in your dark times.

First, on the way home last week, I watched, by chance, the gay soccer team practicing. I was walking to the parking lot and noticed the players looked older than SF State students. And gayer. I knew of the gay team from Manfredo and also from a friend of Peter's, a Lebanese artist who plays on the team. I chatted with players while they scrimmaged. We shared some tears when I described how brave Manfredo had been with his disease. The Lebanese artist wasn't at the practice, but everyone had a strong opinion about him one way or the other.

How appropriate that the gay team practices at Cox Stadium. I'm a little long in the tooth and I've lost too much muscle mass, but in my heart, I wanted to join. I must note that gay soccer players have the sexiest legs, even the ones who shave. The team had just returned from the Gay Games in Vancouver. They earned a silver medal at the first international Gay Games. Not that Vancouver is very far over the border, but the players said soccer teams from Europe competed, so it really is international.

A world of gay teams meeting every four years. A tradition that could outlive me, even if they find a cure. For some reason, this gave me hope for my team, the gay team. Even with teammates dying, this team is figuring out how to keep the gay ball rolling.

The second unexpected event was Leonard Bernstein's death yesterday. Not sure why this news affected me so much. Last time Brice was here, he forced Peter and me to watch *West Side Story*. Actually, he forced me. Peter loves these sorts of entertainment. The movie version came out around the time I moved from Algeria, but I didn't see it. I don't remember ever watching a musical, much less a film when I first moved here and lived with Carl. The only film Carl watched was S&M porn. I don't want to remember the seedy Market Street theaters where Carl forced me to watch that trash.

Bernstein wasn't that old. My first thought, of course, was that it must have been AIDS. Today's obit, however, says lung failure. Bernstein smoked like a chimney, so the obit says. I realized how bad this epidemic has become, that AIDS is always my prime suspect when anyone drops dead. It wasn't so long ago that my first thought would have been heart attack or overdose.

My initial response to Bernstein's death was incorrect because I view the entire world through the lens of AIDS. That led to my second realization, namely that my research is, in its way, my escape from AIDS. Maybe it's Leslie's chance to escape her cancer world, too.

These two unexpected events gave me perspective I needed, gave me a dose of hope after losing my AZT prescription. Life isn't just about AIDS. It's about our gay culture, too, and how we carry on in spite of the death.

27
New York, Jan 17, 2002

Linh entered the gallery while Erica was on a call in her office. Unfortunately, the art on display wasn't Peter's, but it caught Linh's eye. It was abstract, with a primary palette of blues and greens. The colors resonated with Linh, brought back a visceral sense of being on a shore, or in a boat near shoreline, the salty scent of ocean spray on her skin. Linh had been too young when she left Vietnam to remember much, and most of what she remembered she wished she could forget. These abstract colors brought back a lost memory of a walk with her aunt along a warm coast, as if the canvas spritzed her with refreshing water before boarding a cramped boat.

The paintings also contained words whose abstraction was ambiguous. At first they looked like gibberish. As Linh stepped from one work to the next, the language reminded her of immigrant English, of the nonsensical and, in retrospect, the inadvertently comical way she herself had assembled English words. Linh felt these works were making sense of her life, but she didn't understand quite how.

"How may I help you today?" Erica asked, emerging from her office.

"I was admiring this artist," Linh answered.

Linh had come to view Peter's most recent work again, to give herself a head start rejuvenating their friendship in San Francisco, but she was having trouble focusing as she checked out the art. And now Erica. Erica captivated her—the blonde hair, the svelte figure, the perfect smile. If Linh had a sweet spot for women, it was this look, Erica's look. She liked the way Erica was looking back, too.

"I'm admiring your pants," Erica said, checking out Linh's fashion flourish, a large cartoon tongue dangling from the crotch of her bright yellow pants.

"Thanks," Linh said, gyrating her hips so the red tongue licked the air. Erica burst out laughing. Linh started to laugh, too. Then she mumbled some of the gibberish on the art and, with her hand, moved the cartoon tongue in unison with her mumbling. Linh and

Erica giggled and giggled, like two little girls with no parent to shush them. Slowly their laughing subsided.

"How may I help you?" Erica asked again, still gasping.

"Actually, my friend Peter had an opening here in September," Linh answered. A little giggle slipped out. "I wanted to spend time with his work."

"I'm afraid I sold out of Peter's work," Erica said. "How do you know him?"

"Well, we first met at my family's sandwich shop in San Francisco," Linh answered. "When I needed a break, I'd say I was delivering a sandwich to his studio. We'd spend hours talking. I didn't know much about art, except I really liked what Peter was painting."

"Obviously, I like his painting, too," Erica said. The phone started ringing in her office. Erica hesitated, then stepped closer to Linh. A shiver shot up Linh's spine. "I can pick up the message later," Erica continued, ignoring the ringing. "I'm expecting to have another show of Peter's work soon."

"Oh, that's great," Linh said. "I was worried. Our mutual friend Brice told me Peter stopped painting altogether after his show here."

"I think Peter did stop painting," Erica said. "Did I meet Brice on opening night?"

"Probably," Linh said. "Peter stayed at Brice's when he came for the opening night."

"Oh, yes," Erica said. "I wondered if they'd ever been boyfriends."

"That's complicated," Linh said. It was too complicated to explain now. For a second, though, she considered proposing a dinner date to explain the intricacies.

"Would you like a cup of coffee?" Erica asked, placing her hand on Linh's shoulder.

Linh shook her head. Erica headed to the kitchenette.

Perhaps because of Linh's attraction to the green and blue art on the walls, perhaps because of Erica's initial reaction to Linh's lingual pants, Linh felt right away that she and Erica, as opposite as they were physically, shared a kindred spirit. From the kitchenette, Erica seemed to be sizing up the situation before she poured two cups and returned. For Linh, it felt like one of those too rare interactions that would allow its participants to talk about anything, to wander off together in any direction. A bed would be an exciting target.

"If you want to see Peter's works, call my friend Thomas," Erica said, handing Linh a phone number scribbled on a piece of paper along with coffee. "He has the best of Peter's show at his place."

"Thank you," Linh said. "I like the art you have on display."

"The artist is Vietnamese," Erica said, studying Linh's face more closely. "She finished up at NYU recently. I don't usually show artists this young, but I'm interested in the topic and her work is strong. It references her experiences as an immigrant, both in Vietnam and here."

"I'm Vietnamese," Linh said. The memory of walking near the sea with her aunt became very real. It was a memory from Linh's final week in Vietnam. The coastal village provided a respite before the chaotic travel to America.

"I wasn't sure," Erica said. "I didn't want to presume."

"Well, half Vietnamese," Linh continued. "My father was an American soldier. I never met him. My mother was killed when I was four, so I never learned who my father is. Or was. I don't even know whether he's alive."

After this abrupt admission, Erica and Linh were quiet, frozen like statues, holding their cups without sipping. They avoided each other's eyes. Linh almost never spoke about her past. She'd blurted out her family history and she wondered why. Why now? The silence was awkward. She'd seen so much, lived through such horror, watched her own mother die, and now, here, in, of all places, an art gallery, she found herself tongue-tied. The last time Linh told anyone about her past was when she lived in San Francisco, nearly fifteen years ago, during one of her visits to Peter's studio. They'd smoked a lot of pot.

Erica raised her coffee halfway to her lips. Before she took a sip, she looked Linh in the eye. "My father was a soldier in Vietnam, too."

"Are you available later for dinner?" Linh asked.

November 30, 1990 – Internet

Dear Mustafa,

I have to apologize again for taking so long to write you. I put my nose to the grindstone, as they say here. I don't know why anyone would put their nose to a grindstone. It seems dangerous. Anyway, the phrase means I'm working hard. I worked the entire Thanksgiving holiday. Progress is good. At this pace, I'll complete a draft of the book by year's end.

I've learned more about the origins of the Internet since I wrote last time. You're probably as familiar with the Internet, dear Mustafa, as with putting your nose to a grindstone. Allow me to explain the Internet. It's a technology that connects computers, enabling them to communicate with each other. It's a small miracle that government, universities, and industry collaborated to create such free and powerful technology.

Here's a practical example of the Internet's power. Electronic mail, or "email," is easy to understand. Instead of writing a letter on paper and posting it in the mail, someone on the Internet composes a letter on a computer and sends it instantaneously through the Internet to a recipient's computer. The email address tells the Internet how to route the letter to the correct computer.

A piece of email is a modern-day stagecoach. It travels anywhere in the world for free, carrying a small booty of information. I've asked if I could email you in Algeria, but no one can locate a computer in Algeria connected to the Internet. Consider how just this one messaging system will change the way people communicate, Mustafa, and then consider there are plenty of other messaging systems and services the Internet provides. It boggles my mind. I can't wait to see how it evolves.

I feel like I'm close to a substantial intellectual breakthrough. It follows from my earlier entry about Denmark, about the first same-sex unions and identity. I have an intuition the Internet is the information train I've been looking for.

I've visited nearby companies that operate entirely on the Internet. They barely use paper. All records and written communications travel through the Internet. Imagine how this transforms bureaucracy, Mustafa. Instead of printing and distributing regulations, policies, memos, news, etc., employees transmit and access information when they need it. Updates to policies are available to every employee instantaneously. A president can transmit news to employees in seconds. Memos sent via email replace office messengers.

It's not just memos and letters. There's a new service called Gopher that allows sharing entire file systems anywhere in the world. When you get the Internet there, I could send a link that, like a jinn, grants you access to my research and entire book! This is nothing short of transformational.

I've been writing about how this American invention will project American values to other cultures. Imagine how this technology will change business and government in Algeria, whose reputation for bureaucratic speed and transparency is somewhat lacking. Of course, I'm exploring how this Internet technology might have been different had China or France or even Algeria invented it.

But something else is emerging, Mustafa. Something big. I think the Internet's aggregation of personal and corporate information is like a train aggregating stagecoaches in the Wild West. The Internet will become a modern-day robber's dream come true.

I'm exhausted from this work. I should feel great. Unfortunately, I have to return every evening from my research life to the real world of AIDS, the real world of politics.

Back in the real world, Prime Minister Margaret Thatcher, Iron Lady, Defender of the Falklands, Friend Extraordinaire to Ronald Reagan, Perpetrator of Section 28, resigned on the twenty-eighth. With the evil Section 28, Mustafa, Thatcher legalized discrimination against homosexuals. If everyone weren't dying, the Castro would have roared in a gay celebration of her resignation.

I should feel great about this. Instead I feel lousy. Really crappy.

Fuck politics. Who cares? American politics is a straight white man's game.

I feel bad because Brice isn't visiting like he promised. This new window decorating business of his is a smash hit. It practically fell in his lap. Brice said an older gay guy needed someone to take over the business so he could retire. During the days of this plague, "retire" being, of course, a euphemism. Brice planned to wrap up everything in New York by Black Friday and fly west.

I feel bad because Vito Russo died. He was a hero who fought to help everyone with AIDS. His magnificent speech inspires me when I'm down. I reread it today. It helped, it made me feel better. I wish I could express my anger as eloquently as Vito. He was a desperately needed hero.

I feel bad because more friends died. Ricky Smith, Scott Calendar, and Kap Pischel. All, coincidentally, from wealthy California families. The grim reaper's late harvest was plentiful this month. AIDS doesn't care about your bank account. Fuck death. Couldn't attend the services. I wanted to, but I had to stop. The opportunities I have to celebrate a life cut short overwhelm me.

It's okay that Brice didn't come. It's okay that I missed the remembrance services for my friends. The honest reason I feel really crappy is that I'm sick again. I hate admitting it, hate telling anyone, but I have to let you know, Mustafa. I don't need a doctor anymore to know. It's so humiliating. Always happens on a Friday when it's impossible to get into Davies Hospital. The only way I could feel worse is if Brice had wasted his vacation in a hospital.

28

NEW YORK, FEB 25, 2002

Mark returned from the East Village cleaners with his washed and folded clothes to find a package in the lobby. It had been months since Mark received mail from Erica, since before their aborted brunch at the cafe, the meeting Mark thought was a let's-be-friends thing but realized as Erica shot out the door was supposed to be a let's-get-back-together thing. He picked up the box. There was nothing romantic about it. It was the size of a shoebox. The label was typed. The heavy brown wrapping paper provided no clue about its contents. The only way Mark knew it was from Erica was the return address.

As he ascended the flights of stairs to his studio, Mark debated whether to open the box or continue writing up his research. Pretty much anything could distract Mark from writing. He'd even cleaned up his apartment and picked up his laundry. Not that he was expecting anyone else to climb these stairs anytime soon. Still, it was reassuring to know that if anyone made the effort to drop in, he could pour a drink or serve a nosh without cleaning dishes first.

The box rattled as Mark placed it in the center of his writing desk. He took off his jacket and put on a kettle for tea. What a mystery this box was. Erica couldn't possibly be sending love letters again. Sometimes she'd been needy, but never that needy. Nonetheless, the box, by being so devoid of emotion, so the opposite of love, felt like it might be Erica's clever manipulation to re-engage romantically. She wouldn't send anything as dopey as chocolates, although she knew Mark would devour dark chocolate at any hour. Anyway, too heavy for chocolates. Maybe she was returning something Mark had given her. That would be a bit passive-aggressive after all this time.

The kettle whistled. Mark prepared Earl Gray tea and sat at the desk, staring at the box. He liked these kinds of puzzles. What was Erica's motivation to send this box? His entire postdoc was unraveling puzzles, exploring motivations, testing his hypotheses about why people wrote computer code one way and not another. If he solved the puzzles, he hoped to improve coding languages and protocols developed for the burgeoning Internet.

Today Mark was avoiding his current puzzle, the demise of a once promising, but now obscure, Internet protocol called Gopher. The glitzy HTTP protocol that powered the Web left Gopher in the dust. In order to motivate future developers to design longer-lived protocols, Mark was exploring the way Gopher got so close but missed. Gopher's text-only interface was simple, elegant, and snappy. Maybe Gopher's designers failed to anticipate faster networks and computers. Or maybe because Gopher lacked images, porn couldn't drive its adoption. In any case, Brewster from the Internet Archive had emailed some historical leads. Tracking them down might have a payday but was certain to be tedious.

Mark avoided calling Brewster, avoided the tedium. Instead, he shook the box from Erica. The rattling sound didn't provide any clues. What was Erica's motivation?

Mark unlocked his "love letter drawer." It contained, in chronological order, a decade of archived love letters, poems, and drawings, such as they were, from the women he'd dated, most recently from Anna, the seemingly lovely lass he'd met in Knightsbridge last fall. That didn't go quite as planned. Mark racked up a large credit card tab flying to London to attend what turned out to be Anna's hysterical pregnancy. After that manipulation, Mark put the kibosh on dating, in part to recover emotionally from Anna, in part to recover financially from MasterCard and Visa.

Tucked away under Anna's letters were Erica's. Mark hoped to find a signal in those, some indication of what the plain box might contain. Instead, what he found in Erica's letters were memories of their time together. After the brunch incident, after Erica's abrupt exit, he'd tried not to think about Erica. She crept into his thoughts anyway, when he least expected it. This exercise of searching love letters was not serving its purpose. Mark felt exasperated. He remembered crawling into bed with her the first time, in the bed right there across the room, the way they instinctively knew how to pleasure each other. Erica's letters were having the perverse effect of making him question his emotion- and finance-induced celibacy rather than solving the puzzle at hand. He slid the letters back in the drawer and locked it. Didn't need to let that cat out of the bag.

The only thing left to do was open the box. A pair of scissors easily sliced through the brown paper, and a stack of floppy disks scattered across the desk. Mark picked out Erica's folded note from the mess.

Dear Mark,

I never apologized for my behavior at our last meeting. Foolishly, I thought we would make up, that I could talk you out of your affair with Jodie. For that, I apologize.

While I miss our time together, I honestly wish you well in your romances. All I can tell you is that as I've learned more about Peter, the artist whose lover died of AIDS, I've learned more about myself and about relationships.

So I hope you don't mind me asking this favor. It's a big favor to ask. I will understand if you decline.

Peter's late lover, Rano, left behind the floppy disks in this package. Peter gave them to me in San Francisco because I said you might be able to help.

The disks may be unreadable now. If they are readable, though, you are the only person I know who might understand what's on them. Rano wrote about ethics and computers. This is all that's left of his work. Most everything else was lost.

I wouldn't bother you with this except I have a hunch that what's on these disks has significance for Peter, some breakthrough or understanding whose significance Peter doesn't fully appreciate.

At any rate, Peter said he'd lost track of Rano's professional friends, but that he thought the disks contained groundbreaking research. I thought perhaps you also might benefit from Rano's lost work.

Should you deign to help decipher these disks, I would be overwhelmed.

Warmly,
Erica

Mark arranged the disks in a neat stack on his desk, remembering the stupid password drinking game he played with his friend. Ugh. Why hadn't he apologized to Erica for his friend's drunken tomfoolery, sending those amorous emails from Mark's account to Jodie? Their misunderstanding bothered him.

After a few sips of tea, instead of opening the love letter drawer again, Mark placed Erica's letter on top of the disks.

December 31, 1990 – Home

D ear Mustafa,

Returned home yesterday from Davies Hospital. Peter's gone out to celebrate the New Year. I suppose he deserves a break, but I'm worried about being alone. Perhaps I've become too dependent on nurses. Don't want that dependency, but I get scared being alone.

Nice to be home. It's my world now. Glad it's still our home, this fine old Victorian, this *grande dame*. My hospitalization complicated the lease renewal. No financial incentive for the landlord to help us. Asshole offered no flexibility, in spite of my condition. Demanded renewal signed, sealed, and delivered, no matter what god-awful crap was flowing through my IV drip. We've got to change the lease to Peter's name. If I don't make it, Peter won't make it without rent control.

So many memories in this apartment. Why go out to celebrate when I can wax nostalgic inside? I'm resting on the comfy couch like an old man recounting his life to his son. Let me give you a tour of our apartment, Mustafa, in case you never visit me here.

Photos, photos, photos. Friends, trips, vacations. Too many reminders of those who've died during this viral freak show. Wonder what it would be like if either Peter or I had family albums, happy siblings from our years together, smiling nieces and nephews.

Don't remember where I hid that grainy photo of you, dear Mustafa. I wonder if you still look like me or more like Aaliya now. Your eigenface didn't match anyone. I wonder if your recent photos are with your wife and kids. With a man friend. With a beard or a mustache. Or perhaps you didn't make it. Perhaps I've been writing your ghost.

Okay, don't want to think about that. Hospital stay too fresh. It's a relief to be somewhere again that smells of life.

Peter decorated our home in a medley of styles found on furniture forays and treasure hunts. It's something Peter does well, creating cosmic harmony out of the random objects in the apartment. Zebra-skin chair always a hit. A startling contrast to its living-room neighbor, a Louis XV reproduction chair with a frame of exquisitely detailed woodwork. The Berber rug may be cliché. There it is, at the feet of the zebra and Louis XV. Never really a fan of the large Jim Morrison poster Peter kept from his brief Haight-Ashbury days, but everyone else likes it. I admire the way Peter coordinates this movable menagerie. Much livelier than the morbid combo of Scandinavian modern furniture and overstylized Nagel prints that's infecting Castro interiors.

The parties we've had here. Ah, the parties. The very first was my fortieth birthday party, a week after Peter and I moved in. Friends still talk about that. The friends that are alive.

Then there were our *Dynasty* parties. Every Wednesday evening another cliffhanger. All of us adored dreamy Steven, cheering and jeering the love-hate relationship with his straight brother Adam. Homophobic Hollywood cast a straight actor to play the gay son and vice versa. How did we know? Gaydar helped, but *Dynasty* party gossip revealed everything gay. And by gossip, I mean the girls at our parties did a lot of their homework in bed. It's the best place to learn the most important parts of your subjects.

We've had so much fun here. The impromptu drag parties we hosted here. Office drag, military drag, cop drag, S&M drag. And Roman drag. Every Ides of March was an excuse for a toga party. Any uniform or wig, actually, was a good enough excuse. That time Brice flew in the door as a stewardess. The skies couldn't have been friendlier.

Our location isn't quiet. Lots of Market Street noise, especially when the bars let out. It does have the advantage of being a block from the mortuary on Market Street. Easy funereal commute whenever I crave the smell of death.

I'll stop here, Mustafa. I'm exhausted. Besides, I'm writing like an old man giving a tour of a dead friend's house. Not staying up for this year's time-shifted Times Square ball drop. Hard to get excited watching people who were excited three hours ago. It's like a hot trick had an orgasm earlier in the day in a different room, and I'm supposed to get all hot and bothered about it as I turn out the lights. Not happening. That's why I used to go out to the Castro to celebrate. Everyone alive. At least the hospital has reminded me how to sleep without Peter next to me. I missed him.

29

SAN FRANCISCO, FEB 26, 2002

With his self-portrait series complete, Peter was catching up on paperwork. Good excuse to avoid another painting project. The phone rang. Good excuse to avoid paperwork.

"Hey, can I stop by your studio this afternoon?" Linh asked.

"You're already in San Francisco?" Peter responded.

"Yes," Linh answered. "I've decided to rent a place and I need your help. I don't recognize the neighborhoods anymore."

"Come over as soon as you can," Peter said, excited to hear from Linh. She'd be perfect to critique his self-portraits. "And bring sandwiches from your aunt's shop, for old times' sake."

Peter shoved the paperwork in a drawer and prepared for Linh's visit. Of course Linh didn't recognize San Francisco. South of Market had replaced the Castro as the trendy neighborhood. The Embarcadero, cleared of its double-decker freeways, now buzzed with farmers markets and ferries. The seismic dot-com boom and bust had shifted the energy of the city away from the brisk Pacific coast winds towards the milder bay breezes.

What Peter couldn't tell Linh during their short call was that he, too, was contemplating a relocation, except in the opposite direction, from San Francisco to New York. He wasn't sure why, except perhaps because he was an artist and artists did irrational things. A move to New York might light a fire under his uncertain ass. A dozen years ago, he'd told Rano he couldn't move to New York. More and more often now, he had this feeling that he'd exhausted San Francisco and Mendocino, taken everything they had to offer.

As Peter mopped the blue floor, he realized it didn't make any practical sense to move to New York, to give up his studio after he'd just renewed the lease. It made even less sense to give up his rent-controlled apartment in San Francisco for New York's sky-high rents. Other than Erica and a few of her gallery clients, Peter wasn't dialed into the New York art milieu, either. His social circle was in San Francisco. Then, of course, there was Angel,

Peter's long-term, on-again, off-again local attraction, though Angel had been off-again for quite a few months.

All these reasons for Peter to stay were a natural consequence of living in San Francisco his entire adult life. He wondered if this limited him, limited his knowledge, his perspective, his art. It didn't escape Peter that the idea of an adventure, of moving to a new place like New York, could be his decade-delayed midlife crisis. With Rano's death and Peter's subsequent drug-enhanced grieving, there hadn't been time for Peter to indulge in a proper midlife crisis.

Peter straightened up the desk and dusted the shelves. There was Rano's journal, above the desk. Ah, yes, another consideration for moving. He flipped through its pages, scanning the entries he'd nearly memorized, stopping to reexamine the dreaded entry about Carl, the night Carl wielded a knife, the charges Peter pressed against Rano's wishes. Until Peter read this dreadful entry, though, he hadn't known Carl died without disclosing Mustafa's whereabouts.

The final preparation before Linh's arrival was hanging the self-portraits. Once in place, Peter sat down and contemplated his work. It would be the first time anyone else had viewed the entire set of self-portraits. It was a new artistic path, one that both beckoned Peter and worried him about going too far off course. With the entire set on the wall, he was anxious for Linh's feedback.

Linh arrived at the studio wearing one of her more demure getups—demure, Peter was learning, by Linh's standards—perhaps a tacit acknowledgement that potential landlords might prefer less flamboyant tenants.

"You look so conservative today," Peter said, hugging his friend. "Well, except maybe those lavender accents."

"Honey, a simple Dior always opens a few diors," Linh said, squeezing Peter.

As they sat down, Linh's steel-blue eyes reminded Peter of her quiet perseverance. Adversity tried but failed to tame Linh's indomitable spirit. She'd moved to New York against her family's wishes, exploring its underbelly, evading its violence, savoring its sadomasochism. She was the type who talked back to a gunman without hesitation, even in Gucci and high heels. She'd dealt with worse. Much worse. Her toughness paid off. With her new wealth, she would never want for anything. Here she was, back in San Francisco. It felt different and the same to see her.

Peter and Linh hadn't had a long, engaged conversation since forever. At first, it was lighthearted. Linh offered Peter a joint, but Peter declined, claiming he needed to paint. Then the friends cataloged the strains of pot they smoked during her extended sandwich delivery visits. They reminisced about the time Linh asked Mapplethorpe to photograph Rano and his endowment. It didn't take long for the conversation to take a serious turn, although not in the direction of the self-portraits. Linh told Peter about the cold strangeness of her new wealth, the way money opened old family wounds and revealed the ugly agendas of friends. It wasn't a topic Peter could dismiss.

"I'm renting in San Francisco because I can't afford to buy," Linh said. "I mean, I can afford the money, that's not it. If I buy a home, my family will question my motives, ask why I'm not buying something for them, not making them a bigger part of my life. I'll rent because it avoids bad feelings that wouldn't even exist if I didn't have money. The karmic cost of ownership is too high."

"I suppose that explains why you didn't stop by the family shop for sandwiches," Peter said.

Linh didn't answer. They sat silently for what seemed a very long time, looking at Peter's latest work. He couldn't wait to hear Linh's thoughts. Unlike Erica, whose reaction during her visit earlier in the month was as inscrutable as a gallerist's could be, Linh was always forthright about what she saw. She had neither Erica's formal training nor market acumen, but during her time in New York, she'd received a practical education in contemporary art.

New York's art scene had intimidated Peter. Not Linh. Her move to New York coincided with the end of the city's stark era of bankruptcy and abandoned apartment buildings. She arrived after the seminal haunts of that era had vanished—Studio 54 and Mudd Club and *The Times Square Show* were mere memories. Through her Mapplethorpe connection, though, she navigated the new scene, the scene emerging like a phoenix from the ashes of graffiti-covered subway trains—the Basquiats, the Hujars, the Dicksons, the Ahearns. Her encounters with Maplethorpe led to more and more cultural encounters, encounters with the most avant of New York's avant-garde art scene.

Finally, Linh stood to examine the self-portraits up close. The longer the silence stretched on, the more nervous Peter grew waiting for Linh's critique. She wasn't providing clues. When she'd visited Peter's studio in the past, she would talk her way through a viewing, elaborating on details she noticed, asking about color or brush choices. New York seemed to have changed her curiosity.

"There's no way to explain why I'm rich after a few years doing nothing more than talking to customers on the phone," Linh said, "while my family is still struggling after decades making sandwiches. The rich worry about their money, the poor about their bread."

"What?" Peter asked.

Linh sat down again. She explained to Peter in quite some detail how uncertain she felt about her money. She didn't trust it. It felt, she said, like a trick, like something that was sure to be taken away if she ever came to believe it was hers. She knew this feeling was a result of her early life in Vietnam, of events she didn't even remember, a consequence of losing everything precious. But the fear was real. The money made her sad, made her feel she could never allow herself to have things. The money allowed Linh whatever she wanted, yet made her feel she deserved nothing.

This was unexpected. Peter didn't know what to say. He knew how difficult Linh's past had been. She'd told him before that she didn't know who her American father was, that she'd witnessed the napalm attack on her village, witnessed her own mother's fiery death. How could those shitheads, Peter remembered Linh asking, napalm the women they were fucking the night before? When Peter and Linh had talked about all this so many years ago, it seemed like Linh had worked through it, that she'd found a way forward. In all the years since, she hadn't mentioned her early life again. Peter knew how hard her past had been, but hadn't grasped the depth of her despair.

Something must have happened that made Linh revisit the horrors of Vietnam. Peter didn't dare ask for fear it might take him, too, to his own dark place, to those times that powers beyond his control wreaked havoc on his life. Linh's words resonated with Peter. Like Linh, he wasn't sure what he deserved. If he believed what he read in Rano's journal, he should have been the one who died of AIDS.

"You're so quiet," Linh said.

"It's Rano's journal," Peter blurted before considering what he wanted to reveal. From the comment Linh made when they'd met at Cafe Flore, when she said to rip up the journal, it was clear she somehow knew about the journal already. "When I read it, I found out things I didn't know, things about Rano, about his family, about our relationship. It was like finding new parts of him that I have to mourn, like he died a second time. It kept me from painting."

"Yes, I know," Linh said.

"What do you mean?" Peter asked. "How could you know?"

"Dear Peter," Linh answered, "I know. I don't know why it got under your skin, but it's clear the journal got under your skin. I think everyone knows from the way you're hiding it, avoiding talking about it."

Of course Linh was right. He'd told Brice about Rano's journal but kept the actual pages from him. Thomas had seen the journal when the ceiling leak destroyed half of it.

Angel was the only one who'd read the thing, and he was sworn to secrecy. Peter hadn't talked about its contents with anyone, but everyone understood. Looking at himself in the self-portraits made Peter ashamed he'd missed so many opportunities with Rano, ashamed to survive when Rano was the one with so much talent.

"Before I returned to San Francisco, I wanted to spend more time understanding your new work," Linh continued. "So I went down to Erica's gallery, which was interesting in ways I didn't expect. Since Erica had sold all your work, she sent me to Thomas. What a charming man, that Thomas. And beautiful clothes. He told me about his trip out here to visit you. Even Thomas sensed the journal is keeping you from painting."

"Does Erica know about the journal?" Peter asked.

"It doesn't matter," Linh said. "She certainly understands you."

"Did she say anything about my self-portraits?" Peter asked, waving at the paintings on the wall.

"All she said was something like, 'if you squint, you can tell it's Peter,'" Linh answered. "She's right."

"I promised Thomas I would paint the New York skyline," Peter said. "I listened to you, instead. Now I'm worried I've painted something Erica won't show and something that broke my promise to Thomas."

"It was only a suggestion," Linh said.

"There have been days I wanted to burn all these paintings I made of myself," Peter said. "Days that I wanted to move somewhere else and start over again."

January 1, 1991 – Backwards

Dear Mustafa,

I always write resolutions on New Year's Day. What's the point today? After weeks cooped up in the hospital? Doctors and nurses gave me kind words of encouragement. They said they hadn't seen anyone come back from the edge like me. They said to hang on, new drugs coming.

I heard the same encouragement too often last year. Their placebo words have stopped making me feel better.

I'm upset that I didn't finish a draft of the book. Leslie the Librarian worked valiantly while I was in the hospital, but she can't get us over the finish line alone. She hasn't been looking great lately, either.

This year, I would be more comfortable going backwards in time than making resolutions about the future. I reread some of this journal when I woke up, before Peter pulled his hungover ass out of bed. I wrote nice things about him. Perhaps too nice. I think the world of him for taking care of me. He has the right intentions. But the bad things. I'll tell you about those, Mustafa, when I'm in a better mood.

I also read the aspirations I noted when I was diagnosed. I was so scared, maybe even more scared waiting to find out than actually hearing the doctor pronounce what more and more appears to have been my death sentence. "Your test came back positive for HIV." I wanted so bad to be one of the lucky ones who never developed full-blown AIDS—full-blown like HIV is some kind of balloon that, if only I could keep from blowing into it, it wouldn't fill up and burst. I was convinced research would solve my problem. I pledged I would make my mark, show the world an ethics thing or two.

And here I find myself. Home again from the hospital.

Even without a hangover, the future looks bleak today. Very, very, very bleak. A Bloody Mary wouldn't begin to mitigate my anxiety.

Would it be scarier growing younger? Going backwards in time? Knowing I'd regain my faculties, I'd gain back weight, I'd have six-pack abs again, I'd lose the wisdom of age traveling to my innocent youth.

Imagine, dear Mustafa, if I could go backwards. Would I make Old Year's resolutions for the things I want to lose in the next backward year?

My goal this past backward year is to have an accident so my car is like new again.

My goal this past backward year is to have my appendix replaced so I can get rid of the jagged scar across my belly.

My goal this past backward year is to unread more books so I don't have to carry around all that shit in my head.

My goal this past backward year is to come in gay from my family and friends so they can suspect I'm gay, so I can be ashamed of who I am.

My goal this past backward year is to suck my vomit out of toilets more often so I can get rid of hangovers and enjoy being drunk.

Future tense would become past tense. "I will die" is something that happened. Past tense is future tense. "I was born" is something that will happen.

As I grow young, old people gather around to learn the past, what comes before them, so they have an inkling of what they lose as they, too, grow younger. Then they watch as I shrink, shrink until I lose my hair and I suck tits. What a tragedy that is. No cock. Just tits. Oh, well. No shame in that, I suppose. And then the warm slippery slide into darkness. Buried inside my mother, wherever she might be.

As I write this, dear Mustafa, I believe the only way I can see you again is to go backwards in time, to relive that glimpse I had of you in Aaliya's arms, swaddled in blankets. My world is shrinking. There's no time to visit Algeria. I am unbearably sad with that thought.

My resolutions this year are to finish my book and to make peace with Peter, not necessarily in that order. And to figure out how to publish my book even if I don't finish it. (Is that even possible? I keep thinking of the boukalates party.) And to pray the doctors and nurses are right. And to fucking live another fucking year.

30

DANBURY, MARCH 19, 2002

Frank dropped off Erica at the train station. She waited until the drive to let him know she was upset he hadn't come to her gallery, hadn't seen the show she asked him to see. He apologized, unsure why she needed to tell him this, unsure why this particular show was so important. When they hugged at the station, Erica seemed distant.

Frank returned home to finish his breakfast and clean up. He noticed a piece of paper next to Erica's empty orange-juice glass. She must have forgotten it. Frank couldn't decide whether to unfold it. Had to be Erica's. It couldn't be a note he wrote. He didn't recognize the lined paper. He wondered whether Erica left the note for him to find, whether she meant it as a test to see if he'd read something private of hers. That seemed ridiculous when Frank thought about it. There were so many things of hers in the house he could snoop through if he wanted to investigate her private life. Like the treasure trove of high school love notes upstairs in her bedroom closet. He'd opened the shoebox once by accident and, realizing its contents, taped it shut. One day he'd remind Erica of the shoebox. Maybe after she got married and needed a good laugh about romance.

Frank couldn't decide whether to unfold the paper, so he slipped it into his shirt pocket and drove to school. Then he forgot about it. Classes started. Schoolboys suited up, stretched, performed calisthenics, played volleyball, wrestled, ran, showered, roughhoused. Then it was lunch time.

In front of the rusting vending machine, Frank inserted quarters, pressed the worn Sprite button, and watched the aluminum can tumble down. The soda can's landing blocked the dispenser door. As Frank bent over to dislodge the can, the folded paper dropped to the floor, a further interruption to the day's routine. He shook the door of the ancient machine to free the can, picked up the paper from the floor, and found a secluded seat in the teacher's lounge. After arranging his lunch on the table, Frank popped open the soda can. It gushed from all the excitement, overflowing on the folded paper. Horse confetti, Frank said to himself. Either he opened the paper to save its contents or, or, or.

There wasn't really an alternative. He unfolded the note and dabbed it dry with a paper napkin. There it was. Erica's letter to Linh.

Frank started reading the letter as he bit into his tuna fish sandwich. A can of worms, that's what this letter was. He could tell that by the first sentence. A real can of worms. Frank put down his sandwich. He'd lost his appetite by the second sentence.

Erica's letter wasn't exactly a love letter. It was like this Linh, whoever she was, had become a kind of confidante to Erica. As Frank read, the words became more florid. Not quite romantic. Linh seemed more like a sister to Erica. That would be preposterous. Frank waved the letter in the air to dry it out. This was a strange way to learn about Linh. He knew from the context, from the gallery show by the Vietnamese artist, from the spelling of the name, that somehow this Linh character must be Vietnamese. What was Erica thinking when she wrote this letter? Was this why she was upset he hadn't seen the gallery show? After his tour of duty, Frank had trouble trusting anyone Vietnamese. Never knew whether they wanted to swipe your money or to blow you to smithereens. Erica must understand that. How could she not? Frank told her about finding his Purple Heart, about the unexpected combat, the trap the Vietnamese informant set, the flash of gunfire from nowhere, the injury he sustained, the treachery on the battlefield that day. She must have understood that the jagged scars across his left leg ran all the way through his heart.

The letter ended on a practical note, something about an artist named Peter. That must be the artist Erica mentioned all the time, the lucky pansy who survived 9/11 because he postponed his flight. Something about Peter moving to New York and looking for a place. Something about floppy disks. Frank glossed over the rest. His girl had been a good letter writer since he could remember. Always clear, certain, concise.

The school bell rang, signaling afternoon classes. Frank threw his lunch in the trash. He folded the now dry paper and put it back into his shirt pocket. Everything seemed out of control. Afternoon classes were agony. Frank reached for the letter several times, but left it in his pocket. As thin as it was, he could feel its contents pressing against his chest. The afternoon wore on. If only the vending machine dispensed Scotch. Frank's instructions to the students became half-hearted. He stopped paying attention. Rules were broken. Classes ended early. The boys dallied in the locker room, whispering about the coach.

The end of the school day couldn't come soon enough. Frank walked to his car. Sitting behind the steering wheel, he reread the letter. He could drive home and phone Erica. What would they talk about? It seemed as though Erica thought this Linh person might be her sister. Frank could tell Erica that that was impossible, that Erica was his only child.

But he knew Erica, he knew his sweet girl, he knew if she'd made up her mind, that's how things were. The letter made it clear. Erica had concluded she had a Vietnamese half sister. Frank could deny the possibility that Linh was his child until the cows came home but, if Erica believed Linh was her sister, she'd think he was lying, that he was protecting the memory of his wife, of Erica's mother.

The only thing to do with this can of worms was to put it out of his mind. That was always the best way to deal with Vietnam. Frank got out of his car and retraced his steps back to the gym. Yes, he'd had his indiscretion in Vietnam. Who hadn't? He was a horny boy then, not so different from the boys he coached. He'd been a young husband who made a stupid mistake. That would go with him to the grave. A Vietnamese child, though? That was impossible.

Inside the gym, Frank inventoried the high school football equipment—jerseys, helmets, pads by size. It was a mindless chore. He'd avoided it, but today was a good day for something mindless, a good day to fold and count. The cleaner had returned the jerseys weeks ago. They were piled neatly. They just needed to be folded and counted for storage.

It would be better to replace all the gear, but that wasn't in the budget. At least the football program had a budget. Other sports got by on much less. The arts programs survived by the grace of donations from the Danbury community. The band instruments moaned painfully as air pushed its way past their worn valves. Still, as Frank folded the football uniforms, he found more irreparable stains and tears. It wasn't good for team spirit. It wasn't good for school pride. If there was anything the Army taught Frank, it was the significance of a well-groomed uniform, the power of immaculate uniformity. Everything in its place.

Frank took a break from folding to line up the helmets by size. Then he tore up the letter, dropping the shreds in a trash can. Frank stared at the heap of jerseys while his mind turned. He'd never considered the possibility of a Vietnamese child. Why would he? There had been an indiscretion, yes, he wouldn't deny that. But helicopters napalmed the village the following day. No one could have survived, not the handsome Vietnamese woman he paid, not her daughter who played with Frank's radio in the other room.

Today seemed like a good day indeed to inventory the football equipment. Something mindless, something to forget the jagged scar. Frank folded and counted the rest of the jerseys.

January 18, 1991 – Iraq

Dear Mustafa,

I'm starting to feel more like myself. I wanted a night out, so last night Peter and I went to Angel's place to watch the war. The war makes me think of you. I know Algeria is distant from Iraq, but the media describes the Middle East like a neighborhood the size of the Castro. Through my American lens, I fret that you'll get sucked into a ridiculous regional conflict.

On the way to the war show, Peter told me Randy the hairdresser died. That put me in a sour mood. Pretty sure Peter and Randy had a thing, but I never pried. Randy definitely a bottom. Angel reported that tidbit to me after a bathhouse sighting. Randy came to San Francisco five years ago from Hawaii with nothing. Less than what I came with. He starts cutting hair, then opens a hair place in the Haight called Mane Attractions. Boom. Suddenly, Randy rents out six chairs and he's set. The shop is still open, so someone must have taken over. No one has wills. We just figure it out. Or fight it out. Jealous lovers battling each other for furniture or bank accounts, jealous families battling the battling lovers. Randy was humble, practical, self-assured. It tires me to keep losing such resourceful friends.

When Peter and I arrived at Angel's place, we watched the war on his TV. I've been thinking a lot about that, what that even means. The United States and its coalition dropped bombs on Iraq and Kuwait on live TV. I've watched episodes of *The Real World* at the Midnight Sun. It's a show that's supposed to be about real people and their real lives. *The Real World* can't touch the reality of war.

Angel and his boyfriend have cable, so we watched on CNN. I want to write about this. I'm making notes here to remember.

First, it was brilliant theater. Hats off to the Department of Defense. The attack on Iraqi forces was choreographed better than any Super Bowl halftime show. Timed so we could order pizza to be delivered. Controlled so we only saw the distant flashes of rockets and bombs. Narrated so we felt confident in our righteousness, justified in our application of force, awed by our soldiers.

It was a show to make people feel good to be American, feel good about war, to be on the right side, beating the bad guy, Saddam. The military has learned from its Vietnam media missteps. It's not ground troops fighting hideous battles mired in rice paddies against a bad guy who's indistinguishable from a good guy. It's an Arab bad guy with a Hitler bad-guy mustache. Kudos to central casting.

Would the US drop bombs on white people? It's easy when the bad guys have brown skin, easy to dehumanize. But wait, there's more.

My professional interest is technology and ethics. I consider military technology separately from media technology. Some of the reviews in the media are scathing. But why would the DOD care about reviews? It has a political hit on its hands.

Military technology. Weird to watch descending bombs. How does that airplane view of destruction affect the airmen psychologically? What does that say about values? Do future wars even take place with troops on the ground or just through cameras? How much more can we dehumanize the enemy when remote control warfare obsoletes hand-to-hand combat? What does it mean to win?

Media technology. Weird to broadcast bombs hurling towards earth and bursting, to embed reporters with troops rolling in tanks and armored vehicles. Lopsided reporting. The DOD owns the POV. How many more camera angles can the DOD provide? How will the enemy be portrayed? How do we experience future wars? Live surround sound? At movie theaters on large screens? With popcorn?

These are issues we're passing on to your generation, dear Mustafa. I want to talk to you about them. If we never meet, you will find my half of our discussion in my book. Which I'm working on again. Which Leslie the Librarian is quite certain I can finish this summer. She won't be pleased I want to add this new material.

As we munched on pizza, I noticed that Angel's boyfriend was looking skinny. Writing that, I realize I might look the same. That's disheartening. At least, we're both alive and working. He was talking about a six-hour play he's working on. Finding props and costumes. Sounded like a theatrical disaster waiting to happen.

31

New York, Apr 4, 2002

But for the absence of crucifixes, Brice's storage space might have been the set for a surrealistic resurrection film, something out of a David Lynch or a Peter Greenaway fantasy. There were enormous colored eggs everywhere. Brice put a few of these away for next Easter, next to a stack of oversized sateen egg baskets. Sorting through a mound of returned pieces, he set aside two baroque bunnies. Storage was for the timeless pieces that were difficult to acquire or create. The dumpster turned into an anonymous mass grave for the trendy bunnies and eggs.

This part of the window dressing business, the storage and inventory of props, bored Brice. He wanted to hire a helper for this mindless task, except it wasn't quite mindless. An assistant would be hard-pressed to know what would come in handy next year or the year after without good design sense and practical experience. When Brice inherited the business, inventory took one long day. Now, it took up to a week. Surveying the inventory, all he wanted was to put on leotards, blast Miles Davis on the boombox, and improvise a dance with the oversized inanimate objects.

An hour into the day's tasks, Brice came across plastic crates for milk bottles brimming with delicate papier-mâché rabbits. They had a sentimental value to Brice. These particular rabbits were fabricated during a *Día de los Muertos* vacation to Guadalajara. The *fábrica* he'd found there was so good at making anything, he'd kept it a business secret.

The precious *conejos* needed to be stored where nothing could mangle them, preferably up high. Brice secured a ladder next to a high shelf. One by one, he placed the rabbits on the shelf that looked more spacious from below than it turned out once atop the ladder. The colony didn't quite fit its warren, requiring Brice to balance several fragile bunny props on top of others. As the crates emptied and the shelf overfilled, as Brice balanced the penultimate bunny precariously, the phone in his office rang. He let go of the wobbly papier-mâché object and climbed down. In his office, he picked up the phone.

"I'm about to burn my self-portraits," Peter said without a salutation.

"Slow down, buddy." As Brice sat at his desk, a synchronicity dawned on him. Waking up that morning, he'd fantasized about Peter. "Funny, I was going to call you, but it was too early."

"I'm using these fucking self-portraits for a bonfire at the beach."

"What self-portraits?"

"Erica wants to put up a show of my new work," Peter answered. "She wants a 9/11 anniversary show featuring me, ostensibly because art saved my life. The only new paintings I have are these self-portraits I'm beginning to detest."

"September isn't so far away." This conversation was different from the one Brice imagined waking up, lollygagging in his cozy bed. "Your self-portraits must be good. After all, they feature you."

"They have nothing to do with 9/11," Peter said. "They have nothing to do with New York. They make no sense for a 9/11 anniversary show. I don't even like them."

"You haven't painted anything else?" Brice asked. This call wasn't going to be about pleasure.

"I told myself to paint something, anything," Peter replied. "With these self-portraits, I painted myself into an emotional corner."

Then there was one of those silences that happened with Peter. Well, he'd painted something, even if he hated it. How bad could it be? Brice twirled the curly phone cord around his pinky, thinking of some way to encourage Peter. As much as Brice missed dancing, the world hardly noticed when he stopped. Hundreds and thousands of lithe boys followed in his footsteps. In Brice's estimation, though, the world was worse off without Peter's art. Twirl, untwirl. Sometimes it was better to wait out these silences, force Peter to reveal what he didn't want to discuss. There were, however, only so many times Brice could wrap and unwrap the curly phone cord around his pinky.

"It's Rano's stupid journal," Peter said at last. "What's left of it, anyway. I can't find answers for all the questions I have. I feel like I didn't know who I was living with, like he didn't respect me, and now it's too late."

"Did Rano write something in particular that bothers you?" Brice asked, relieved that Peter brought up the journal so he didn't have to.

"He kept a big secret from me," Peter answered. "Like he didn't trust me."

"You know that Rano loved you," Brice said. "I imagine it's tough to read things you didn't know about Rano, but that doesn't mean he didn't love you."

"I blew it with Rano," Peter said. "I was so selfish about my painting, I kept him from his work. I kept him from so much more. I read the journal and all I see is missed opportunities for us. I kept us from moving to New York. Now when I paint, I feel like I'm slapping Rano in the face, demeaning his memory, declaring again that my painting is more important than his life."

Over the phone, Brice heard Peter start crying and then covering up the handset so Brice wouldn't hear. Peter was opening up, revealing more about Rano's journal than before, although it wasn't clear exactly what it was that bothered him so much. Brice stopped playing with the phone cord. Peter's reaction to Rano's journal seemed a bit overboard. Of course Rano didn't tell Peter everything. If diaries didn't hold secrets, they wouldn't need clasps and locks.

"Listen," Brice said at last, "it sounds like you could use a change in scenery. If you're painting about 9/11, why don't you visit New York? You know you're welcome at my place any time."

"That's sweet of you," Peter said, uncovering his handset. "But I have to stay in the studio and work. Erica gave me a deadline."

"At least, join me on Fire Island," Brice said. Sharing a place smack-dab on the Atlantic seemed like an appropriate way to celebrate a healthy year. No friends had died of AIDS in recent memory. Island fever was back. A share would be more fun with Peter. Potentially, much more fun. "My business has been great—an embarrassment of riches, really, after 9/11—so I'm taking a share for the season. Join me for a week or two and clear your mind."

"You know I'm still skittish about flying, but it's tempting."

Brice and Peter continued on for a time about everything in general and nothing in particular, Brice giving Peter one opportunity after the next to talk about romance. Peter seemed distracted and unable to focus until he ended the call abruptly. He'd forgotten he was supposed to meet Linh at an S&M club. As strange as that sounded at this hour, Brice didn't ask questions. He nudged Peter once more to visit Fire Island.

After they hung up, Brice returned to the storage area. Shit. He looked beneath the sky-high warren. A dozen rabbits had tumbled to their papier-mâché deaths. Brice knelt to collect the remains. At least if he couldn't repair them, his secret place in Guadalajara could fabricate new ones.

As Brice examined the lifeless bunny pieces, other secrets came to mind, the secrets Rano told him on his deathbed, the secret of having a son, the more unbelievable secret that Carl somehow abused this son. The final secret Rano gasped was that his son lived in Orem. That made no sense. Orem was Brice's hometown. Eventually Brice attributed these secrets to deathbed delirium, but maybe it wasn't delirium, maybe these secrets were explained in the diary. Any of them could debilitate Peter emotionally. There wasn't time before Rano died to ask why he wanted to keep his son secret. Rano's journal must have revealed something unnerving, something about the secrets Brice kept. Rano had to have written about his son.

March 15, 1991 – Betrayal

Dear Mustafa,

Beware the Ides of March.

I want to teach you, Mustafa, a thing or two about Caesar, partly because you should know the history, mostly because, in spite of our fabulous toga parties of yore, Peter appreciates neither Rome nor his betrayal of me.

The Ides of March is a day of treachery. I should have no fear of dying. I am no Caesar, no great commander of armies, no absolute dictator. Why would anyone betray a mere professor?

I certainly cannot change the calendar by snapping my fingers, as Caesar did. Wouldn't that be a fabulous superpower? I would make myself eighteen again, disappear Carl from our lives, regain my vigor, watch you grow.

The only thing I control are these pages. Even those I'm not so sure about. I'm stuck at home today, so bored that I'm commanding myself to write to you about Caesar, even if it kills me.

For the record, I lectured on Caesar, examining how Shakespeare rearranged Plutarch's history to create a fiction about power and corruption. Shakespearean English is a bitch. At least, Plutarch has modern translations.

The comparison to Plutarch reveals Shakespeare's intent. That's a hallmark of my research, comparison of things. What's important to me about Caesar is entirely different from what's important to Shakespeare. The bard examines how absolute power corrupts absolutely.

Allow me to compare Caesar's power to mine.

My realm, Mustafa, is quite compact compared to Caesar's. It is a classroom of ethics where my few fawning plebes are students and my hodgepodge government consists mainly of overqualified faculty and overpaid administrators. I am, if I may say so myself, a benevolent dictator. My orations are lively, interactive, inquisitive, and occasionally, against the wishes of the government, accompanied by celebratory food and music.

Food and music disrupt study, say the administrators. It helps education succeed memorably, say I. The administrators want to limit my power but cut me some slack because even they have figured out how groundbreaking my research is. I promise repeatedly I will serve less food and play less music, although I forget to mention I'm uncertain when. The people rejoice, eating well, drinking, and singing in the reign.

Like my administrators, the Roman Senate wanted to limit Caesar's power. When he was my age, the Senate handed him walking papers. Caesar chose instead to march, bringing along a single legion of his soldiers. They crossed the Rubicon and challenged his friend, his former son-in-law, and finally his political rival Pompey. Although vastly outnumbered, Caesar put Pompey on the run, consolidating power as he chased Pompey through Spain, Greece, and Egypt.

Egypt.

Egypt, where King Ptolemy arranged Pompey's stabbing and presented noble Pompey's head to a sorrowful Caesar. Egypt, where a twenty-year-old Cleopatra seduced a fifty-one-year-old Caesar; she in need of his forces to thwart Ptolemy, he in need of her wealth to pay the staff. Egypt, a hop, skip, and jump over the Mediterranean to Algeria.

Algeria.

Algeria, where fifty-four-year-old Caesar lost a third of his troops putting down insurrections, two years before the Roman senators would put him down. Those were the days when battles were up close and personal, where soldiers smelled the blood and shit of the vanquished. Nothing like today's televised wars, enjoyed from the lavender-scented comfort of home.

Algeria, where Caesar's earliest political rival, Sulla, had made his name thirty years prior by convincing King Bocchus of Mauretania to arrest his Berber son-in-law, King Jugurtha of Numidia, an on-again, off-again Roman enemy. After parading the prized Jugurtha through the streets of Rome, Sulla got a big promotion. For his part, Bocchus got Numidia, not far from where you were conceived, dear Mustafa, not so far from the shores where Carl and I would meet two millennia later.

I didn't learn this last part about Algeria from Plutarch. I saw the ruins, locals told me the history. Carl impressed me one afternoon with stories of Jugurtha's treachery while his hands explored my netherlands. Carl had a thing for tyrants.

In truth, my power has more in common with Cleopatra's than Caesar's. At twenty, Cleopatra knew Caesar would get her Egypt. At twenty, I knew Carl would get me

America. It's just that Cleopatra had ways to keep control of the situation. I may have had Cleopatra's talents, but she had better options.

I digress.

When Caesar was my age, he had six more glorious years before his friends stabbed him in the back. He must have been full of himself not to see it coming. I, glorious professor of ethics, on the other hand, I am suffering from a death sentence delivered up the ass. Caesar has no idea what a blessing his quick death was. In the midst of this fucking crisis, I would be ecstatic to have half as many years remaining as Caesar, to have enough time to finish my research, to finish my book, to find you, Mustafa.

Peter refuses to test, so I don't know if he infected me. It wasn't Carl. That was too long ago, before the pandemic. But that's beside the point. There were others.

It is Peter, though, who has stabbed me in the back, in a manner of speaking. I'm not referring to his prosecution of Carl. He kept me from finding you, Mustafa, but he doesn't know that. I'm referring to his art. Peter kept me from my power, kept me from my best work, in order to do his. He says his work is ready now, but no gallery, no show, no significant sales. Not only will I die without finding you, I may die without publishing my groundbreaking work.

My power is more durable than Caesar's. Caesar's power is muscle, mine knowledge. I can see the future of digital identity; I foresee the danger of its theft. Like Cassandra, I'm helpless to warn the world. Peter has taken my power. He betrayed me, betrayed our relationship. Not on purpose, otherwise I would have left already.

Et tu, Peter?

32

SAN FRANCISCO, APR 4, 2002

Linh walked down the stairs to a subterranean S&M space equipped for even the most esoteric of fetishes. She was evaluating Safeword, San Francisco's new bondage-by-the-hour club. There were perhaps a dozen stations spread uniformly across the floor, all visible to one another, each with its own system of restraints. One station featured an examination table with stirrups. Another enabled a dom to secure a sub to a steel frame in a variety of positions. By comparison, the leather sling hanging in the corner looked rather pedestrian. It was eleven o'clock in the morning, so no one was there besides Linh. The sales rep, a dyke with orange spiky hair and serious nose piercings, had outlined the basic membership options and waited upstairs for other prospects. Linh examined a cart loaded with whips that could be wheeled to any of the stations for a reasonable upcharge. She would bring her favorite switch when she came here, of course, but it was a useful amenity if she forgot.

Peter was a no-show. Safeword was only a few blocks from his studio. He'd told Linh he'd never been inside and was curious to view it. After fifteen minutes upstairs waiting for Peter, there wasn't much more Linh could think of to ask the sales rep. Linh was disappointed that Peter hadn't joined her, but excited nonetheless to tour the downstairs.

Peter had never shown much interest in S&M beyond his annual excursions to the Folsom Street Fair. Some years he hosted a gathering at his studio, providing friends a convenient place to change from street clothes into leather drag. Most years he walked the block to the fairground wearing nothing other than a jockstrap and high leather boots. As far as Linh could tell, Peter still could pull off that look if he wanted, still could have everyone swooning, gathering close enough for a grope shot.

People sometimes had strange reactions to S&M. Linh was pretty sure Peter's absence this morning wasn't because he was avoiding some perversion that creeped him out. All Linh got was busy signals when she tried calling earlier. More likely he'd overslept. Folsom Street seemed to satisfy Peter's basic S&M cravings. Still, Linh had been surprised at S&M

sessions, when someone she didn't expect to show up got into it completely, or when someone she thought would get into it completely didn't show up. Not that she and Peter had planned on any activity this morning, but still.

Linh walked past the bathtub over to the cage. She wasn't intrigued by watersports or scat, but cage play wearing leather chaps and dog masks was beyond titillating with the right partner. Or partners. Caged canines forced to touch each other wherever and whenever Linh commanded, forced to sniff each other, lick one another. Sometimes it went all the way. Those sessions became Linh's treasured fantasies for months and years. Linh had analyzed her own excitement. She wasn't stupid. She knew it had something to do with working out her Vietnam shit, processing an indecipherable desire for control. Sometimes the excitement of cage play overwhelmed her. Her heart thumped so wildly she had to bring the session to a head prematurely. It was an exquisite excitement she didn't share with anyone, not even her therapist.

Looking around the space, Safeword seemed too good to be true. Linh's experience of sadomasochism in New York was completely different from her experience after returning to San Francisco. The cities had different attitudes about fetish. Sure, New York had its late-night clubs and back rooms, but San Francisco celebrated fetish in broad daylight with an enormous street fair, a half-million people gawking or being gawked at along a half dozen of Folsom Street's city blocks. Safeword removed the stigma of S&M. With different fittings, Safeword might as well have been a boutique grocery. Here, at this station, are the cheeses, and over there the handcuffs, and that station has a nice variety of fruits and vibrators. San Francisco treated S&M as though it were a healthy main course at an exciting restaurant filled with outrageously dressed diners.

Returning to the sales rep, Linh stopped halfway up the stairs. She had wanted Peter to see this space with her. They would have giggled about a few of the contraptions, fantasizing out loud about the possible antics of doms and subs in a barber chair or on a dancing pole. Linh wondered if she would tell Peter about her puppy fetish, about the encounters she'd had, how they excited her. It was a dark side she wasn't comfortable exposing, but she knew it would be safe to tell Peter, and good for Peter to hear it.

Peter's absence bothered Linh more now. Looking over the subterranean space, she realized that she'd wanted him here so he'd see how S&M affected her. Sure, that was selfish, but how else could she help Peter? He needed a push down the path to change. His self-portraits weren't cutting it. Unlike the self-portraits of artists she'd met in New York, Peter's seemed too obvious to Linh, obvious in the way they allowed Peter to fool himself that he was moving forward when, in fact, he was avoiding the hard work of change. The self-portraits looked to Linh like nothing more than busywork.

Change never came for free. For Linh, it came with significant discomfort, if not outright pain. Puppy play was difficult as well as titillating or, perhaps, titillating because of its difficulties. In the midst of its power dynamics, it forced her to confront her losses, her unhappiness. Even if change for Peter didn't involve S&M, Linh had hoped the S&M Disneyland she was surveying below would inspire Peter to find his own medium for change.

Peter's absence this morning elevated Linh's anxiety about his New York remark, that a change of scenery might be good for him. It was selfish of her to be anxious about Peter leaving, but he was one of the main attractions of her return to San Francisco. She worried that Peter might not even be aware that a move to New York was another way to avoid his issues with Rano and with the journal. A New York move could turn out to be just another diversion like the self-portraits. But maybe she was projecting her desires on Peter.

If Peter moved to New York, Linh would mourn another extended absence from him. During his absence at Safeword, a hollowness had filled Linh, the horrible hollowness that haunted her life. Starting with her parents, absence shaped Linh's interior. She was tired of one absence following another and upset by Peter's no-show and now more upset by the possibility of his move to New York. No amount of puppy play would compensate for more absence.

It was out of her hands. Maybe a move to New York was exactly the change Peter needed to move past his issues with Rano. If she understood more about those issues, she might know. At least, she had enough money now to visit New York whenever she pleased. Perhaps it would be better for Peter to be close to Brice. Linh always wondered why those two hadn't hitched their wagons.

As Linh turned to continue her ascent up the stairs, she heard Peter's voice. He was chatting with the sales rep with spiky orange hair. Happiness flooded the horrible hollowness inside Linh.

"Sorry I'm late," Peter said, turning from the sales rep to hug Linh. "I was blabbing with Brice and lost track of time."

"Talking with Brice is a decent excuse," Linh said after she let go of Peter. "Are you moving in together?"

"I decided to stay in San Francisco," Peter answered. "I have to get a show ready for Erica. I don't have time to set up a new studio in New York. Anyway, how am I going to afford New York rent?"

Linh was even happier to hear Peter was staying, although he didn't sound entirely enthusiastic about this decision. She liked this growing feeling of happiness. On the other hand, she didn't like Peter spending more time apart from Brice. She also didn't want to depend on Peter, or anyone else, to feel happy. Safeword was a place she could learn to find happiness within herself.

"You know I kept my New York apartment," Linh said. "You can stay there for free as long as you'd like."

"Oh, wow," Peter said. "That's kind of you. I'd love to take your offer, but I need to work in my studio to make Erica's deadline."

"Well, I can't solve all your problems," Linh said, "but Erica must know about good studio space in New York."

"Funny you should mention that," Peter said. "Erica said Thomas would let me use a space in one of his buildings, a space with skyline views to inspire my painting."

"So what's the problem?" Linh asked, wondering not only what possibly could cause Peter to decline such a great offer, but also whether the well-dressed art collector had eyes on Peter. "Thomas or New York?"

"It's a bit awkward with Thomas," Peter answered. "I feel like I owe him so much already."

Linh knew from Peter's answer that he would find the change he needed in New York. All the resources he needed there were available. The excuses he was making to stay in San Francisco were just that, excuses.

"If you're painting a show about 9/11," Linh said, "the obvious place to paint it is New York."

Peter was quiet. Linh didn't have more time to wait for Peter today. As per usual, he was lost in his thoughts. Linh realized that Safeword was the place for her to explore change, not the place for Peter. She couldn't force him to New York, but she could encourage him.

"Can you show me around?" Peter asked. "The equipment here looks amazing."

"I'd love to," Linh replied, "but I'm late for a fitting."

APRIL 2, 1991 – ANGER

Dear Mustafa,

Nancy from SF State phoned to ask if I would teach fall term. That's not why she called, though. She really wanted to know if I'm well enough to research. They must have landed funding. Did that Silicon Valley guy come through? Nancy sounded relieved when I said I'm still writing.

I'm angry at Peter. I'm angry because I depend on him and he will survive me. I've seen this anger in other men who are approaching the end. It doesn't make my anger go away.

I'm also angry at Peter because we didn't move to New York. Maybe that's why I'm angry. Sometimes unsure. I should be angry at myself for staying here.

So many things going wrong in my body. Getting those headaches again, like just before my brain inflammation. Told Peter this morning. I got mad about it. He sighed and held my hand. He wants me to see the doc. He's right.

33

NEW YORK, APR 7, 2002

Mark sat in the same chair at the same table in the same East Village cafe where he'd met Erica last. Miniature cyclones formed outside in the brisk spring wind, swirling a newspaper and leaves in a dance across the sidewalk. Mark had asked Erica to meet him there. He could have chosen any restaurant in New York, but he thought it important to acknowledge their last meeting didn't go well, to continue where they left off. Erica had provided an excellent example of her volatility at that aborted meeting and Mark meant her to consider it. He didn't plan to discuss it explicitly. He would order the same breakfast, the lumberjack breakfast, and this time she would watch as he ate it. She was smart. She would figure out what he was up to.

Erica arrived, cheeks ruddy, hair disheveled from the wind. The first few minutes after she sat down at the table were awkward. Other than scheduling this meeting, the only communication between Mark and Erica since they'd met here had been the impersonal package of floppy disks, the same floppies now stacked on the table. Erica and Mark exchanged pleasantries, complained about how extraordinarily cold this particular spring season seemed, agreed that the few days it warmed up were even more miserable because of the humidity, and then studied their menus in silence.

On this weekday morning, the cafe was quiet. The only waiter was slow to reach their table. Mark ordered the lumberjack breakfast.

"Would you mind sharing that?" Erica asked.

Mark was surprised. Already things weren't going as planned. However, it seemed a small concession. Mark agreed. The waiter sauntered to the kitchen to place their order.

"I've been craving pancakes and eggs," Erica said. "Splitting a serving is perfect since I'm on a diet."

"You look fine," Mark said.

In fact, Erica never looked better. Mark caught himself staring at her. Her figure put his dating abstinence program at risk. The only activities on his mind when he'd set up this meeting were a breakfast chat and the return of the floppy disks. Her animal magnetism, a magnetism that never seemed to wear thin, was rearing its head. He sat forward so it wouldn't be so obvious.

"So, how are things with Jodie?" Erica asked.

"Jodie?" Another unexpected turn. "Um, there was never anything with Jodie. I should have apologized before. Someone hijacked my account and sent those emails."

"What?!"

Watching Erica quietly work through the implications of his disclosure, Mark realized he didn't want to work through it with her. Stick with light banter and returning the floppies.

"So, how's your dating life?" Mark asked, convincing himself his only intent was to change topics.

"Nothing special," Erica replied, looking up. "Met someone I liked who ended up moving to San Francisco. Seemed more like sisterly love, really."

"Oh, I see," Mark said, suppressing his interest. Sisterly love? What did that mean? They'd only teased about sexuality. It never crossed Mark's mind that Erica might be bisexual. This was supposed to be a friendly little chat, not some Book of Revelation. Mark sipped ice water to cool any incipient sexual fantasies.

"Thanks for bringing the floppies," Erica said after another silence. "Did you find anything?"

"Nothing," Mark answered, sliding the floppies toward Erica.

From the disappointment in Erica's demeanor, Mark understood these disks had more significance than he expected. The note she sent with the disks indicated that she was helping the artist from San Francisco, or perhaps that she thought the contents of the disks might provide an insight into her own life. As he thought about her note now, he was less and less sure why Erica wanted to know what was on these disks. Regardless of her motivation, the leeway she provided Mark to decline her request to examine the disks implied disappointment would not be a consequence.

"I didn't find anything because I didn't look," Mark continued. "I've been too busy with research."

"I thought you'd finished your postdoc," Erica said. "It's vital to find what's on these disks."

"I have a new project," Mark said. "My research is due soon. Even if I thought I could help, I don't have the time right now."

Then Erica told Mark about Rano, Peter, and the floppy disks. When she'd visited Peter at his gallery in San Francisco in February, Erica noticed how Peter kept Rano's journal, or what was left of the journal, in a special place, on a shelf above his desk, next to his sketches of the New York skyline. This journal was an obsession that had become a roadblock. Something in it stopped him from painting.

"I asked myself what it would take to get Peter painting again." Erica said. "The poor guy is emotionally paralyzed. I don't see any way he'll be able to paint until he has a conversation with Rano about the journal, except how can he have a conversation with notes from a dead man?"

"But you have plenty of other artists," Mark said.

"Peter is talented beyond belief," Erica said. "It's just that he can't bring himself to paint. That's not completely true. He did paint these odd self-portraits. They seem all wrong to me, too self-absorbed. He's reflecting on himself. His self-portraiture looks more like art therapy than art."

"Wasn't Peter supposed to be on that flight that crashed?" Mark asked. "Maybe that's why he can't paint."

"Whatever is blocking him, that missed flight is exactly the reason a 9/11 anniversary show by Peter would sell out in a heartbeat," Erica replied, fidgeting with the rubber band that bound the stack of floppies. "Anyway, I asked him what's on the floppy disks next to Rano's journal. Well, that got him going. Peter went on about Rano's writing, about how smart Rano was, about Rano's disappointment never publishing his book. 'The world never had a chance to appreciate Rano's brilliance,' Peter said to me. 'No one except Rano could finish that book.' When Peter said that, I realized he needed someone, anyone, to read Rano's words."

"If Rano was that good, I'm sure you'll find someone to read these floppies."

"If Peter knew Rano's words had been freed from the magnetic bonds of these disks, knew that just one person had read and appreciated what Rano discovered, it would lift a weight off Peter's shoulders. Peter would have the sort of spiritual reconciliation he needs to paint again."

Mark wasn't sure what to think about this story. When he first opened the package Erica mailed, he suspected her actual agenda was to start dating again. However, her story was sincere. Of course, she was helping Peter because Peter would help her gallery. She had walls crying for inventory. Her concern about Peter seemed genuine, though, not motivated by money, as though she herself were learning something from the disks. It was a nurturing side of Erica he rarely saw. After all, Mark thought, there could be something to these disks, something that warranted their examination. Nevertheless, he had a deadline.

The waiter returned, placing the coffee and the lumberjack breakfast on the table. The food smelled as good as Mark remembered. It was nice to share it with Erica, much better than eating alone. He didn't want to talk about the disks anymore. He opened one of the small plastic containers and stirred sterilized cream into his coffee.

"How is your gallery?" Mark asked. "You have a new show up."

"I had a show by a young Vietnamese artist that just came down," Erica answered. "Perhaps too young, but I see a talent in her. Her work is strong."

"Didn't your father serve in Vietnam?"

"Yes, he did." Erica said, poking her fork at the pancakes. "I suppose that's a reason I'm interested in this artist."

Erica chewed on a bite of pancake. After Mark's questions, she kept chewing, She seemed lost in thought. Mark waited to hear more about the show. When they'd dated, Erica told him the backstories of her shows, whom the artist was diddling when he painted a piece, how an artist stole these elements or those subjects from this artist or that, why the relationship of the visual elements wouldn't work any other way.

"The strangest thing happened," Erica said after she swallowed. "One of Peter's friends stops by the gallery to see if I have any of his works left. She's wearing this outlandish outfit. She spends a lot of time looking at the art. She's mesmerized. After I tell her the show is by a Vietnamese artist, she tells me that she herself is Vietnamese. Right as she says this, a shiver shoots up my spine. I can't figure out why. It's something about the way she looks, but I can't place it. I ask her if she'd like coffee and, while I'm pouring a cup, I remember her eyes. They're blue."

"Blue?" Mark asked, wondering if this gallery visitor was Erica's sisterly love. "As in, her father's a soldier?"

"The same blue as my father's eyes."

— ???

M ustafa,
Not sure where I am. Found journal. Confused.
Free Algeria!

34

SAN FRANCISCO, APR 11, 2002

During the past week, the same depressing scene repeated itself every day at the studio. Peter slipped a recording into the music player and squeezed fresh colors on a palette. Some days it was the classical or jazz music Brice gave Rano, other days it was Queen, The Cure, or another random recording from the stash at home. While music played, Peter stared at the blank canvas. The skyline sketches lay on the table for inspiration. By the time the wet paint on the palette dried, Peter knew it wasn't the day to start painting.

When the paint on the palette dried on this particular day, Peter did something different. He phoned Thomas. It was Thomas to whom Peter had promised the paintings of the New York skyline, and it was Thomas he wanted to ask about painting something different. He didn't need Thomas' permission. He'd already painted the self-portraits. Peter liked Thomas a lot, respected his wisdom. Thomas thought through things, weighed the alternatives, came to a decision with an appreciation of its implications.

"It's nice to hear from you," Thomas said. "I was thinking about you yesterday. Well, I think of you most days because I'm enjoying your landscapes."

"I'm glad you like those," Peter said, surprised Thomas picked up. He wanted to discuss alternatives to skyline paintings with Thomas but hadn't thought through any actual alternatives before calling. What Peter usually remembered about Thomas was how kind Thomas had been after the flood in the studio. All that came to mind now, though, was the series of Armistead Maupin interactions he had with Thomas, a series of silly interactions that fed on themselves during Thomas' trip to San Francisco. Both of them had been adolescent about that.

"To what do I owe the pleasure of your call today?" Thomas asked after a bit.

"I made you a promise," Peter answered.

"Yes, I'm so excited," Thomas said. "Erica told me you'll show new New York skyline paintings for a 9/11 memorial show at her gallery."

"I know," Peter said, looking at the blank canvas across the studio. How did he get himself into this predicament?

"That didn't sound very enthusiastic," Thomas said. "Are you stuck again?"

"Yes," Peter said. Armistead Maupin kept going through his head. It kept him from thinking of a way to ask about painting. "You know that time I said I would invite Armistead to join us at my studio?"

There was an awkward silence on the phone. Peter sensed Thomas was just as embarrassed about the Armistead Maupin stories they'd made up.

"Of course." Thomas cleared his throat.

"I wanted to let you know that, while I've met Armistead, I don't actually know him well enough to invite him to my studio."

"Thank you for saying that," Thomas said. "I embellished my story about Armistead, too. I guess we both did. I wanted to impress you. Instead I ended up feeling uncomfortable."

"Did you eat dinner with Armistead?" Peter asked, wondering why he couldn't let go of the whole episode, and then realizing he would like to hear Thomas admit once more how much he wanted to impress Peter.

"Let's just say that my late lover was great at breaking the ice with strangers," Thomas said. "I don't have that knack."

"I'm the same," Peter said. "I guess that's why I paint."

"So, what do you want to paint?" Thomas asked. "If you don't mind me asking."

"That's just it," Peter said. "I'm stuck. I need to change up my direction. That's what I wanted to talk to you about."

"Okay," Thomas said. "I'm not sure how I can help you, except to say that, as much as I would like to see how you transform your skyline sketches into paintings, I would never hold an artist to a promise about what to paint."

"My friends tell me I need a change of scenery," Peter said. "They say I should go to New York to paint New York skylines. They're probably right, but I've never painted anywhere besides my studio. It's comfortable for me here."

There was another silence, a longer silence than before. Peter wasn't used to other people's silence during a conversation. This time he had no idea what Thomas was thinking about. Maybe Thomas was waiting for him to say something. The silence was becoming uncomfortable. Looking again at the blank canvas, Peter wondered if his friends felt this uncomfortable when he was this quiet.

"This is what worries me," Thomas said at last. "Perhaps I shouldn't say this, but I worry that if you paint something else, you're simply avoiding whatever it is that keeps you from painting the New York skylines."

Of course Thomas was right. Peter had known when he phoned that Thomas would say something useful. Peter's friends were telling him to go to New York. Thomas gave him the reason to go. He was good at helping Peter find clarity. The main thing Peter lacked if he painted his skyline project in New York was a studio he could work in.

"You're so quiet sometimes," Thomas said. "Did something I said offend you?"

"Quite the contrary," Peter replied. "I was thinking about how to ask a favor. When Erica visited, she said you had a perfect studio space. It's in a building with views of Manhattan's skyline."

"Oh, yes, that," Thomas said. "Well, Erica is right. It has great views, but it's tricky to offer you that space because I'm negotiating a deal there. I could offer you a bedroom at my place or at one of my unoccupied apartments. You might be able to work in one of those."

"That's very kind of you." With the previous offers of living space from Brice and Linh, Peter had plenty of housing options. That wasn't the problem, although if he wanted to get to know Thomas better, a penthouse bedroom would be a nice perk. "I don't know if I can go to New York and paint in just any apartment. Having the skylines to inspire me would be useful, but the right lighting is critical."

"I understand," Thomas said. "The building Erica is talking about has great light. It's just that there's a complicated and rather significant deal I'm working on there."

"Brice's place is small, but I suppose the lighting would work," Peter said. "That has great views, too."

"Well, let me see what I can do," Thomas said. "My attorney is negotiating the deal. If we can work out something, I'll let you know."

MAY 15, 1991 – BETTER

Dear Mustafa,

Writing easier now. Brain inflammation brutal. Second time. Don't remember parts of hospital stay. Look at diary. Still can't remember all that happened. Trying. Trying. Tiring.

Get angry now. Don't know why. Just happens. Fuck, fuck, fuck.

At least writing easier. Couldn't hold pen sometimes. Fucking pen pisses me off. Didn't know how to think sometimes. Peter tells me things happened. Don't remember. Did not hit nurse. Liar. Peter is a liar.

Please don't lose mind. Please. Fuck. Keep writing. Keep sane. Must take journal to hospital next time. Remember stuff.

Home again. Good. Can't find stuff. Where are foot things? Can't go outside anyway. Get lost. Know I'm home. Feet cold here.

Doc says it'll get better. Says mind will work. Like writing again. Holding pen. Drawing stuff. It's cool.

Naked boy walked into house this morning. Wanted to fuck. Didn't tell Peter. Shhhhh. Don't always know stuff. Not sure who. Was it Peter?

Want to go outside. Don't know why Peter won't let me. Makes me mad. ANGRY! FUCK PETER. Tells me to write. Fuck him. Hard to write. Can't write. Stop now.

35

San Francisco, Apr 21, 2002

Angel couldn't remember. The days ran together in spite of sobriety. On the subway to meet Peter for dinner, he was trying to remember. It had been like, what, two or three months since the weird meeting at Peter's studio where he interrupted Peter's naked painting? Two or three months since he fucked up and got drunk, missed the celebration he'd planned for Peter?

Angel disembarked Muni Metro at Church Street and ascended to a dark evening fog. The cold, moist air blanketed his arms and legs. He scurried across Market Street to reach the warmth of Chow. Peter was waiting at a table in the back. Angel sat down and shivered. He couldn't warm up. Or he was nervous. Or both.

"Are you high?" Peter asked.

"No," Angel answered, lowering his eyes. Then he remembered. It was New Year's Eve he'd fucked up. Angel had asked Peter to celebrate the miracle that he'd rescheduled his flight, the flight that nosedived in a Pennsylvania field. So that made it more than three months since he messed up. Three months of shitty AA meetings practicing his apologies to Peter. "Sober for almost four months."

"You've got goosebumps from your knees to your ass," Peter said. "Why are you wearing shorts in April?"

That, cabrón, is a good question, Angel thought to himself. Okay, wanted to be attractive. Was that like a crime or something? Too gordo to wear a tight shirt. How about showing some leg? Yeah? No. Goosebumps everywhere. How attractive. Fucked up. Again. Typical.

"Here," Peter said, handing Angel his jacket. "You need to warm up."

Angel wanted to leave. This was beyond humiliating, the only person for miles wearing shorts. He looked like a puta. Living sober, working in the bakery, holed up in his Tenderloin room like a hermit, these were things that were not helping him socialize. It had been so hard to call Peter, to apologize again on the phone, to make this date.

"Thanks," Angel said, taking Peter's green bomber jacket. The warmth felt nice. "It's been almost four months, and there isn't a day I don't feel bad about messing up with you."

"I know that," Peter said. "I worried about you."

These words were like love syrup dripping into Angel's ears, running all the way down to his heart, melting his soul. He couldn't remember what it sounded like to have someone care about him—without offering a drink. As his goosebumps smoothed, he kept his expectations in check. Just because Peter worried about him didn't mean wedding bells. It was nice, though, hearing Peter say this. It wasn't one of those coke-induced declarations of love whose primary intent is another snort. The words came from Peter's heart.

"At least someone has been feeding you," Peter said after a bit.

Ugh. Why did Peter say this? Now the bomber jacket felt snug. Uncomfortably snug. Snug like it made him look fat. How many thousands of conchas and orejas had he baked since he got sober again? Pobrecito Angel tried focusing on the menu. He'd developed his first ever panza. His midlife crisis made a crash landing on his stomach. The abdomen that once was the six-pack everyone admired had grown into a keg everyone ignored. Fat and sober. If he could just be happy. Angel wanted to give the jacket back to Peter. Instead he pushed his menu away. A drink would be great right now. Angel hated this fragile vulnerability. Each word felt like a step through a field of emotional landmines. Make love, not war, as Rano once said.

"Hazard of the trade," Angel said.

The waiter came to take their order. Peter asked for chicken soup and Thai noodles. Angel said he wasn't hungry. The waiter hurried off to a table complaining obnoxiously about cold food.

"Sure you don't want something?" Peter asked. "I'm paying."

"As you noticed, I eat too much at the bakery," Angel replied. Okay, that was muy estúpido. It was just that Angel, after calling attention to himself with these shortest of pink shorts, didn't want so much attention. What would he tell Peter about, anyway? His dawn commute to the bakery with the drunks sleeping on the bus? His new roommate, the television? "Tell me what's been going on with you."

"Not much," Peter said. "I finished that set of self-portraits. Haven't painted anything else for a few weeks. Can't find the energy, the interest. No muse."

"That's not good," Angel said. He knew what that meant. He knew Rano's journal was still a problem. "You've got something I don't have, which is talent. You should use it."

"Why do you sell yourself short like that?" Peter asked, looking past Angel.

"You're thinking of the me you know from our drug days," Angel said. "We said all kinds of crazy shit. We were going to conquer the world. I'm a baker now. I bake bread and pastries. That's my talent. It's not so special."

"I knew you from before the drugs," Peter said. He picked up his empty wine glass and rolled it between his hands. "I know there is something special inside you."

It was comfortable talking with Peter tonight. It had been a long time since they'd had a sober face-to-face. Well, there was that weird meeting at the studio when Angel brought flowers. Peter was a little distant tonight after a glass of wine, but that was nothing compared to their booze and coke sessions. Peter spoke to Angel differently now. His tone was thoughtful.

"Do you ever wish we could go back?" Angel asked. "You know, before AIDS, before our boyfriends died."

"That seems so distant, further than ever," Peter replied. "I mean, there are some things I'd like to ask Rano. But all of us were different people then."

Angel wanted to know what questions Peter would ask Rano. Rano was like a father to Peter. Peter took Rano's words seriously. Angel knew the journal had to make Peter feel inadequate. How would Peter move forward without getting answers to his questions?

"Do you want another glass of wine?" Angel asked. "I'm having one."

"You know you can't drink wine." Peter looked Angel in the eye.

"I'm tired of this baking shit," Angel said. "Tired of riding to work in a bus full of drunks. Tired of spending evenings with the television when I return to my room."

"What are you talking about?" Peter asked, putting down his wine glass. "You're going to start drinking and snorting again? Asking for a third strike is lame."

"And fuck you, too, for not painting," Angel said, a smile filling his face. "Of course I'm not ordering wine. Why are you not painting?"

"I'm going to New York to paint," Peter replied. "Leaving next month."

"Is that the end for us?" Angel asked after he caught his breath. This was news he didn't expect. His primary support system was splitting town. "I mean, can I come visit you?"

"I don't know any more than that," Peter answered, "but I have to go to New York to paint."

The waiter brought soup for Peter. Peter handed the waiter his glass, declining more wine. After the waiter withdrew, the conversation paused while Peter ate his soup. His slurping noise both annoyed and charmed Angel. The gurgling in Angel's stomach, however, was annoying, but not charming. It protested for a tardy dinner order, even if such an order were to expand his paunch and diminish his pride. Angel slid his menu close enough to read. It would be embarrassing to call for the waiter after his obstinate assertion that he wasn't hungry. Peter mopped up his soup with bread and smiled back at Angel as though he knew the conflict brewing between Angel's stomach and his pride.

"That jacket looks great on you," Peter said. "Keep it. It'll always be there to keep you warm."

June 1, 1991 – Culture

Dear Mustafa,

Pity party for one. Peter at studio. I'm alone with my mind. At least I'm home. At least mind working. Sick of hospitals. My myriad of maladies exhausts me.

Finding hope in culture, dear Mustafa. It's all that's left for me. Die once when heart stops. Die again when buried. Die forever last time someone speaks name. Culture keeps us alive after our physical demise.

Consider Mapplethorpe, for instance. Controversies swirl years after death. All those big black cocks no one knows how to mount on gallery walls. Coulda been mine. Linh knew Mapplethorpe, made an introduction. I lost weight, worked out to model for him. Didn't get to New York in time. What a scandal if SF State had found out. Younger than me when he died.

Keith Haring died last year. Don't know much about art, but Haring's art getting more attention posthumously. Thomas Fogerty dead, too. Love dancing to "Proud Mary" at Trocadero when they play the oldies. "Rollin', rollin', rollin' on the river." Remember how songs like this taught me English.

Gays have to leave more culture behind before we're extinct.

If I'm lucky, I'll leave book no one reads. Internet protocols and digital identity. Who cares?

Keep getting new primary care doctor. Fucking medical musical chairs. First doc died. Second one needed break after boyfriend died. Like third one. Who will outlast whom this time? Getting doc harder than gay dating these days.

Have to face it. Not great prognosis. New doc says I'm doing fine. Without enthusiasm. Preoccupied with onslaught of new patients. He means doing fine relative to dead guys. He means no promises about time on planet. He means enjoy today.

Without knowing it, he means I'm stuck with Peter forever. Dance contest over. No new partners.

Of course, known this for quite some time. Just got real after seeing new doc.

Could be worse. Much worse. Peter like baklava—sweet, but too sweet. Relief when he goes to studio, to bars, to market. Can taste crisp salty skin of roast chicken, can savor oil and vinegar dripping off tender artichoke heart when he's away. Can taste life.

Sweet intentions. Wants me to stay alive. Is that enough? Keep breathing. Has that been enough?

Angel showed up this morning with sweet intentions in form of pot brownies. Thank Goddess. Calms mind. Maybe gain weight.

Told me about backstage shenanigans at *Angels in America*. His lover worked on set. Angel asked how gay play could go five, maybe six hours. Told him six seems hardly long enough for gays. Good buzz about this new AIDS play at Eureka even if it goes on forever. Play that won't die. Don't know playwright, but he lives on even if he dies.

Angel also told me John Lemon died. Poor John. Twenty-seven years old. About your age, Mustafa. Fuck. Just finished master's program. John told me masters was in language. Told him, no, in handsome.

Angel said John went fast. First symptoms a month ago. Couldn't tolerate meds.

36

NEW YORK, MAY 6, 2002

Mark fidgeted outside Thomas' door. He'd skipped lunch to arrive on time. Thomas whisked Mark to the living room, explaining he needed to finish a phone call, something about a caterer menu that couldn't wait. Sitting in an overstuffed chair, Mark looked at his wrist and remembered he'd left his watch at home because its battery was dead. Mark was too stingy to store extra watch batteries and too forgetful to buy a replacement. For someone working against deadlines, it was a miracle he completed anything on time. There was no clock in Thomas' living room, no way to keep track of time.

It seemed impolite to make him wait. Mark had made the trek from the Lower East Side to Harlem as a favor to Erica. At her insistence, really. Now he found himself cooling his heels. It wasn't like he didn't have a major research paper due. Erica had impressed upon him the importance of reporting what he'd found on Rano's disks to Thomas. The timing was vital, she said. Mark would lend gravity to his findings by presenting them in person, she said.

Since their shared lumberjack brunch, Erica had been signaling interest in Mark again, phoning more frequently over the course of the spring, forwarding silly jokes to initiate short email banter. These flirtations were friendly, not insistent. She was dangling the bait, not forcing it down his throat. Or at least that's how it seemed to Mark. He still wanted space to recover from the misadventure with Anna. Anna's romantic theatrics had made Erica's look amateur by comparison.

Erica's flirtations could have been a ruse, a manipulation to cajole him into examining Rano's disks. Mark's involvement had been cautious. He didn't want to get caught biting on Erica's bait only to have her cut him loose again. Right now, his only hunger was for lunch. He had no appetite for romantic disappointment.

To Mark's delight, the content on the disks fascinated him. On a rainy weekend, when he'd been looking for a new excuse to avoid his own research, Mark set off on a downtown Manhattan expedition to find a cheap floppy drive. A few of the disks were damaged beyond repair, some were partly readable, but Mark salvaged enough to cut and paste a veritable digital palimpsest of Rano's manuscript into a word processor. During breaks from his own research, Mark plowed his way through Rano's work. It was first-draft material with first-draft flaws, but cogent and persuasive. Rano's writing was intelligent, solidly academic, more wry than dry.

Halfway through, Mark grasped the possible implications of Rano's research and regretted not starting sooner. Rano's book contained many veins of research gold, a pre-World Wide Web examination of culture and technology that predicted, or at least hinted at, many of the ethical quandaries of digitally connected societies. The big breakthroughs were in identity theft. Rano argued that different cultures would have implemented the Internet differently, and that any one of these culturally diverse implementations of the underlying technology would have led to significantly different outcomes for ownership, security, and a host of other attributes. Rano had latched onto Wild West stagecoaches and trains as a metaphor to navigate this goldmine of research topics. What he wrote about identity theft was a decade ahead of its time. Mark checked with a few associates, but no one knew of Rano or his specific line of research.

Still no sign of Thomas.

Mark recognized the paintings on the wall. They were landscapes by Peter, the artist from San Francisco, Rano's surviving lover. If Thomas' phone call went on much longer, Mark would have time to paint his own landscape. Even after dating Erica, Mark was not much of a visual arts aficionado. She had taught him some of the basics about composition, color, and technique. Mark began to recognize the styles of a few modern artists they viewed at New York's museums. He learned to distinguish jagged Clyfford Still from messy Willem de Kooning from iconographic Jasper Johns. Going back in time, though, all the Dutch Masters blurred together as did the Italian Renaissance artists. Erica would go on and on describing each of these ancient artists. Mark would smile to suppress a yawn. He mustered a connection to twentieth-century art, but found no interest in older art. The Dutch Masters might as well have been photographers with great studio lighting. The main point of the Italian Renaissance art seemed to be lapis blue everywhere. The thing that made any show worth viewing was Erica's excitement about and deep understanding of the artists and their works. Mark never dared ask Erica whether she noticed the correlation between their trips to see art and her desire afterwards for a great fuck. After Erica broke things off, Mark no longer found himself drawn to galleries and museums.

Trapped in Thomas' living room, there wasn't much else to do but pass time with the landscapes. To suppress his pangs of hunger, Mark played a mind game. He imagined what Erica might say about Peter's painting. She'd explain the arrangement of the objects, the way the easily identifiable man-made structures—the old house, the distant shed—were placed in an abstract natural setting. She'd point out the contrast between the insistent industrial colors of the structures and the eery coloring of an abstract pond or patch of berries. She'd explain how Peter's brushwork revealed emotion in each element, lines of the realistic structures reinforcing the abstract elements of the setting. It was as if, Erica might say, the structures somehow emerged from the landscape they were once part of. Mark understood how these works appealed to Erica. He could hear the excitement growing in Erica's voice as she explained Peter's landscapes. The landscapes had all the characteristics Erica looked for in art. It was just that the landscapes didn't do much for Mark. That, and, even if Erica were in Thomas' living room right now, they wouldn't be shagging afterwards. That was something he missed more and more with her ongoing flirtations. His stomach growled. He looked at his bare wrist and reminded himself to buy watch batteries.

"My apologies for that prolonged phone call," Thomas said, carrying a tray of tastefully arranged cheeses and crackers. "The caterer claimed I missed the deadline to place an order for next weekend's fundraiser."

"I was beginning to think I'd be marooned among these landscapes until dinner," Mark said. Ravenous, he gnawed on a hunk of cheese he hacked off even before Thomas sat down.

"Yes," Thomas said, looking a bit put off. "Well, sorry to strand you in this rat-infested gallery."

This wasn't starting well. As hungry as Mark was, he placed the large piece of cheese back on the tray and cut exacting slices of cheddar to fit on the octagonal crackers. He noticed from the luster of Thomas' sweater that Thomas had an appreciation for quality in more than painting and food. The wait had annoyed Mark, but he was relieved by such a luxurious appetizer. The scents wafting from the tray reminded him of family vacations to Vermont, the picnics where his parents spread out cheeses they'd discovered at the local dairies and rated them. Mark offered cheddar-topped crackers to Thomas.

"Erica told me you'd found something exciting on Rano's disks," Thomas said, taking a cracker and resting more comfortably on the sofa.

"Rano's writing is quite brilliant, actually," Mark said. He slowed down to enjoy the cheese flavors. Already his blood sugar was normalizing, his mood stabilizing. The whole point of this visit was to explain Rano's work to Thomas, not get hot under the collar because Erica's best client took an unexpected phone call. As he crunched through another cracker, Mark's appetite to explain what was on the disks subsumed his hunger for food. "It breaks ground in something called 'identity theft' as well as significant topics of ethics and culture."

"As I suspected," Thomas said. "It seems that even though they lived together, neither Peter nor Rano fully appreciated each other's brilliance."

"Would you like to know what Rano wrote?" Mark asked.

"No," Thomas answered. "I don't think I'd understand it."

"Wasn't the whole point of this meeting to explain Rano's work to you?" Mark considered leaving. Everything Thomas said this afternoon seemed dismissive, as if Thomas had an entirely different agenda for their meeting, as if the disks didn't matter. Mark reminded himself how important this meeting was to Erica and sat still. He couldn't stand anyway. The cheese aroma had formed invisible handcuffs, tethering the hungry prisoner to his seat. "I thought that's why Erica asked me to come."

"What matters now is that Peter paints," Thomas said. "Peter has been consumed with guilt since he read Rano's journal, but I don't think he knows exactly why. He doesn't appreciate the significance of Rano's book, the book you've extracted so ingeniously from the disks. It's as if Rano left his masterpiece hidden behind a drape and somehow this masterpiece humiliates Peter. My hunch is that once the drape is pulled back, Peter will be freed from his humiliation."

Mark grabbed a handful of crackers from the tray. He already knew all about Peter's painting block. Erica couldn't have made that any clearer the thousand times she'd mentioned it in her emails. If Thomas didn't want to know what was on the disks, what was the point of skipping lunch and waiting a lifetime in Thomas' living room? Mark was annoyed again, but he couldn't leave. Maybe he was overthinking this. As his hunger returned, he began eating crackers in rapid succession.

"It's kind of you to come here to tell me what you learned about the disks," Thomas continued. "What matters to me, though, is not their content. I don't care what kind of masterpiece Rano created. What matters is that someone pulls back the drape and reveals Rano's masterpiece, that someone who appreciates the content completes and publishes his work. That's what I believe will free Peter, allow him to move on, to paint again."

"So why did Erica insist I come here?" Mark asked. "I can email Rano's manuscript to anyone you choose to publish his book."

"I asked Erica if you would come because I did want to learn something from you today. I wanted to find out who can complete Rano's book. I believe you've just told me that person is you."

"I'm afraid I'm not your man for a book about identity theft or ethics." Mark's frustration subsided. This meeting was different from what he expected. At least, Mark thought to himself while slicing through another of the soft cheeses; at least, Thomas was treating him to the best array of cheeses he'd tasted since those family trips to Vermont. As he slathered this particular soft cheese on a cracker, it reminded him of a special cheese, a specific cheese associated with an event he couldn't place. He held the cheese under his nose and inhaled before he spoke again. "You want someone who knows security and ethics."

"You clearly understand the topics well enough," Thomas said. "How else would you know the significance of Rano's work? I also want someone with your enthusiasm to reveal Rano's masterpiece to the world."

"I'd love to help if I could," Mark said. This meeting was turning out better than Mark could have imagined. He didn't have the opportunity he expected to tell Thomas about Rano's work, but he'd helped Erica, given Thomas the confirmation he wanted, and enjoyed one of the tastiest lunches he'd had in months. Better yet, he had no further obligations other than eating more. "I have to finish writing up my research. Then I'm interviewing for teaching positions. Then I'll be teaching. Even if I could help, it would be at least a year before I'd have the time."

"I can make it worth your while to reconsider," Thomas said. "But if you won't help complete Rano's book, will you at least help find the right person?"

"Yes, of course," Mark answered, intrigued by the offer of compensation. He chewed off a bit of the soft cheese and rolled it around his tongue. "Where is this cheese from?"

"A family dairy farm in Vermont," Thomas answered. "I visit every few years. They ship cheese for my events. This is for next week's fundraiser."

"Is this from a dairy near Hardwick?" Mark asked.

"Yes," Thomas replied. "How could you possibly know?"

"My family vacationed there in the summer," Mark said. "We tried a lot of cheese around Hardwick."

"What a coincidence!"

"That's part of the coincidence, part of the reason I remember it," Mark said. "The other reason I remember it is that it's the first cheese Erica and I tasted together. I still remember telling her about visiting the dairy as a kid."

"I asked Erica once how she met you," Thomas said. "She gave Vermont cheese a great deal of credit for understanding you'd be fun to date.

"She's been flirting with me lately."

"So I heard," Thomas said. He picked up the cheese and cracker on his plate and took a minute to enjoy it. "Knowing Erica, she won't stop until you propose."

June 24, 1991 – Distraction

Dear Mustafa,

Breakfast in bed. Luxury. Fresh peaches in yogurt. Fresh OJ. Peter a genius. All stayed down. Food has been friend lately. Gained two pounds last week. The magic of Angel's pot brownies.

Lounging in bed. Your father deserves a distraction from work and AIDS. Reading Sunday papers snatched from Cafe Flore yesterday. Disturbing *Washington Post* story on Gulf War. Reminder of televised images of bombs striking targets in Iraq and Kuwait. War as video game. Beautiful silent explosions. Can't see "collateral damage." Can't feel heat. Can't hear destruction whizzing by. Can't smell the carnage.

Article says some bombs targeted civilian infrastructure. Punish Iraqis for Saddam's hubris? Who thought of that brilliant strategy? Bush? Couldn't have been Quayle. Too dumb. Cheney more likely. He's evil.

Isn't it punishment enough Saddam still in charge? No! Cut off power. Cut off water. Cut off jobs. Kill innocent Iraqis. Fuck ragheads.

Plus Palestinians flooding out of Kuwait on way to Goddess knows where. Algeria is too far, but who knows? Americans never understand. Creating generations of bad karma. Win Kuwait battle, lose Middle East war.

This is not a good distraction. Made me angry. Lashed out at Peter just now. So stupid. How do I tell him?

37

FIRE ISLAND, MAY 24, 2002

Brice lazed by the pool, awaiting Peter's arrival at the Fire Island house that featured songs from the gay divas of yore, the Barbra Streisands, the Billie Holidays. In earlier decades, these ravishing sirens were the Pines' soundtrack. During the past week, Brice found they'd become gay counterculture, a nostalgic counterpoint to the repetition of omnipresent electronic dance music.

Fire Island dance still was about posing, about sex. The dancers chose music to show off, if not their bodies or their scanty swimwear, then their knowledge of obscure European bands or of new electronic music effects. This summer was the same as every summer. Fire Island dance coalesced around a few songs, the songs that became anthems for the season. When the island boys ventured back to the outside world, they'd hum these songs like roaming villagers as a badge of their identity.

Brice watched the pool boy clean to the accompaniment of *Appalachian Spring*. The pool boy posed frequently, flaunting his muscular charms. As tempting as it might have been to seduce this somewhat mature boy, what Brice wanted was to dance. Not a dance of seduction, though, at least not until Peter arrived. Brice needed one of his transformational dances, a dance to help him understand Peter and Rano and Carl. Dancing in the pool boy's presence would confuse both of them.

Instead, Brice closed his eyes. The music reminded Brice of those days with Rano, those days listening to Bernstein play Copland, to Louis Armstrong accompany Ella Fitzgerald. Those days seemed like a lifetime ago now. A few times when Brice visited Rano, he'd danced, shown Rano how the steps worked. He told Rano that dancing was a way he worked out things he wasn't sure about, that he would find a place to dance and often a confusion would transform into an understanding.

The long-distance arrangement with a mature man, an attentive man more than twenty years his senior, suited Brice. It was a secret he kept from his friends, a secret he fantasized about alone in his own bed at night. It anchored him in the tides of New York's gay dating scene. Sometimes Brice wanted more with Rano, and sometimes he was sure Rano felt the same. Long after Rano's offer from Columbia came and went, Brice still wanted Rano to move to New York. That fantasy flew out the window the day Rano called to say he couldn't join Brice on Fire Island because he was recovering in the hospital. New York was off the table. Brice knew Rano would rely on Peter in ways he couldn't rely on someone like Brice, someone who ran a business a continent away.

And then Rano went downhill.

And then Rano whispered those crazy secrets on his deathbed, secrets about a biological son, about the ways Carl must have molested that son.

And then Brice ended up in bed with Peter the night Rano died. A decade later, where was all this going?

Brice opened his eyes. The pool boy was nowhere to be seen, a mirage. For that matter, Peter, too, was nothing more than a mirage. Brice glanced at the clock inside the house. Where was Peter? He said he'd be here by now to share the bedroom with Brice for the week. Maybe he was coming on a later ferry. After 9/11, Peter disappeared and reappeared, stopped returning calls and then phoned repeatedly to apologize for not calling. At first, Brice thought he should do something, maybe an intervention. Then, on Brice's most recent trip to San Francisco, when he'd hopped on a flight after Peter panicked about his heart, it became clear Peter had to find his own way. All Brice could do was be there when Peter reached out.

House to himself, Brice went inside to start *Appalachian Spring* again from the beginning. Time to dance. Brice wanted to step through a decision whether to tell Peter Rano's secrets, reveal the son, reveal Carl's abuse. Stretching felt good while he waited for his favorite number. He cleared his mind. He'd taught Rano all about this number. As it came up, Brice finished his stretches and leapt through the door to the pool.

"Hey," Peter yelled as he pushed through the gate with a rainbow knapsack on his back and a ravishing brunette in tow. "I wasn't sure of the way, but Ken showed me."

Ken waved sheepishly. Brice caught himself midstride and waved back. This was unexpected. There was something endearing about Ken, like a bartender about to tell an amusing story. Unsure about the story between Peter and Ken, Brice met Peter at the pool's edge with a modest hug and then shook Ken's hand.

"Peter and I struck up a conversation about art on the ferry," Ken said, smiling at Peter and then at Brice. "Since he's a first-timer here, I wanted to give the artist a friendly island welcome. Nice place you have."

"Thanks," Brice said. "Peter, do you want to drop your bag in our room?"

"No, I'm exhausted," Peter answered, plopping himself on a lounge chair. "It turns out Ken and I have a lot in common."

"Oh, really," Brice said, less sure where this was going. "Would either of you like something?"

"Don't worry about me," Ken said, lowering his brown canvas bag next to Peter.

"I'd love a glass of whatever to take off the edge," Peter said. "Ken has something he wants to show me."

"Okay, sure." Inside, Brice poured two glasses of white wine and looked for an album to set the proper mood. There it was. The original cast recording of *Hello, Dolly!* Carol Channing's rasp was the perfect antidote for Viagra, even when its help wasn't required.

Back outside, the two glasses sweat with condensation. Ken huddled next to Peter on the lounge chair, their backs to Brice. Unperturbed, Brice walked around to face them. On a table, Ken was fanning out snapshots from his bag.

"Thanks," Peter said, taking a long sip from the glass. "You're not going to believe this. Ken, go ahead, tell Brice."

"As we were walking here from the ferry," Ken said, brushing his mustache with his fingers, "Peter said you guys watched the first jet strike the World Trade Center."

"Yes," Brice said. He sat down in the other lounge chair. The memory still took away his breath. "It was unimaginable."

"So, my boyfriend," Ken said, "he worked in the North Tower."

"Holy shit," Brice said, putting down his wine. Carol Channing's voice was discordant as *Hello, Dolly!* played. "Holy shit."

"Charles is okay," Ken said, resting his hands on his legs. "He hated that building, hated working there. Loved the people, but hated the tower."

"I can't imagine working there," Peter said.

"The enormity of the structure drove Charles crazy," Ken said. "It became this neurotic albatross around his neck, a symbol of the enormity of the social structure that crushed our gay friends, that stopped the world from fighting AIDS. He had this intuition the tower would crush him as well."

"Oh, wow," Peter said. "Was Charles in his office when the plane hit?"

"Yep." Ken's fingers pressed into his thighs. "He was so convinced the structure would crush him physically or spiritually or whatever that, to cope, he'd map out escape routes. He'd memorized the best ways out, but only managed to save a couple of his colleagues."

"God, he must've felt terrible," Brice said. Carol's cackle was a sonic disaster for this conversation.

"He's better now," Ken said, leaning forward. "Look, I was showing Peter these snapshots I took of Charles in front of the North Tower."

"While you guys look at those," Brice said, "I'm running inside for a minute."

Back in the house, Brice switched off the sound system and poured a glass of wine for Ken. This jealousy Brice had felt with Ken was strange, unusual. Never happened with Rano. On his way outside, he detoured through the bedroom to snag a joint. Now he wanted to get to know Ken better. Wine and pot would help.

"I could use that," Ken said, sitting erect as Brice offered the wine glass. "I was just seeing if there are any duplicates in my bag for Peter."

"These photos are what I've been looking for," Peter said, moving the photos around the table like chessmen. "I know what I'm painting for Erica's 9/11 memorial show."

July 6, 1991 – Charm

Dear Mustafa,

Behold, my late, late, late forties. Never expected fifty to look this emaciated. One week away.

Feel better after decent week of writing. Miss teaching, miss inquisitive young minds. At least, there's writing. And no grading.

Told Peter no party. Got angry when he pressed. No fucking fiftieth party. It'd be pitiful. Gift ideas? Rainbow urns, mortuary parking passes, glitter paddles for River Styx. Have to credit glitter paddles to Brice. Funny.

Cesar Casado and Ron McEachern died last month. Couldn't keep track without *Bay Area Reporter* obits. Cesar dashing. Dazzling smile. Worked at Wilkes Bashford selling fashionable threads. Loved watching Cesar on tennis court. Toothpick legs, but who cares. That million-dollar smile.

Ron sold real estate. His lover, Rob, died last year. They had a beautiful house on Buena Vista Park. Views for days. Both bridges. Peter says Ron's family fighting with late lover's family over their house. This, of course, after both families disowned their gay sons.

Student stopped by Thursday. Bright boy. Sweet gesture. Not a beauty, but could charm pants off anyone. Too bad I'm so thin now my pants fall off without charm. Asked smart questions about Internet, identity, and ethics—concepts from lecture last year. Avoided my health so assiduously I'm sure that's all he wanted to talk about. How to reassure twenty-year-old it will be okay? So clear looking at me that it's not.

Billy said "I love you" as he left. Sounded like goodbye.

38

SAN FRANCISCO, MAY 30, 2002

Linh fished in her purse for keys to Peter's studio. It was foggy in the rest of San Francisco but clear in this pocket of South of Market microclimates. Clear but cool. Linh entered and waited for Angel inside. The Ghesquière jacket, with its leather sleeves and tailored wool bodice, kept Linh stylishly warm. She sat down, placing her styrofoam cup of coffee on Peter's desk. His request for a very specific photo of Rano was strange. To Linh, the specificity of this request signified a likely return to painting. If Peter could change, Linh thought to herself, if Peter could get past another painting block, perhaps there was hope for her, too, hope that she would be able to invite people into her life without fear of abandonment.

The buzzer. Linh opened the studio door. Here was Angel, eons since their last visit. Linh managed a smile. Angel had changed—less hair, more belly. His clothes spoke the language of cheap midlife crisis. He smelled like flour and sugar. At least, he wasn't dying his hair some hideous shade of aubergine.

"It's so nice to see you," Linh said, feigning a smile. She knew Angel's resume. Despite his recent transition from pharmaceuticals to baking, it didn't please her that he continued to garner Peter's attention. "You look great."

"Thanks," Angel said, smiling genuinely. Angel dropped a bag in the kitchenette and looked around. "The last time I saw you was with Rano."

"Oh, that's right," Linh said.

It was a dozen years ago that she'd flown in from New York to see Rano in the hospital. She carried a bouquet into Rano's room and there was Angel, holding Rano's hand. Angel was the sexiest thing under the sun. His beaming smile lit up the darkest corners of Davies Hospital. In the midst of the AIDS crisis, his visage of naïveté gave hope that some vestige, any vestige, of innocence would survive the slaughter. Too bad he became a dealer.

"I can't believe it's been since Rano's final hospital stay," Linh said. "Just before he died."

That was a conversation killer. Angel draped his fitted green bomber jacket over a chair, a contrast to his threadbare shirt and soiled sweatpants. While he pondered the New York skyline sketches taped to the wall, Linh finished her coffee. The visage of naïveté had matured, not in a way anyone a dozen years ago would have predicted.

Angel's presence was awkward. Peter wanted Linh to ship the skyline sketches to him in New York along with the photograph of Rano in front of the World Trade Center. What possessed Peter to ask Angel to help her? He'd said Angel would know where to find everything, but it was clear to Linh that Peter's sketches were right there, right above all his self-portraits leaning against the wall. It didn't seem too hard to figure out where the photographs might be.

"What's in the bag?" Linh asked.

"Pastries I baked," Angel answered. He found a clean plate in the kitchenette and presented a half-dozen Mexican pastries to Linh. "They're still warm."

"That's sweet of you," Linh said, trying to mean it. She'd spent too much of her life in the food business not to recognize the danger. One nibble from these Mexican lard pillows and her jacket would burst into rags. It was more than that, though. She wasn't comfortable. She couldn't adjust to Angel's appearance, Angel the virile stud turned sleazy drug dealer turned middle-aged baker.

"I have to stop eating these," Angel said, patting his belly. Then he took a bite of a bright blue and red cookie. "If I want a boyfriend."

"Too bad Peter is moving to New York," Linh said, pushing the plate of pastries away.

"For sure?" Angel asked, eyes wide open with surprise. Angel's rich brown eyes surprised Linh. She recognized something from the past. His eyes were as caring now as they were a dozen years ago when he held Rano's hand at the hospital. They hadn't changed—not even crow's-feet.

"Well, I'm not absolutely sure," Linh said. "But he's borrowing my apartment. Now he's asking for his sketches. Seems like he's moving. I thought you'd know."

"All I know is that he went to New York to paint," Angel said, chewing the last of the cookie. "I didn't think he'd move. He's my last hope for a boyfriend."

Something about the honesty of these words changed the way Linh saw Angel. Her mental picture seemed off. She was expecting drug dealer speak. Instead, Angel was unguarded, unpretentious. He wasn't afraid to share his doubts, fears, desires. That was different from Linh. She was honest about things she saw, honest about what she saw in others, but hid her own feelings. Her S&M adventures helped. S&M protocols provided boundaries for her feelings, emotional guardrails. Linh was still afraid when she started letting go, though, afraid she wouldn't be able to stop once the genie oozed out of the bottle. Angel, on the other hand, seemed to be able to reveal himself by doing nothing more esoteric than eating a cheap pastry. She sensed a sincerity under Angel's awkward middle-aged exterior. It was attractive.

"I don't want Peter to move," Linh said. "He was an important factor in my decision to return to San Francisco."

"I don't want him to move, either," Angel said. "I care about him, care about his painting, his sanity. If New York is all it takes for that, I suppose he has to move. What did he want shipped?"

"Peter said you'd know where to find his sketches of the New York skyline and a photograph of Rano," Linh answered. There was one thing she hadn't seen in the studio, one thing Angel might be able to help her find. "Do you know where Peter keeps Rano's journal?"

"It's usually around his desk," Angel answered.

"I'd like to read it," Linh said. "Like to find out what it was that Rano said about Peter."

"It's a tough read," Angel said. He looked around Peter's desk and then walked to the far end of the gallery, to the alcove. He poked around unsuccessfully for a couple minutes and turned back to Linh. "Peter said he was going to burn it last month. Maybe he did."

Linh was surprised that Peter let Angel—of all people, the recovering addict Angel!—read Rano's journal. Those two were closer than she realized. The more time she spent with Angel, the more she liked him. Still, it seemed like Brice, or maybe that art collector in New York, the one who wore such magnificently understated outfits, had more to offer. But who was she to judge Peter's taste in men, she reminded herself.

"Peter also asked me to send a specific photo, a photo of Rano standing in front of the World Trade Center," Linh said. "I wonder if that's in Rano's journal."

"I didn't see any photos in the journal," Angel said. "Drawings and clippings, but no photos. It's probably in here."

Angel returned with the remnants of a mildewy box that contained remnants of Rano's possessions. Linh saw postcard-sized photos, some like they'd just arrived from Fotomat, others glommed together or stained beyond recognition.

"I remember this dildo," Linh said, poking through the box.

"How did you know about it?" Angel said.

"Peter showed it to me one day at his house," Linh answered. "I told him I was learning about S&M. This was the entirety of what he had to show me. This and his leather boots."

"I found Rano's dildo by accident," Angel said. "At the same time I found his journal by accident."

"How did that happen?" Linh asked, organizing stacks of photos.

"I was searching for a bedpan under Rano's bed with my foot," Angel replied. "Kicked the journal by accident. I think I was the only one who knew about it until Peter found it last year. Rano asked me to destroy it. I wish I had."

Linh looked up from the photos. That was some news. Whatever Rano wrote must have been a nightmare. "Why didn't you destroy it?"

"I don't remember," Angel answered, flipping through a stack of photos from the box. "You know how crazy it got after Rano died. Why does Peter want a photo of Rano in front of the World Trade Center?"

"No clue," Linh replied. What Linh wouldn't give, she realized, to read such a diary from her mother, nightmares and all. "I'm glad you didn't destroy the journal."

They rifled through stacks of photos. A few times Angel had to stare at a photo to remember the names, or at least to tell Linh how he knew the people, or, if not how he knew them, at least whether they'd had sex. After a bit, Linh found a set of four photos with Rano, Peter, and Brice.

"This must be right after I introduced these three," Linh said, holding up one of the photos.

"When did you meet Brice?" Angel asked.

"I met Brice right after I moved to New York," Linh replied. "I snuck into the Mineshaft wearing teen-boy drag and caught Brice checking out the leather daddies. We became fast friends. He wanted to get naked with leather dads. So did I. We drank and smoked and shared our sex fantasies, our desires to have anonymous sex in the dark back rooms at the S&M clubs."

Linh placed the photo with the other three. Angel examined them, looking at each for a moment. When he was done, Linh pushed the four to the side to keep them separate. Linh and Angel took a break from the photos.

"Brice never judged my sexual proclivities," Linh continued, nibbling the pink corner of a Mexican pastry. "It was refreshing not to be judged. It's why I had to leave my family, to leave San Francisco. Too much judgment. That, and I couldn't prepare one more fucking bánh mì sandwich."

Angel laughed. "So when did you introduce them?"

"Ah," Linh answered, "Brice told me he'd never been to San Francisco. I said that I had some friends in the Castro and that he had no choice but to stay with them. After I found out Brice was sleeping with Rano, I was scared to death he would get AIDS."

Angel was quiet after Linh said that. He started sorting through photos again. Linh put the rest of the pastry back on the plate and joined Angel in the search. She hoped she hadn't offended Angel with something she said about AIDS. It wasn't like she didn't have friends who died.

Then, bingo! At last, Linh dug out the photo of Rano in a suit and tie, beaming cheek to cheek, right in front of a World Trade Center tower. His suit was a weird plaid, and the low camera angle made him look enormous, as large as the tower behind him. She chuckled with Angel about that.

In the same part of the box, Angel found a couple more blurred photos of the towers that Rano must have taken. From the very bottom of the box, Linh rescued an errant photo and held it up for Angel.

"I've never seen a photo of Rano this young. It's so grainy." Linh turned over the snapshot. "Is this Rano? There's no date. Why is 'Mustafa' written on the back? Who's Mustafa?"

"Jesús, María y José," Angel said, crossing himself. He took the grainy photo from Linh and examined it. "I can't tell you anything about Mustafa because I've never met him. Peter would know more about him."

July 13, 1991 – Fifty

D ear Mustafa,

Fifty. Seemed so far away. Here it is. How many more birthdays? Felt okay this week until today.

Fifty made me think of family, family who forsook me. Algeria not great place for queers, especially in countryside. At least tourist towns tolerated gays for attracting businessmen. In some ways, I'm lucky Carl found me. Don't talk about him much. Not even Peter knows everything.

Carl, the ripped blond American Carl, vacationing at beach hotel. Me, street urchin who knew how to wear bathing suit. Him, sadist who knew young catch when he saw one. He got me to America all right. Made sure of it. Could have been worse. Got out of Algeria alive. Got away from Carl alive. Would hate him if he weren't dead. AIDS got the asshole early. Can't say I wasn't happy to read his obit. Pray he never hurt you.

What of my parents? Sister? Brothers? Practically, they are dead to me. Don't hate them. May hate culture, but can't hate them. Could write them if I knew where. You must have many cousins by now, Mustafa. Unlikely to make it back to find out.

Joke of a birthday party. Barely ate. Bad mezze. I don't blame Peter, although maybe I should. Blamed him for plenty already.

39

NEW YORK, JUNE 8, 2002

Erica was patching the gallery walls, filling in the nail holes, then sanding the fillings. When Erica wasn't filling and sanding, the only sound was the cool rain, rain that kept the streets clear of the few remaining souls who hadn't fled Manhattan this summer weekend. On afternoons as dark as this, the flood lights transformed the gallery into a neighborhood lantern. Soon, Erica would touch up the paint and, after the paint dried, she'd start her favorite gallery activity, installing a new show. Now that her morning sickness had subsided, Erica could concentrate. Soon she'd be able to afford an assistant to prepare the walls and help her mount the work. For now, she enjoyed working alone, the repetition of repairing one hole after the next, the dust scent from sanding.

Erica's anticipation of installing the new art grew. She relished finding relationships between the works, balancing the colors and moods in the space until each piece was in exactly the right place. It was like introducing an artist's children to one another. Sometimes artists would disagree with Erica's placement, but more often they saw new ways their works related. These few hours of vacation from artists' nerves and clients' egos revitalized her.

As Erica placed the sandpaper in the toolbox, a man knocked on the door. Erica wasn't expecting anyone and didn't recognize the bundle dripping outside in the storm. She opened the door anyway. The weather was too miserable to shoo away anyone.

"This space is just what I was looking for," the man said, looking at the bare gallery walls after he pulled off his baseball cap and mussed his hair. "However, looks like I missed the Vietnamese artist."

"That show's long gone," Erica said. The man looked familiar without his cap. "Weren't you at Peter's show?"

"Peter said I should see the Vietnamese show," the man said. "Asked me to tell him what I thought. Seems he was more confused than normal."

"Why doesn't he fly out himself?" Erica asked, walking over to an imperfection, a small ding she'd missed in the wall. "And bring along something I can sell."

"He's been afraid of flying since 9/11," the man answered. Dripping from the rain, he struggled to unzip his jacket. "But Peter flew to New York a few weeks ago."

How strange for Peter to fly to New York without telling her. Erica remembered this dripping man now. Peter holed up in this man's apartment after missing his flight on 9/11. What *was* his name? Peter had been a nervous Nellie after opening night. He couldn't wait for the reviews of the gallery show, then couldn't wait to break out of New York. That nervous energy spilled out into the sketches he drew while he was stuck in this man's apartment, the drawings of New York's skyline. The highlight of Erica's trip to Peter's San Francisco studio was viewing these drawings. The lines were intense, not relaxed. The destruction was clear, monumental. So was a brighter future for New York, hope for its redemption. New York, however, was recovering better from 9/11 than Peter. These skylines were the direction Erica thought Peter should take, not the sniveling self-portraits he'd shown her.

"What's he doing in New York?" Erica asked.

"I wish I knew," the man said as he stopped tugging his zipper. "We spent a few days on Fire Island, then he cut short his stay and raced to Manhattan. No clue what he's doing, but he said he was going to paint."

"That would be fantastic," Erica said, remembering the man's name at last. "Are you chilled, Brice? Would you like a cup of coffee?"

"Yes, please," Brice answered. "There's something about this gallery space. Maybe I'm remembering Peter's show here."

"Why is Peter being so mysterious?" Erica asked. She made a mental note to fill the defect in the wall and walked to the kitchenette to brew a fresh pot.

Brice was scoping out the gallery silently. Erica wondered what he was examining so intently. The only art in the space was stacked together, leaning against a wall. While the coffee dripped, Brice fidgeted with his zipper again. Erica returned to the new artwork, flipping through the pieces she had to hang by the end of the day. She loved the new paintings, couldn't wait to see them fill the gallery walls. Part of her mind was planning where the new pieces would go. Another part considered how Brice might help her encourage Peter to paint the New York skylines, the skylines Peter promised for a 9/11 memorial show in two months. If Brice couldn't help with that, she wanted him gone so she could install the art show. Right now, he seemed as useful as wet laundry.

"I don't know why Peter is being so quiet," Brice said, unzipping at last. His coat dropped to the floor. "Quieter than normal. At least, he said he's painting again."

"Have you seen his latest work?" Erica asked.

Brice plopped the rest of his outerwear and his umbrella into a heap on the floor and walked to the kitchenette. He took a cup from the pantry, poured himself coffee, and grabbed milk from the fridge. Erica felt as though Brice didn't see her. He treated the space as if he owned it.

"Have you seen Peter's latest work?" Erica repeated.

Brice gulped down the coffee, then rubbed his hands on his forearms and his thighs to warm them. Erica looked down at the new art. She wanted to help the paintings to their places, but this silent man was stretching and bending in her kitchenette. Erica didn't want to repeat her question. She didn't know what else to say to this intruder.

Then, with his arms outstretched, Brice stepped across the gallery floor in rhythmic steps. One-two-three, one-two, one-two-three, one-two. He stopped, turned, raised his arms above his head, and improvised a dance without music. From one side of the gallery to the other, Brice leapt, twirled, grunted, swayed, kicked, clapped. His percussive and sibilant sounds created a musical accompaniment for his dance. He commanded the space with his graceful movement.

Erica retreated, although she was almost backed into the corner already. It was like nothing she'd ever seen. Her heart pounded. She didn't understand why Brice was dancing, but she didn't want it to end. Normally, she was protective of her gallery space. Brice flew through it with power and grace. There were no paintings to protect, only the expanse of empty walls. Erica's shoulders relaxed. She watched as Brice's improvisation grew in intensity, admiring the smooth physique under his loose tank top. Brice moved close to her, teased her. She felt as if she could surrender to him, even though she had nothing to surrender. Brice dropped his arms and collapsed at her feet, his body forming a second heap on the floor. He was still except his chest pumping for air.

"That was something," Erica said after Brice's breathing slowed.

"I've been craving a space like this," Brice said, sitting upright and pulling his knees to his stomach. "Sometimes I have to do that. I know it's strange." He took more deep breaths. "The last time I danced that was years ago, for Peter's late lover, for Rano, at Rano's funeral. I was upset that Rano left me. Now I'm upset about Peter. When I'm upset and don't know how to talk about it, I dance about it. And the answer to your question is that, no, I haven't seen Peter's latest painting, but I know he's stuck. He says he's painting, but I think he's still stuck, stuck like something died inside him. That's the only reason he'd be so quiet. I don't understand why Peter is stuck. I keep asking myself why. It could be Rano's journal, it could be the 9/11 flight he missed, it could be the color of the sky. It's been a year, though, and it's time for him to get unstuck. I'm confused about what he wants, maybe because I seem to be confused, too."

Now Erica was the quiet one. Weirder things had happened in the gallery. Like the time an artist wanted to pose naked between his self-portraits to challenge viewers to compare art and reality. That lasted a few days before the artist grew tired of being overlooked. Brice's dance was moving sculpture—weird, unannounced, out of nowhere. It also was touching. It seemed like he was making love. Erica wasn't sure who the object of Brice's desire was. Was she the object? Peter? Rano? It didn't matter. In Erica's effort to get Peter back on track, Brice was turning out to be more of an ally than she could have hoped for.

"I think I understand why Peter got stuck, as you say, why he's not painting."

"How can you know?" Brice asked.

"A collector who likes Peter's work is paying to have Rano's book edited," Erica said. "He flew to San Francisco to see Peter's studio last year. I told this collector I'd obtained the disks containing the book. He's sure that getting Rano's book out for academic review will help Peter move forward."

"You mean Thomas?" Brice asked. "The collector?"

"Yes, Thomas," Erica said. She was more than a little surprised Brice knew Thomas, but it was a small gay world. "Thomas does wonderful things for artists he likes. Thomas' intuition seems correct to me. Releasing Rano's book to at least a few academics strikes me as a kind and loving gesture to help Peter."

"I hope you're right," Brice said. "Did Thomas ask you to bring Rano's disks to New York?"

"No," Erica answered. She didn't want to tell Brice the whole story, that originally the disks were part of her stratagem to rekindle a relationship with Mark and that, unexpectedly, they so enthralled Mark that he would have edited Rano's book regardless of whether Thomas paid. "I had a hunch the disks would be more valuable if an expert examined them than if they deteriorated on Peter's shelf."

Brice stood up without saying anything, walked over to his pile of garments, dressed himself, and picked up his umbrella. In a moment, the two piles on the floor had transformed back into the bundle that had walked in twenty minutes earlier. Just before Brice opened the gallery door to let himself out, he pointed at one of the walls. "By the way, I noticed a small ding right there that you might want to patch."

AUGUST 5, 1991 – DAHMER

D ear Mustafa,

Hideous Jeffrey Dahmer story everywhere. I fear you know this, Mustafa, this story. Depressing.

Anyone who met Carl got taste of Dahmer's insane depravity. Feels like Carl haunting me.

Monster rapes and dismembers dozens of boys. Fucking eats them. Now a gay lifestyle headline. Dahmer presses every homophobia button, ticks every homophobia box.

Gays deserve to die because now we're all Jeffrey Dahmers. Another big step away from cure.

Dahmer lured poor boys to their deaths. They never returned home. Was Dahmer more terrifying than months of AIDS? Than years of praying for cure? Did victims have time to pray? To grasp how it ended?

Tired of watching TV. Makes me worry what Carl did to you. Too tired to do much else.

40

DANBURY, JUNE 14, 2002

Frank knew he'd crossed a line the instant the word escaped his lips.

"If you ever use the word 'gook' again," Erica said, "I won't bother coming home."

Erica's warning sounded like the warnings Frank himself gave school kids using inappropriate language. Erica was right, of course, but she'd been impossible this morning. All over the map. Making him crazy. He couldn't figure out what was bugging her, whether it was their heated discussion about Linh, or Mark's imminent arrival, or some problem Erica was holding back. She continued cleaning the kitchen frantically, the same way her mother did when something upset her.

Something was bothering Frank, too. A lot. Maybe he was a little old-fashioned but, when Erica invited Mark to Danbury to spend the night, Erica intended Mark to share her room upstairs. Frank wanted to discuss sleeping arrangements before Mark arrived. That wasn't going to happen now. Erica dropped the sponge on the counter and declared it was time to go to the station.

"I still can't believe you called Linh a gook," Erica said in the car.

"I'm sorry," Frank said, driving a little faster than usual to minimize conversation time. "You upset me when you asked if I could be her father."

"Why?" Erica asked. "Mom once told me I might have a Vietnamese sister."

"No," Frank said, pulling over the car. "You do not have a Vietnamese sister. Can we stop this discussion?"

"What's wrong with a Vietnamese sister?" Erica asked.

"It would mean I cheated on your mother," Frank answered.

After a silence on the side of the road, Frank switched on the radio. It was news about casualties in Afghanistan. He pressed the preset to a light rock station which, it happened, was playing the Creedence Clearwater Revival song his captain played incessantly in Vietnam. War was getting under Frank's skin today. The train horn blared and he silenced the radio.

"It's not that important," Erica said. "Let's get to the station."

After they returned to the house, Erica toured Mark around and then served the five-star lunch she'd prepared earlier. The salad was bright red, white, and green, something she called a "caprese." The tomatoes tasted homegrown and the cheese was softer than the Kraft spread in the refrigerator. Through the entire meal Erica was uncharacteristically lovey-dovey, hardly acknowledging Frank—not even a peep about the square-dancing club Frank joined to rejuvenate his social life.

Although Erica hadn't made an official proclamation, Frank began to feel certain about the purpose of Mark's visit. He grew more certain after Erica served her best lasagna and Mark commented more than once how he looked forward to Frank's version. Sure enough, after strawberry shortcake for dessert, Erica retrieved a bottle of champagne hidden in the refrigerator and announced the engagement. The morning's stress bubbled over. Frank congratulated his future son-in-law. It was odd that Mark hadn't asked for Erica's hand. Better to keep that bottled up. Frank wanted to maintain his young truce with Erica. He loved seeing Erica in such a good mood.

After an hour of stories recounting the on-again, off-again courtship, Erica said she was taking the car to buy things for a barbeque. She ordered the men to prepare the backyard for a cookout while she shopped. Frank found himself alone with Mark for the first time, unsure what to say.

"Should we go out back?" Mark asked.

"Sure," Frank replied. "The backyard is fine. There's nothing to prepare, really."

Stepping outside, the two of them stared at the yard. Frank had no idea what to say. He was processing what took place over lunch. It was a monumental change. Much more important than starting square-dancing lessons. It still bothered him that Mark hadn't asked for Erica's hand.

"Why don't I mow the lawn?" Mark said out of nowhere. Before Frank could respond, Mark had walked over to the mower and yanked the pull cord.

"You don't have to mow the lawn," Frank shouted over the motor. "I did that last Sunday."

"It's fun," Mark yelled back, wiping his brow with the back of his hand. "I haven't mowed a lawn since high school."

Frank watched as Mark pushed the lawnmower back and forth a few more times. Mark's hair was as bright red as it was well-groomed. Frank wanted to tell Mark to do a better job at the edges, where the lawn intersected the hedge and the brick patio, but held his tongue. Mark was trying to please him. That didn't matter to Frank. What mattered was that Mark was sleeping with his baby girl. There wasn't any way to imagine otherwise. Erica didn't seem to care what Frank thought.

"I'm making some lemonade," Frank announced, going inside to mix the frozen concentrate with tap water. He stirred in extra ice. When he returned outside, Mark was nearly done. The back of Mark's shirt was drenched. Nice to be young, have so much energy. As Mark finished, Frank placed the round glass pitcher of lemonade on the porch table along with two glasses and sat down.

"Perfect," Mark said, sitting next to Frank and gulping his lemonade.

"Glad you like it," Frank said. It was easier to hear Mark without the lawnmower running. "The lawn looks nice. Thanks."

Frank was almost unaware of the awkward silence that ensued. He enjoyed the sweet smell of freshly cut grass. It reminded Frank how Erica, when she was a young girl, would run out of the house and follow him, raking piles from the cut grass left in the lawnmower's wake. Now she was grown up, about to graduate to married life. Frank had a thousand questions for Mark, a thousand and one things he wanted to tell Mark.

"Erica mentioned you're researching an old book related to one of her artists," Frank said.

"I'm trying to teach," Mark said. "Or prepare to teach. This manuscript research for Erica isn't helping."

"I know the drill," Frank said, taking his first sip of lemonade. "Eventually, you'll find your own course preparation system, know what you have to teach and what you can put aside."

"I worry about answering all the students' questions," Mark said. "I love this manuscript, but it's taking over my prep work."

"Can't it wait until you're done preparing?" Frank asked.

"Erica found someone to pay me to edit the manuscript," Mark answered. "Plus, it's amazingly relevant stuff. Brilliant foresights. Ideas the world needs now."

"You should postpone the manuscript work," Frank said. "There can't be a deadline for a manuscript."

"No," Mark said. "It's just that we have to get ready for the . . ."

Mark stopped midsentence to pour himself a second glass of lemonade. Frank understood what this meant. Mark's pause was as surreal as the afternoon the sheriff stopped by the high school to tell Frank about the car accident. Surreal in a happier way, of course, but still disorienting. At the sight of the sheriff, Frank had sensed something was horribly wrong. It was worse than that long-ago afternoon in Vietnam, the afternoon Frank learned from a radio call that the slant-eyed asshole had betrayed them, the afternoon he'd felt the bullets ripping apart his leg.

It was much, much worse waiting for the sheriff's news. Frank didn't know whether it was his wife or his daughter. The moment the sheriff said there'd been a car accident, it was as though Frank himself had absorbed the impact of the cars colliding head on. By the way the sheriff looked down at the ground, Frank knew that instant, before this uniformed stranger had uttered her name, that it was his wife, knew his whole life had turned upside down, knew he hadn't said all the things he'd wanted to say.

It was different today. Frank was overwhelmed in a different way. He sipped lemonade again while he felt his whole life tumbling upside down. No control. At least this time, there would be more life, not less. This time there might be a chance to say what needed saying.

"When is the baby due?" Frank asked. He couldn't help the disappointment in his voice, the disappointment of hearing this news from a stranger.

"I wasn't supposed to tell you!" Mark answered, his face turning nearly as red as his hair. "Early next year. Erica is sure it's going to be a girl." Mark sipped more lemonade. "Either way, she wants to name it Lynn."

August 10, 1991 – Disaster

Dear Mustafa,

Blood work a disaster. Coughing spasms. No beds at Davies Hospital. Never enough administrators on weekends. They said I'll be okay at home. They should've checked that with Peter. They. Depending on Them. Despising Them and depending on Them.

I got sick on the zebra chair. Blood and vomit. Ruined fabric. Living-room harmony disrupted without the zebra stripes balancing everything.

Peter playing new *Queen* album. Told him to blast it. That way he can't hear me weep. Want to be alone, contemplate death. On 1 to 10 scale, discomfort at 11. On and off for days. More comfortable to fall out window and hit concrete. Splat.

Just this, Mustafa. Peter watched new *Queen* music video at Midnight Sun, said Freddie Mercury gaunt. "Gaunt." Code, of course, for someone who won't acknowledge having AIDS.

Fuck closet queens. Dying in the closet for what? Reputation? Protect loved ones? I'll take ACT UP ethics any day. Break the law. Fuck system. Fuck reputation. Fuck Them.

Get me to fucking hospital. That's all.

Silence = Death

41

NEW YORK, JUNE 15, 2002

Peter was anxious, ready at last to paint. It was a year to the day that he'd found Rano's journal. Light flooded the impromptu studio. From the corner space this many floors up, Peter looked south and west over Manhattan's vast skyline, skyscrapers touching the cotton candy clouds, sun glinting off glass, rivers refreshing the shores.

The refreshing rivers. Peter had found his way back into painting as he traversed Manhattan, searching for river access. From his accommodations at Linh's Upper West Side apartment, it was a quick walk to observe the Hudson River. The East River, on the other hand, required a treacherous crosstown bus trip through Central Park or a subterranean adventure uptown.

Peter believed that the water flowing around Manhattan influenced in ineffable ways the ebb and flow of life on the island, that the way to render the city's tallest skyscrapers was to indulge its outer riparian features. It was something he learned from his boyhood visits with Grandma Eunice. The two of them spent hours on the banks of the Kansas River, talking, reading, telling stories, or just listening to the cool water rippling by.

The river, Grandma Eunice remarked wisely one sweltering afternoon, whispers everything you need to know about life. The river did, in fact, teach Peter what he needed to know about his otherwise solitary Kansan life, and Grandma Eunice's wisdom stuck. Like the Kaw, her words always sparkled in Peter's memory. Now, after decades of listening to San Francisco's ocean and bay waters, Manhattan's rivers murmured reinvigorating messages for him.

The catalyst to paint again, though, came not from the fluvial explorations that Peter's grandmother inspired, not from his surveys of the man-made alluvium along the edge of Manhattan, but from the photos he now carried with him everywhere, the photos of Ken's boyfriend, Charles, standing in front of the World Trade Center where he once worked.

For his first painting, Peter didn't want Rano or Charles as the subject. These were too close to home. Instead, Peter chose a related black and white he'd found, an overexposed gay couple holding hands at the base of the North Tower. The tall one, the one on the left with dark skin, was leaning in to kiss his white boyfriend on the cheek. It was exciting mixing the paint, adding drops of pigment to the white to give the image an imperceptible cast. Peter stared at the empty canvas, unsure where to start.

"Oh, good, you're here!" Thomas said, pushing open the door without knocking. "And you're painting!"

Peter sighed to himself. It was always nice seeing Thomas, but the excitement of painting oozed onto the floor as Thomas placed two plastic cups with iced drinks and two bags on a corner table.

"I'm sorry," Thomas said, turning toward Peter. "I interrupted you. Should I leave?"

"It's okay," Peter said, putting down his brush. Thomas had been more than generous to provide such lovely studio space. Dispatching with his social call would take no time. Peter summoned his manners with a smile. "Better now than after I got started."

"What inspired you to paint again?" Thomas asked.

"These photos," Peter answered, nodding at photos taped to the walls.

"How did you find all these photos of the Twin Towers?" Thomas asked.

"People at GMHC found some for me," Peter said. "The staff at the LGBT Community Center said tourists usually took photos from the Top of the World observation deck, so I collected that perspective, too. Once I knew what I wanted, I found it everywhere—flea markets, garage sales, trash bins."

Thomas continued viewing the photos. Most were color prints, a few black and white. The ones taped to the wall were photos Peter planned to paint, gay men at the base of the towers along one wall, gay men on the South Tower observation deck along another. Among the first set was the photo of Rano in front of the South Tower, the photo Linh mailed from Peter's San Francisco studio, the photo in which Rano wore that unfortunate plaid suit he'd always treasured. Like Rano, many of the subjects in these snapshots hadn't survived AIDS, had no way to have known while posing with the solid Twin Towers that those also would crumble prematurely to the ground.

"Wow," Thomas said, moving from one snapshot to the next. "I see common elements in each photo. You found so many. I like the visual connection between AIDS and 9/11."

Thomas always seemed to understand Peter's work better than Peter did. It was uncanny. He read Peter's art as if it were a fairy tale, a story so apparent even a child could comprehend. Few critics came close to describing Peter's work the way Peter thought of it. Thomas got it right away.

"I saw the first of these snapshots after I met this guy Ken on the ferry to Fire Island." Peter pointed to a photo of Charles. "Ken gave me a few photos of his boyfriend standing in front of the tower where he worked. Like me, his boyfriend surprisingly survived 9/11. The realism of the photos set off something inside me. The image felt concrete, the medium fragile. I had to chase my intuition, had to understand what they were telling me."

"Something that had to do with Rano?" Thomas asked. "Or his journal?"

"Yes, I suppose so," Peter replied, although he hadn't thought of this exact connection before. Even after the success of his first New York gallery show, Rano's journal crippled Peter subconsciously in ways that only now were coming to light, ways different from what he'd thought initially. "I don't know for sure. For a long time I felt humiliated by the secrets in Rano's journal, the things he kept from me. I wondered how much I didn't know about this man I lived with."

"I know what you mean," Thomas said. "After Maurice died, I found saucy notes to a cantor at his synagogue. At first, I wanted to know everything about this cantor, find other secrets Maurice might have kept. Then, I learned that the cantor was married with children. That's why the secret. I didn't want to know any more."

"These photos give me a different angle," Peter said. "A different angle on my work, a different angle on Rano. There is something uncompromising in the structures of the World Trade Center towers, something absolute. They exude a kind of everlasting truth, like two longtime lovers standing together. But sometimes compromise collides with the uncompromising."

Peter picked up a black and white on the table next to his brushes, the photo from Algeria that Linh and Angel found, the one Peter overlooked all those years. He handed the grainy photo to Thomas.

"Spending time with these snapshots," Peter continued, "I've come to understand that my hang-ups with Rano weren't about our compromises or about his secrets. They were about Rano's son, Mustafa, the young man in that photo. They were about the insanity of watching things vanish in ways you can't imagine."

"Rano had a son?"

Thomas was quiet for a bit, contemplating the snapshot. Peter surprised himself at the truth he'd revealed to Thomas, at how much sense this explanation made. Since he first laid eyes on the journal, he'd let Rano's secrets get under his skin. In the end, Rano's secrets were nothing more than that.

While Thomas studied Mustafa's photo, Peter looked again at the black-and-white photo of the black and white couple in front of the North Tower. Peter was certain now that Rano's secrets were not what had kept him from painting. He wondered what happened to the couple in this photo, whether he should paint them as though their lives came crumbling down after AIDS, or after 9/11, or not at all.

"I never would have barged in like I did," Thomas said, returning the photo of Mustafa and fetching the cups of iced drinks on the corner table, "except I brought something very exciting for you."

All Peter wanted to do now was to paint, but he was polite enough to wait for Thomas' exciting show-and-tell. It couldn't take long. First, Thomas offered an iced coffee to Peter. It had milk, the way Peter liked. Then, Thomas pulled out two muffins from one of the bags on the corner table. From the other bag, he pulled out a stack of paper held together with a metal binder clip. On the cover page, Peter recognized the author's name and the title of his book.

"Is this possible?" Peter asked. "Is this Rano's book?"

"I asked Erica's boyfriend to edit it," Thomas said. "Mark extracted the contents from the computer disks you gave Erica. He told me Rano's work was splendid. More than splendid. I believe Mark used the word 'groundbreaking,' something about passwords and identities."

"Rano occasionally got excited about something he'd refer to as 'identity theft.' " Peter said. "I forgot about that."

"Yes, that's it," Thomas replied. "I asked Mark to edit it for academic publication. With Rano's help, it seems Mark's becoming recognized as something of an expert in the field."

Peter stood up and took the paper stack from Thomas. Touching Rano's book overwhelmed him. He flipped through the pages. It felt so different from holding the remnants of Rano's journal, its heft, the clarity of its print. Scanning a sentence here and there, he heard Rano's voice, the intonation of Rano practicing a lecture. The loose-bound book was his reincarnation.

Thomas sipped lemonade and gazed at the million-dollar views, allowing Peter the time to appreciate Rano's book. Peter had no words. Rano got the reincarnation he wanted. There was, however, something deeply disturbing about this, something Peter had never quite understood before about Mustafa and the journal. It meant there had to be one more reincarnation for Rano. The guilt pressing on Peter's shoulders lightened.

"I have to start painting before my palette dries," Peter said, squeezing Thomas and kissing him on the cheek.

"I'm so delighted you're painting these snapshots instead of the skyline," Thomas said. He was radiant as Peter let go. "May I stay and watch?"

"I'd love that."

AUGUST 31, 1991 – DEATH

D ear Mustafa,

Unusual Saturday. Wrote all day. No nausea. Maybe because I'm home again. More energy. Perhaps energized by homecoming.

Ignored Peter most of day. Not on purpose, just writing. Seemed like he appreciated time for himself. No chance for my anger to erupt. I'll tell him about my breakthroughs tonight about identity theft. That will bore him and keep me from anger.

Felt good writing. Reworked ideas scribbled during hospital stay. Maybe not as breakthrough as other material, but maybe good construct for wrap-up?

Hospital strange. Stranger than other times. Glad not to be there. Morbid roommate camaraderie encourages honesty. Or forces honesty. Can't ignore dying guy in next bed, can't say, "Oh, he's just having a shitty day."

Doctors and nurses, our augurs, each speak a different tongue. Some hide behind jargon, others ask if we have what we need. After they examine or palpate or comfort, though, each one honest, saying what was seen, saying what was felt, revealing what it means (if they honestly know). Nothing to hide. No closets. A virtue of facing death.

Mustafa, my dearest Mustafa, I feel well enough today to know with certainty that I am facing death. I will never see you. I don't know if these words will reach you. I pray they do. I once asked Angel to destroy this journal if I die. I wanted only to protect you, keep these words from prying eyes, keep you and your mother safe. I pray Angel forgets my request. I've found another way to get my words to you just in case. However, I'll have no control soon.

I'm inserting Vito's speech here in my diary to remind you, dear Mustafa, never to acquiesce. I never accepted HIV as a death sentence. I have persisted against ignorance and intolerance. Even today, I continue to write. Soon you will carry on for me. You must fight for what you believe in. Make me proud, dearest son.

Whenever you lose your way, sweet Mustafa, read Vito's words. In good times and bad, they are a blessing and a comfort. I'm writing below the part of his speech that brought tears to my eyes today.

If I'm dying from anything, I'm dying from the fact that not enough rich, white, hetero-sexual men have gotten AIDS for anybody to give a shit. You know, living with AIDS in this country is like living in the twilight zone. Living with AIDS is like living through a war which is happening only for those people who happen to be in the trenches. Every time a shell explodes, you look around and you discover that you've lost more of your friends, but nobody else notices. It isn't happening to them. They're walking the streets as though we weren't living through some sort of nightmare. And only you can hear the screams of the people who are dying and their cries for help. No one else seems to be noticing.

I love you.

42

NEW YORK, SEPT 5, 2002

Mark killed time at Grand Central Station waiting for Frank's delayed train. He was doing Erica a favor, guiding her father from Grand Central to Peter's summer studio. According to Erica, she'd insisted Frank view Peter's portrayals of the Twin Towers because her father was so obsessed with 9/11. It seemed to Mark, though, that Erica was devising every possible opportunity before their wedding for Mark to bond with Frank. Regardless, he hadn't brought anything to amuse himself while waiting. A crumpled newspaper on the bench had stories about upcoming events commemorating the first anniversary of 9/11. Mark leafed through the pages while monitoring the arrivals board.

One article gave a timeline of 9/11 events the day of the attack, another the timeline of next week's anniversary events. Yet another article listed the dignitaries who would join Mayor Bloomberg at the official ceremony marking the anniversary. These included former Mayor Giuliani, Secretary of State Powell, leaders from ninety foreign countries, and the celebrated cellist Yo-Yo Ma.

Mark read with most interest an article describing *The Sphere*, a twenty-five-foot-diameter sculpture composed of fifty-two bronze pieces. Once dwarfed by the Twin Towers, the article explained, *The Sphere* survived the towers' 9/11 collapse largely intact. In the aftermath it had been moved to a salvage facility near JFK airport before it came to rest in Battery Park. At next week's ceremony, Mayor Bloomberg would rededicate the damaged artwork with an eternal flame. The German sculptor of *The Sphere*, Fritz Koenig, was quoted as saying, "It now has a different beauty, one I could never imagine. It has its own life—different from the one I gave to it."

A loudspeaker blurted the arrival of Frank's train. Mark found the sculptor's observation poignant, something Erica would appreciate. He tore out the article and slipped it into his pocket before he walked to the track. Frank waved from the platform, wearing blue jeans and a black T-shirt. As he approached, Mark recognized a photo of the actor Tom Cruise sporting shoulder-length hair on Frank's *Born on the Fourth of July* T-shirt

Mark wasn't sure what to make of this anti-war sentiment, and Frank wasn't talking much. The invitation to tonight's studio preview requested office casual attire. Frank's decade-old movie promotion T-shirt seemed a bit too casual, even by Danbury standards. Perhaps too provocative. Mark spotted a menswear store as they walked along one of Grand Central's corridors, but there wasn't time to spruce up Frank. Nothing to do now except remind him of the crosstown subway route. As they approached Thomas' midtown office building, the innocuous twenty-story structure that housed Peter's temporary studio, Frank finally perked up.

"Football season's starting," Frank said. "Should've been at practice today."

"Erica's very jazzed about this exhibit," Mark said.

"I'm not sure why she wanted me to see a gay art show."

"Erica said 9/11 was important to you," Mark said, navigating both the building lobby and his future father-in-law's politics. "She thought this show was an excellent anniversary tribute."

"At least the artist isn't Vietnamese this time," Frank said as the elevator door opened. "I know this artist is important to Erica, that he was supposed to travel on one of the hijacked flights. Does that make him some kind of an authority on 9/11?"

Mark pressed the elevator button and they reached the studio at twilight, just as the space blushed red. The view downtown and across the Hudson was dazzling. The gathering was already buzzing like one of those well-lubricated tourist excursions circling the island, full steam ahead. Frank darted straight away to the safety of Erica. He seemed out of his league here.

Mark had another task on his mind. Erica had asked a second, perhaps more important favor, to keep Linh and Frank separated or, at least, to maintain the peace should they end up together. Erica was worried Frank's prejudices might incite a war of words in the presence of Linh, or a disruptive discourse about Vietnam, or some other spectacle at an event meant to celebrate Peter and his art. Frank's T-shirt wasn't a good omen.

Thomas was across the room and many of Erica's other clients were scattered throughout the packed studio. From the configuration of the throng, Mark determined which person had to be the artist. The obvious candidate for Linh was the slender fashionista across the studio speaking with Thomas. She wore a simple gold lamé minidress topped with a glittering jade baseball cap. Luckily, Frank remained glued to Erica, about as distant from the jade baseball cap as possible. That gave Mark ample opportunity to snatch a glass of wine on his way to Thomas and his sparkling companion.

As Mark negotiated his way past the beverage table toward the baseball cap, he checked out the art. There were a dozen oil paintings, half on one wall, half on another. Together they resembled an album of supersized family snapshots. Mark remembered the afternoon he cooled his heels in Thomas' apartment, viewing Peter's landscapes there. Those paintings were a combination of abstract and representational painting, very different from this evening's hyperreal paintings. Wine in hand, he thought about how Erica would describe this art to her clients.

Most of the painted snapshots were in color, but a few looked like old black and whites. The works on the near wall featured single men and male couples posing in front of the Twin Towers. The towers loomed ominously, uniform dark metal monoliths overshadowing the animated figures in the foreground.

The far wall had different paintings of men. In these, couples or groups of friends posed atop the Twin Towers on the observation deck. They floated like angels over vistas of New York and New Jersey, vistas rendered in painstaking detail with majestic rivers separating the various landmasses.

The men in all the photos looked gay. They held hands or made fawning gestures. They wore natty suits, leather jackets, hippy tie-dye, Lycra gym shorts. Some had stylishly colored hair, others pornstaches. There were T-shirts with "Silence = Death" or "AIDS Walk" or other gay rallying cries. One man wore a snappy head-to-toe outfit of what Mark recognized as Keith Haring figures.

Mark passed a painting of a man wearing a hideous plaid suit and turned back. For some reason, this man had to be Rano. It wasn't just the dark skin or the carefree attitude of the subject. The intensity of the eyes was somehow familiar. The world's knowledge dwelled behind those eyes. They had to be the eyes of the researcher whose brilliant ideas he'd resurfaced. Who else besides Rano would have the self-confidence to wear fashion so blatant while grinning ear to ear without a care in the world?

"Pardon," a man said, accidentally brushing against Mark. The man was examining the same painting. He was short and moved economically.

"Do you know if this is the painter's partner?" Mark asked the man. "The one who died of AIDS."

"Yes, you can tell by the bulge," the man answered, extending his hand to Mark. "That's a snapshot of Rano, and I'm Brice."

"Nice to meet you," Mark said, shaking hands. "Something about the eyes makes me think I've seen him somewhere before."

"It's more than a memory for me," Brice said. "I took the photo that Peter painted."

"Oh, wow," Mark said, finishing his glass of wine. "That's an odd angle, pointing the camera from the ground toward the sky. It makes Rano look larger than life."

"In many ways he was," Brice said. "Perhaps you slept with him, too?"

"Um, no," Mark replied, puzzled. "I'm here because my fiancée is the gallerist representing Peter."

"Oh, sorry," Brice said, laughing at his own faux pas. "You must be Mark, the one promoting Rano's book."

Both Mark and Brice turned to face the painting. Mark didn't know anything about Brice, but Brice seemed to know a lot about him. He considered asking Brice the questions about Rano that he'd wanted to ask Peter. He wanted to know what inspired Rano to investigate the topic of identity theft. He wanted to know about someone named Leslie, what role she played in writing Rano's book. Erica wouldn't grant Mark access to Peter all summer. Don't dare contact Peter, she warned Mark, until he finishes painting. Technically, Mark could ask Peter questions about Rano right now since the paintings were on the wall. Mark checked the throng. Peter would be trapped in the press of art aficionados the rest of the evening.

"I didn't mean to imply you were gay," Brice said, turning back to Mark. "It's just that I dig redheads."

"I'm flattered, actually," Mark said, feeling himself blush. Men had hit on him, but this felt more personal because of the mutual connection to Rano. At any rate, Brice seemed innocent enough, if a little stoned. "I wish I had an ounce of gay sensibility. What do you think of Peter's work?"

"I'm envious," Brice answered. "The beauty of Peter's art makes me wish I'd continued on my own creative course. If I hadn't left dance to build a business, maybe I could have created something this beautiful."

"It's amazing how all the figures in these paintings have vanished and Peter's interpretations of the snapshots are the only things left," Mark said, looking at Rano's image again. "Like a trace of a trace, a memory of a memory. Too bad Rano never saw this conceptual brilliance."

"What was in Rano's book that allowed Peter to start painting again?" Brice asked. "I'd ask Peter, but I haven't seen much of him since he started painting this series. Was there some reference? Some story?"

"Rano's book is pretty technical," Mark answered. "I can't imagine anything would've been relevant to Peter's painting."

"Maybe Peter figured out something about Rano's journal," Brice said. "I don't know what it was, but somehow these snapshots inspired Peter to paint again."

"I did run across something personal on the Internet," Mark said, realizing why the eyes in the painting looked familiar. "I can't imagine Peter has seen it, though. Rano used this passé protocol called Gopher to post information about Algeria. Luckily a guy named Brewster at the Internet Archive helped me find it."

"What kind of personal information?" Brice asked.

"Did Rano have a son?"

Before Brice could answer, a commotion broke out on the other side of the studio. Frank was pushing through the crowd, yelling something that ended with, "I would have fucked more in Vietnam if all the girls dressed like you." When he reached the woman with the jade baseball cap, Frank strummed an air guitar and belted out a Bruce Springsteen song, a song Mark recognized from the Tom Cruise film. All the attention in the room shifted from Peter and his art to Frank and his pathos.

"That guy is certifiably crazy even by New York standards," Brice said to Mark. "Poor Linh shouldn't have to deal with Vietnam shit like this."

Mark grimaced as he weaved towards the outburst. He saw Erica pushing through the crowd from the other side of the room. Frank had gone way over the edge. Thomas stepped between Frank and Linh, as if to protect her. Linh stepped around Thomas and had indistinct words with Frank. Thomas looked shocked, almost paralyzed by her words. As Mark and Erica reached Frank, he dropped to his knees and hummed while rocking back and forth.

"Who is this crazy grandpa," Thomas snapped, stepping close. "He's like the soldiers at Saigon clubs, taunting women they planned to pay."

"I need to deal with the guests," Erica said to Mark, handing him keys. "Can you take Dad down to my gallery?"

"Oh, geez," Thomas said, stepping back to Linh.

"Of course," Mark answered, taking the keys with one hand and putting his other on Frank's shoulder.

"Don't touch me," Frank growled. "And never fucking call me 'grandpa.' "

"You will be," Mark said, without removing his hand. "You will be Grandpa soon."

September 2, 1991 – Future

Dear Mustafa,

Feeling crappy. Hanging on. Health so fucking unpredictable now. No control.

Why am I writing you? Won't meet you. Don't know you.

You religious? Gay? Kids? Work? Happy?

Aaliya?

You wonder about me?

Huge disappointment not meeting you. Father without son. No future.

43

New York, Sept 9, 2002

"Yes," Peter replied. "I packed up the studio this weekend and Erica helped move all the paintings to the gallery this morning."

"Sorry work kept me from helping," Brice said. "Did Thomas help?"

"He's been too kind already," Peter answered. It didn't seem appropriate to discuss Thomas with Brice, the disappointment that Thomas disappeared after the preview without saying a word.

"I hope Erica's father isn't coming to opening night." Brice extricated a joint from his cargo shorts. "Smoke?"

Peter shook his head. Pot was the last thing on his mind. The New York buzz was wearing off now and Peter looked forward to getting home, sleeping in his own bed. It had been a longer stay than anticipated, a sweet cocktail of contemplation, painting, and urban discovery, topped with the cherries of Rano's book and a successful preview—well, except for the bitter taste of Frank's insane Vietnam rant.

"I've got to clean up Linh's place before I leave," Peter said. "I'd hoped to fly today in case there's a repeat 9/11 attack."

"You never could've got everything packed by today," Brice said, waving the joint over Peter's newfound treasures. On the coffee table, guides and program books Peter collected while surveying the city. By the wall, a sizable Statue of Liberty tchotchke recovered during a walk along the Hudson River. Stacked on a chair, six I ♥ NY T-shirts purchased in a rainbow of colors during the first giddy days searching for snapshots. "Besides, your plane won't get off the ground carrying all this stuff."

"I should donate it to an AIDS charity," Peter said, remembering everything else stashed in the bedroom.

"Even Housing Works won't touch this," Brice said, holding out the joint. "Come on. Could be your last opportunity to smoke with me."

"Sorry I was too busy working to spend more time together." Peter couldn't read Brice, whether the pot was a lure for sex. "Anyway, Linh comes back from the Hamptons tonight. I promised I'd clean up."

"Suit yourself." Brice sounded disappointed as he put the joint in his pocket. "I'm quitting marijuana for 9/11."

"That's symbolic," Peter said. The main reason for getting together with Brice today was to show him Rano's diary and tell him about Mustafa, not run some kind of twelve-step session.

"I learned a few things at your preview," Brice said, sitting on the couch. "One is that I'm envious of you."

"What?!" Peter couldn't read Brice at all this afternoon. Was he on the verge of some Big Announcement? Maybe pot wasn't such a bad idea. They should've spent more time together.

"I envy your dedication to painting," Brice continued. "Your work is so rich. I wish I'd stayed with dance the same way."

"Are you having a midlife crisis?" Peter asked, sitting next to Brice.

"Are you?" Brent replied.

"No," Peter said. "I am, however, all these years later, feeling closure with Rano. Or clarity. Something."

"Your painting of Rano." Brice rested his hand on Peter's knee. "It took me back."

Brice's delicate touch was monumental. Significant. As if he'd moved exactly the right way at exactly the right time. It wasn't a let's-fuck gesture. It was a pay-attention gesture.

"I have to show you something," Peter said, trying to remember where he'd hidden Rano's journal. "First, though, tell me why you're giving up pot."

"Because I'm going to dance again," Brice said.

"Really?" Peter asked. Brice was a thing in his day. The world, however, was not wanting for talented middle-aged dancers. "Are you sure? What about your business?"

"Quite sure," Brice said. "I'll find someone to run it."

"Aren't you a little long in the tooth?" Peter asked.

"Maybe," Brice said. "Maybe I'll teach or start a dance company. Whatever. I have to get back to dance." He removed his hand from Peter's knee. "There was something else I learned during the preview."

"Wait," Peter said, heading to the bedroom. "I want to show you Rano's diary."

"Before you do, I have to tell you about Rano's son."

"You knew Rano had a son?" Peter stopped and turned around. He'd been humiliated by this secret that suddenly seemed not to have been a secret at all. "Why keep that from me?"

"I promised Rano," Brice answered, stopping a moment to compose himself. "I pray he's safe and sound."

As difficult as these words seemed for Brice, they stung Peter. He felt betrayed, a year ago by Rano and now by Brice. What made Rano tell Brice about Mustafa? Why did Peter have to wait for the journal to find out? It was so unsettling.

"It's okay," Peter said, remembering parts of the journal, calming himself. "Rano wanted to protect Mustafa. He was paranoid that somehow his journal would fall into the hands of religious zealots, would put Mustafa in danger, so he asked Angel to destroy it. On his deathbed, he must have wanted to make sure someone knew about Mustafa."

"The son's name is Mustafa?" Brice asked, wiping away tears. "Rano didn't tell me that."

"When did he tell you?"

"Just before he died." Brice needed another moment. "After Rano died, I concluded he suffered some kind of deathbed delirium. He said his son was living in Orem, where I was born in Utah. Nothing made sense."

Peter turned and continued to the bedroom. Things with Rano were feeling less clear than before Brice's visit. When Peter had completed the painting of Rano, he had a sense of resolution, like he'd captured Rano's essence between its four corners, put all the pieces back in the box. Now there seemed to be pieces he'd missed. Peter pushed aside his roller bag and dug out a plastic bag under the bed.

"Here's what's left of Rano's journal," Peter said, returning with the mildewy bag. "What made you decide to disclose your secret today?"

"Well, I met Erica's fiancé, Mark, at the preview," Brice said, more to himself. "And Mark told me Rano had a son, so I figured Mustafa wasn't a secret anymore."

"Wait, wait, wait. What?"

"Mark said Rano posted some personal information on some obscure Internet thingy, something about gophers. Who knows? Anyway, Mark definitely found something online about the son."

"What else did he tell you about Mustafa?" Peter asked.

"Nothing," Brice answered. "That's when Frank went ballistic."

Peter placed the mildewy bag on the coffee table. While Brice rotated it to examine Rano's journal, Peter sat next to Brice again, relieved he wasn't learning all this while he was high. Why would Rano put personal information on the Internet and then hide it? How did Mark find it? This news made no sense.

"When half the journal was destroyed by water," Peter said after a while, "I went to pieces. It was like watching Rano get washed out to sea. I'm excited that Mark knows where to find more about Rano and Mustafa online."

"Can I read the journal?" Brice asked.

The journal hadn't left Peter's possession since he found it. It would be strange to leave it in New York. However, it might help Brice remember more details about Mustafa. "Will you promise to return it before I leave?"

A key rattled in the lock and the apartment door flew open.

"Look at the lovebirds," Linh said, putting down a weekend bag by the door.

"You're back early from the Hamptons," Peter said, surveying the mess.

"Thomas offered me a lift." Linh took off her baseball cap and wiped her forehead. "This air conditioning is delicious."

"Wait, you went with Thomas?" Peter asked. "How am I the last to know where Thomas went this weekend?"

"Bumped into him at a party," Linh said. "I thought *I* knew a lot of artists. Watching Thomas, though. Wow. He's connected."

"Are you okay?" Brice asked, standing up to hug Linh.

"You mean about Erica's father?" Linh replied. "Yeah. I'm more worried about Erica."

"I probably should get going, then," Brice said. "I know Peter needs to clean up and pack."

"Oh, please don't go," Linh begged. "Or, if you go, at least come to our picnic lunch tomorrow in Central Park. Thomas and I will bring everything."

"Peter gave me a big reading assignment," Brice said, lifting the plastic bag from the coffee table. "Besides, I think before Peter leaves, he may need some time to thank Thomas."

September 4, 1991 – Waiting

Dear Mustafa,

Better now. As always, Peter an angel. Served breakfast in bed.

I barely slept. Not from working on my book—although between heaving and shitting, had occasional presence of mind to scratch out thoughts. Mind still working. Not worst of nights. Didn't drown in sweat or shit the sheets.

No appetite. Too bad for Peter. Another meticulous presentation. Melons perfect. No idea where he found time. He must have stopped at farmers market. Past peak peach season and yet—and yet vibrant yellow slices ringing orange cantaloupe balls. Veritable festival Ferris wheel. Couldn't taste sweetness, but abundant freshness in my nostrils scaring death out of my sinuses. Ha!

Stomach gurgled warnings, mind demanded to know whether I'd savor next year's crop. Body a fucking minstrel show of grotesque surprises. Tired, tired, tired of corporeal dramas. I may have pushed too hard to leave hospital. Peter mentioned hospice.

Obviously better now. I'm writing this. Like rebirth, coming back to life. Never know. Every hour a surprise. Could die tomorrow. Need cure today. Ten years since first AIDS deaths here. No cure is insanity.

Sporadic time to work on book today. Leslie the Librarian stopped by to order floppy disks by chapter. At least, that was her excuse.

Leslie brought important news, Mustafa. Scientist named LeVay says hypothalamus of gay men smaller than hypothalamus of straight men. She laughed. Sang "If I Only Had a Brain" from *Wizard of Oz*. Homosexuality is genetic. If you didn't inherit the gay gene, dear Mustafa, don't hold it against me. I did my best.

The not knowing, dear Mustafa, is fucking confusing. Will I finish chapter? Want food? Will it stay down? Shoot through?

How do I tell Peter? I exhaust him. He asked friends to help. So hard to ask when entire San Francisco gay community exhausted. Nurse gives Peter a couple hours off. When she can get here. Angel gave him a night off this week. What did Peter do? Cried himself to sleep. Didn't want anyone to hear. Even Angel gave me a look after a while.

Fuck, Mustafa. Forgot to ask Angel not to destroy this. Fuck, fuck, fuck. Must remember next time. Must, must, must.

Brice flies in tomorrow. Not sure I want Brice to see me like this. Skinny.

What vanity.

Only you, great Vanity, ignore Death.

Does this hospital gown make my ass look fat?

Sometimes seems harder on Peter. Maybe it is. If you meet him, Mustafa, treat him as a relative. You must meet him.

Get angry with him sometimes. Sorry, sorry, sorry. But I'm the one who's fucking dying. Thin as a rail, frail as a great-grandfather.

I should feel guilty for writing this instead of chapter. Peter insists I finish book. Don't know what that means. Finish before I die? Finish so I can die? Finish so next book keeps me breathing, keeps me alive? Can't be dead if I'm writing. Keep writing.

For all I know, I'll be the only one reading the book (or this journal, if Angel destroys it). Culmination of five years of research and class presentations. Why did I choose ethics in computer age? Seems complete. Then technology evolves. They say nothing stops technology. They say an AIDS cure is right around the corner. Fucking Reagan administration killed that technology. Bush no better. "Government for the people."

Not sure I can finish book because not sure it's finishable. Sorry, Peter. In your hands.

At least, it will be clear when journal finished, dear Mustafa. Stiff fingers can't type. Will brain work until end? Memory? Where do memories go?

44

NEW YORK, SEPT 10, 2002

No more morning sickness. That was excellent timing because Erica had no time left to install Peter's show. Mark would be along any second to take her to lunch. As Erica suspended the final painting of Peter's Twin Tower series, she questioned her unconventional presentation. The exhibit had to live up to the occasion, honor the memories of so many lost. If the paintings were mounted on the wall, it would have made Erica's life easier, but it wouldn't be special. Maybe she'd gone overboard. She took one last look at Peter's new work and pushed aside the ladder.

"Thank goodness for your air conditioning," Thomas said as he entered the gallery, legs bare and hands straining under the weight of shopping bags. He stopped to consider the way Erica displayed Peter's work.

Erica had no time for social calls, but she always made time for her best client. She hoped Thomas wasn't here to discuss her father's outburst at Peter's preview. She'd already spent too much time on the phone with Frank trying to understand what set him off, why he hijacked the event. At least he'd come clean about having sex in Vietnam, but there was so much more. No time to rehash all that. The Fifth Avenue shopping bags in Thomas' hands were an indication that he stopped by for a quick look, not for a serious talk.

"What do you think?" Erica asked, wiping her hands on her pants before hugging Thomas. She'd thought for days about how to position Peter's works. It was harder than usual because her exhibition concept was so different from the way Peter had arranged his own work.

"Peter's display was a practical solution for the preview space," Thomas said. "You've conjured up something quite special."

"These paintings are about unparalleled buildings and end times," Erica said. "With the gravity of the first anniversary of 9/11, I wanted a symbolic way to present Peter's series."

Erica had secured Peter's works with wires attached to the ceiling and anchored to the floor. The artwork floated in the air, a bit higher than eye level, swaying slightly like heavy muslin sheets put out to dry. She arranged the paintings in two circles, one small circle with the six paintings of men posing at the base of the towers, the other large circle with the six paintings of men on the observation deck.

The paintings in the small circle faced outwards so that viewers could walk outside the circle of artworks as though they were walking around a miniature tower. Above the small circle, a placard read *It now has a different beauty, one I could never imagine.*

The paintings in the large circle faced inwards. Viewers could step inside this circle and rotate as though they were on the observation deck looking out at the vistas. Above the larger circle was another placard. *It has its own life—different from the one I gave to it.*

"I imagine this small circle of paintings as one of the Twin Towers," Erica said as Thomas surveyed the gallery, "and the center of the larger circle of paintings over there as the observation deck. I want the viewer to sense the physicality of the towers and the observation deck as they view the artwork."

"Do I need an entrance ticket for the observation deck?" Thomas said, grinning. He toted his shopping bags around Erica's imaginary tower and over to her imaginary observation deck without another word.

Erica worried whether she'd got this arrangement right. Thomas would be honest enough to let her know. She watched his movements while he looked at the paintings, noting the time he spent looking at paintings and interacting with the space.

"It's an unconventional presentation," Thomas said, placing his shopping bags on the ground next to Erica. "Very conceptual."

Conceptual. Hmm. Smart choice of words. It could be a good criticism or bad, but it was a criticism. Thomas was letting Erica know her display could upstage the artwork it was meant to enhance. There wasn't much Erica could change now. The show opened the next day, on the anniversary of 9/11. After lunch with Mark, there was still cleanup and marketing work left in the afternoon. The entire exhibit preparation was on a tight timeline as it was.

"Also," Thomas said, smiling wryly, "there's no mention of me."

"Oh, dear," Erica said, unsure how to take this. Museums sometimes mentioned patrons who sponsored an exhibition. She couldn't think of a gallery show that explicitly acknowledged a patron. Erring on the side of caution, she addressed Thomas' offhand remark seriously. "You've done so much for Peter, validating the market for his art, providing him a makeshift summer studio. This exhibit wouldn't be here without you. I should have thought to give you some kind of credit."

"It's not credit I want, or even deserve," Thomas said after a pause. "What's getting under my skin is my uncertainty about Peter. I have no idea where I stand, as a friend, or a supporter, or anything else."

"He's always thankful for your support, Thomas," Erica said. Even though it was obvious Thomas had a romantic interest, there was nothing but risk talking about romance with her best customer, especially when the love interest was her best artist. This topic felt more fraught than Frank's outburst at the preview. "He has nothing but the kindest words for you."

"I wish I'd heard a few of them," Thomas said. "But Peter is a quiet one, so it's his actions that trouble me. Even after providing a studio, I was the one who had to initiate all our interactions. Maybe he's involved with Brice or someone I don't know about."

"It's funny you should mention that," Erica said, recalling Brice's complaints about Peter when he'd performed his extemporaneous dance in her gallery. "Brice said the same thing, in so many words, when he stopped by the gallery."

"Did he?" Thomas asked. "That's amusing. Well, maybe I can chalk up Peter's distance to his time in front of the canvas."

"He was under tremendous pressure to deliver the series in time for tomorrow's anniversary," Erica said, digging into the romance conversation she'd just advised herself to avoid. "Perhaps, Thomas, you're like those movie fans who fall in love with an actor only to discover they fell in love with the character."

"Yes, my interest might be misguided," Thomas said. "Peter's art is spectacular. I consulted a rabbi friend about that. Artists sometimes wear masks, he said, and masks make poor companions. I do feel like I'm peering behind the artist's mask, though, when I look at this new series. Don't you think it reveals more about Peter?"

"That's a good point," Erica said, impressed at how Thomas always found new attributes in art. "The Twin Towers have a sincerity unlike Peter's previous work."

"I've searched my heart," Thomas said, "and I believe my interest in Peter to be distinct from my interest in his art."

As always, Thomas' deliberations were thorough. His current state of romantic uncertainty reminded Erica of herself. It was only a year ago that she was running away from Mark, afraid of the thornier sides of his personality. Thomas was wiser. He wouldn't run from Peter's imperfections. He would bide his time. If things worked out, it would be well worth Thomas' wait.

"I wonder if Peter is available for a relationship yet," Erica said. "Has he resolved his feelings about Rano?"

"Is it just me?" Thomas asked. "Did you sense that Rano pervades the Twin Tower series?"

"Yes," Erica said, relieved at the change of subject. "I had the same feeling at Peter's preview. The works are a dialogue not only between the certain structure of the towers and the unpredictable lives of gay men during times of crisis, but also between Rano and Peter. There's, of course, the explicit dialogue between them in the painting of Rano wearing that odd suit, but their dialogue runs throughout the rest of the series as well." Erica paused a moment. "Actually, it was Mark who pointed that out to me afterwards. He said he felt a bit like he was seeing Rano's ghost."

"After editing Rano's book, Mark may have a better sense of the ghost than anyone, even Peter," Thomas said. From the assortment of fancy shopping bags, he selected the one from Tiffany and offered it to Erica. "I know it's early, but I saw this and thought it would be perfect for your baby."

"Thomas, you shouldn't have," Erica said, accepting the aqua-blue bag. She was delighted. There were so many things on her mind with this exhibit and with her father, she hadn't even thought about a baby shower, let alone the myriad of baby things she and Mark needed for the Brooklyn apartment they now shared. Let alone wedding plans. "I'll wait to open it until Mark arrives."

"Of course," Thomas said. "By the way, I've read the first chapter of the book Mark's working on."

"You mean Rano's book?" Erica asked.

"Yes," Thomas answered. "I don't understand everything, but the concepts seem impressive. I mentioned it to Linh. She knew Rano rather well."

"Linh did know Rano quite well," Erica said. "She's friends with Peter and Brice, too."

"We're having a picnic in Central Park this afternoon if you'd care to join," Thomas said, holding out one of the bags. "Linh asked me to bring cheese."

"As tempting as it smells, Mark is taking me to lunch," Erica said. She had noticed Thomas and Linh during Peter's studio party. Everyone had. Linh wore that over-the-top jade baseball cap. The two spoke at length, as though no one else was in the room. At first, it seemed the two wealthiest people at the event were ignoring the peons. Then, it became clear how much the two of them clicked, that they had a great deal in common, starting with their interest in fashion. Their obliviousness to the rest of the crowd was sweet to watch. "Linh lost everything in Vietnam," Erica continued, "then moved here and made bazillions. She has an extraordinary firsthand knowledge of New York artists."

"I've enjoyed getting to know her. You know, I couldn't speak with anyone Vietnamese after I returned from the war." Thomas turned to look at Peter's work. "Maurice encouraged me to see a therapist. Once I understood how my distrust of Vietnamese was like white people's distrust of me, I worked through it."

"As you seemed to have guessed from my father's performance at the preview, he served in Vietnam, too," Erica said. She didn't want to rehash the conversation about Frank's outburst. "Maybe you two should meet."

"That was something, your father strumming the air guitar and singing Bruce Springsteen," Thomas said, turning back to look at Erica.

"I'm not sure what's happening with my father," Erica replied, dreading this conversation. "He keeps it bottled up. I don't remember him saying a word about Vietnam until he found his Purple Heart at Christmas. Even then, he doesn't talk about it. Then that outburst. I'm not sure what to do."

"War destroys lives," Thomas said. "The conditions of war require keeping secrets to survive. That, and smoking a lot of dope. I returned from Vietnam with some very poor habits. I hope your father finds his way."

This was the first conversation Erica had about her father with someone who'd served in Vietnam. Even this brief exchange was useful, more useful than other conversations she'd had about Frank and the war. There was so much more for Frank to process, but there wasn't enough time to discuss this with Frank. She saw Mark down the block, approaching the gallery.

"I haven't told anyone this," Erica said, "but when I met Linh, I had an odd sensation that she was my sister. It was the look in her eyes. But suppose my father got someone pregnant during the war, something he, of course, denies. What are the chances Linh could be his child?"

"A lot of crazy shit happened in Vietnam," Thomas said. "Starting with the fact that we were even fighting a war there."

"I don't think I told you," Erica said. Mark was close enough that she could see the bouquet in his hand. "We decided to name the baby Lynn."

"That's good," Thomas said. "It's the name I had them emboss on your present."

September 4, 1991

F uck, fuck, fuck. Don't want to die. Hope Peter understands, moves on without me. Thank Goddess he tested negative.

I pray you're unharmed, too, Mustafa.

45

New York, Sept 10, 2002

Thomas had his eyes out for Linh when he spotted Peter in the shade of a mature tree, snoozing on a blanket. A pleasant surprise. Peter was exactly where Linh said to meet, the lawn on the opposite side of 79th Street transverse from the Delacorte Theater. Hotter than Hades in the sun. Thomas chided himself. He'd spent too long downtown with Erica. No time to drop the shopping bags at home before coming to Central Park. And the cheese. Even the parmigiano would be limp by now.

Under the canopy of the graceful elm, Thomas stood over Peter quietly, studying his face. They were not so far from the Ramble and a memory flashed through Thomas' mind, a glimpse of Maurice that first hot, smoggy evening thirty-some years ago. Thomas spoke softly to wake Peter. "Hey."

Peter's eyes fluttered as he stretched his arms and legs.

"I was looking for Linh," Thomas said. "I found you."

"Lucky me." Peter smiled hello as he sat up. "I'm not sure Linh is coming. She said it's hotter than Vietnam today."

"She's right," Thomas said, dropping his bags and sitting by Peter's side. As tempting as it was to put his arm around Peter, it would be uncomfortably hot. And perhaps a little forward. "I'd make you a grilled cheese sandwich if I had any bread."

"Sorry I didn't bring any food," Peter said. "Linh said she was going to shop and then, I don't know, the heat must have gotten to her."

"Poor thing," Thomas said, disappointed not to visit with Linh again, but thrilled to have time alone with Peter. "Hey, I just came from the gallery."

"Really?" Peter asked. "How does the show look? I'm supposed to be there in an hour to check it out myself."

Such a short rendezvous would quench Thomas' thirst for Peter as much as a thimble of beer on a hot Vietnamese beach. Thomas described Erica's presentation of Peter's art, the small circle of paintings facing outwards and the large circle of paintings facing inwards.

"That's a little conceptual," Peter said after Thomas finished. "I mean, the display might overwhelm the art."

"Erica's found a smart way to market your work for 9/11," Thomas said, digging for a rationalization to keep Peter from flying downtown in a panic. "So what are your plans after tomorrow's opening?"

"After I go home, I'm not sure, actually," Peter said. There was one of those silences with Peter. He seemed to be cogitating about Erica's conceptual installation, but Thomas couldn't be sure. Then Peter rested his hand on Thomas' bare knee. "I'm thinking about a trip."

This was the first unprovoked physical interest Peter had expressed. Thomas kept his hands to himself. He wanted to be sure of Peter's intent. "Where?"

"Algeria," Peter replied.

"Algeria?" Thomas asked. Why would Peter travel to Algeria? Why not New England? New England landscapes were legendary, perfect for Peter. "Part of Maurice's family was from Algeria," Thomas continued as though Algeria were an obvious destination for Peter, "a small town called Oran. I only remember that because Maurice reminded me a hundred times that Camus set one of his books in Oran."

"Orem?" Peter asked.

"Orem is in Utah," Thomas replied. "Oran is in Algeria."

"Is Oran on the coast?" Peter asked. "Rano worked somewhere on the coast."

"Yes, but it's a long coast," Thomas answered, thinking about Erica's question, about whether Peter had resolved his feelings for Rano. Thomas had to find out. "I could show you Maurice's photos of Oran, of the Jewish neighborhood when there was a Jewish neighborhood."

"Can I see them now?" Peter asked, squeezing Thomas' leg.

"It's physically impossible for you to come to my place and then meet Erica downtown in an hour," Thomas said, resting his hand on top of Peter's.

"Erica would understand if I were waylaid at your place," Peter said, leaning so their shoulders touched. "I'm sure her installation is fine. Anyway, it's not like she has time to change it."

Thomas pressed into Peter and closed his eyes. As their lips touched, he felt again what he'd felt thirty-some years ago with Maurice, when rain drenched him with love.

SEPTEMBER 11, 2002 – INSANITY

D ear Mustafa,

I have so many things to tell you. Too many. I have to dash off to the opening of my new show at Erica's gallery soon. First, though, it's a pleasure to meet you.

I'll start with my Grandma Eunice. She lived on the Kansas River her entire life. She moved once, after she married, a distance of two miles from the farm where she grew up. Eunice said the river gave her everything she needed—her children, her joy, her sorrow, her everyday wisdom, even her riveting vocabulary.

In New York this year, I spent time along the Hudson River, contemplating what Eunice taught me and remembering your father. I sat for hours, listening to the Hudson the way Eunice taught me to listen to the Kaw. As I watched birds, tugboats, rowers, I imagined Rano might wash up on shore.

Earlier today, he did. Imagine my joy. You should have seen him. In the version of Rano's story the river told me this morning, Rano rowed his boat up the River Styx, pulling those glitter paddles Brice dreamed up, and landed near me. I couldn't miss his antiretroviral pills, the ones that saved his life. As he approached, he rattled them in a yellow plastic pharmacy bottle. Then he sat down next to me. Words were pointless. We held hands and listened to the water flowing by.

After a while, what I understood was that Rano had two regrets. First and foremost, of course, never finding you, Mustafa. He let me know it was important that I give you his journal. I already knew that. It will be difficult. I don't know much about where you live or what you look like. I speak neither Arabic nor French. All I know for sure is your first name. And a grainy photo of you when you must have been a teen. You probably live in Oran. I just found out your father posted details about your mother and her family on the Internet. When I think I know everything about Rano, miraculously there's more.

Regardless of what Rano posted about online, I promised him I would find you in person, Mustafa. I also let him know that I would ask a man named Thomas to accompany me, a man who's supported my work, a man I trust, the man I slept with last night. Rano smiled that loving smile of his.

Rano also regretted that he and I never moved to New York. He was right, as always. We should have moved. In his journal—the journal you will read someday, Mustafa—Rano unfairly compared me to Brutus murdering Caesar on the Ides of March, implying my refusal to move with him to New York betrayed him violently. Nothing, Mustafa, nothing could be further from the truth.

Sitting on the shore, I let Rano know I never intended to sabotage our relationship, though I might have. I let Rano know that, all those years ago, when I said I had to continue painting in San Francisco, I didn't understand at the time it was a lie.

The truth, Mustafa, wasn't that I needed to stay in San Francisco. The truth was different. The truth, as I explained to Rano, was that I had been too scared of New York to move, too terrified by the pressure of New York's art scene, the ferocity of its galleries and critics.

I didn't comprehend this different truth until recently, not until I saw some snapshots. On a ferry to Fire Island, I struck up a conversation with a man named Ken, complimenting his Tom of Finland mustache. At some point, Ken said his boyfriend had worked in the World Trade Center and survived 9/11. I told Ken that I, too, survived the attack. I'd booked a flight home that day but postponed it to have dinner with an art collector named Thomas, the same Thomas, it turns out, whose bed I shared last night. The flight I missed was hijacked. Everyone on board perished.

That tragedy, Mustafa, happened one year ago today. Every day since, I have thought about you and about Rano.

The conversations with Ken were the catalyst for my epiphany about New York. During my first day on Fire Island, he pulled out photos of his boyfriend, Charles, standing in front of the North Tower. Charles was adorable, a lithe young redhead with a blissful smile. Holding his photos in my hand triggered something inside me, something I didn't understand.

After a few days talking with Ken and examining the photos, I was lounging by a pool that faced the expansive Atlantic. I watched a plane fly by and connected Charles' story to mine, realized a truth I hadn't recognized before. Charles hated the structure of the tower, felt somehow it would crush his spirit. Like Charles, I also had feared a structure. I'd feared the structure of New York's art scene the way Charles had feared the structure of the North Tower.

Sitting with Rano on the riverbank, I explained all this, how it was a subconscious fear that kept me from New York. Then something unheard beckoned Rano to return to the Styx. I had to tell him about his book, about Mark editing it. Mustafa, you will be proud of the astonishing book your father wrote. Its reincarnation is a miracle. I quickly described how Mark extracted a draft from the remnants of Rano's disks and created a version for academics to review, how Mark was evangelizing Rano's ideas far and wide. At this news, Rano jumped and waved his arms.

I wasn't sure when I would see Rano again. Before he could digest the good news about his book, I blurted out what I'd painted for the gallery show, paintings of Charles' snapshot and similar snapshots I'd found later. Rano winked approvingly. As he got back into his boat and waved farewell, I knew he still loved me.

I left without telling Rano everything. That's why I'm writing you, Mustafa. It's why I have to meet you.

During the past year, I was too upset to paint, but I wasn't sure why. I was upset that I'd kept Rano from New York. I was mad at Rano for the attention he gave you and ashamed that Rano kept you secret from me. I never understood why Rano got angry with me, why he would lash out unexpectedly.

When I connected Charles' snapshot with my fear of New York, I thought I was ready to paint again. As I was putting brush to canvas, Thomas interrupted to show me Rano's book, the one that Mark restored. That's when it struck me. It was as disturbing as watching the jet vanish inside the North Tower. The thing that stopped me from painting wasn't my fear of New York. I'd had a successful gallery show. Like Charles, I'd navigated the structure.

What kept me from painting was a man named Carl, a man I hope you don't know, but fear you do. If you do, you'll understand why I wanted him in jail. After Carl attacked Rano and me one night, I had no choice. I prosecuted Carl against Rano's wishes. Rano, who always made sense, didn't make any sense. Why was he protecting his ex-lover? Jailing Carl was our only protection from his insanity.

I was innocent of the harm I did until I read Rano's journal. Rano never told me Carl was his best possible connection to you. Rano never told me I destroyed his best hope to meet his son. Rano never told me Carl might have abused you.

The insanity of Carl is the insanity of life. It's the insanity of wars destroying soldiers and civilians. It's the insanity of Rano dying so young along with so many other gay men. It's the insanity of airplanes flying into towers.

Carl is the insanity that damaged Rano's trust in me. The insanity is that it's my fault, but I could not have known. For Rano's memory, I need to make sure you're okay. For my sanity, I have to present you his journal.

I love your father now more than ever. I'll never reconcile with Rano entirely about New York. It's too late for that. But I can put us back together again if I give you what's left of his journal. When Thomas handed me Rano's ethics book—this miraculous reincarnation of Rano—I realized Rano needed one more reincarnation. You, Mustafa, you will realize this, too, after reading the remnants of the journal. After that, Rano will reconcile with me. I'm sure of it. As a gesture of goodwill, I painted a splendid snapshot of him. He might regret the plaid suit he wore, but Rano would be proud of my painting.

I will see you soon, Mustafa. I promise.

ACKNOWLEDGEMENTS

Deborah Constable for reading along.

Leslie Tomkins for her empathy for me and my characters.

Rabih Alameddine for his reading tips and writing tricks.

Frederick Johnston for introducing me to Peter.

Peter Poskas II for the diary story.

Rano Guerfi, may he rest in peace, for his humor.

Jim Constantine for Fire Island time.

David Spitzer for Tales of the City introductions.

Ebet Roberts for her composition.

Jimmy Seeger because Jimmy Seeger.

Brad Rubenstein for ethics, technology, and feminism tips.

Janet L. Ference for reading.

Cristián Morales Olavarría for enthusiastic corrections.

James Wiggin for art tips.

Tim Miller for early feedback.

Kristen Vera for ♥.

Sherif M El-azma for Middle Eastern sanity checks.

Hào Anh Lê for Vietnamese sanity checks.

Dana Treadwell for finding my deepest, darkest grammar mistakes.

Michael Jarnebro for finding even more.

Francis Potter for turning pages.

Ana Islas for her elucidating interview.

David Groff for his perceptive editing.

Kathleen Damron for her encouragement.

About the Author

As a witness to AIDS and a Manhattanite on 9/11, Steven Damron draws on personal experiences to render *Dear Mustafa*. Damron studied English at Dartmouth College and Creative Writing at The Writing Salon in San Francisco. His tech start-up career includes a stint at Artify, a fine art subscription business where he honed his knowledge of art. Damron currently lives and writes in Barcelona.